Napoleon Dynamite ™

Napoleon Dynamite ™

Chris Ryall, President and Publisher/CCO

Cara Morrison, Chief Financial Officer

Matt Ruzicka, Chief Accounting Officer

David Hedgecock, Associate Publisher

John Barber, Editor-In-Chief

Justin Eisinger, Editorial Director, Graphic Novels and Collections

Scott Dunbier, Director, Special Projects

Jerry Bennington, VP of New Product Development

Lorelei Bunjes, VP of Digital Services

Jud Meyers, Sales Director

Anna Morrow, Marketing Director

Tara McCrillis, Director of Design & Production

Mike Ford, Director of Operations

Rebekah Cahalin, General Manager

Shauna Monteforte, Manufacturing Operations Director

Ted Adams and Robbie Robbins, Founders of IDW

Series Assistant Editors
MEGAN BROWN
& RILEY FARMER

Series Editor
TOM WALTZ

Collection Editors
ALONZO SIMON
and ZAC BOONE

IDW

ISBN: 978-1-68405-637-8   23 22 21 20   1 2 3 4

NAPOLEON DYNAMITE: IMPEACH PEDRO. MAY 2020. FIRST PRINTING.
™ & © 2020 Twentieth Century Fox Film Corporation and Paramount Pictures Corporation. All Rights Reserved.

© 2020 Idea and Design Works, LLC. All Rights Reserved. IDW Publishing, a division of Idea and Design Works, LLC.
Editorial offices: 2765 Truxtun Road, San Diego, CA 92106. The IDW logo is registered in the U.S. Patent and Trademark Office.

Originally published as NAPOLEON DYNAMITE issues #1–4 and NAPOLEON DYNAMITE VALENTINE'S DAY SPECIAL.

Special thanks to Nicole Spiegel for her invaluable assistance.

For international rights, contact licensing@idwpublishing.com

Tina, you fat lard!

IMPEACH PEDRO

Written By
Carlos Guzman-Verdugo &
Alejandro Verdugo

Art and Colors By
Jorge Monlongo

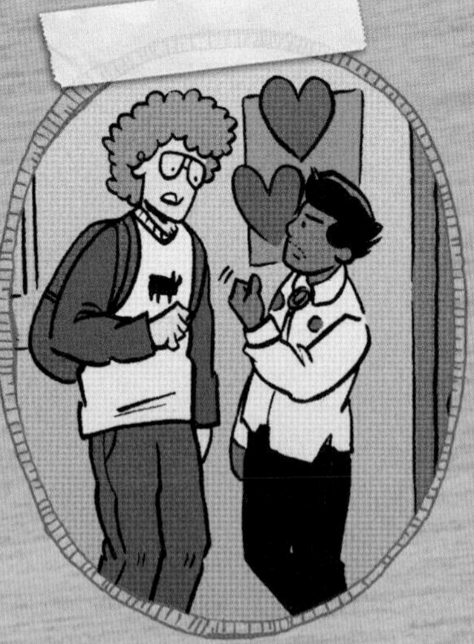

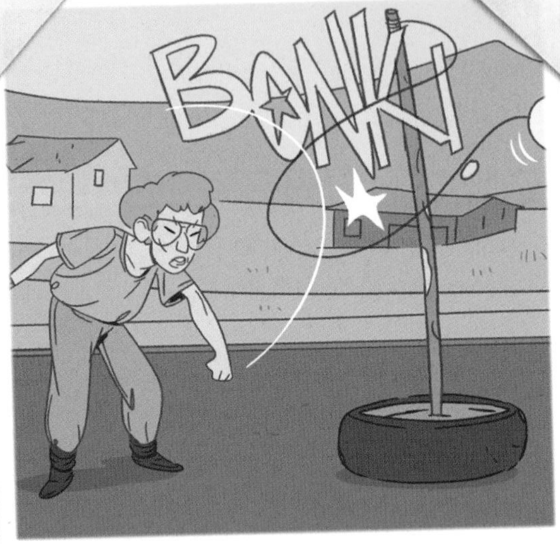
BONK

setting a new record!

VALENTINE'S DAY SPECIAL

Written By
Megan Brown

Art and Colors By
Christine Larsen

Cover Art By
Jorge Monlongo

Design and Letters By
Christa Miesner

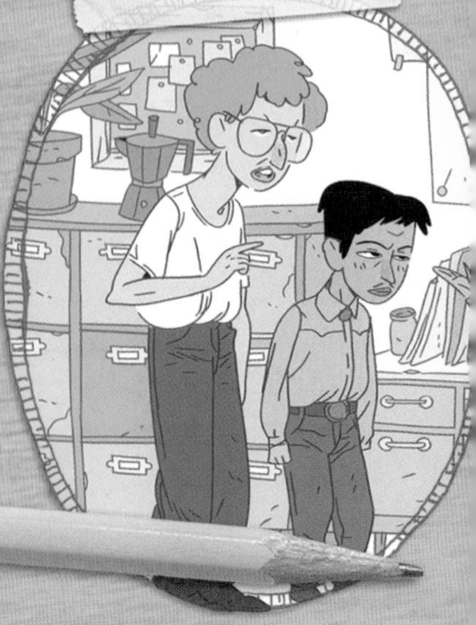

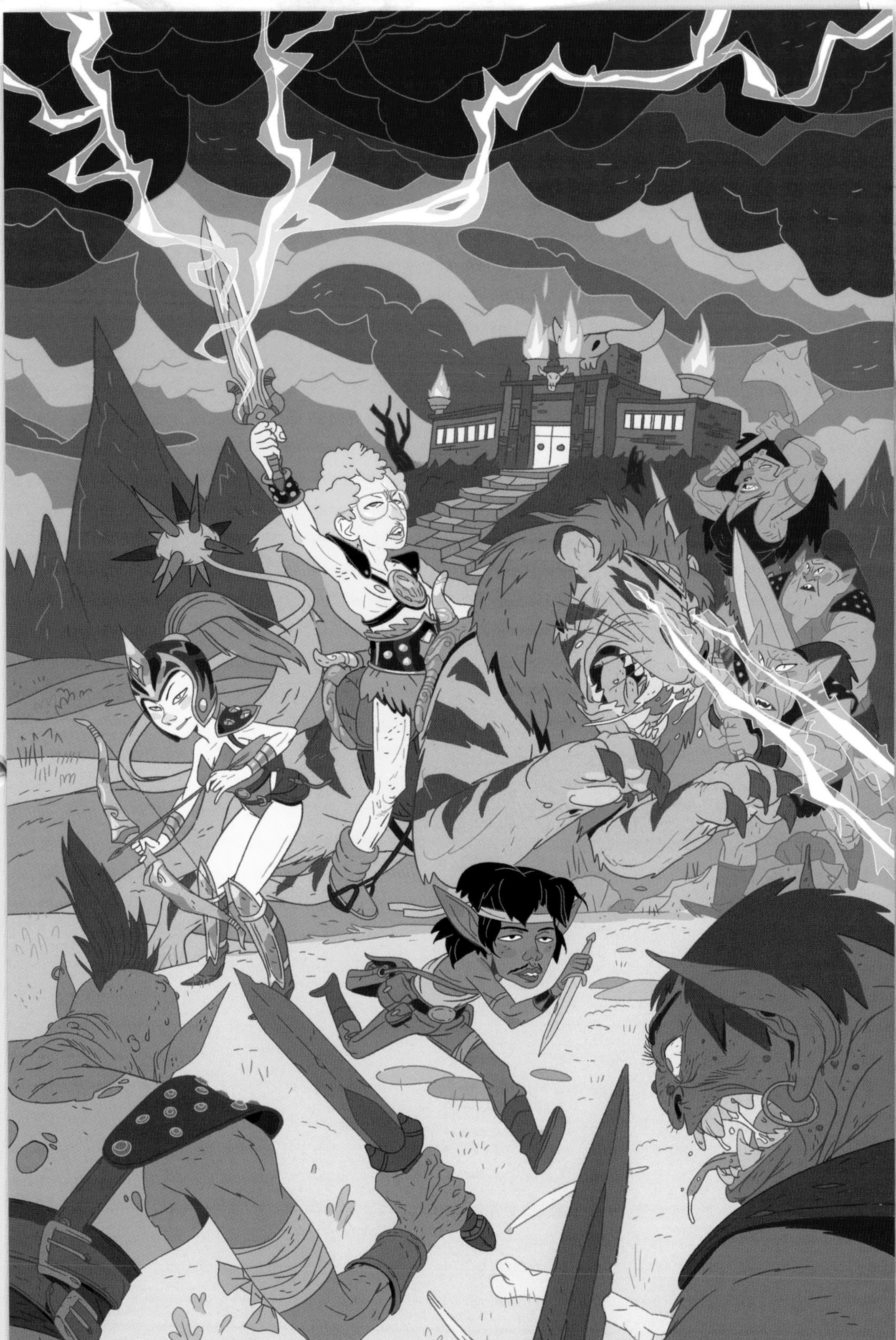

Art by Jorge Monlongo

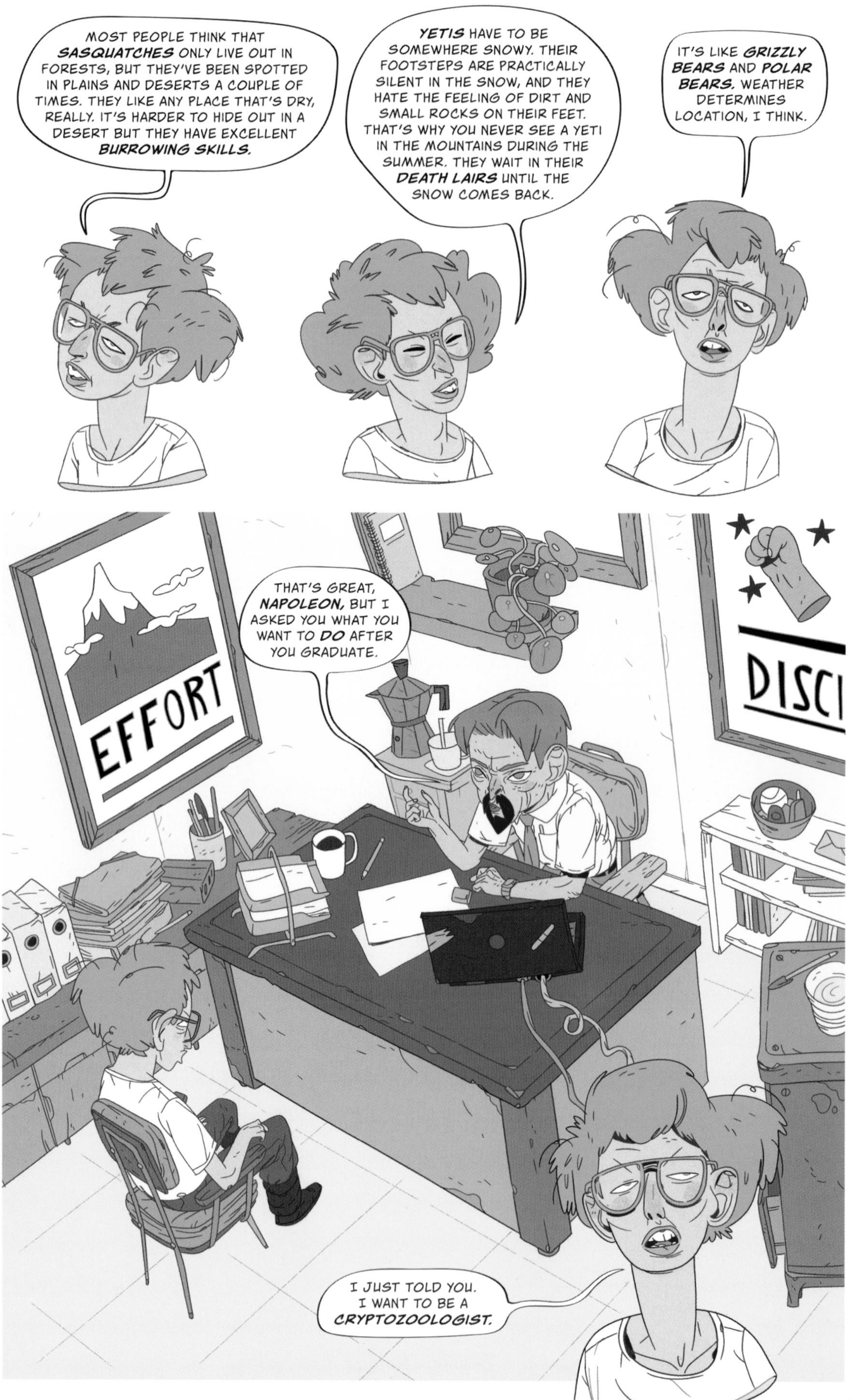
MOST PEOPLE THINK THAT SASQUATCHES ONLY LIVE OUT IN FORESTS, BUT THEY'VE BEEN SPOTTED IN PLAINS AND DESERTS A COUPLE OF TIMES. THEY LIKE ANY PLACE THAT'S DRY, REALLY. IT'S HARDER TO HIDE OUT IN A DESERT BUT THEY HAVE EXCELLENT BURROWING SKILLS.
YETIS HAVE TO BE SOMEWHERE SNOWY. THEIR FOOTSTEPS ARE PRACTICALLY SILENT IN THE SNOW, AND THEY HATE THE FEELING OF DIRT AND SMALL ROCKS ON THEIR FEET. THAT'S WHY YOU NEVER SEE A YETI IN THE MOUNTAINS DURING THE SUMMER. THEY WAIT IN THEIR DEATH LAIRS UNTIL THE SNOW COMES BACK.
IT'S LIKE GRIZZLY BEARS AND POLAR BEARS. WEATHER DETERMINES LOCATION, I THINK.
EFFORT
THAT'S GREAT, NAPOLEON, BUT I ASKED YOU WHAT YOU WANT TO DO AFTER YOU GRADUATE.
DISCI
I JUST TOLD YOU. I WANT TO BE A CRYPTOZOOLOGIST.

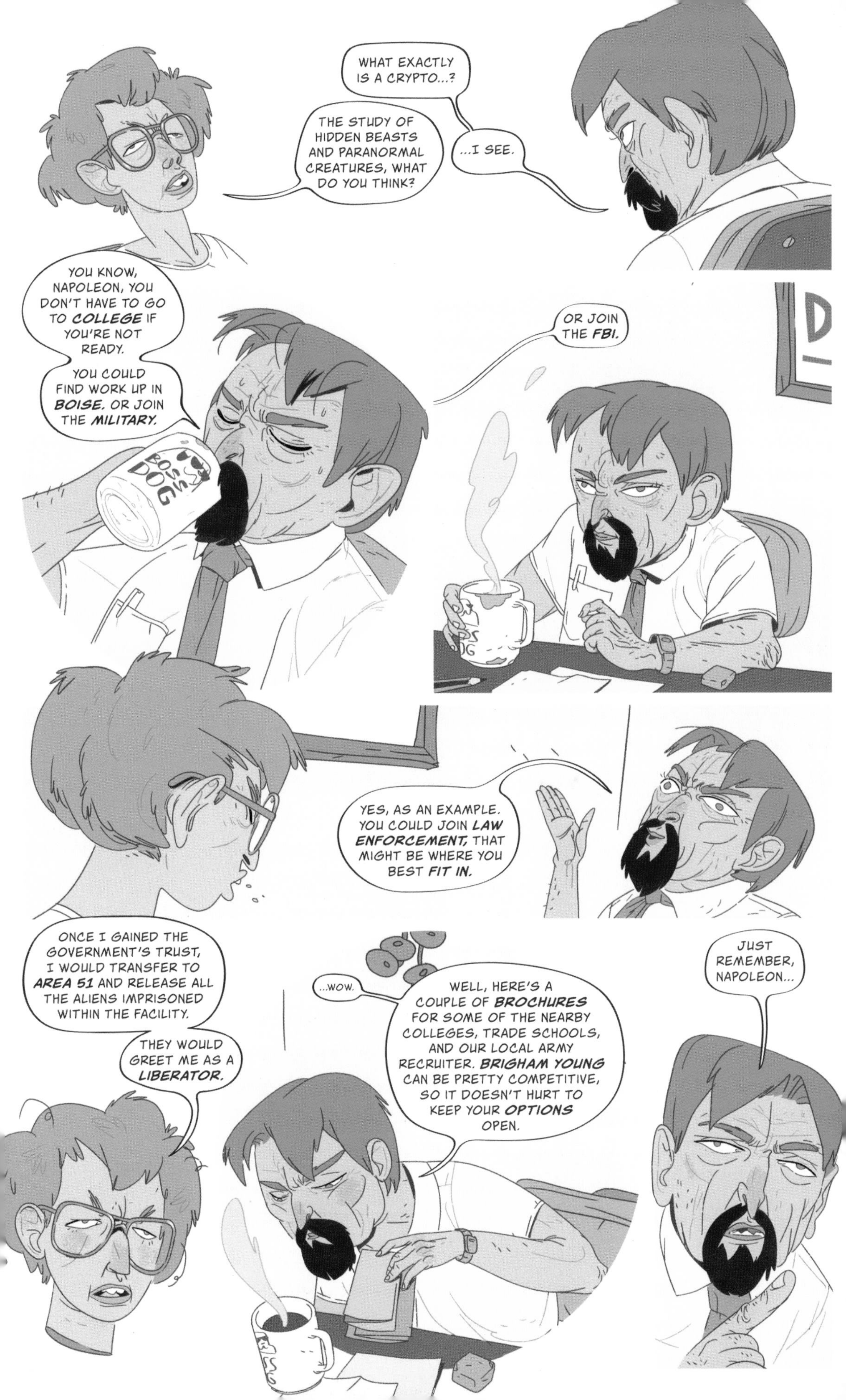
WHAT EXACTLY IS A CRYPTO...?
THE STUDY OF HIDDEN BEASTS AND PARANORMAL CREATURES, WHAT DO YOU THINK?
...I SEE.
YOU KNOW, NAPOLEON, YOU DON'T HAVE TO GO TO COLLEGE IF YOU'RE NOT READY.
YOU COULD FIND WORK UP IN BOISE. OR JOIN THE MILITARY.
BOSS DOG
OR JOIN THE FBI.
YES, AS AN EXAMPLE. YOU COULD JOIN LAW ENFORCEMENT, THAT MIGHT BE WHERE YOU BEST FIT IN.
ONCE I GAINED THE GOVERNMENT'S TRUST, I WOULD TRANSFER TO AREA 51 AND RELEASE ALL THE ALIENS IMPRISONED WITHIN THE FACILITY.
THEY WOULD GREET ME AS A LIBERATOR.
...WOW.
WELL, HERE'S A COUPLE OF BROCHURES FOR SOME OF THE NEARBY COLLEGES, TRADE SCHOOLS, AND OUR LOCAL ARMY RECRUITER. BRIGHAM YOUNG CAN BE PRETTY COMPETITIVE, SO IT DOESN'T HURT TO KEEP YOUR OPTIONS OPEN.
JUST REMEMBER, NAPOLEON...

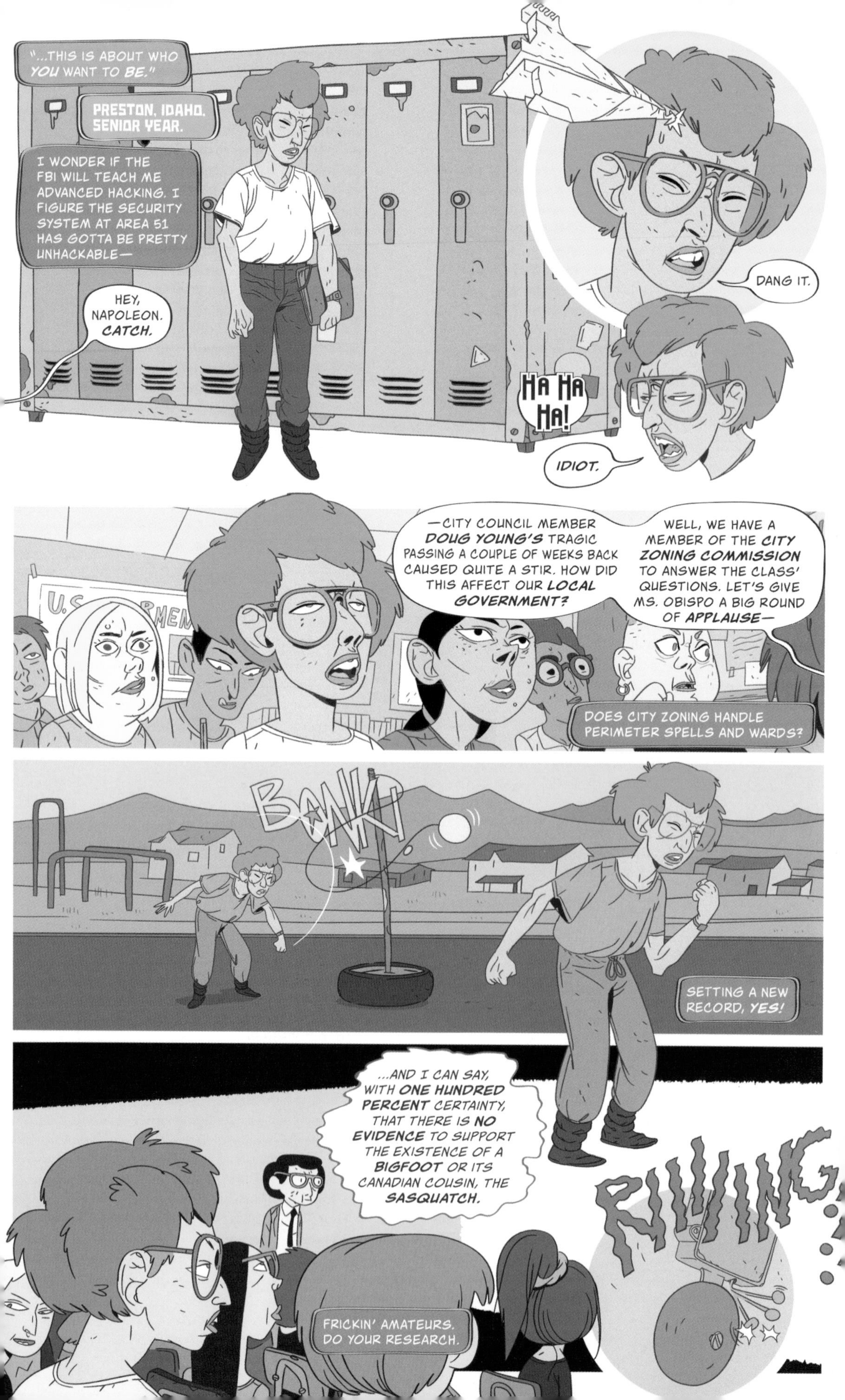
"...THIS IS ABOUT WHO YOU WANT TO BE."
PRESTON, IDAHO. SENIOR YEAR.
I WONDER IF THE FBI WILL TEACH ME ADVANCED HACKING. I FIGURE THE SECURITY SYSTEM AT AREA 51 HAS GOTTA BE PRETTY UNHACKABLE—
HEY, NAPOLEON. CATCH.
DANG IT.
HA HA HA!
IDIOT.
—CITY COUNCIL MEMBER DOUG YOUNG'S TRAGIC PASSING A COUPLE OF WEEKS BACK CAUSED QUITE A STIR. HOW DID THIS AFFECT OUR LOCAL GOVERNMENT?
WELL, WE HAVE A MEMBER OF THE CITY ZONING COMMISSION TO ANSWER THE CLASS' QUESTIONS. LET'S GIVE MS. OBISPO A BIG ROUND OF APPLAUSE—
DOES CITY ZONING HANDLE PERIMETER SPELLS AND WARDS?
BONK!
SETTING A NEW RECORD, YES!
...AND I CAN SAY, WITH ONE HUNDRED PERCENT CERTAINTY, THAT THERE IS NO EVIDENCE TO SUPPORT THE EXISTENCE OF A BIGFOOT OR ITS CANADIAN COUSIN, THE SASQUATCH.
RIIIING...
FRICKIN' AMATEURS. DO YOUR RESEARCH.

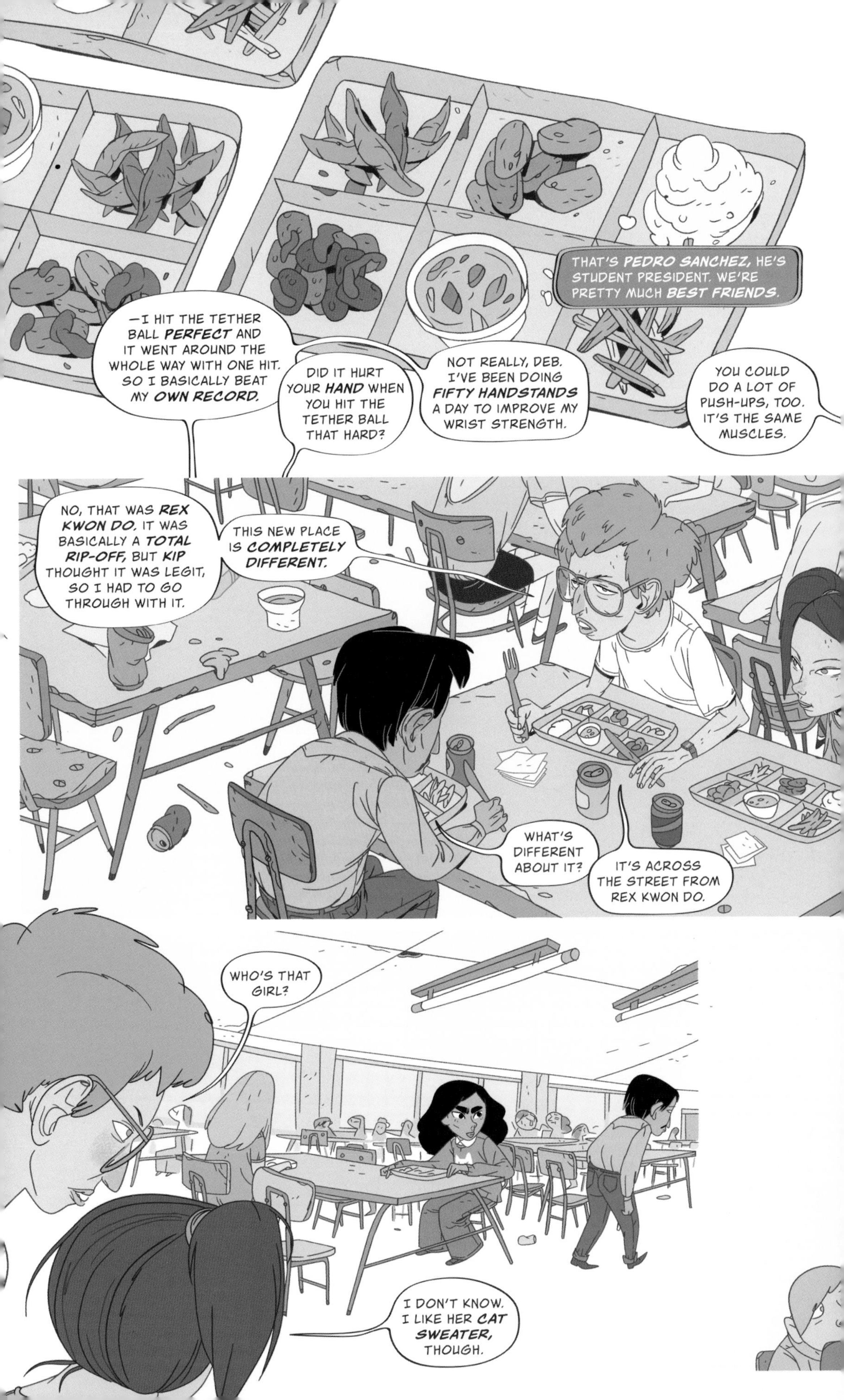
THAT'S PEDRO SANCHEZ, HE'S STUDENT PRESIDENT. WE'RE PRETTY MUCH BEST FRIENDS.
—I HIT THE TETHER BALL PERFECT AND IT WENT AROUND THE WHOLE WAY WITH ONE HIT. SO I BASICALLY BEAT MY OWN RECORD.
DID IT HURT YOUR HAND WHEN YOU HIT THE TETHER BALL THAT HARD?
NOT REALLY, DEB. I'VE BEEN DOING FIFTY HANDSTANDS A DAY TO IMPROVE MY WRIST STRENGTH.
YOU COULD DO A LOT OF PUSH-UPS, TOO. IT'S THE SAME MUSCLES.
NO, THAT WAS REX KWON DO. IT WAS BASICALLY A TOTAL RIP-OFF, BUT KIP THOUGHT IT WAS LEGIT, SO I HAD TO GO THROUGH WITH IT.
THIS NEW PLACE IS COMPLETELY DIFFERENT.
WHAT'S DIFFERENT ABOUT IT?
IT'S ACROSS THE STREET FROM REX KWON DO.
WHO'S THAT GIRL?
I DON'T KNOW. I LIKE HER CAT SWEATER, THOUGH.

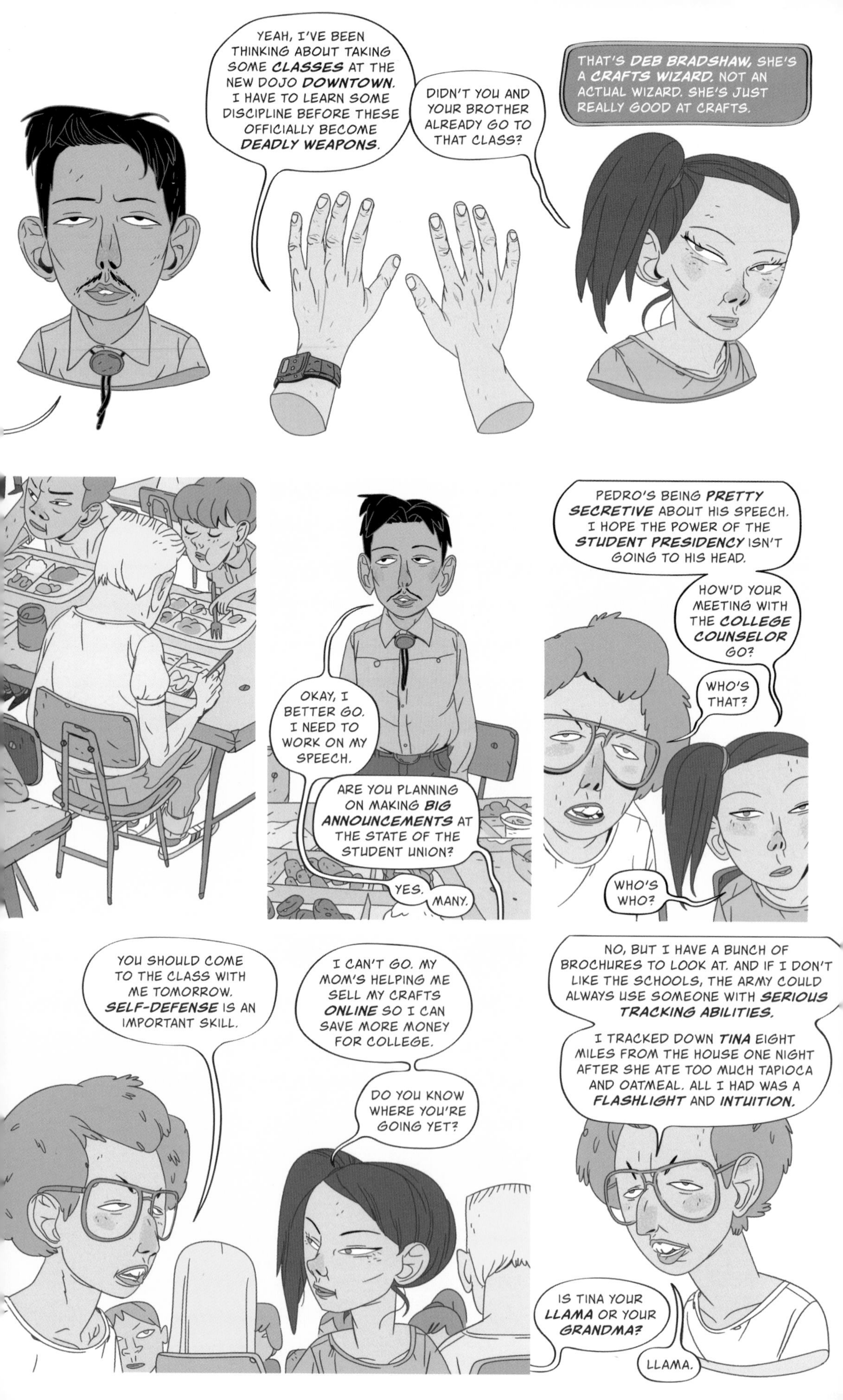
YEAH, I'VE BEEN THINKING ABOUT TAKING SOME CLASSES AT THE NEW DOJO DOWNTOWN. I HAVE TO LEARN SOME DISCIPLINE BEFORE THESE OFFICIALLY BECOME DEADLY WEAPONS.
DIDN'T YOU AND YOUR BROTHER ALREADY GO TO THAT CLASS?
THAT'S DEB BRADSHAW, SHE'S A CRAFTS WIZARD. NOT AN ACTUAL WIZARD. SHE'S JUST REALLY GOOD AT CRAFTS.
OKAY, I BETTER GO. I NEED TO WORK ON MY SPEECH.
ARE YOU PLANNING ON MAKING BIG ANNOUNCEMENTS AT THE STATE OF THE STUDENT UNION?
YES.
MANY.
PEDRO'S BEING PRETTY SECRETIVE ABOUT HIS SPEECH. I HOPE THE POWER OF THE STUDENT PRESIDENCY ISN'T GOING TO HIS HEAD.
HOW'D YOUR MEETING WITH THE COLLEGE COUNSELOR GO?
WHO'S THAT?
WHO'S WHO?
YOU SHOULD COME TO THE CLASS WITH ME TOMORROW. SELF-DEFENSE IS AN IMPORTANT SKILL.
I CAN'T GO. MY MOM'S HELPING ME SELL MY CRAFTS ONLINE SO I CAN SAVE MORE MONEY FOR COLLEGE.
DO YOU KNOW WHERE YOU'RE GOING YET?
NO, BUT I HAVE A BUNCH OF BROCHURES TO LOOK AT. AND IF I DON'T LIKE THE SCHOOLS, THE ARMY COULD ALWAYS USE SOMEONE WITH SERIOUS TRACKING ABILITIES.
I TRACKED DOWN TINA EIGHT MILES FROM THE HOUSE ONE NIGHT AFTER SHE ATE TOO MUCH TAPIOCA AND OATMEAL. ALL I HAD WAS A FLASHLIGHT AND INTUITION.
IS TINA YOUR LLAMA OR YOUR GRANDMA?
LLAMA.

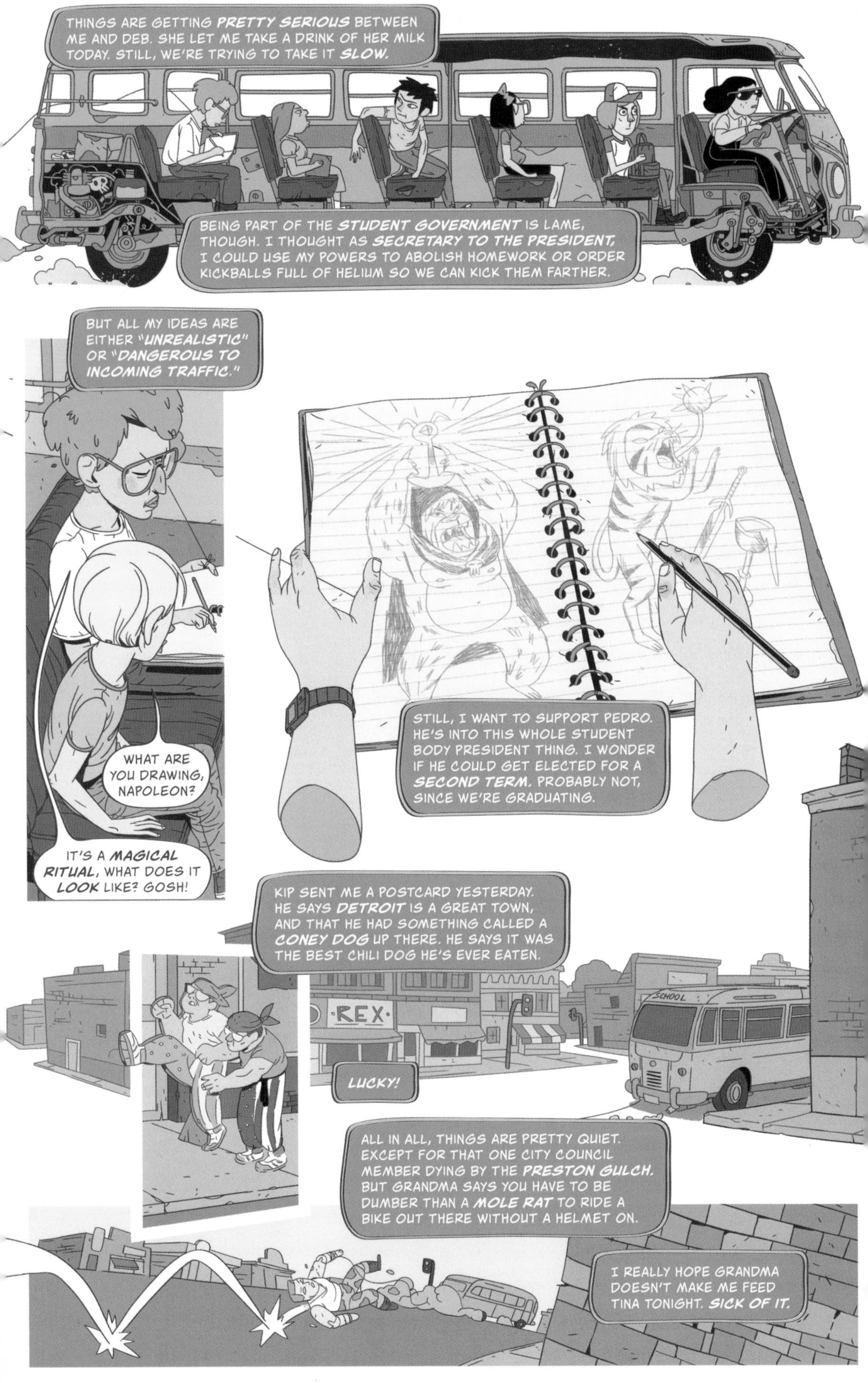
THINGS ARE GETTING PRETTY SERIOUS BETWEEN ME AND DEB. SHE LET ME TAKE A DRINK OF HER MILK TODAY. STILL, WE'RE TRYING TO TAKE IT SLOW.
BEING PART OF THE STUDENT GOVERNMENT IS LAME, THOUGH. I THOUGHT AS SECRETARY TO THE PRESIDENT, I COULD USE MY POWERS TO ABOLISH HOMEWORK OR ORDER KICKBALLS FULL OF HELIUM SO WE CAN KICK THEM FARTHER.
BUT ALL MY IDEAS ARE EITHER "UNREALISTIC" OR "DANGEROUS TO INCOMING TRAFFIC."
WHAT ARE YOU DRAWING, NAPOLEON?
IT'S A MAGICAL RITUAL, WHAT DOES IT LOOK LIKE? GOSH!
STILL, I WANT TO SUPPORT PEDRO. HE'S INTO THIS WHOLE STUDENT BODY PRESIDENT THING. I WONDER IF HE COULD GET ELECTED FOR A SECOND TERM. PROBABLY NOT, SINCE WE'RE GRADUATING.
KIP SENT ME A POSTCARD YESTERDAY. HE SAYS DETROIT IS A GREAT TOWN, AND THAT HE HAD SOMETHING CALLED A CONEY DOG UP THERE. HE SAYS IT WAS THE BEST CHILI DOG HE'S EVER EATEN.
REX
SCHOOL
LUCKY!
ALL IN ALL, THINGS ARE PRETTY QUIET. EXCEPT FOR THAT ONE CITY COUNCIL MEMBER DYING BY THE PRESTON GULCH. BUT GRANDMA SAYS YOU HAVE TO BE DUMBER THAN A MOLE RAT TO RIDE A BIKE OUT THERE WITHOUT A HELMET ON.
I REALLY HOPE GRANDMA DOESN'T MAKE ME FEED TINA TONIGHT. SICK OF IT.

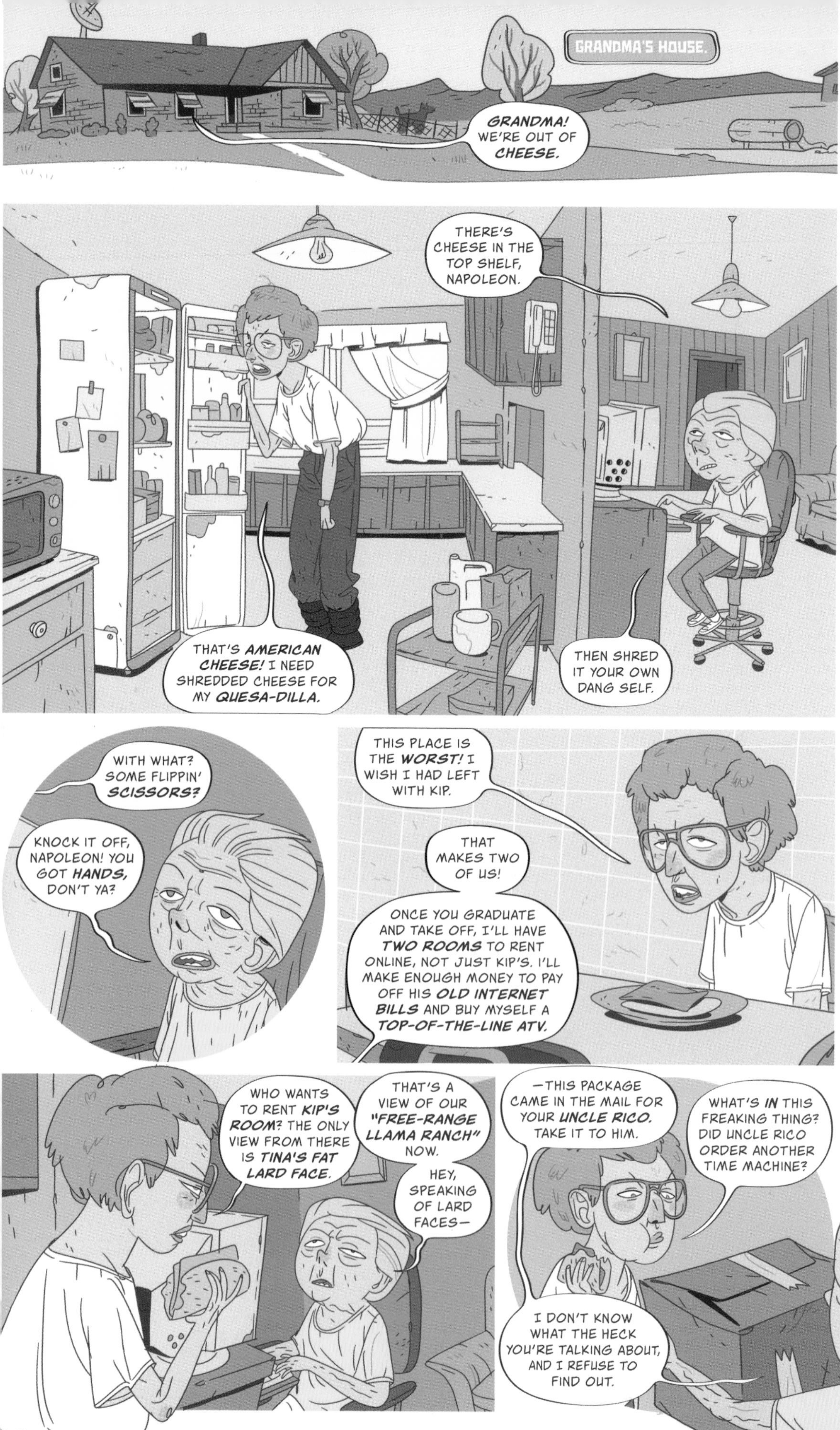
GRANDMA'S HOUSE.
GRANDMA! WE'RE OUT OF CHEESE.
THERE'S CHEESE IN THE TOP SHELF, NAPOLEON.
THAT'S AMERICAN CHEESE! I NEED SHREDDED CHEESE FOR MY QUESA-DILLA.
THEN SHRED IT YOUR OWN DANG SELF.
WITH WHAT? SOME FLIPPIN' SCISSORS?
KNOCK IT OFF, NAPOLEON! YOU GOT HANDS, DON'T YA?
THIS PLACE IS THE WORST! I WISH I HAD LEFT WITH KIP.
THAT MAKES TWO OF US!
ONCE YOU GRADUATE AND TAKE OFF, I'LL HAVE TWO ROOMS TO RENT ONLINE, NOT JUST KIP'S. I'LL MAKE ENOUGH MONEY TO PAY OFF HIS OLD INTERNET BILLS AND BUY MYSELF A TOP-OF-THE-LINE ATV.
WHO WANTS TO RENT KIP'S ROOM? THE ONLY VIEW FROM THERE IS TINA'S FAT LARD FACE.
THAT'S A VIEW OF OUR "FREE-RANGE LLAMA RANCH" NOW.
HEY, SPEAKING OF LARD FACES—
—THIS PACKAGE CAME IN THE MAIL FOR YOUR UNCLE RICO. TAKE IT TO HIM.
WHAT'S IN THIS FREAKING THING? DID UNCLE RICO ORDER ANOTHER TIME MACHINE?
I DON'T KNOW WHAT THE HECK YOU'RE TALKING ABOUT, AND I REFUSE TO FIND OUT.

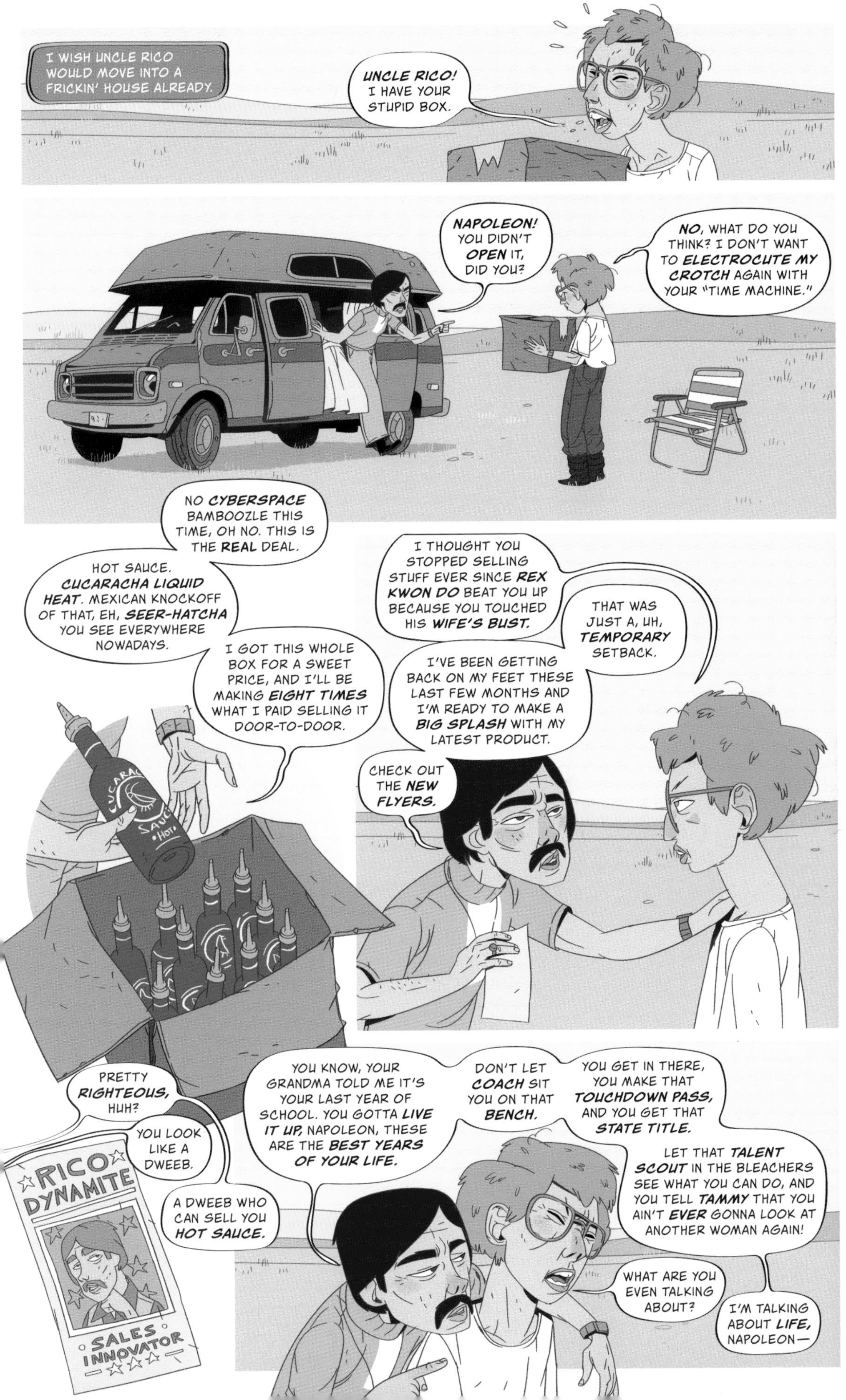

I WISH UNCLE RICO WOULD MOVE INTO A FRICKIN' HOUSE ALREADY.
UNCLE RICO! I HAVE YOUR STUPID BOX.
NAPOLEON! YOU DIDN'T OPEN IT, DID YOU?
NO, WHAT DO YOU THINK? I DON'T WANT TO ELECTROCUTE MY CROTCH AGAIN WITH YOUR "TIME MACHINE."
NO CYBERSPACE BAMBOOZLE THIS TIME, OH NO. THIS IS THE REAL DEAL.
HOT SAUCE. CUCARACHA LIQUID HEAT. MEXICAN KNOCKOFF OF THAT, EH, SEER-HATCHA YOU SEE EVERYWHERE NOWADAYS.
I GOT THIS WHOLE BOX FOR A SWEET PRICE, AND I'LL BE MAKING EIGHT TIMES WHAT I PAID SELLING IT DOOR-TO-DOOR.
CUCARACHA SAUCE HOT
I THOUGHT YOU STOPPED SELLING STUFF EVER SINCE REX KWON DO BEAT YOU UP BECAUSE YOU TOUCHED HIS WIFE'S BUST.
THAT WAS JUST A, UH, TEMPORARY SETBACK.
I'VE BEEN GETTING BACK ON MY FEET THESE LAST FEW MONTHS AND I'M READY TO MAKE A BIG SPLASH WITH MY LATEST PRODUCT.
CHECK OUT THE NEW FLYERS.
PRETTY RIGHTEOUS, HUH?
YOU LOOK LIKE A DWEEB.
A DWEEB WHO CAN SELL YOU HOT SAUCE.
RICO DYNAMITE
SALES INNOVATOR
YOU KNOW, YOUR GRANDMA TOLD ME IT'S YOUR LAST YEAR OF SCHOOL. YOU GOTTA LIVE IT UP, NAPOLEON, THESE ARE THE BEST YEARS OF YOUR LIFE.
DON'T LET COACH SIT YOU ON THAT BENCH.
YOU GET IN THERE, YOU MAKE THAT TOUCHDOWN PASS, AND YOU GET THAT STATE TITLE.
LET THAT TALENT SCOUT IN THE BLEACHERS SEE WHAT YOU CAN DO, AND YOU TELL TAMMY THAT YOU AIN'T EVER GONNA LOOK AT ANOTHER WOMAN AGAIN!
WHAT ARE YOU EVEN TALKING ABOUT?
I'M TALKING ABOUT LIFE, NAPOLEON—

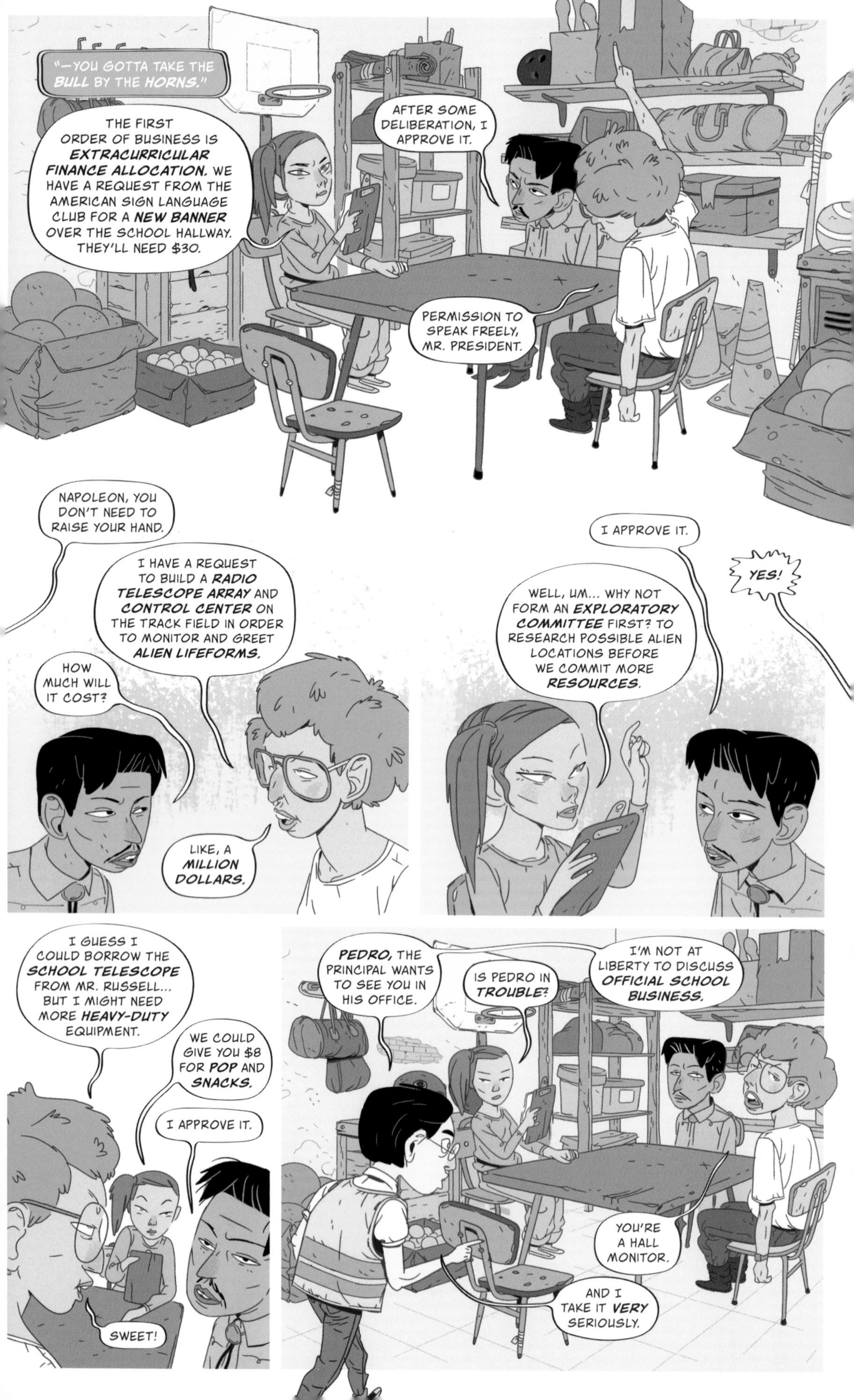
"—YOU GOTTA TAKE THE BULL BY THE HORNS."
THE FIRST ORDER OF BUSINESS IS EXTRACURRICULAR FINANCE ALLOCATION. WE HAVE A REQUEST FROM THE AMERICAN SIGN LANGUAGE CLUB FOR A NEW BANNER OVER THE SCHOOL HALLWAY. THEY'LL NEED $30.
AFTER SOME DELIBERATION, I APPROVE IT.
PERMISSION TO SPEAK FREELY, MR. PRESIDENT.
NAPOLEON, YOU DON'T NEED TO RAISE YOUR HAND.
I HAVE A REQUEST TO BUILD A RADIO TELESCOPE ARRAY AND CONTROL CENTER ON THE TRACK FIELD IN ORDER TO MONITOR AND GREET ALIEN LIFEFORMS.
HOW MUCH WILL IT COST?
LIKE, A MILLION DOLLARS.
WELL, UM... WHY NOT FORM AN EXPLORATORY COMMITTEE FIRST? TO RESEARCH POSSIBLE ALIEN LOCATIONS BEFORE WE COMMIT MORE RESOURCES.
I APPROVE IT.
YES!
I GUESS I COULD BORROW THE SCHOOL TELESCOPE FROM MR. RUSSELL... BUT I MIGHT NEED MORE HEAVY-DUTY EQUIPMENT.
WE COULD GIVE YOU $8 FOR POP AND SNACKS.
I APPROVE IT.
SWEET!
PEDRO, THE PRINCIPAL WANTS TO SEE YOU IN HIS OFFICE.
IS PEDRO IN TROUBLE?
I'M NOT AT LIBERTY TO DISCUSS OFFICIAL SCHOOL BUSINESS.
YOU'RE A HALL MONITOR.
AND I TAKE IT VERY SERIOUSLY.

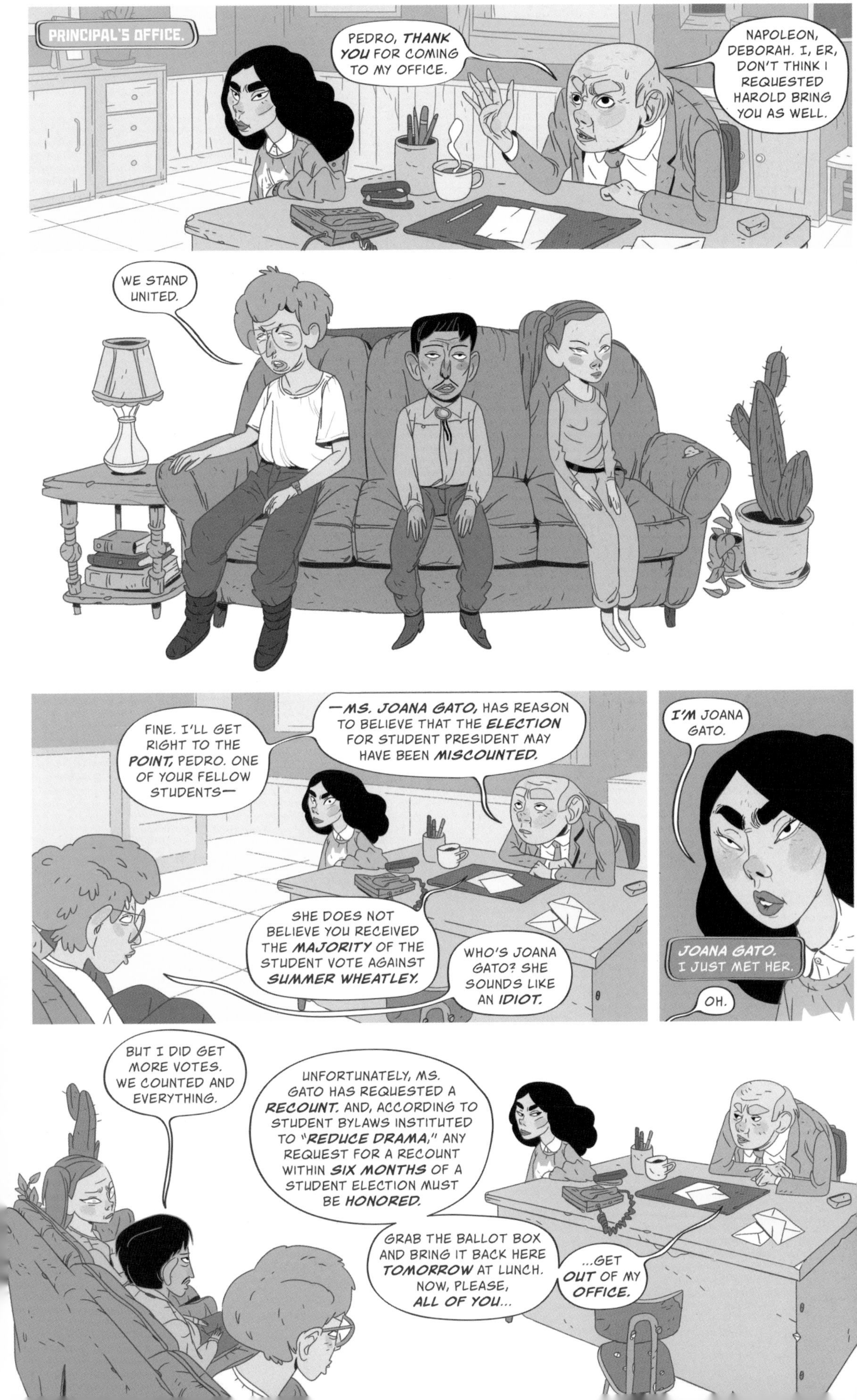
PRINCIPAL'S OFFICE.
PEDRO, THANK YOU FOR COMING TO MY OFFICE.
NAPOLEON, DEBORAH. I, ER, DON'T THINK I REQUESTED HAROLD BRING YOU AS WELL.
WE STAND UNITED.
FINE. I'LL GET RIGHT TO THE POINT, PEDRO. ONE OF YOUR FELLOW STUDENTS—
—MS. JOANA GATO, HAS REASON TO BELIEVE THAT THE ELECTION FOR STUDENT PRESIDENT MAY HAVE BEEN MISCOUNTED.
SHE DOES NOT BELIEVE YOU RECEIVED THE MAJORITY OF THE STUDENT VOTE AGAINST SUMMER WHEATLEY.
WHO'S JOANA GATO? SHE SOUNDS LIKE AN IDIOT.
I'M JOANA GATO.
JOANA GATO. I JUST MET HER.
OH.
BUT I DID GET MORE VOTES. WE COUNTED AND EVERYTHING.
UNFORTUNATELY, MS. GATO HAS REQUESTED A RECOUNT. AND, ACCORDING TO STUDENT BYLAWS INSTITUTED TO "REDUCE DRAMA," ANY REQUEST FOR A RECOUNT WITHIN SIX MONTHS OF A STUDENT ELECTION MUST BE HONORED.
GRAB THE BALLOT BOX AND BRING IT BACK HERE TOMORROW AT LUNCH. NOW, PLEASE, ALL OF YOU...
...GET OUT OF MY OFFICE.

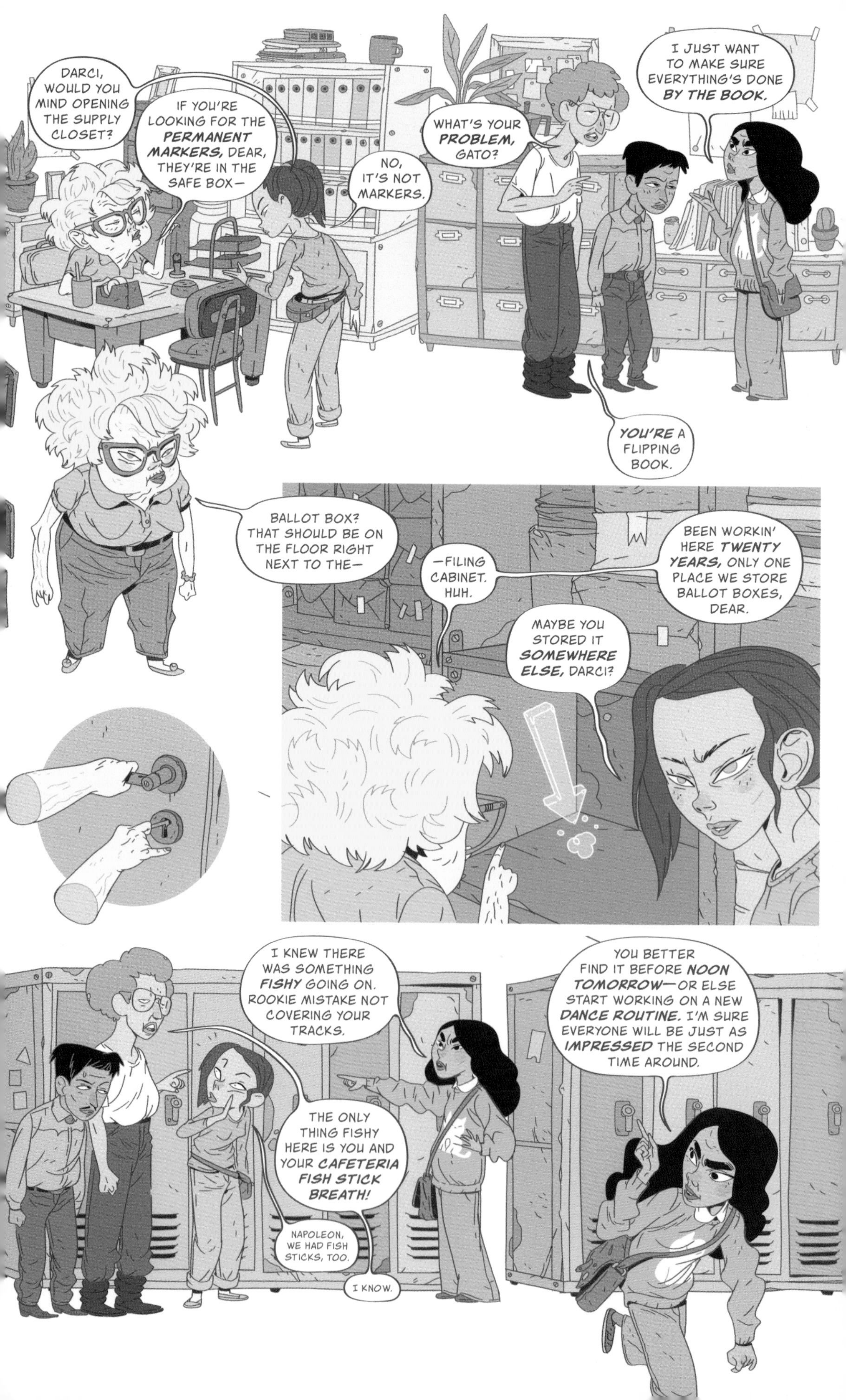
DARCI, WOULD YOU MIND OPENING THE SUPPLY CLOSET?
IF YOU'RE LOOKING FOR THE **PERMANENT MARKERS,** DEAR, THEY'RE IN THE SAFE BOX—
NO, IT'S NOT MARKERS.
WHAT'S YOUR **PROBLEM,** GATO?
I JUST WANT TO MAKE SURE EVERYTHING'S DONE **BY THE BOOK.**
YOU'RE A FLIPPING BOOK.
BALLOT BOX? THAT SHOULD BE ON THE FLOOR RIGHT NEXT TO THE—
—FILING CABINET. HUH.
BEEN WORKIN' HERE **TWENTY YEARS,** ONLY ONE PLACE WE STORE BALLOT BOXES, DEAR.
MAYBE YOU STORED IT **SOMEWHERE ELSE,** DARCI?
I KNEW THERE WAS SOMETHING **FISHY** GOING ON. ROOKIE MISTAKE NOT COVERING YOUR TRACKS.
THE ONLY THING FISHY HERE IS YOU AND YOUR **CAFETERIA FISH STICK BREATH!**
NAPOLEON, WE HAD FISH STICKS, TOO.
I KNOW.
YOU BETTER FIND IT BEFORE **NOON TOMORROW**—OR ELSE START WORKING ON A NEW **DANCE ROUTINE.** I'M SURE EVERYONE WILL BE JUST AS **IMPRESSED** THE SECOND TIME AROUND.

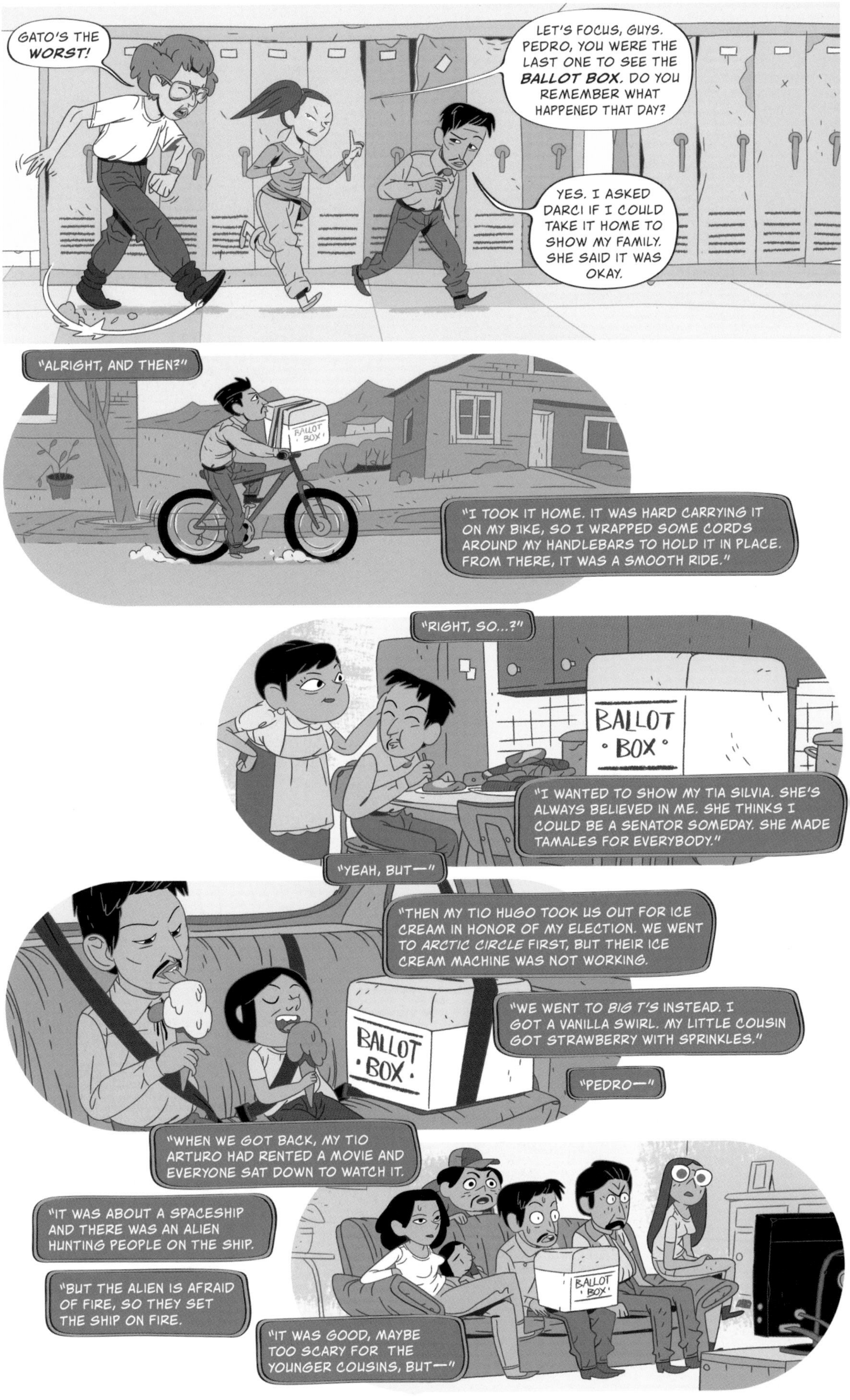
GATO'S THE *WORST!*
LET'S FOCUS, GUYS. PEDRO, YOU WERE THE LAST ONE TO SEE THE *BALLOT BOX.* DO YOU REMEMBER WHAT HAPPENED THAT DAY?
YES. I ASKED DARCI IF I COULD TAKE IT HOME TO SHOW MY FAMILY. SHE SAID IT WAS OKAY.
"ALRIGHT, AND THEN?"
BALLOT BOX
"I TOOK IT HOME. IT WAS HARD CARRYING IT ON MY BIKE, SO I WRAPPED SOME CORDS AROUND MY HANDLEBARS TO HOLD IT IN PLACE. FROM THERE, IT WAS A SMOOTH RIDE."
"RIGHT, SO...?"
BALLOT BOX
"I WANTED TO SHOW MY TIA SILVIA. SHE'S ALWAYS BELIEVED IN ME. SHE THINKS I COULD BE A SENATOR SOMEDAY. SHE MADE TAMALES FOR EVERYBODY."
"YEAH, BUT—"
"THEN MY TIO HUGO TOOK US OUT FOR ICE CREAM IN HONOR OF MY ELECTION. WE WENT TO *ARCTIC CIRCLE* FIRST, BUT THEIR ICE CREAM MACHINE WAS NOT WORKING.
BALLOT BOX
"WE WENT TO *BIG T'S* INSTEAD. I GOT A VANILLA SWIRL. MY LITTLE COUSIN GOT STRAWBERRY WITH SPRINKLES."
"PEDRO—"
"WHEN WE GOT BACK, MY TIO ARTURO HAD RENTED A MOVIE AND EVERYONE SAT DOWN TO WATCH IT.
"IT WAS ABOUT A SPACESHIP AND THERE WAS AN ALIEN HUNTING PEOPLE ON THE SHIP.
"BUT THE ALIEN IS AFRAID OF FIRE, SO THEY SET THE SHIP ON FIRE.
BALLOT BOX
"IT WAS GOOD, MAYBE TOO SCARY FOR THE YOUNGER COUSINS, BUT—"

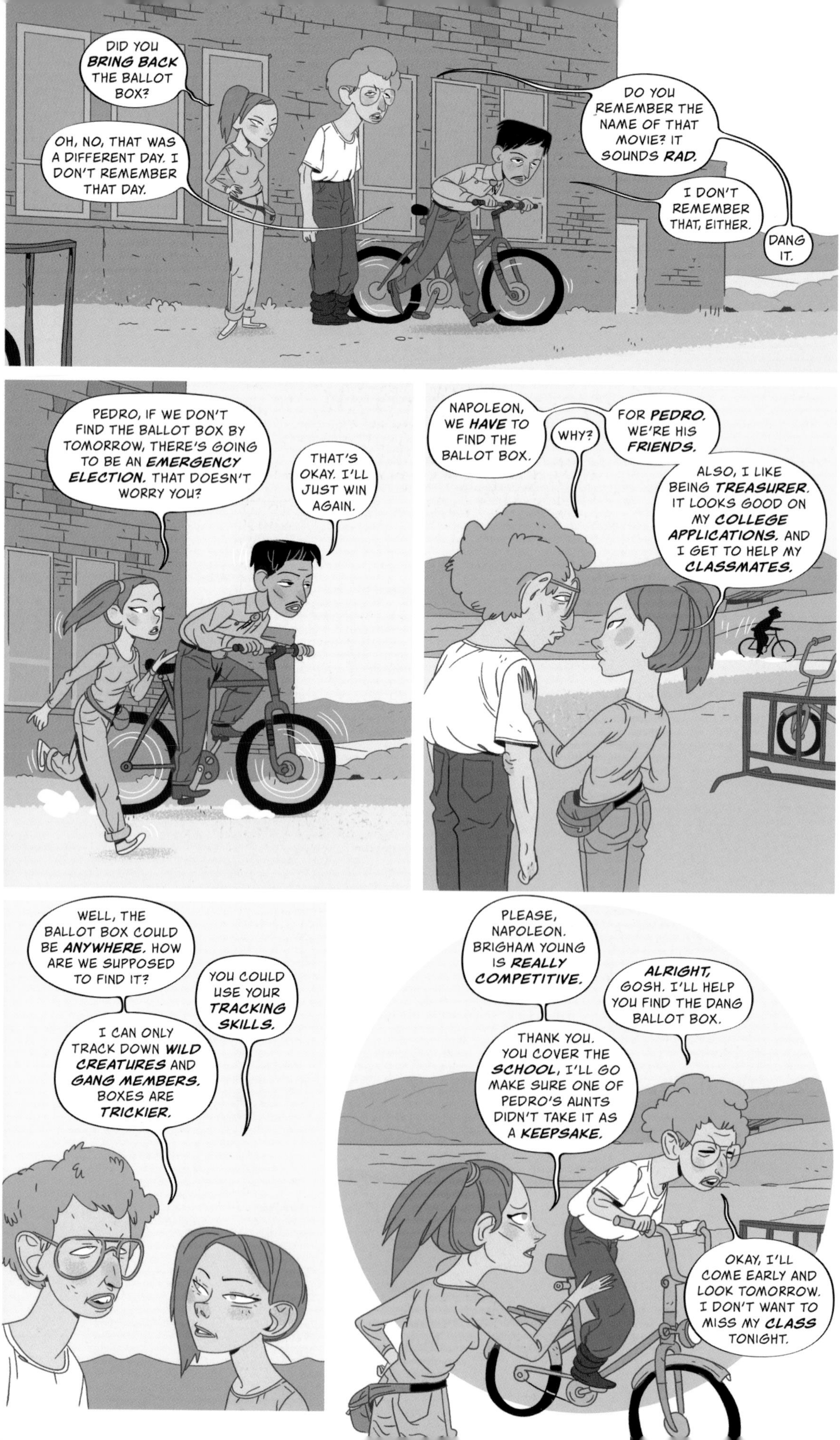
DID YOU BRING BACK THE BALLOT BOX?
OH, NO, THAT WAS A DIFFERENT DAY. I DON'T REMEMBER THAT DAY.
DO YOU REMEMBER THE NAME OF THAT MOVIE? IT SOUNDS RAD.
I DON'T REMEMBER THAT, EITHER.
DANG IT.
PEDRO, IF WE DON'T FIND THE BALLOT BOX BY TOMORROW, THERE'S GOING TO BE AN EMERGENCY ELECTION. THAT DOESN'T WORRY YOU?
THAT'S OKAY. I'LL JUST WIN AGAIN.
NAPOLEON, WE HAVE TO FIND THE BALLOT BOX.
WHY?
FOR PEDRO. WE'RE HIS FRIENDS.
ALSO, I LIKE BEING TREASURER. IT LOOKS GOOD ON MY COLLEGE APPLICATIONS. AND I GET TO HELP MY CLASSMATES.
WELL, THE BALLOT BOX COULD BE ANYWHERE. HOW ARE WE SUPPOSED TO FIND IT?
YOU COULD USE YOUR TRACKING SKILLS.
I CAN ONLY TRACK DOWN WILD CREATURES AND GANG MEMBERS. BOXES ARE TRICKIER.
PLEASE, NAPOLEON. BRIGHAM YOUNG IS REALLY COMPETITIVE.
ALRIGHT, GOSH. I'LL HELP YOU FIND THE DANG BALLOT BOX.
THANK YOU. YOU COVER THE SCHOOL, I'LL GO MAKE SURE ONE OF PEDRO'S AUNTS DIDN'T TAKE IT AS A KEEPSAKE.
OKAY, I'LL COME EARLY AND LOOK TOMORROW. I DON'T WANT TO MISS MY CLASS TONIGHT.

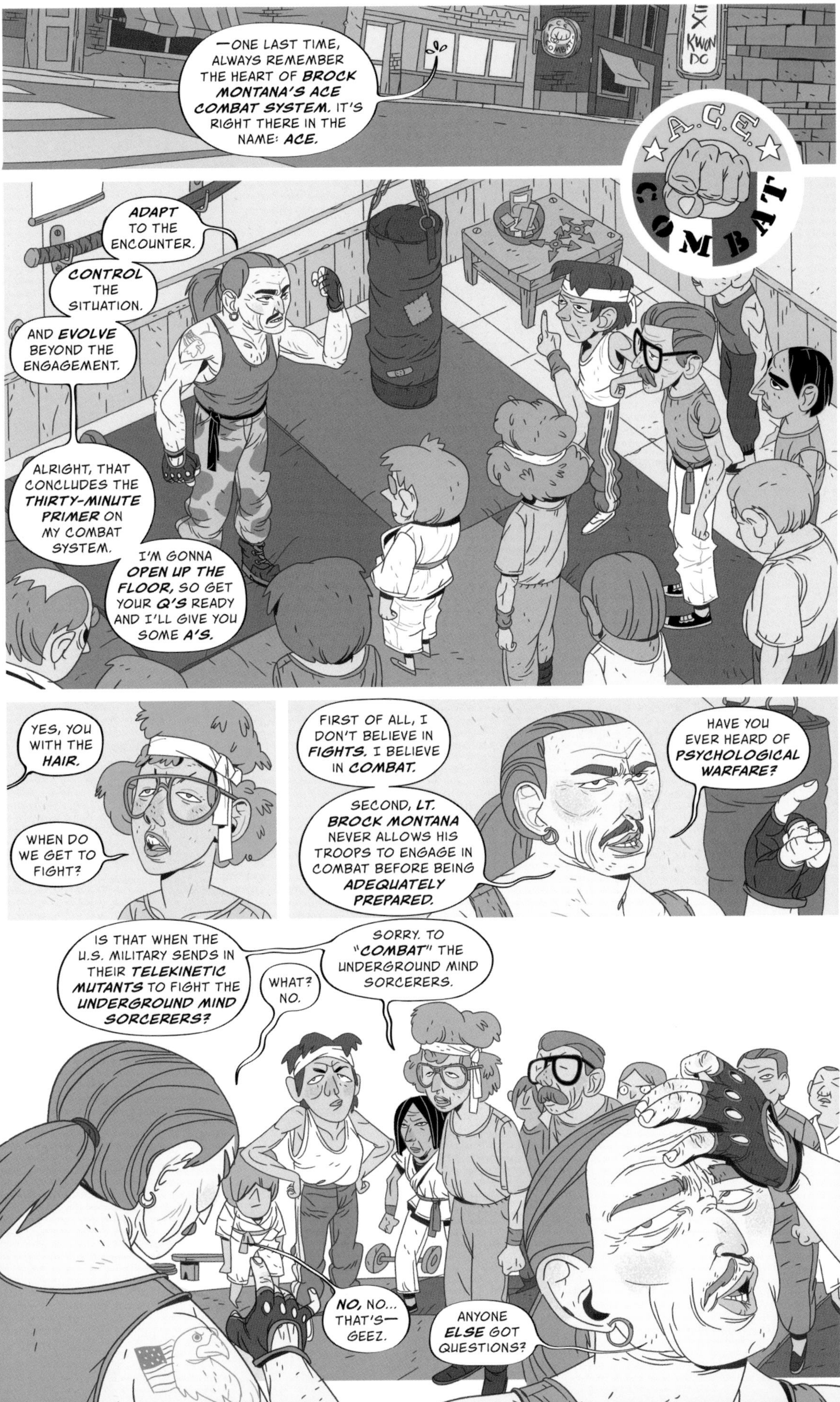

—ONE LAST TIME, ALWAYS REMEMBER THE HEART OF BROCK MONTANA'S ACE COMBAT SYSTEM. IT'S RIGHT THERE IN THE NAME: ACE.
TAE KWON DO
A.C.E. COMBAT
ADAPT TO THE ENCOUNTER.
CONTROL THE SITUATION.
AND EVOLVE BEYOND THE ENGAGEMENT.
ALRIGHT, THAT CONCLUDES THE THIRTY-MINUTE PRIMER ON MY COMBAT SYSTEM.
I'M GONNA OPEN UP THE FLOOR, SO GET YOUR Q'S READY AND I'LL GIVE YOU SOME A'S.
YES, YOU WITH THE HAIR.
WHEN DO WE GET TO FIGHT?
FIRST OF ALL, I DON'T BELIEVE IN FIGHTS. I BELIEVE IN COMBAT.
SECOND, LT. BROCK MONTANA NEVER ALLOWS HIS TROOPS TO ENGAGE IN COMBAT BEFORE BEING ADEQUATELY PREPARED.
HAVE YOU EVER HEARD OF PSYCHOLOGICAL WARFARE?
IS THAT WHEN THE U.S. MILITARY SENDS IN THEIR TELEKINETIC MUTANTS TO FIGHT THE UNDERGROUND MIND SORCERERS?
WHAT? NO.
SORRY. TO "COMBAT" THE UNDERGROUND MIND SORCERERS.
NO, NO... THAT'S— GEEZ.
ANYONE ELSE GOT QUESTIONS?

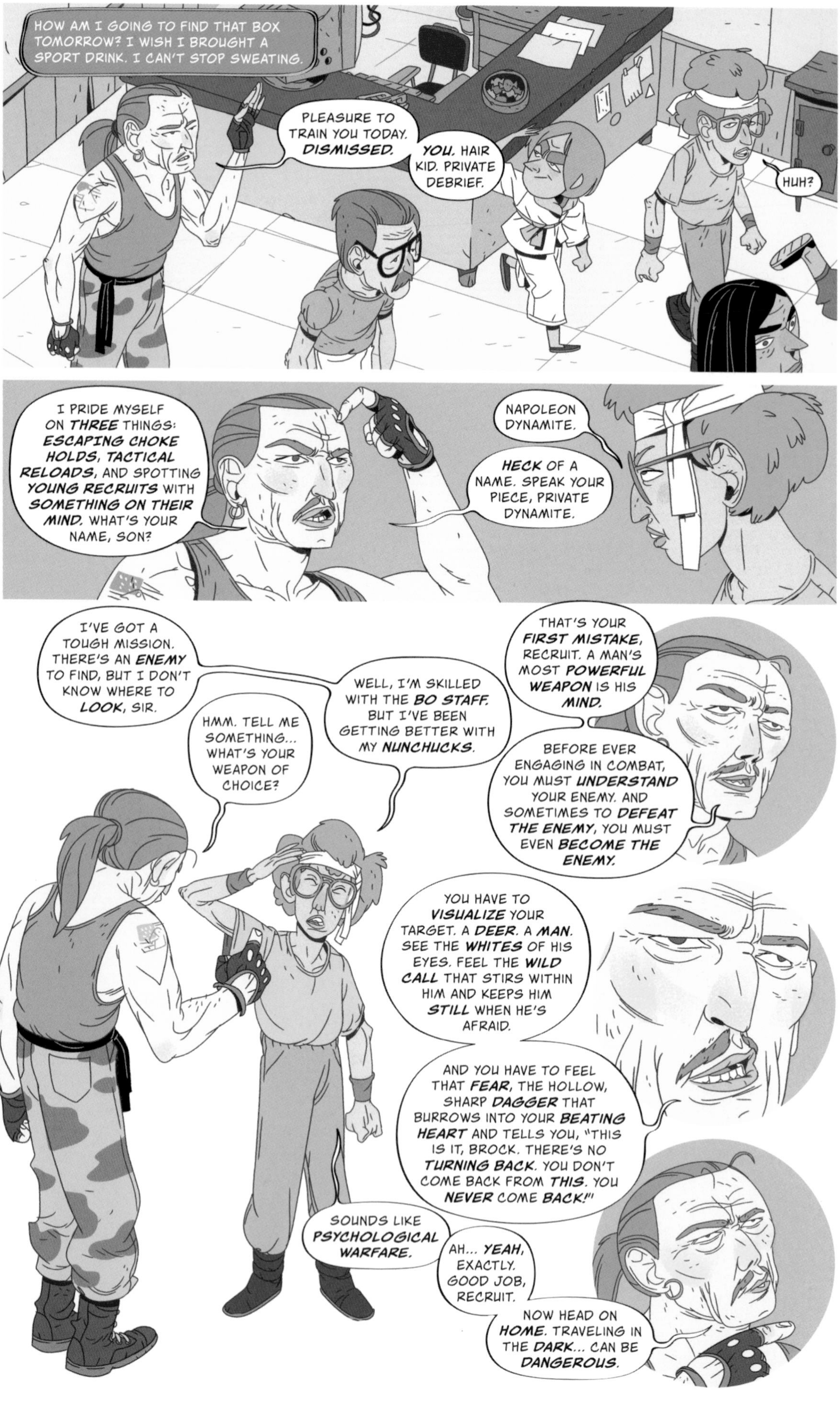
HOW AM I GOING TO FIND THAT BOX TOMORROW? I WISH I BROUGHT A SPORT DRINK. I CAN'T STOP SWEATING.
PLEASURE TO TRAIN YOU TODAY. DISMISSED.
YOU, HAIR KID. PRIVATE DEBRIEF.
HUH?
I PRIDE MYSELF ON THREE THINGS: ESCAPING CHOKE HOLDS, TACTICAL RELOADS, AND SPOTTING YOUNG RECRUITS WITH SOMETHING ON THEIR MIND. WHAT'S YOUR NAME, SON?
NAPOLEON DYNAMITE.
HECK OF A NAME. SPEAK YOUR PIECE, PRIVATE DYNAMITE.
I'VE GOT A TOUGH MISSION. THERE'S AN ENEMY TO FIND, BUT I DON'T KNOW WHERE TO LOOK, SIR.
HMM. TELL ME SOMETHING... WHAT'S YOUR WEAPON OF CHOICE?
WELL, I'M SKILLED WITH THE BO STAFF. BUT I'VE BEEN GETTING BETTER WITH MY NUNCHUCKS.
THAT'S YOUR FIRST MISTAKE, RECRUIT. A MAN'S MOST POWERFUL WEAPON IS HIS MIND.
BEFORE EVER ENGAGING IN COMBAT, YOU MUST UNDERSTAND YOUR ENEMY. AND SOMETIMES TO DEFEAT THE ENEMY, YOU MUST EVEN BECOME THE ENEMY.
YOU HAVE TO VISUALIZE YOUR TARGET. A DEER. A MAN. SEE THE WHITES OF HIS EYES. FEEL THE WILD CALL THAT STIRS WITHIN HIM AND KEEPS HIM STILL WHEN HE'S AFRAID.
AND YOU HAVE TO FEEL THAT FEAR, THE HOLLOW, SHARP DAGGER THAT BURROWS INTO YOUR BEATING HEART AND TELLS YOU, "THIS IS IT, BROCK. THERE'S NO TURNING BACK. YOU DON'T COME BACK FROM THIS. YOU NEVER COME BACK!"
SOUNDS LIKE PSYCHOLOGICAL WARFARE.
AH... YEAH, EXACTLY. GOOD JOB, RECRUIT.
NOW HEAD ON HOME. TRAVELING IN THE DARK... CAN BE DANGEROUS.

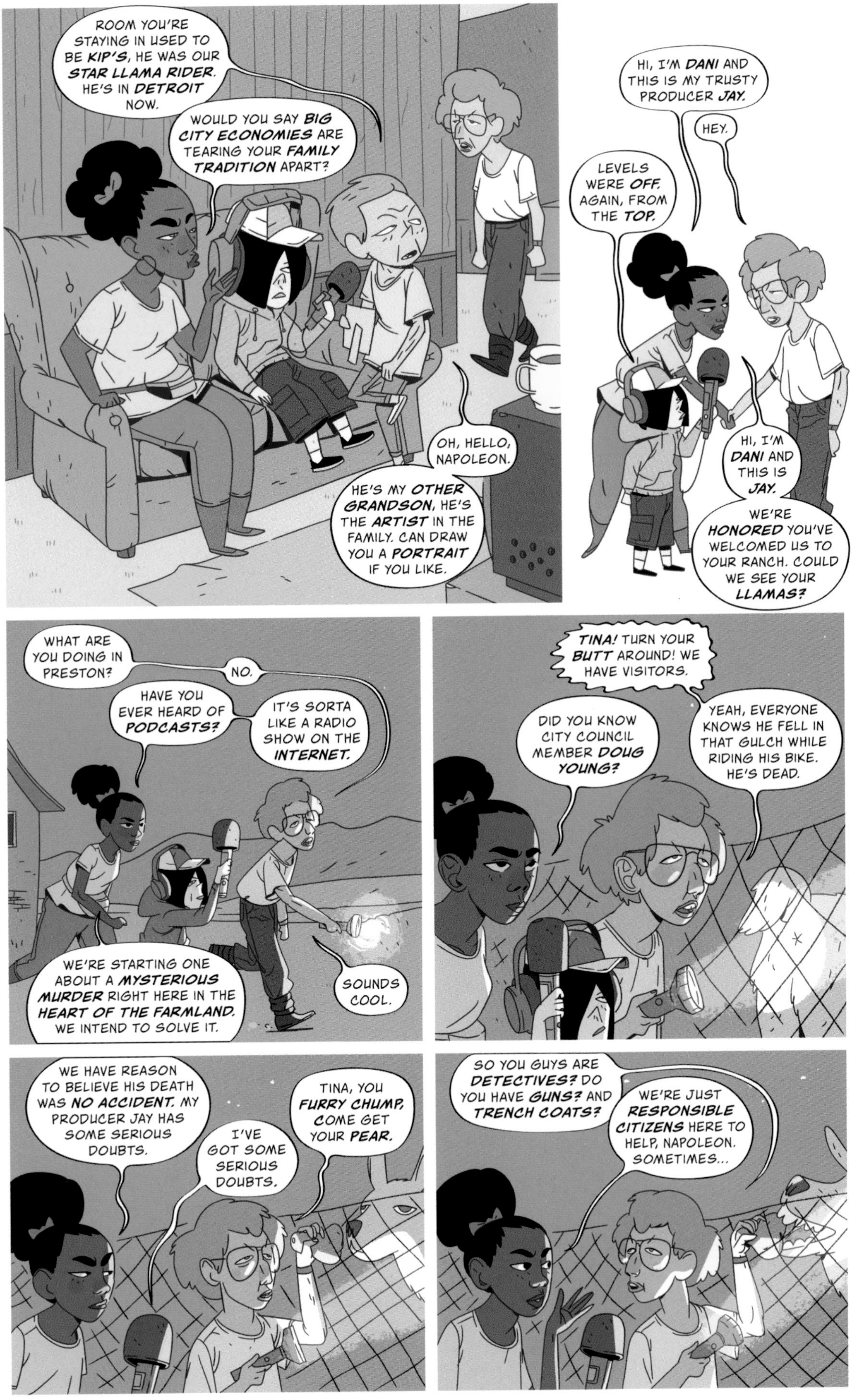
ROOM YOU'RE STAYING IN USED TO BE KIP'S, HE WAS OUR STAR LLAMA RIDER. HE'S IN DETROIT NOW.
WOULD YOU SAY BIG CITY ECONOMIES ARE TEARING YOUR FAMILY TRADITION APART?
OH, HELLO, NAPOLEON.
HE'S MY OTHER GRANDSON, HE'S THE ARTIST IN THE FAMILY. CAN DRAW YOU A PORTRAIT IF YOU LIKE.
HI, I'M DANI AND THIS IS MY TRUSTY PRODUCER JAY.
HEY.
LEVELS WERE OFF. AGAIN, FROM THE TOP.
HI, I'M DANI AND THIS IS JAY.
WE'RE HONORED YOU'VE WELCOMED US TO YOUR RANCH. COULD WE SEE YOUR LLAMAS?
WHAT ARE YOU DOING IN PRESTON?
NO.
HAVE YOU EVER HEARD OF PODCASTS?
IT'S SORTA LIKE A RADIO SHOW ON THE INTERNET.
WE'RE STARTING ONE ABOUT A MYSTERIOUS MURDER RIGHT HERE IN THE HEART OF THE FARMLAND. WE INTEND TO SOLVE IT.
SOUNDS COOL.
TINA! TURN YOUR BUTT AROUND! WE HAVE VISITORS.
DID YOU KNOW CITY COUNCIL MEMBER DOUG YOUNG?
YEAH, EVERYONE KNOWS HE FELL IN THAT GULCH WHILE RIDING HIS BIKE. HE'S DEAD.
WE HAVE REASON TO BELIEVE HIS DEATH WAS NO ACCIDENT. MY PRODUCER JAY HAS SOME SERIOUS DOUBTS.
I'VE GOT SOME SERIOUS DOUBTS.
TINA, YOU FURRY CHUMP, COME GET YOUR PEAR.
SO YOU GUYS ARE DETECTIVES? DO YOU HAVE GUNS? AND TRENCH COATS?
WE'RE JUST RESPONSIBLE CITIZENS HERE TO HELP, NAPOLEON. SOMETIMES...

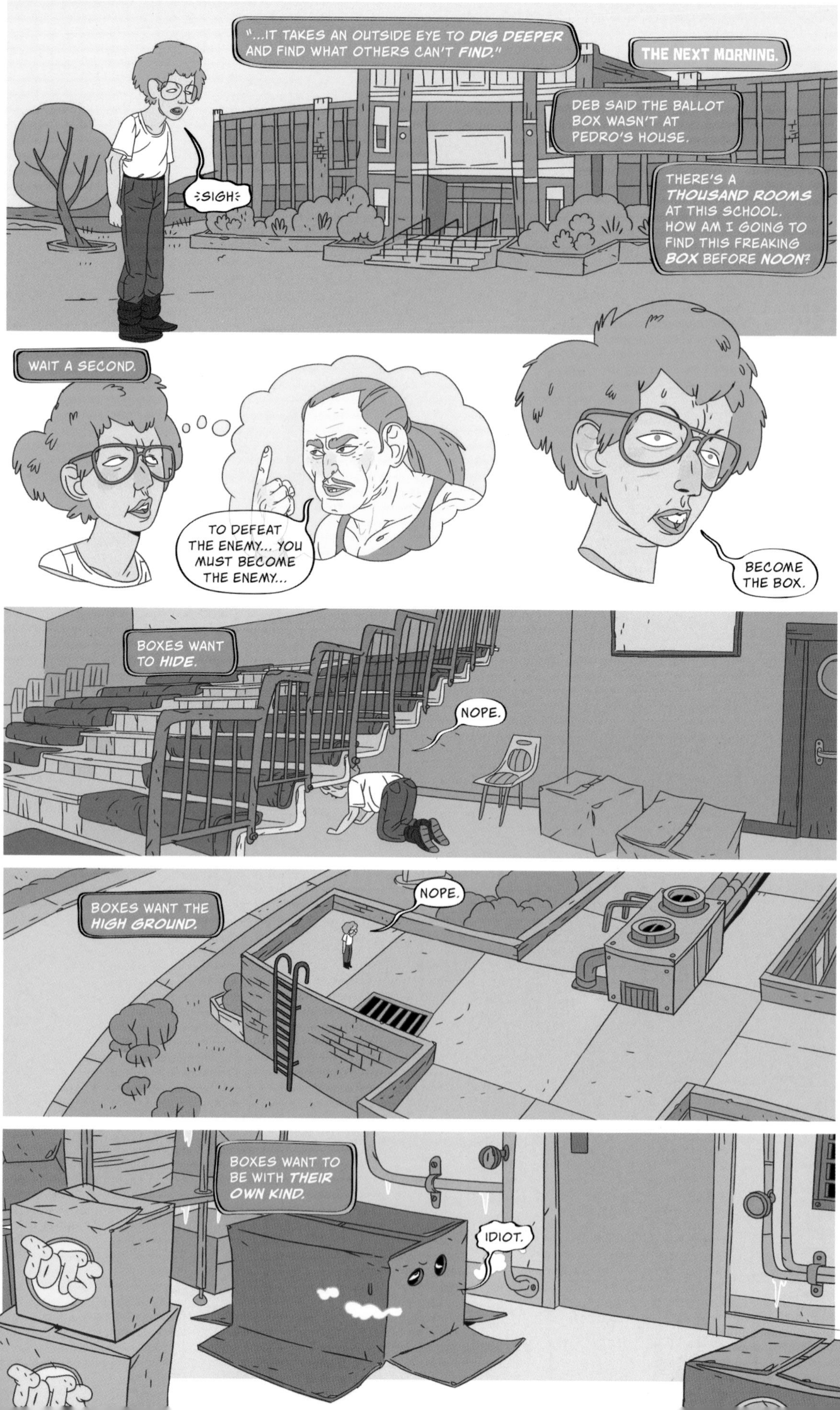
"...IT TAKES AN OUTSIDE EYE TO DIG DEEPER AND FIND WHAT OTHERS CAN'T FIND."
THE NEXT MORNING.
DEB SAID THE BALLOT BOX WASN'T AT PEDRO'S HOUSE.
SIGH
THERE'S A THOUSAND ROOMS AT THIS SCHOOL. HOW AM I GOING TO FIND THIS FREAKING BOX BEFORE NOON?
WAIT A SECOND.
TO DEFEAT THE ENEMY... YOU MUST BECOME THE ENEMY...
BECOME THE BOX.
BOXES WANT TO HIDE.
NOPE.
BOXES WANT THE HIGH GROUND.
NOPE.
BOXES WANT TO BE WITH THEIR OWN KIND.
IDIOT.
TOTS
TOTS

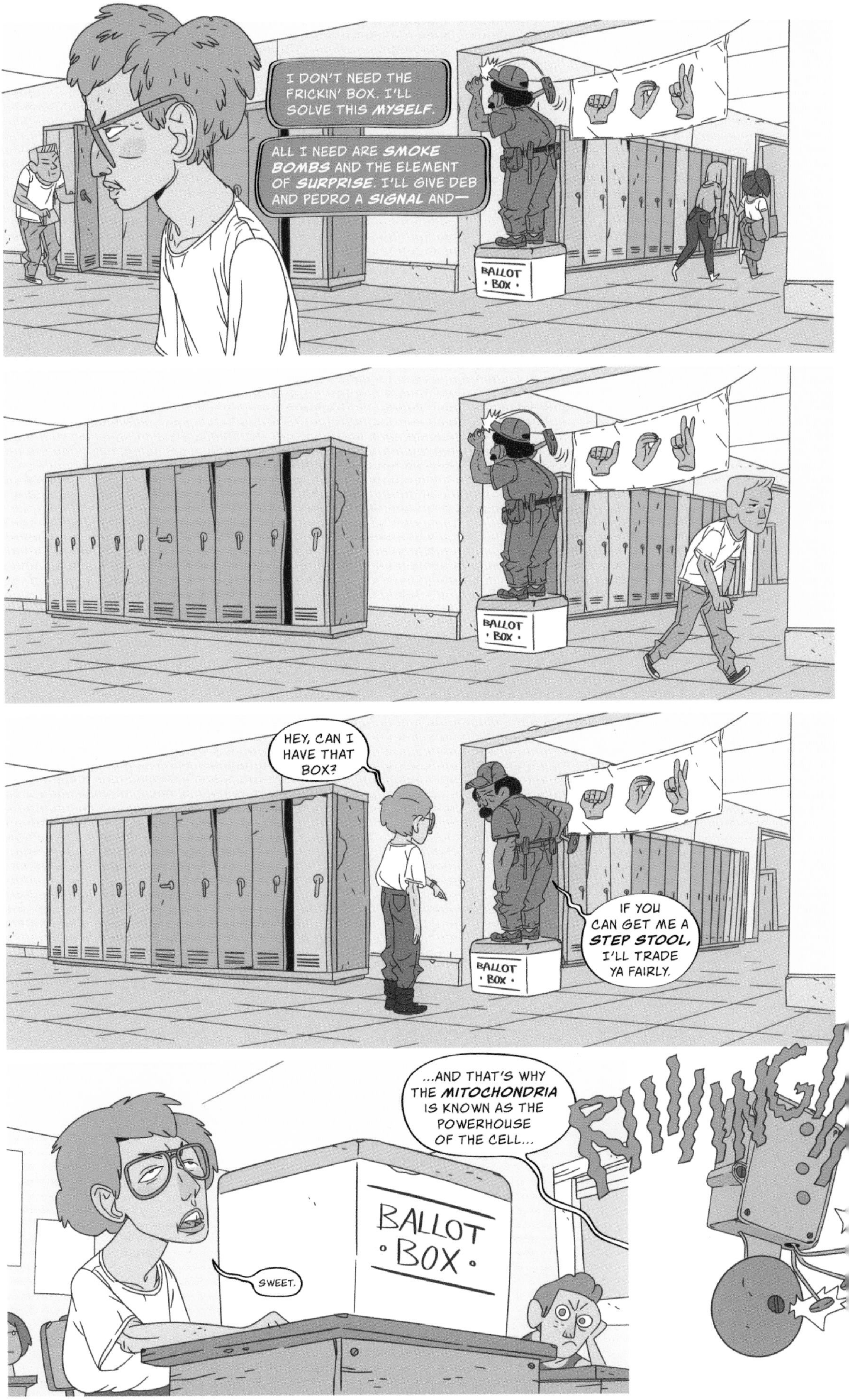
I DON'T NEED THE FRICKIN' BOX. I'LL SOLVE THIS MYSELF.
ALL I NEED ARE SMOKE BOMBS AND THE ELEMENT OF SURPRISE. I'LL GIVE DEB AND PEDRO A SIGNAL AND—
BALLOT • BOX •
BALLOT • BOX •
HEY, CAN I HAVE THAT BOX?
IF YOU CAN GET ME A STEP STOOL, I'LL TRADE YA FAIRLY.
BALLOT • BOX •
...AND THAT'S WHY THE MITOCHONDRIA IS KNOWN AS THE POWERHOUSE OF THE CELL...
RIIIING!
BALLOT • BOX •
SWEET.

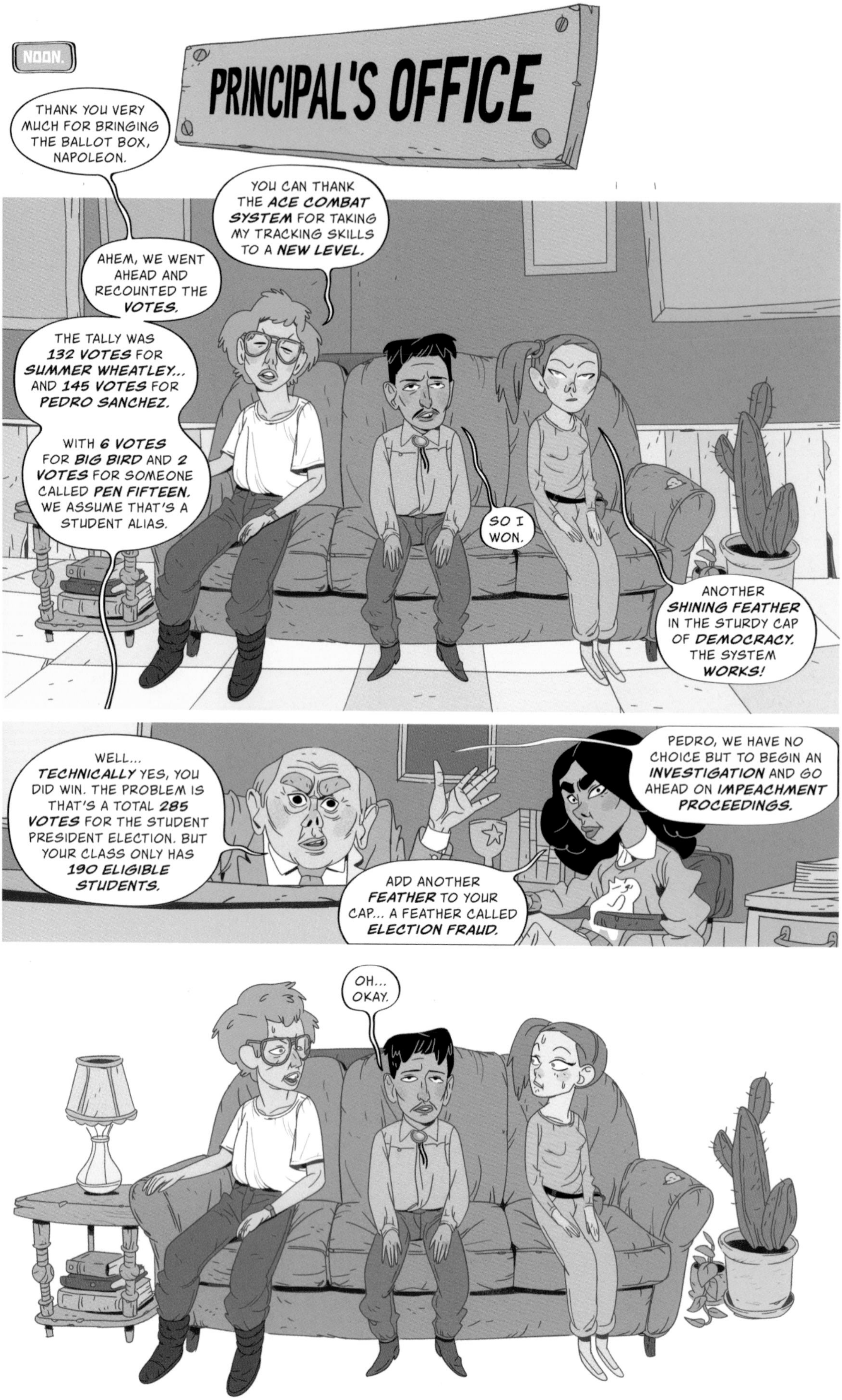
NOON.
PRINCIPAL'S OFFICE
THANK YOU VERY MUCH FOR BRINGING THE BALLOT BOX, NAPOLEON.
YOU CAN THANK THE ACE COMBAT SYSTEM FOR TAKING MY TRACKING SKILLS TO A NEW LEVEL.
AHEM, WE WENT AHEAD AND RECOUNTED THE VOTES.
THE TALLY WAS 132 VOTES FOR SUMMER WHEATLEY... AND 145 VOTES FOR PEDRO SANCHEZ.
WITH 6 VOTES FOR BIG BIRD AND 2 VOTES FOR SOMEONE CALLED PEN FIFTEEN. WE ASSUME THAT'S A STUDENT ALIAS.
SO I WON.
ANOTHER SHINING FEATHER IN THE STURDY CAP OF DEMOCRACY. THE SYSTEM WORKS!
WELL... TECHNICALLY YES, YOU DID WIN. THE PROBLEM IS THAT'S A TOTAL 285 VOTES FOR THE STUDENT PRESIDENT ELECTION. BUT YOUR CLASS ONLY HAS 190 ELIGIBLE STUDENTS.
PEDRO, WE HAVE NO CHOICE BUT TO BEGIN AN INVESTIGATION AND GO AHEAD ON IMPEACHMENT PROCEEDINGS.
ADD ANOTHER FEATHER TO YOUR CAP... A FEATHER CALLED ELECTION FRAUD.
OH... OKAY.

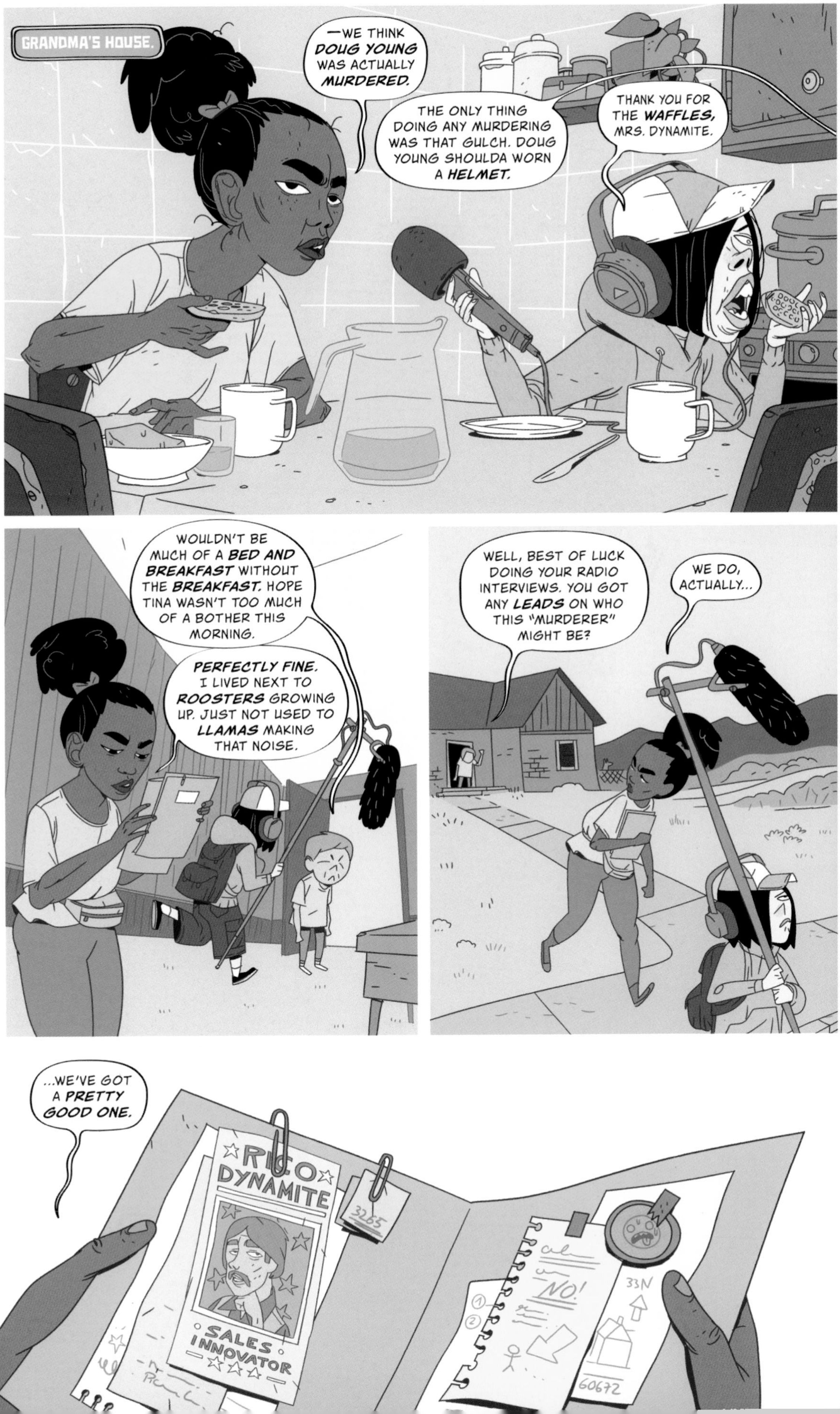
GRANDMA'S HOUSE.
—WE THINK DOUG YOUNG WAS ACTUALLY MURDERED.
THE ONLY THING DOING ANY MURDERING WAS THAT GULCH. DOUG YOUNG SHOULDA WORN A HELMET.
THANK YOU FOR THE WAFFLES, MRS. DYNAMITE.
WOULDN'T BE MUCH OF A BED AND BREAKFAST WITHOUT THE BREAKFAST. HOPE TINA WASN'T TOO MUCH OF A BOTHER THIS MORNING.
PERFECTLY FINE. I LIVED NEXT TO ROOSTERS GROWING UP. JUST NOT USED TO LLAMAS MAKING THAT NOISE.
WELL, BEST OF LUCK DOING YOUR RADIO INTERVIEWS. YOU GOT ANY LEADS ON WHO THIS "MURDERER" MIGHT BE?
WE DO, ACTUALLY...
...WE'VE GOT A PRETTY GOOD ONE.
RICO DYNAMITE
SALES INNOVATOR
3265
NO!
33N
60672

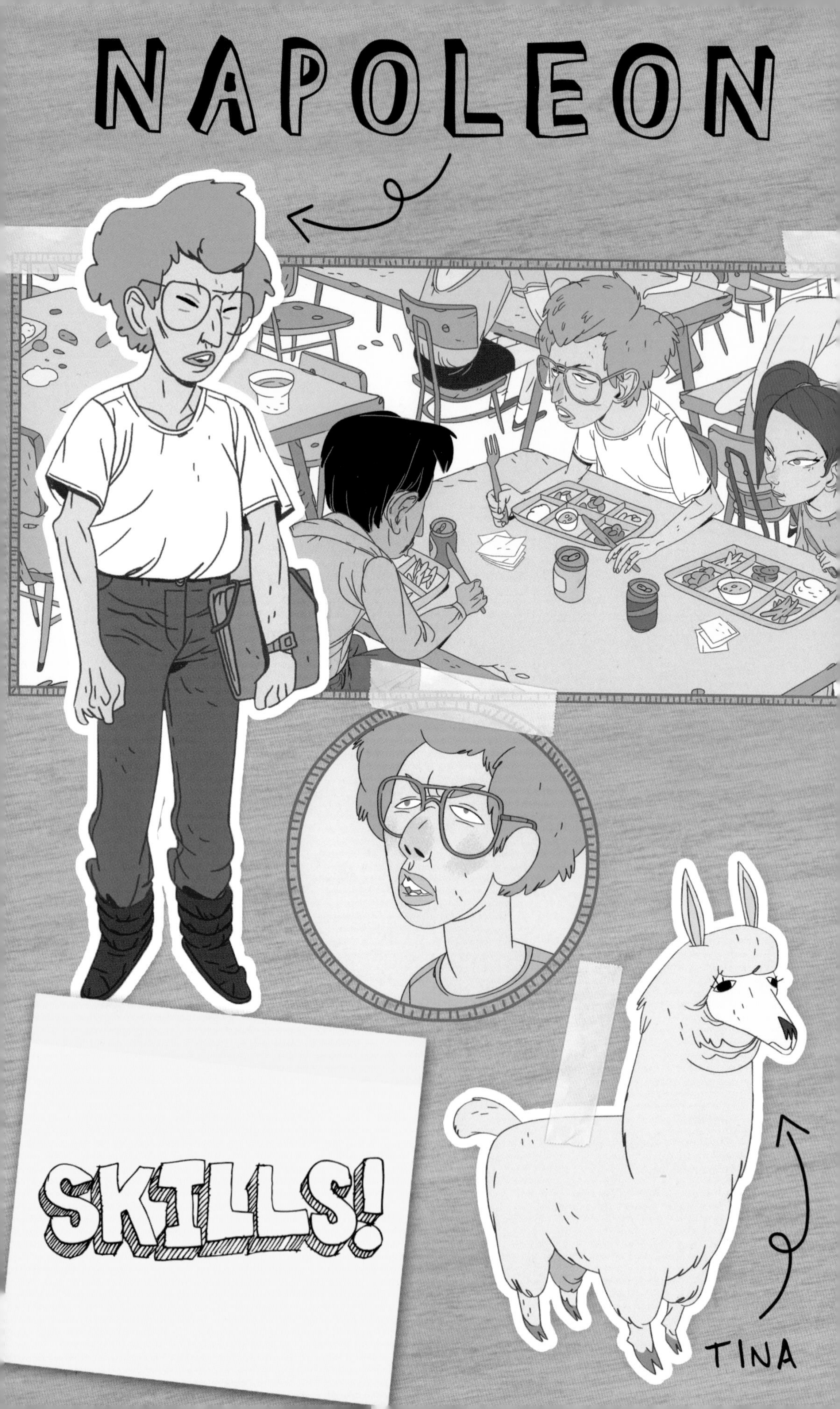
NAPOLEON
SKILLS!
TINA

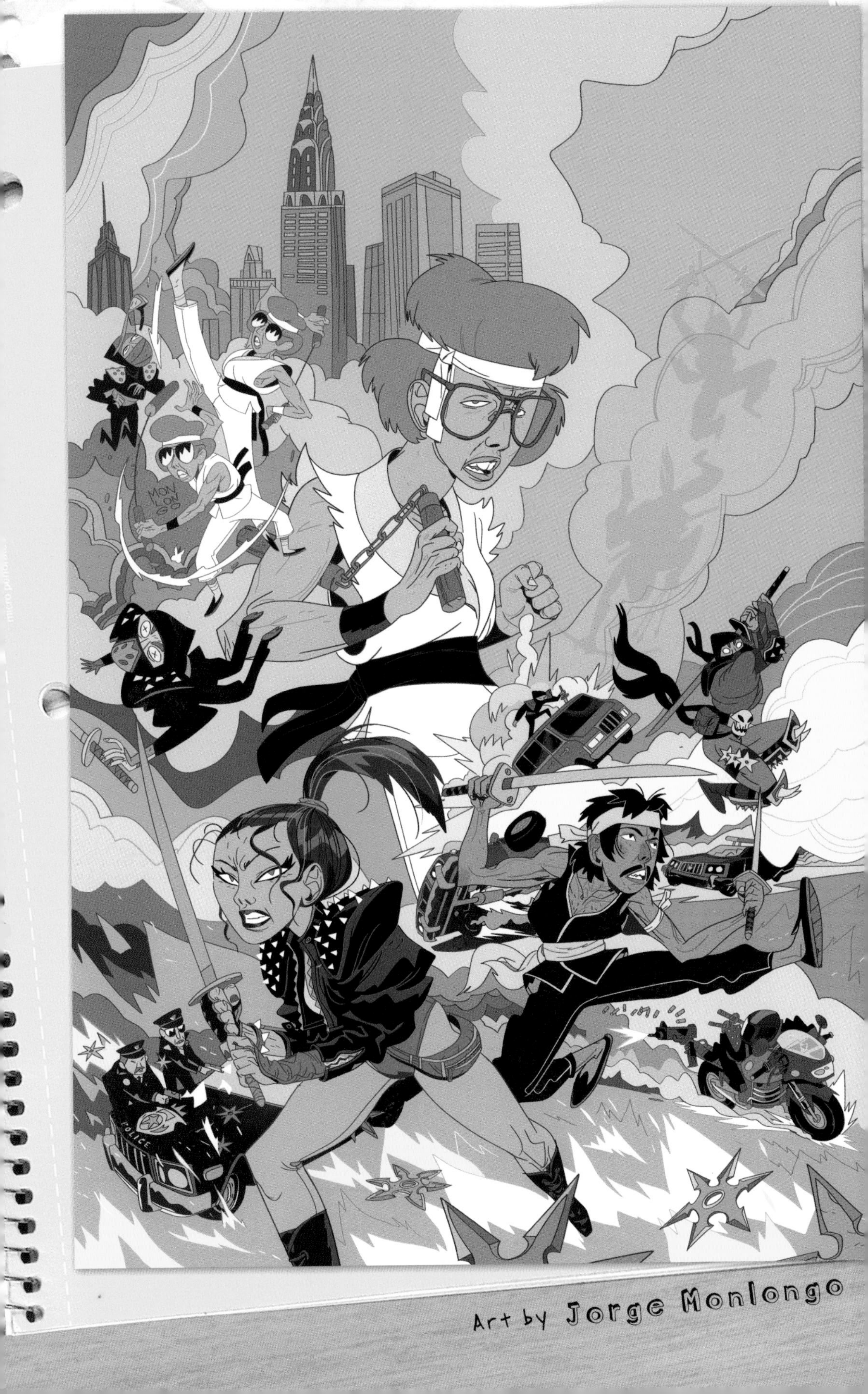
MON LON GO
POLICE

Art by Jorge Monlongo

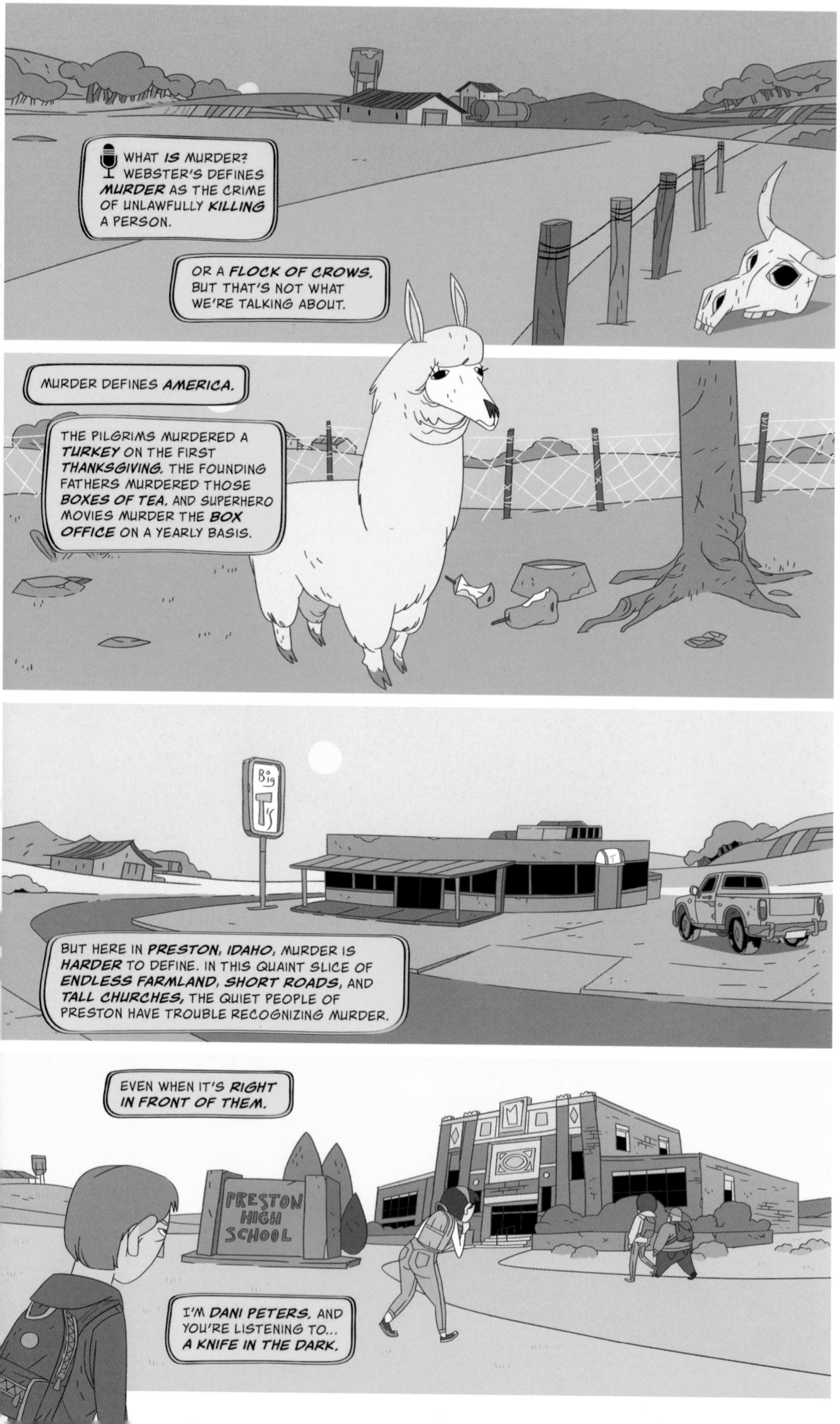
WHAT IS MURDER? WEBSTER'S DEFINES MURDER AS THE CRIME OF UNLAWFULLY KILLING A PERSON.
OR A FLOCK OF CROWS. BUT THAT'S NOT WHAT WE'RE TALKING ABOUT.
MURDER DEFINES AMERICA.
THE PILGRIMS MURDERED A TURKEY ON THE FIRST THANKSGIVING, THE FOUNDING FATHERS MURDERED THOSE BOXES OF TEA, AND SUPERHERO MOVIES MURDER THE BOX OFFICE ON A YEARLY BASIS.
Big T's
BUT HERE IN PRESTON, IDAHO, MURDER IS HARDER TO DEFINE. IN THIS QUAINT SLICE OF ENDLESS FARMLAND, SHORT ROADS, AND TALL CHURCHES, THE QUIET PEOPLE OF PRESTON HAVE TROUBLE RECOGNIZING MURDER.
EVEN WHEN IT'S RIGHT IN FRONT OF THEM.
PRESTON HIGH SCHOOL
I'M DANI PETERS, AND YOU'RE LISTENING TO... A KNIFE IN THE DARK.

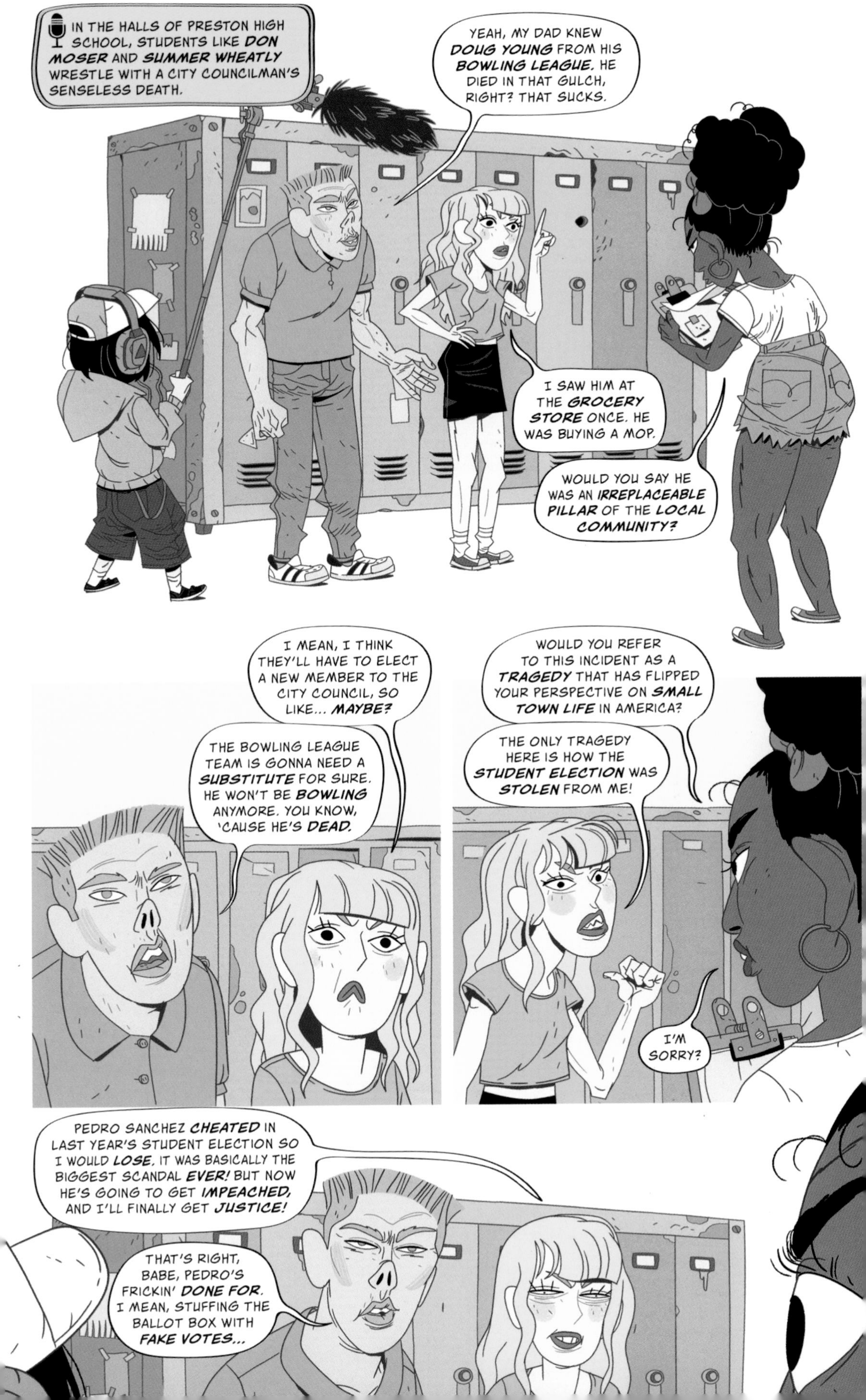
IN THE HALLS OF PRESTON HIGH SCHOOL, STUDENTS LIKE DON MOSER AND SUMMER WHEATLY WRESTLE WITH A CITY COUNCILMAN'S SENSELESS DEATH.
YEAH, MY DAD KNEW DOUG YOUNG FROM HIS BOWLING LEAGUE. HE DIED IN THAT GULCH, RIGHT? THAT SUCKS.
I SAW HIM AT THE GROCERY STORE ONCE. HE WAS BUYING A MOP.
WOULD YOU SAY HE WAS AN IRREPLACEABLE PILLAR OF THE LOCAL COMMUNITY?
I MEAN, I THINK THEY'LL HAVE TO ELECT A NEW MEMBER TO THE CITY COUNCIL, SO LIKE... MAYBE?
THE BOWLING LEAGUE TEAM IS GONNA NEED A SUBSTITUTE FOR SURE. HE WON'T BE BOWLING ANYMORE. YOU KNOW, 'CAUSE HE'S DEAD.
WOULD YOU REFER TO THIS INCIDENT AS A TRAGEDY THAT HAS FLIPPED YOUR PERSPECTIVE ON SMALL TOWN LIFE IN AMERICA?
THE ONLY TRAGEDY HERE IS HOW THE STUDENT ELECTION WAS STOLEN FROM ME!
I'M SORRY?
PEDRO SANCHEZ CHEATED IN LAST YEAR'S STUDENT ELECTION SO I WOULD LOSE. IT WAS BASICALLY THE BIGGEST SCANDAL EVER! BUT NOW HE'S GOING TO GET IMPEACHED, AND I'LL FINALLY GET JUSTICE!
THAT'S RIGHT, BABE, PEDRO'S FRICKIN' DONE FOR. I MEAN, STUFFING THE BALLOT BOX WITH FAKE VOTES...

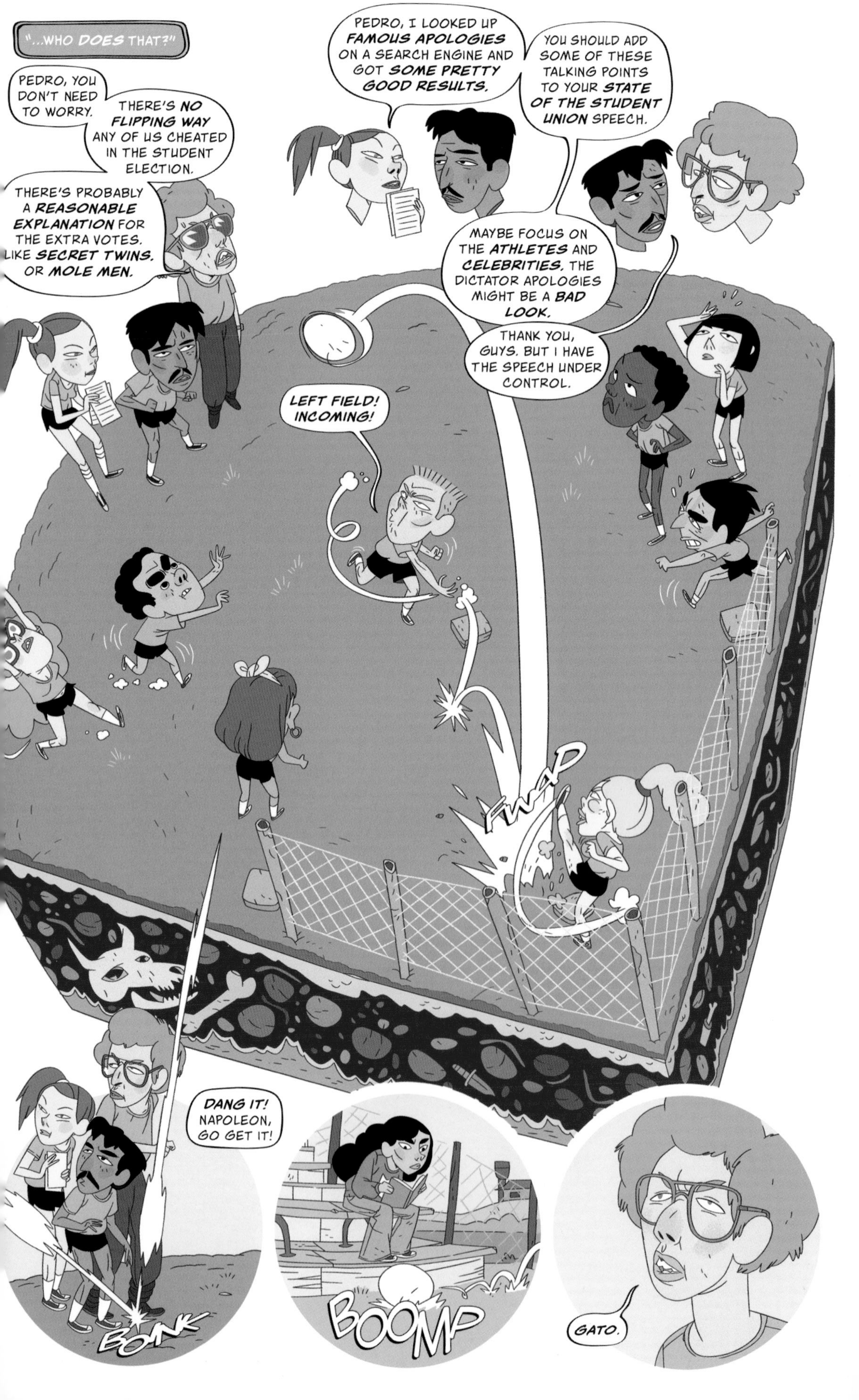
"...WHO DOES THAT?"
PEDRO, YOU DON'T NEED TO WORRY.
THERE'S NO FLIPPING WAY ANY OF US CHEATED IN THE STUDENT ELECTION.
THERE'S PROBABLY A REASONABLE EXPLANATION FOR THE EXTRA VOTES. LIKE SECRET TWINS. OR MOLE MEN.
PEDRO, I LOOKED UP FAMOUS APOLOGIES ON A SEARCH ENGINE AND GOT SOME PRETTY GOOD RESULTS.
YOU SHOULD ADD SOME OF THESE TALKING POINTS TO YOUR STATE OF THE STUDENT UNION SPEECH.
MAYBE FOCUS ON THE ATHLETES AND CELEBRITIES. THE DICTATOR APOLOGIES MIGHT BE A BAD LOOK.
THANK YOU, GUYS. BUT I HAVE THE SPEECH UNDER CONTROL.
LEFT FIELD! INCOMING!
FWAP
DANG IT! NAPOLEON, GO GET IT!
BOINK
BOOMP
GATO.

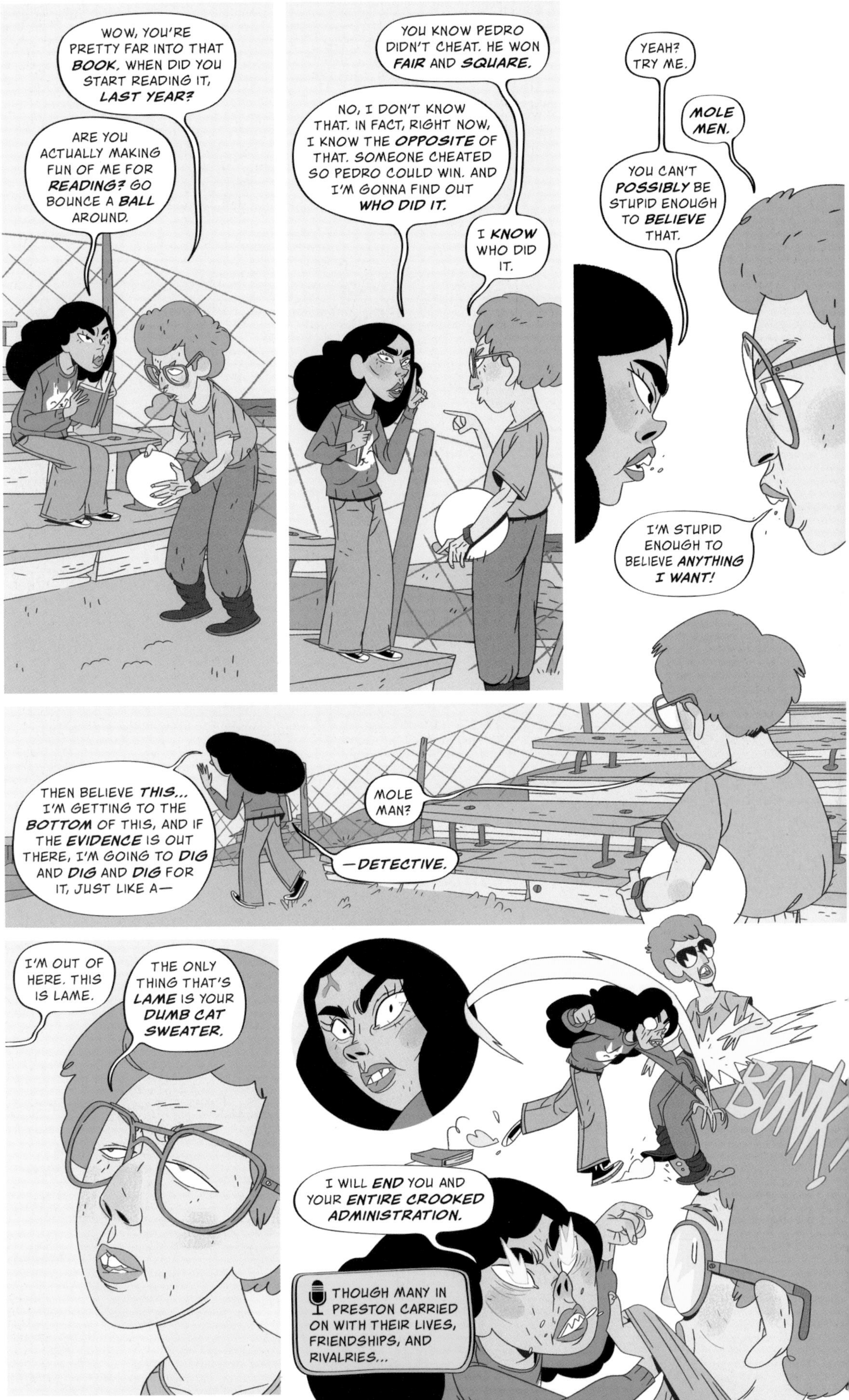
WOW, YOU'RE PRETTY FAR INTO THAT **BOOK.** WHEN DID YOU START READING IT, **LAST YEAR?**
ARE YOU ACTUALLY MAKING FUN OF ME FOR **READING?** GO BOUNCE A **BALL** AROUND.
YOU KNOW PEDRO DIDN'T CHEAT. HE WON **FAIR** AND **SQUARE.**
NO, I DON'T KNOW THAT. IN FACT, RIGHT NOW, I KNOW THE **OPPOSITE** OF THAT. SOMEONE CHEATED SO PEDRO COULD WIN. AND I'M GONNA FIND OUT **WHO DID IT.**
I **KNOW** WHO DID IT.
YEAH? TRY ME.
MOLE MEN.
YOU CAN'T **POSSIBLY** BE STUPID ENOUGH TO **BELIEVE** THAT.
I'M STUPID ENOUGH TO BELIEVE **ANYTHING I WANT!**
THEN BELIEVE **THIS...** I'M GETTING TO THE **BOTTOM** OF THIS, AND IF THE **EVIDENCE** IS OUT THERE, I'M GOING TO **DIG** AND **DIG** AND **DIG** FOR IT, JUST LIKE A—
MOLE MAN?
—DETECTIVE.
I'M OUT OF HERE. THIS IS LAME.
THE ONLY THING THAT'S **LAME** IS YOUR **DUMB CAT SWEATER.**
BONK!
I WILL **END** YOU AND YOUR **ENTIRE CROOKED ADMINISTRATION.**
THOUGH MANY IN PRESTON CARRIED ON WITH THEIR LIVES, FRIENDSHIPS, AND RIVALRIES...

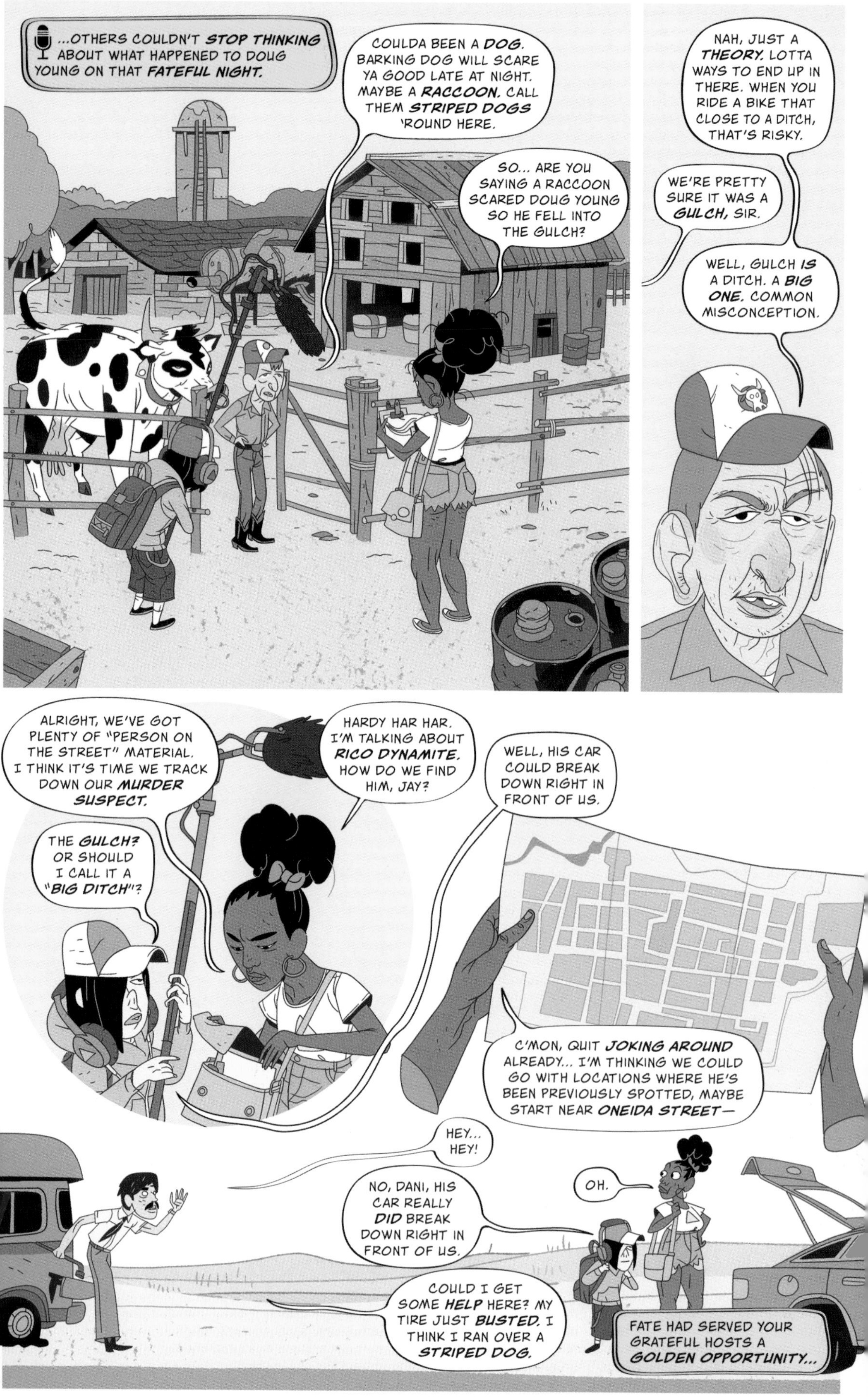
...OTHERS COULDN'T STOP THINKING ABOUT WHAT HAPPENED TO DOUG YOUNG ON THAT FATEFUL NIGHT.
COULDA BEEN A DOG. BARKING DOG WILL SCARE YA GOOD LATE AT NIGHT. MAYBE A RACCOON. CALL THEM STRIPED DOGS 'ROUND HERE.
SO... ARE YOU SAYING A RACCOON SCARED DOUG YOUNG SO HE FELL INTO THE GULCH?
NAH, JUST A THEORY. LOTTA WAYS TO END UP IN THERE. WHEN YOU RIDE A BIKE THAT CLOSE TO A DITCH, THAT'S RISKY.
WE'RE PRETTY SURE IT WAS A GULCH, SIR.
WELL, GULCH IS A DITCH. A BIG ONE. COMMON MISCONCEPTION.
ALRIGHT, WE'VE GOT PLENTY OF "PERSON ON THE STREET" MATERIAL. I THINK IT'S TIME WE TRACK DOWN OUR MURDER SUSPECT.
THE GULCH? OR SHOULD I CALL IT A "BIG DITCH"?
HARDY HAR HAR. I'M TALKING ABOUT RICO DYNAMITE. HOW DO WE FIND HIM, JAY?
WELL, HIS CAR COULD BREAK DOWN RIGHT IN FRONT OF US.
C'MON, QUIT JOKING AROUND ALREADY... I'M THINKING WE COULD GO WITH LOCATIONS WHERE HE'S BEEN PREVIOUSLY SPOTTED, MAYBE START NEAR ONEIDA STREET—
HEY... HEY!
NO, DANI, HIS CAR REALLY DID BREAK DOWN RIGHT IN FRONT OF US.
OH.
COULD I GET SOME HELP HERE? MY TIRE JUST BUSTED. I THINK I RAN OVER A STRIPED DOG.
FATE HAD SERVED YOUR GRATEFUL HOSTS A GOLDEN OPPORTUNITY...

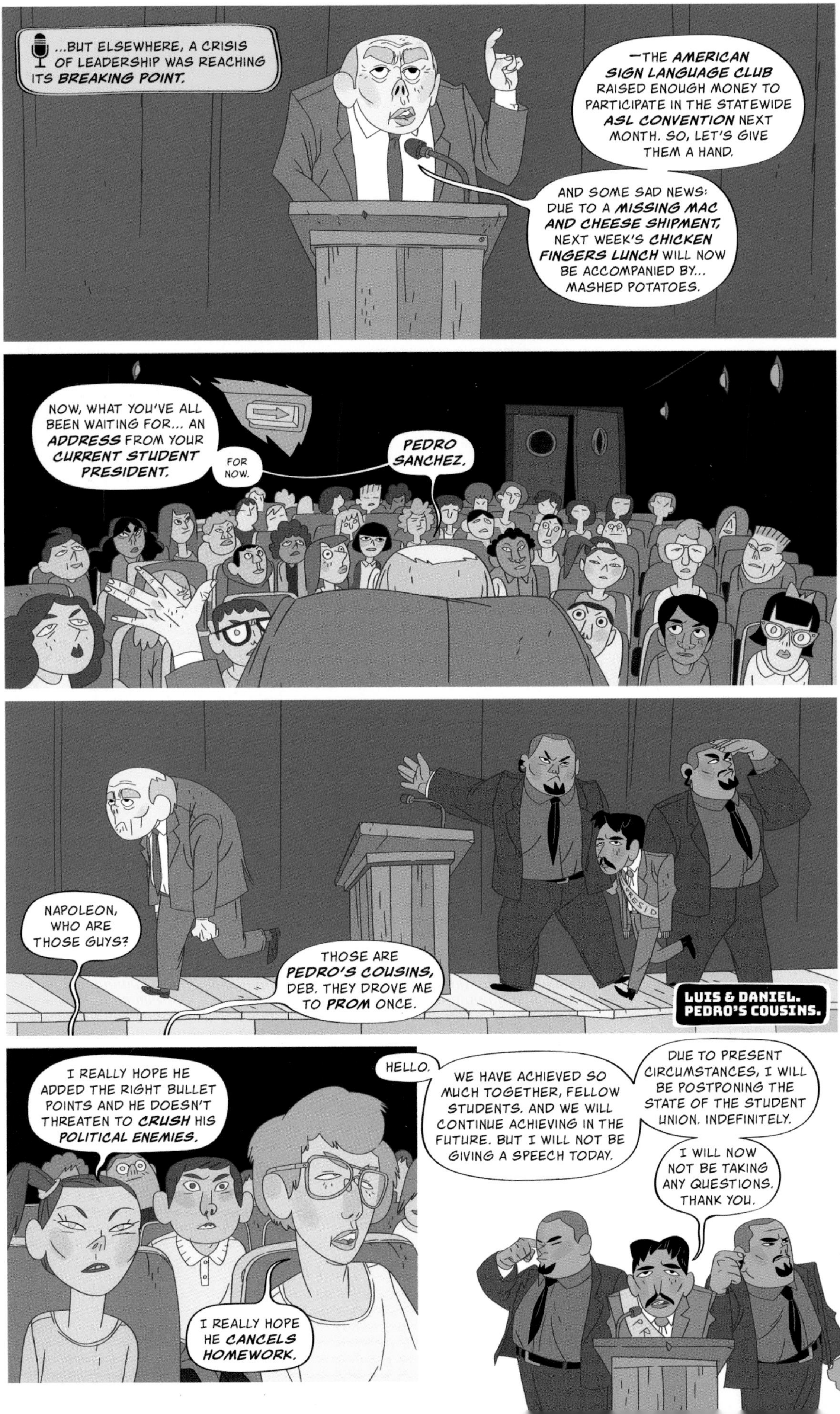
...BUT ELSEWHERE, A CRISIS OF LEADERSHIP WAS REACHING ITS BREAKING POINT.
—THE AMERICAN SIGN LANGUAGE CLUB RAISED ENOUGH MONEY TO PARTICIPATE IN THE STATEWIDE ASL CONVENTION NEXT MONTH. SO, LET'S GIVE THEM A HAND.
AND SOME SAD NEWS: DUE TO A MISSING MAC AND CHEESE SHIPMENT, NEXT WEEK'S CHICKEN FINGERS LUNCH WILL NOW BE ACCOMPANIED BY... MASHED POTATOES.
NOW, WHAT YOU'VE ALL BEEN WAITING FOR... AN ADDRESS FROM YOUR CURRENT STUDENT PRESIDENT.
FOR NOW.
PEDRO SANCHEZ.
NAPOLEON, WHO ARE THOSE GUYS?
THOSE ARE PEDRO'S COUSINS, DEB. THEY DROVE ME TO PROM ONCE.
LUIS & DANIEL. PEDRO'S COUSINS.
I REALLY HOPE HE ADDED THE RIGHT BULLET POINTS AND HE DOESN'T THREATEN TO CRUSH HIS POLITICAL ENEMIES.
I REALLY HOPE HE CANCELS HOMEWORK.
HELLO.
WE HAVE ACHIEVED SO MUCH TOGETHER, FELLOW STUDENTS. AND WE WILL CONTINUE ACHIEVING IN THE FUTURE. BUT I WILL NOT BE GIVING A SPEECH TODAY.
DUE TO PRESENT CIRCUMSTANCES, I WILL BE POSTPONING THE STATE OF THE STUDENT UNION. INDEFINITELY.
I WILL NOW NOT BE TAKING ANY QUESTIONS. THANK YOU.

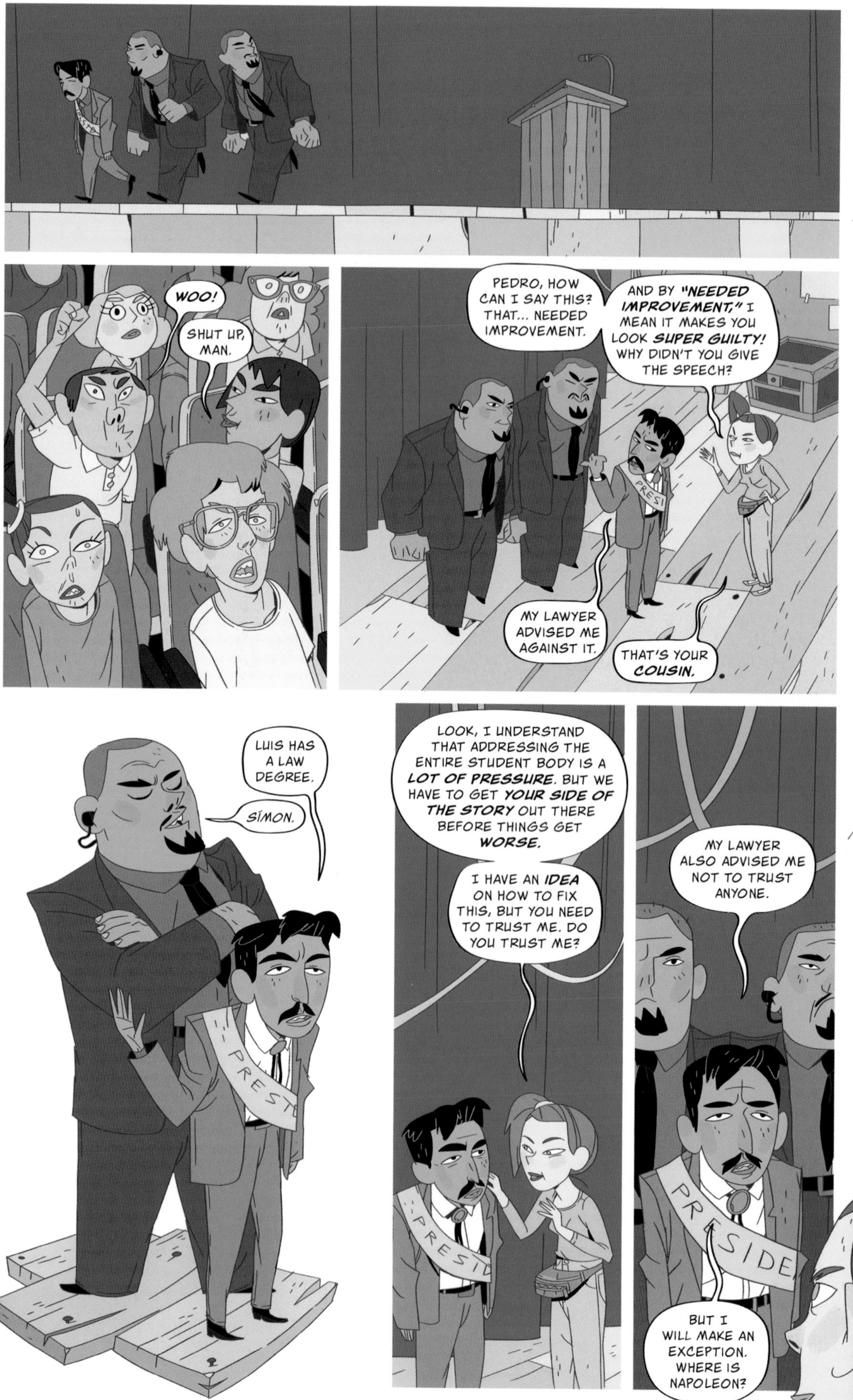
WOO!
SHUT UP, MAN.
PEDRO, HOW CAN I SAY THIS? THAT... NEEDED IMPROVEMENT.
AND BY "NEEDED IMPROVEMENT," I MEAN IT MAKES YOU LOOK SUPER GUILTY! WHY DIDN'T YOU GIVE THE SPEECH?
MY LAWYER ADVISED ME AGAINST IT.
THAT'S YOUR COUSIN.
LUIS HAS A LAW DEGREE.
SÍMON.
LOOK, I UNDERSTAND THAT ADDRESSING THE ENTIRE STUDENT BODY IS A LOT OF PRESSURE. BUT WE HAVE TO GET YOUR SIDE OF THE STORY OUT THERE BEFORE THINGS GET WORSE.
I HAVE AN IDEA ON HOW TO FIX THIS, BUT YOU NEED TO TRUST ME. DO YOU TRUST ME?
MY LAWYER ALSO ADVISED ME NOT TO TRUST ANYONE.
BUT I WILL MAKE AN EXCEPTION. WHERE IS NAPOLEON?

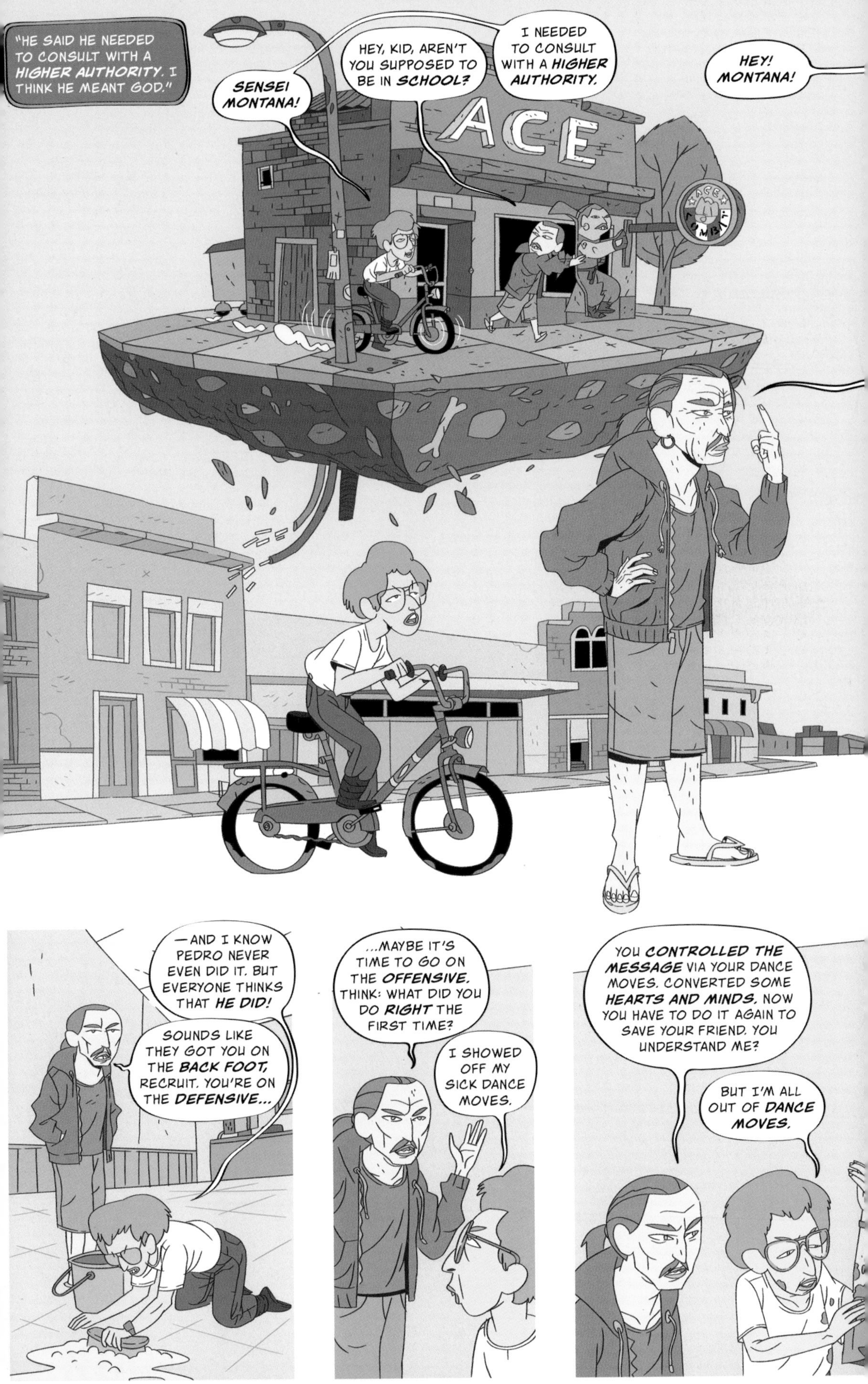
"HE SAID HE NEEDED TO CONSULT WITH A HIGHER AUTHORITY. I THINK HE MEANT GOD."
SENSEI MONTANA!
HEY, KID, AREN'T YOU SUPPOSED TO BE IN SCHOOL?
I NEEDED TO CONSULT WITH A HIGHER AUTHORITY.
HEY! MONTANA!
ACE
ACE COMBAT
—AND I KNOW PEDRO NEVER EVEN DID IT. BUT EVERYONE THINKS THAT HE DID!
SOUNDS LIKE THEY GOT YOU ON THE BACK FOOT, RECRUIT. YOU'RE ON THE DEFENSIVE...
...MAYBE IT'S TIME TO GO ON THE OFFENSIVE. THINK: WHAT DID YOU DO RIGHT THE FIRST TIME?
I SHOWED OFF MY SICK DANCE MOVES.
YOU CONTROLLED THE MESSAGE VIA YOUR DANCE MOVES. CONVERTED SOME HEARTS AND MINDS. NOW YOU HAVE TO DO IT AGAIN TO SAVE YOUR FRIEND. YOU UNDERSTAND ME?
BUT I'M ALL OUT OF DANCE MOVES.

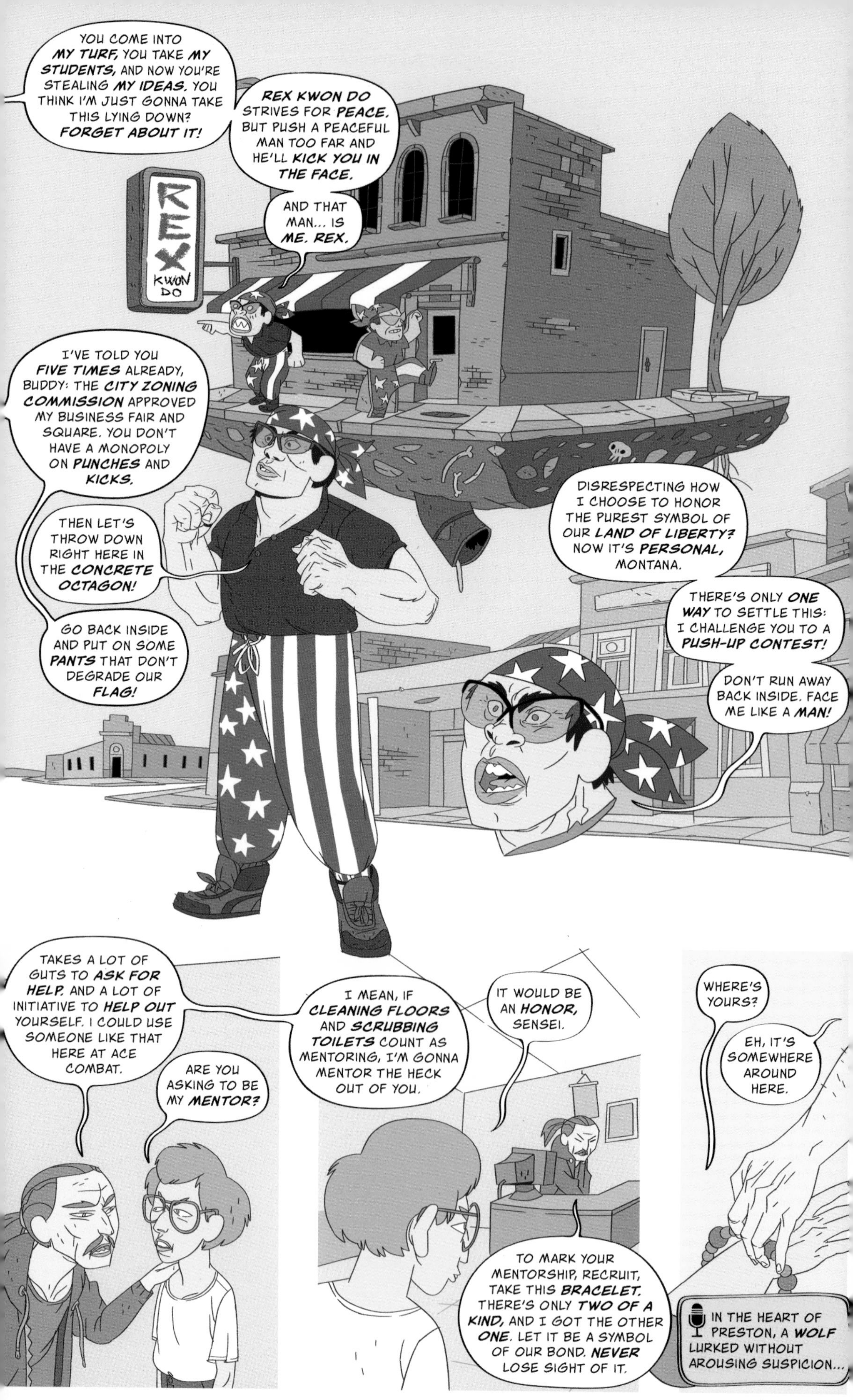
YOU COME INTO MY TURF, YOU TAKE MY STUDENTS, AND NOW YOU'RE STEALING MY IDEAS. YOU THINK I'M JUST GONNA TAKE THIS LYING DOWN? FORGET ABOUT IT!
REX KWON DO STRIVES FOR PEACE. BUT PUSH A PEACEFUL MAN TOO FAR AND HE'LL KICK YOU IN THE FACE.
AND THAT MAN... IS ME. REX.
REX KWON DO
I'VE TOLD YOU FIVE TIMES ALREADY, BUDDY: THE CITY ZONING COMMISSION APPROVED MY BUSINESS FAIR AND SQUARE. YOU DON'T HAVE A MONOPOLY ON PUNCHES AND KICKS.
THEN LET'S THROW DOWN RIGHT HERE IN THE CONCRETE OCTAGON!
GO BACK INSIDE AND PUT ON SOME PANTS THAT DON'T DEGRADE OUR FLAG!
DISRESPECTING HOW I CHOOSE TO HONOR THE PUREST SYMBOL OF OUR LAND OF LIBERTY? NOW IT'S PERSONAL, MONTANA.
THERE'S ONLY ONE WAY TO SETTLE THIS: I CHALLENGE YOU TO A PUSH-UP CONTEST!
DON'T RUN AWAY BACK INSIDE. FACE ME LIKE A MAN!
TAKES A LOT OF GUTS TO ASK FOR HELP. AND A LOT OF INITIATIVE TO HELP OUT YOURSELF. I COULD USE SOMEONE LIKE THAT HERE AT ACE COMBAT.
ARE YOU ASKING TO BE MY MENTOR?
I MEAN, IF CLEANING FLOORS AND SCRUBBING TOILETS COUNT AS MENTORING, I'M GONNA MENTOR THE HECK OUT OF YOU.
IT WOULD BE AN HONOR, SENSEI.
TO MARK YOUR MENTORSHIP, RECRUIT, TAKE THIS BRACELET. THERE'S ONLY TWO OF A KIND, AND I GOT THE OTHER ONE. LET IT BE A SYMBOL OF OUR BOND. NEVER LOSE SIGHT OF IT.
WHERE'S YOURS?
EH, IT'S SOMEWHERE AROUND HERE.
IN THE HEART OF PRESTON, A WOLF LURKED WITHOUT AROUSING SUSPICION...

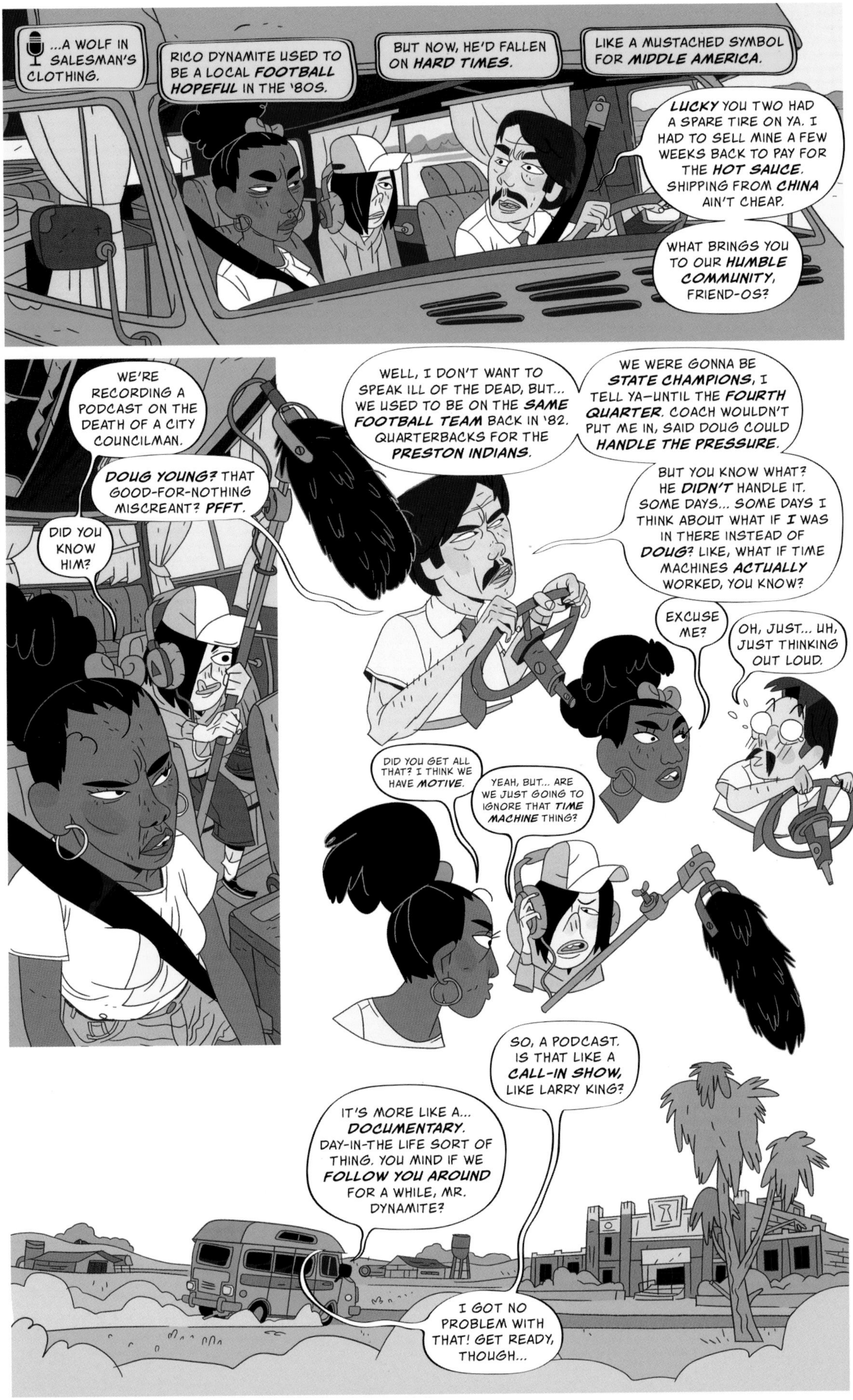
...A WOLF IN SALESMAN'S CLOTHING.
RICO DYNAMITE USED TO BE A LOCAL FOOTBALL HOPEFUL IN THE '80S.
BUT NOW, HE'D FALLEN ON HARD TIMES.
LIKE A MUSTACHED SYMBOL FOR MIDDLE AMERICA.
LUCKY YOU TWO HAD A SPARE TIRE ON YA. I HAD TO SELL MINE A FEW WEEKS BACK TO PAY FOR THE HOT SAUCE. SHIPPING FROM CHINA AIN'T CHEAP.
WHAT BRINGS YOU TO OUR HUMBLE COMMUNITY, FRIEND-OS?
WE'RE RECORDING A PODCAST ON THE DEATH OF A CITY COUNCILMAN.
DOUG YOUNG? THAT GOOD-FOR-NOTHING MISCREANT? PFFT.
DID YOU KNOW HIM?
WELL, I DON'T WANT TO SPEAK ILL OF THE DEAD, BUT... WE USED TO BE ON THE SAME FOOTBALL TEAM BACK IN '82. QUARTERBACKS FOR THE PRESTON INDIANS.
WE WERE GONNA BE STATE CHAMPIONS, I TELL YA—UNTIL THE FOURTH QUARTER. COACH WOULDN'T PUT ME IN, SAID DOUG COULD HANDLE THE PRESSURE.
BUT YOU KNOW WHAT? HE DIDN'T HANDLE IT. SOME DAYS... SOME DAYS I THINK ABOUT WHAT IF I WAS IN THERE INSTEAD OF DOUG? LIKE, WHAT IF TIME MACHINES ACTUALLY WORKED, YOU KNOW?
EXCUSE ME?
OH, JUST... UH, JUST THINKING OUT LOUD.
DID YOU GET ALL THAT? I THINK WE HAVE MOTIVE.
YEAH, BUT... ARE WE JUST GOING TO IGNORE THAT TIME MACHINE THING?
SO, A PODCAST. IS THAT LIKE A CALL-IN SHOW, LIKE LARRY KING?
IT'S MORE LIKE A... DOCUMENTARY. DAY-IN-THE LIFE SORT OF THING. YOU MIND IF WE FOLLOW YOU AROUND FOR A WHILE, MR. DYNAMITE?
I GOT NO PROBLEM WITH THAT! GET READY, THOUGH...

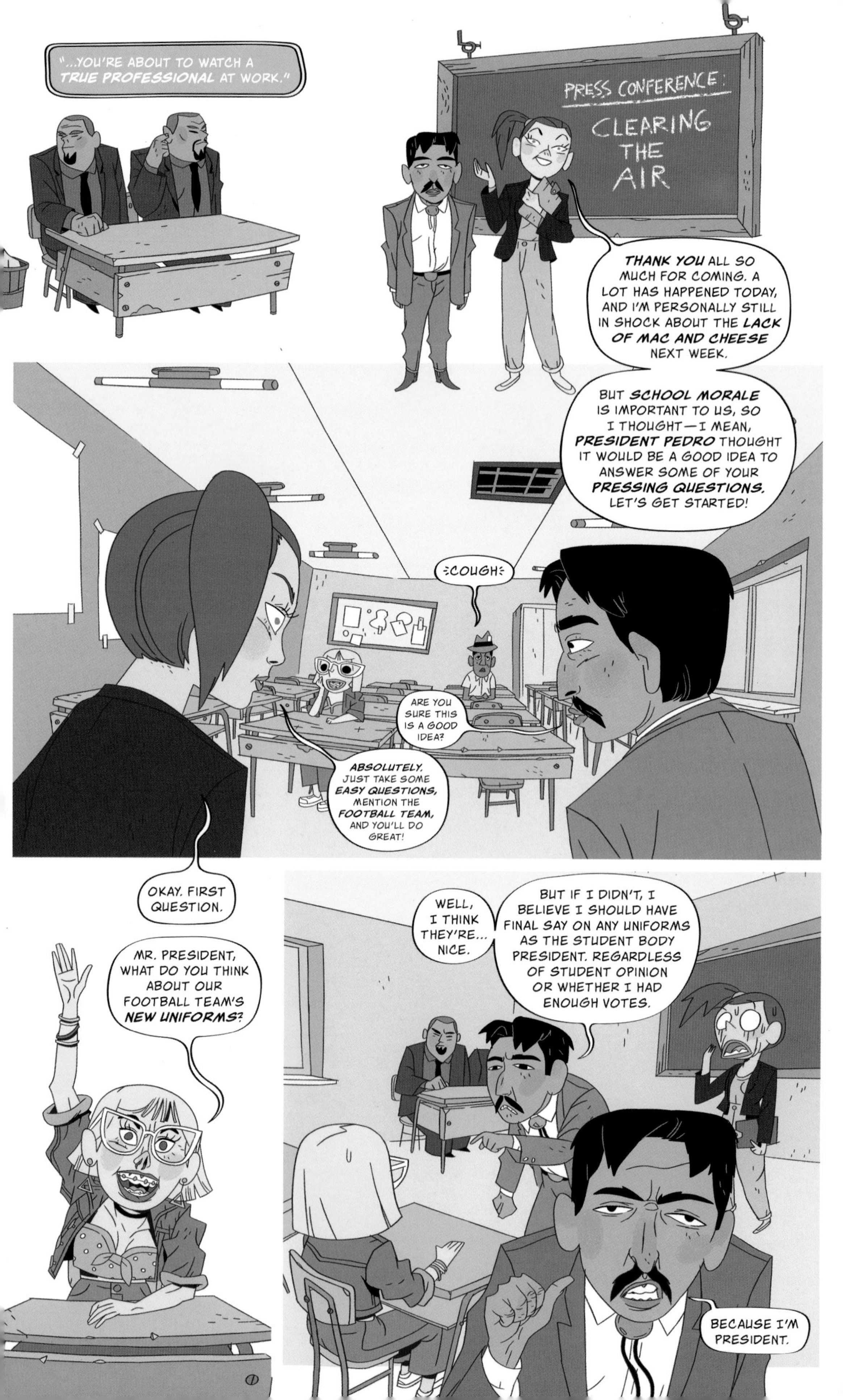
"...YOU'RE ABOUT TO WATCH A TRUE PROFESSIONAL AT WORK."
PRESS CONFERENCE: CLEARING THE AIR
THANK YOU ALL SO MUCH FOR COMING. A LOT HAS HAPPENED TODAY, AND I'M PERSONALLY STILL IN SHOCK ABOUT THE LACK OF MAC AND CHEESE NEXT WEEK.
BUT SCHOOL MORALE IS IMPORTANT TO US, SO I THOUGHT—I MEAN, PRESIDENT PEDRO THOUGHT IT WOULD BE A GOOD IDEA TO ANSWER SOME OF YOUR PRESSING QUESTIONS. LET'S GET STARTED!
COUGH
ARE YOU SURE THIS IS A GOOD IDEA?
ABSOLUTELY. JUST TAKE SOME EASY QUESTIONS, MENTION THE FOOTBALL TEAM, AND YOU'LL DO GREAT!
OKAY. FIRST QUESTION.
MR. PRESIDENT, WHAT DO YOU THINK ABOUT OUR FOOTBALL TEAM'S NEW UNIFORMS?
WELL, I THINK THEY'RE... NICE.
BUT IF I DIDN'T, I BELIEVE I SHOULD HAVE FINAL SAY ON ANY UNIFORMS AS THE STUDENT BODY PRESIDENT. REGARDLESS OF STUDENT OPINION OR WHETHER I HAD ENOUGH VOTES.
BECAUSE I'M PRESIDENT.

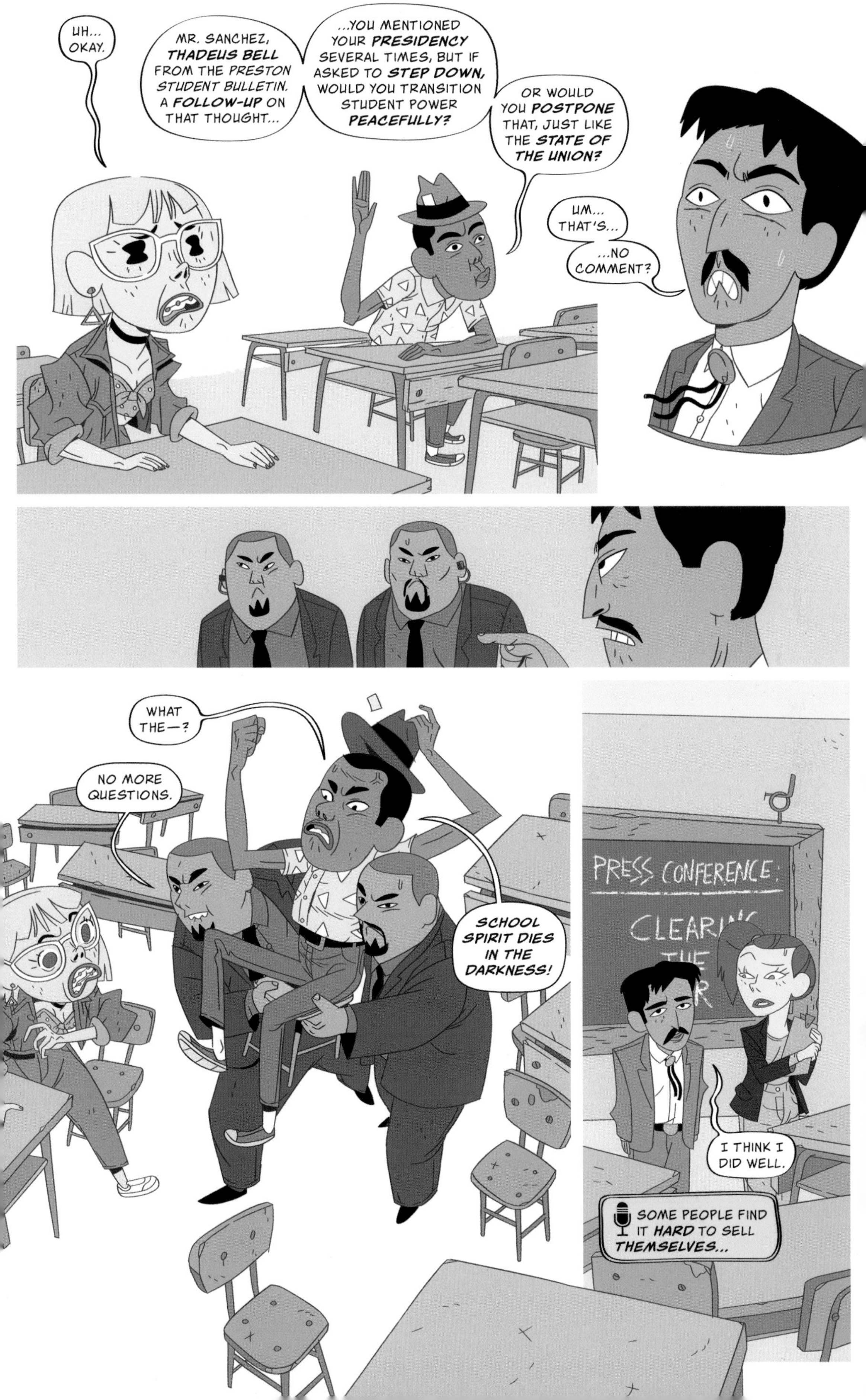
UH... OKAY.
MR. SANCHEZ, THADEUS BELL FROM THE PRESTON STUDENT BULLETIN. A FOLLOW-UP ON THAT THOUGHT...
...YOU MENTIONED YOUR PRESIDENCY SEVERAL TIMES, BUT IF ASKED TO STEP DOWN, WOULD YOU TRANSITION STUDENT POWER PEACEFULLY?
OR WOULD YOU POSTPONE THAT, JUST LIKE THE STATE OF THE UNION?
UM... THAT'S...
...NO COMMENT?
WHAT THE—?
NO MORE QUESTIONS.
SCHOOL SPIRIT DIES IN THE DARKNESS!
PRESS CONFERENCE:
I THINK I DID WELL.
SOME PEOPLE FIND IT HARD TO SELL THEMSELVES...

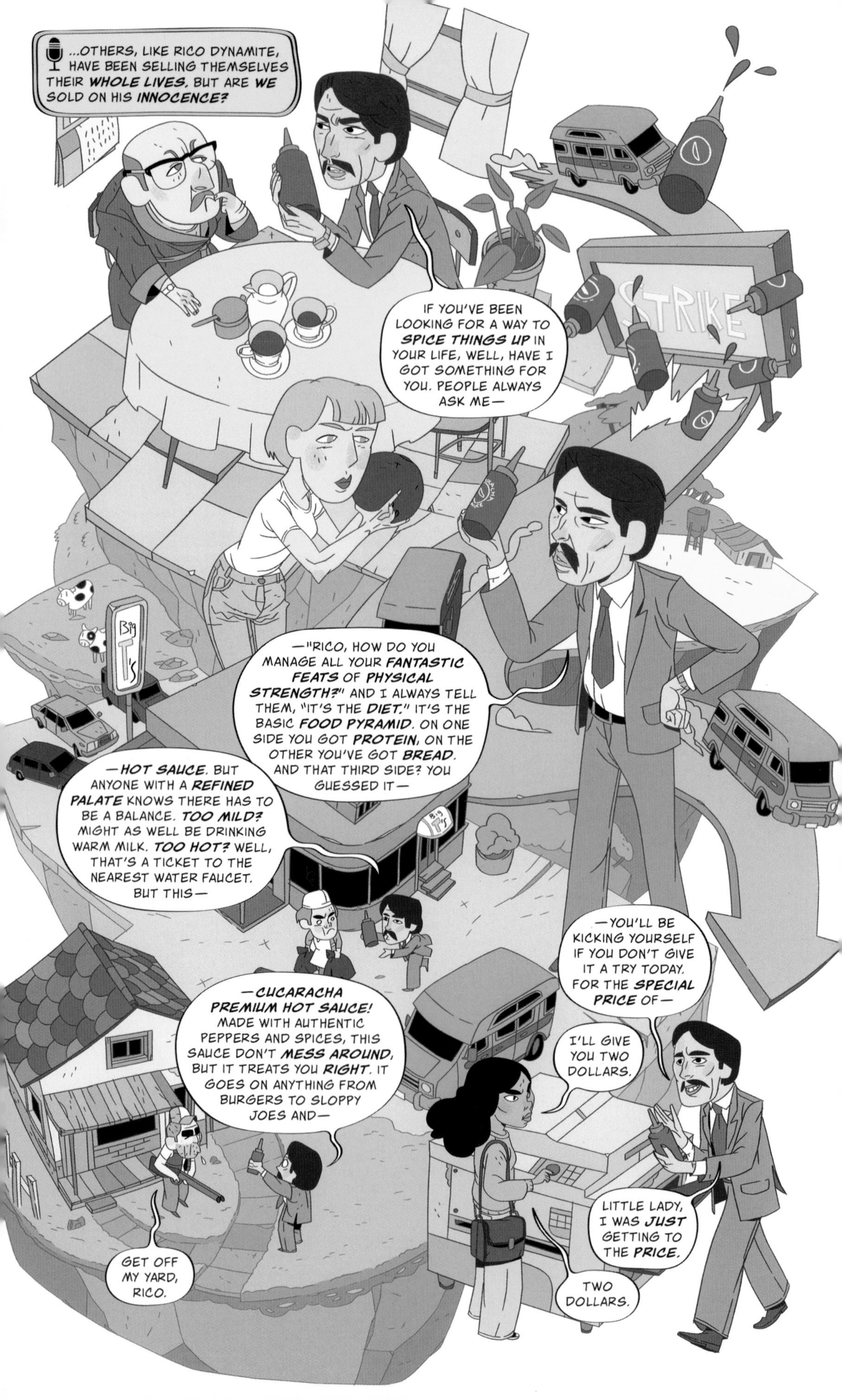
...OTHERS, LIKE RICO DYNAMITE, HAVE BEEN SELLING THEMSELVES THEIR WHOLE LIVES. BUT ARE WE SOLD ON HIS INNOCENCE?
IF YOU'VE BEEN LOOKING FOR A WAY TO SPICE THINGS UP IN YOUR LIFE, WELL, HAVE I GOT SOMETHING FOR YOU. PEOPLE ALWAYS ASK ME—
STRIKE
Big T's
—"RICO, HOW DO YOU MANAGE ALL YOUR FANTASTIC FEATS OF PHYSICAL STRENGTH?" AND I ALWAYS TELL THEM, "IT'S THE DIET." IT'S THE BASIC FOOD PYRAMID. ON ONE SIDE YOU GOT PROTEIN, ON THE OTHER YOU'VE GOT BREAD. AND THAT THIRD SIDE? YOU GUESSED IT—
—HOT SAUCE. BUT ANYONE WITH A REFINED PALATE KNOWS THERE HAS TO BE A BALANCE. TOO MILD? MIGHT AS WELL BE DRINKING WARM MILK. TOO HOT? WELL, THAT'S A TICKET TO THE NEAREST WATER FAUCET. BUT THIS—
Big T's
—YOU'LL BE KICKING YOURSELF IF YOU DON'T GIVE IT A TRY TODAY. FOR THE SPECIAL PRICE OF—
—CUCARACHA PREMIUM HOT SAUCE! MADE WITH AUTHENTIC PEPPERS AND SPICES, THIS SAUCE DON'T MESS AROUND, BUT IT TREATS YOU RIGHT. IT GOES ON ANYTHING FROM BURGERS TO SLOPPY JOES AND—
I'LL GIVE YOU TWO DOLLARS.
LITTLE LADY, I WAS JUST GETTING TO THE PRICE.
GET OFF MY YARD, RICO.
TWO DOLLARS.

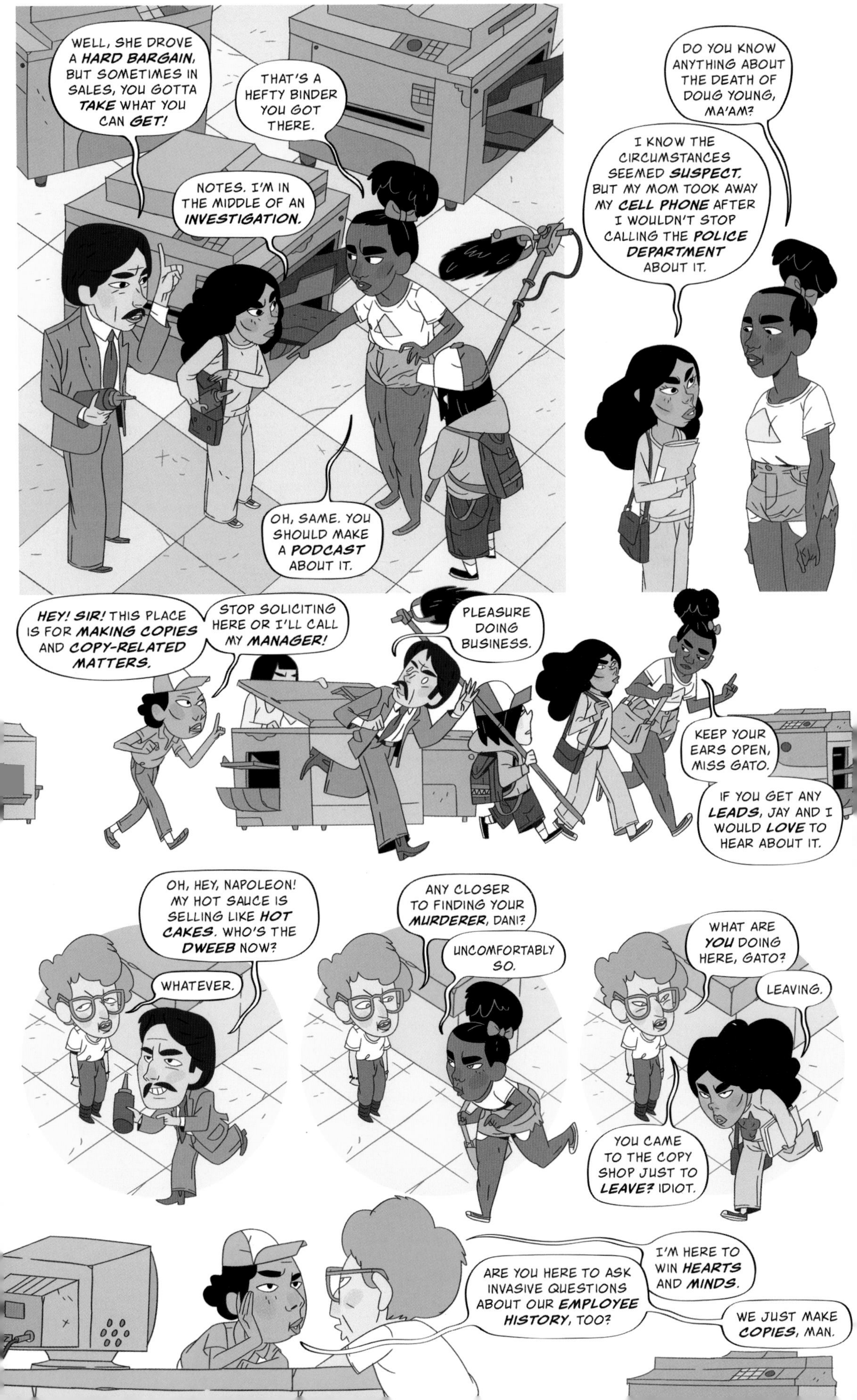

WELL, SHE DROVE A HARD BARGAIN, BUT SOMETIMES IN SALES, YOU GOTTA TAKE WHAT YOU CAN GET!
THAT'S A HEFTY BINDER YOU GOT THERE.
NOTES. I'M IN THE MIDDLE OF AN INVESTIGATION.
OH, SAME. YOU SHOULD MAKE A PODCAST ABOUT IT.
DO YOU KNOW ANYTHING ABOUT THE DEATH OF DOUG YOUNG, MA'AM?
I KNOW THE CIRCUMSTANCES SEEMED SUSPECT. BUT MY MOM TOOK AWAY MY CELL PHONE AFTER I WOULDN'T STOP CALLING THE POLICE DEPARTMENT ABOUT IT.
HEY! SIR! THIS PLACE IS FOR MAKING COPIES AND COPY-RELATED MATTERS.
STOP SOLICITING HERE OR I'LL CALL MY MANAGER!
PLEASURE DOING BUSINESS.
KEEP YOUR EARS OPEN, MISS GATO.
IF YOU GET ANY LEADS, JAY AND I WOULD LOVE TO HEAR ABOUT IT.
OH, HEY, NAPOLEON! MY HOT SAUCE IS SELLING LIKE HOT CAKES. WHO'S THE DWEEB NOW?
WHATEVER.
ANY CLOSER TO FINDING YOUR MURDERER, DANI?
UNCOMFORTABLY SO.
WHAT ARE YOU DOING HERE, GATO?
LEAVING.
YOU CAME TO THE COPY SHOP JUST TO LEAVE? IDIOT.
ARE YOU HERE TO ASK INVASIVE QUESTIONS ABOUT OUR EMPLOYEE HISTORY, TOO?
I'M HERE TO WIN HEARTS AND MINDS.
WE JUST MAKE COPIES, MAN.

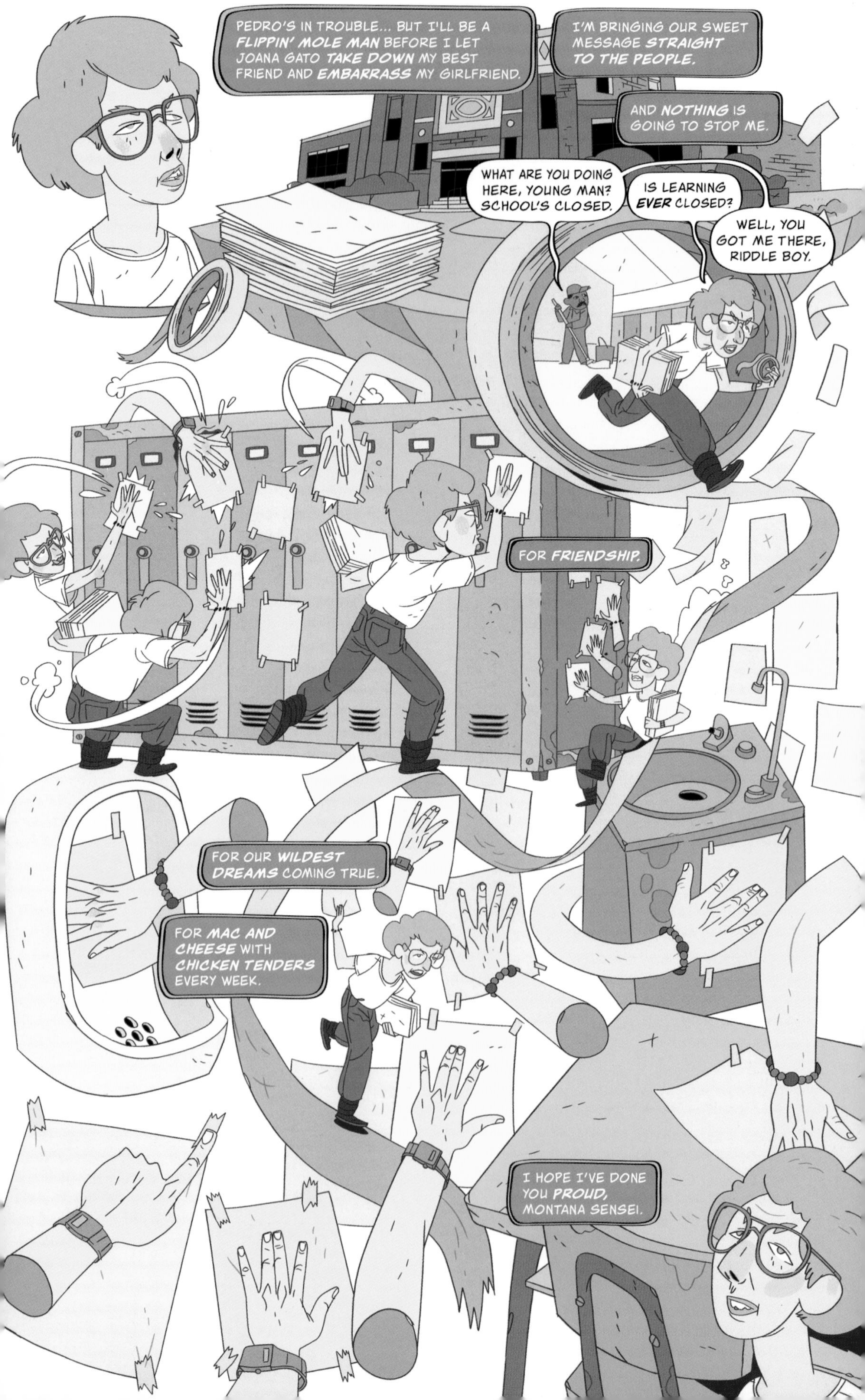
PEDRO'S IN TROUBLE... BUT I'LL BE A FLIPPIN' MOLE MAN BEFORE I LET JOANA GATO TAKE DOWN MY BEST FRIEND AND EMBARRASS MY GIRLFRIEND.
I'M BRINGING OUR SWEET MESSAGE STRAIGHT TO THE PEOPLE.
AND NOTHING IS GOING TO STOP ME.
WHAT ARE YOU DOING HERE, YOUNG MAN? SCHOOL'S CLOSED.
IS LEARNING EVER CLOSED?
WELL, YOU GOT ME THERE, RIDDLE BOY.
FOR FRIENDSHIP.
FOR OUR WILDEST DREAMS COMING TRUE.
FOR MAC AND CHEESE WITH CHICKEN TENDERS EVERY WEEK.
I HOPE I'VE DONE YOU PROUD, MONTANA SENSEI.

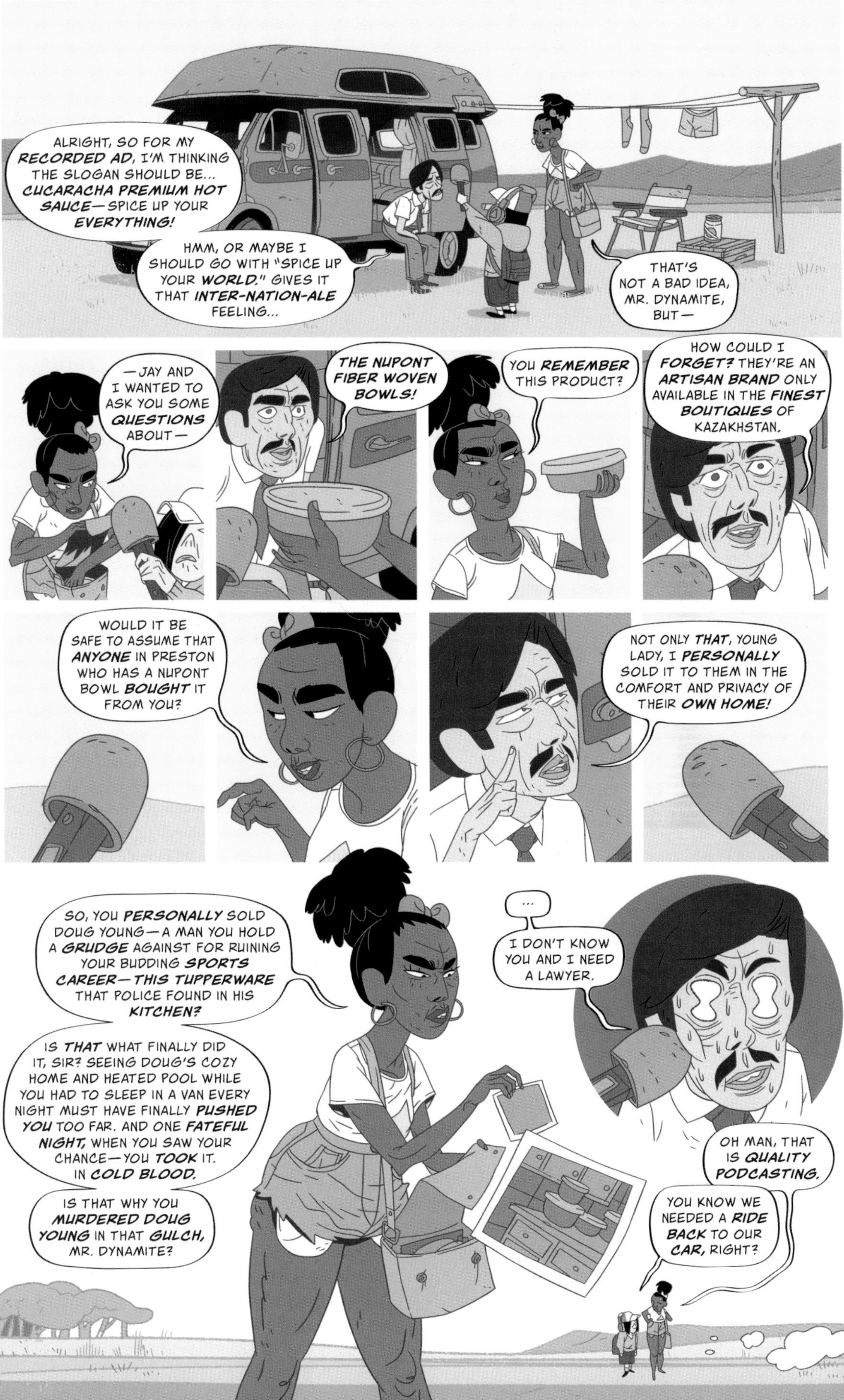
ALRIGHT, SO FOR MY RECORDED AD, I'M THINKING THE SLOGAN SHOULD BE... CUCARACHA PREMIUM HOT SAUCE—SPICE UP YOUR EVERYTHING!
HMM, OR MAYBE I SHOULD GO WITH "SPICE UP YOUR WORLD." GIVES IT THAT INTER-NATION-ALE FEELING...
THAT'S NOT A BAD IDEA, MR. DYNAMITE, BUT—
—JAY AND I WANTED TO ASK YOU SOME QUESTIONS ABOUT—
THE NUPONT FIBER WOVEN BOWLS!
YOU REMEMBER THIS PRODUCT?
HOW COULD I FORGET? THEY'RE AN ARTISAN BRAND ONLY AVAILABLE IN THE FINEST BOUTIQUES OF KAZAKHSTAN.
WOULD IT BE SAFE TO ASSUME THAT ANYONE IN PRESTON WHO HAS A NUPONT BOWL BOUGHT IT FROM YOU?
NOT ONLY THAT, YOUNG LADY, I PERSONALLY SOLD IT TO THEM IN THE COMFORT AND PRIVACY OF THEIR OWN HOME!
SO, YOU PERSONALLY SOLD DOUG YOUNG—A MAN YOU HOLD A GRUDGE AGAINST FOR RUINING YOUR BUDDING SPORTS CAREER—THIS TUPPERWARE THAT POLICE FOUND IN HIS KITCHEN?
IS THAT WHAT FINALLY DID IT, SIR? SEEING DOUG'S COZY HOME AND HEATED POOL WHILE YOU HAD TO SLEEP IN A VAN EVERY NIGHT MUST HAVE FINALLY PUSHED YOU TOO FAR. AND ONE FATEFUL NIGHT, WHEN YOU SAW YOUR CHANCE—YOU TOOK IT. IN COLD BLOOD.
IS THAT WHY YOU MURDERED DOUG YOUNG IN THAT GULCH, MR. DYNAMITE?
...
I DON'T KNOW YOU AND I NEED A LAWYER.
OH MAN, THAT IS QUALITY PODCASTING.
YOU KNOW WE NEEDED A RIDE BACK TO OUR CAR, RIGHT?

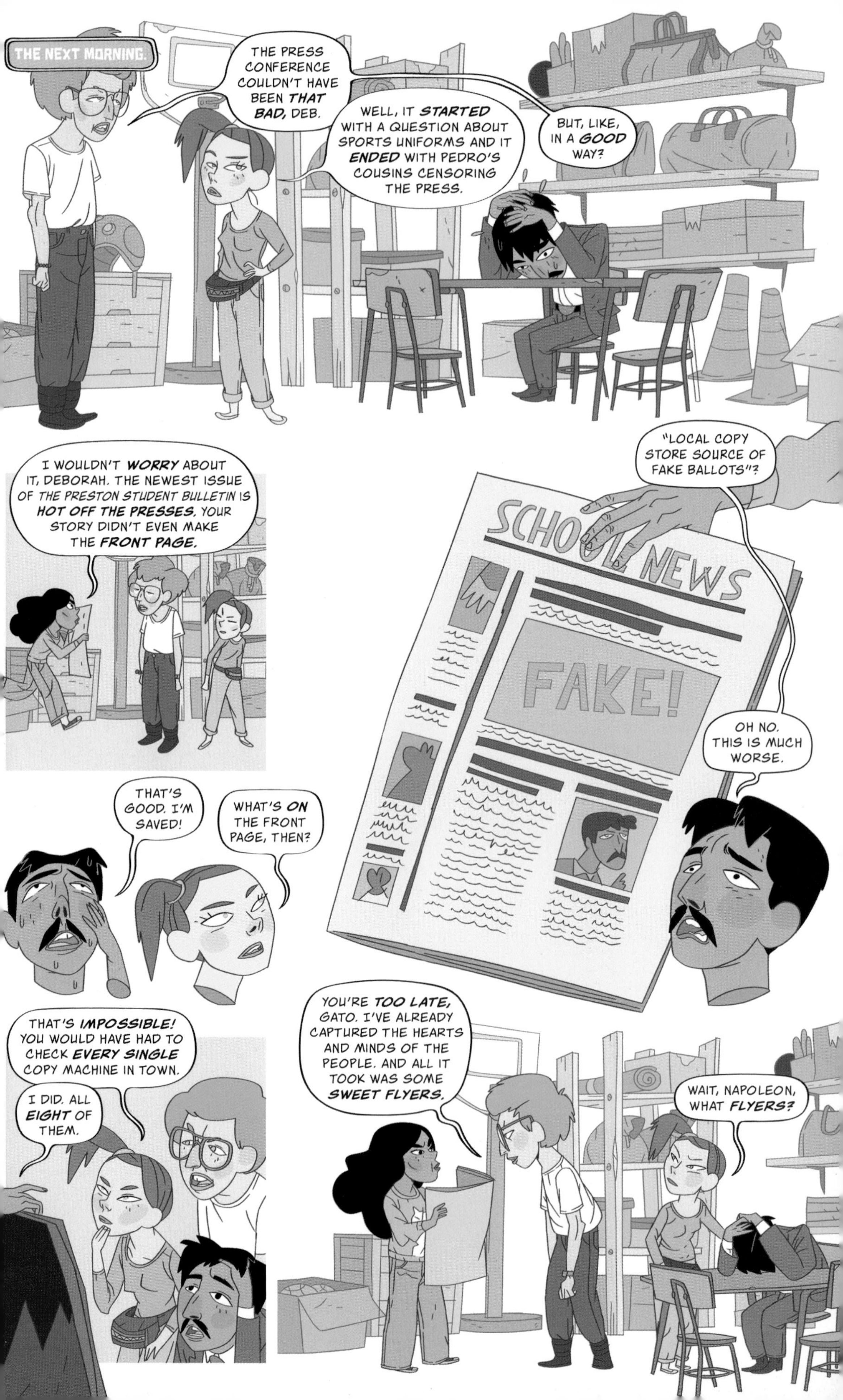

THE NEXT MORNING.
THE PRESS CONFERENCE COULDN'T HAVE BEEN THAT BAD, DEB.
WELL, IT STARTED WITH A QUESTION ABOUT SPORTS UNIFORMS AND IT ENDED WITH PEDRO'S COUSINS CENSORING THE PRESS.
BUT, LIKE, IN A GOOD WAY?
I WOULDN'T WORRY ABOUT IT, DEBORAH. THE NEWEST ISSUE OF THE PRESTON STUDENT BULLETIN IS HOT OFF THE PRESSES. YOUR STORY DIDN'T EVEN MAKE THE FRONT PAGE.
THAT'S GOOD. I'M SAVED!
WHAT'S ON THE FRONT PAGE, THEN?
"LOCAL COPY STORE SOURCE OF FAKE BALLOTS"?
SCHOOL NEWS
FAKE!
OH NO. THIS IS MUCH WORSE.
THAT'S IMPOSSIBLE! YOU WOULD HAVE HAD TO CHECK EVERY SINGLE COPY MACHINE IN TOWN.
I DID. ALL EIGHT OF THEM.
YOU'RE TOO LATE, GATO. I'VE ALREADY CAPTURED THE HEARTS AND MINDS OF THE PEOPLE. AND ALL IT TOOK WAS SOME SWEET FLYERS.
WAIT, NAPOLEON, WHAT FLYERS?

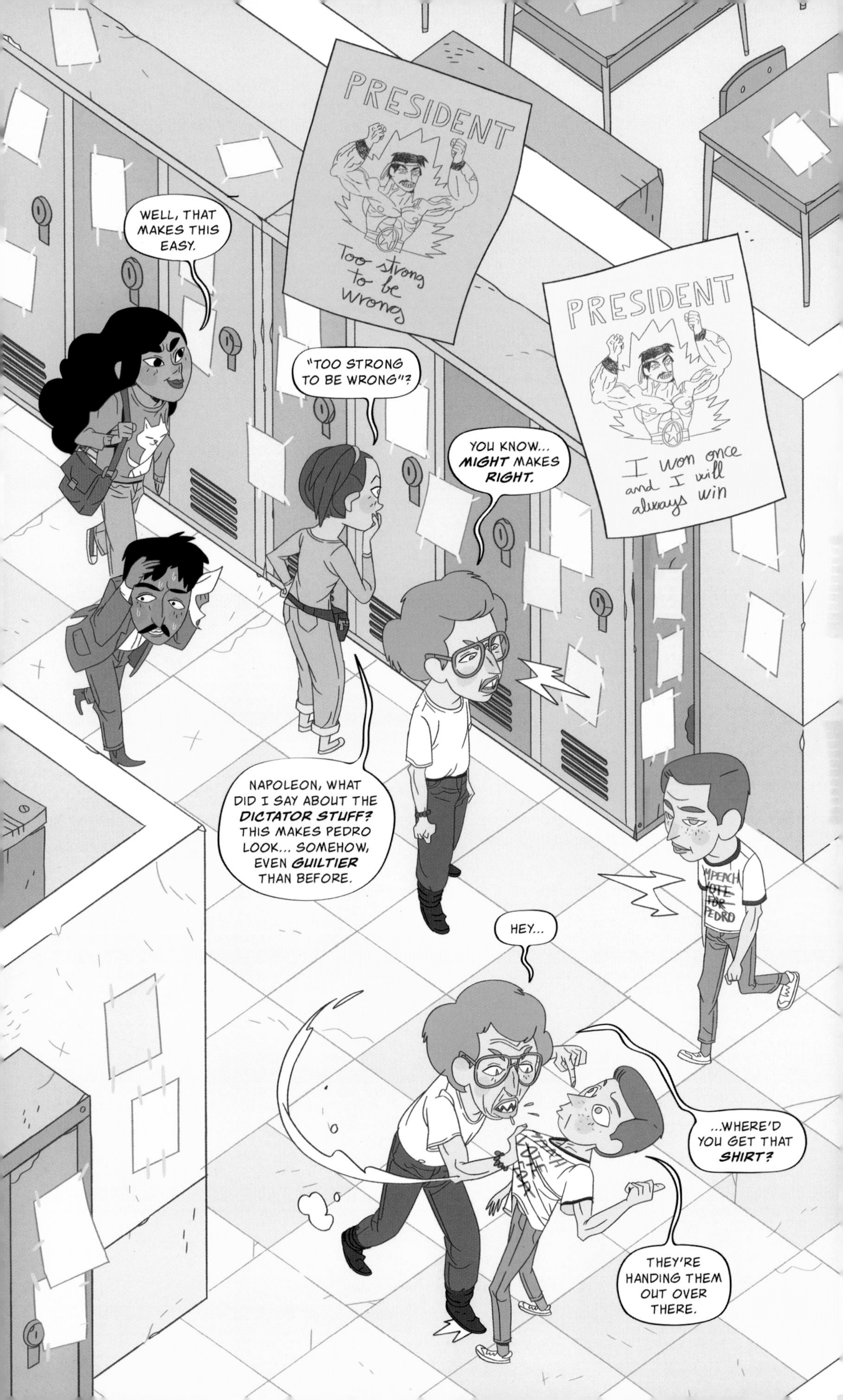
PRESIDENT
Too strong to be wrong
PRESIDENT
I won once and I will always win
WELL, THAT MAKES THIS EASY.
"TOO STRONG TO BE WRONG"?
YOU KNOW... MIGHT MAKES RIGHT.
NAPOLEON, WHAT DID I SAY ABOUT THE DICTATOR STUFF? THIS MAKES PEDRO LOOK... SOMEHOW, EVEN GUILTIER THAN BEFORE.
IMPEACH VOTE FOR PEDRO
HEY...
...WHERE'D YOU GET THAT SHIRT?
THEY'RE HANDING THEM OUT OVER THERE.

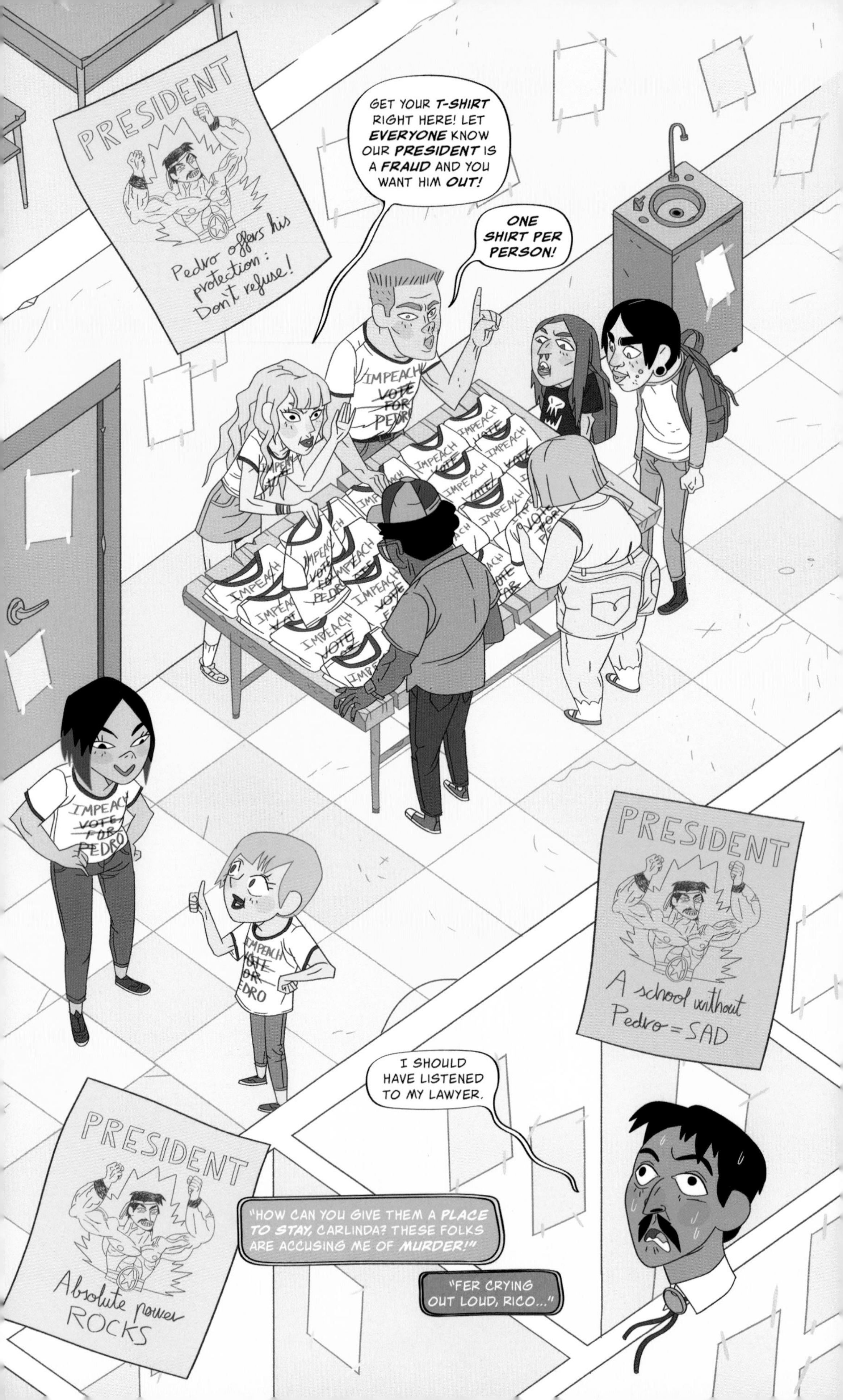
PRESIDENT
Pedro offers his protection: Don't refuse!
GET YOUR T-SHIRT RIGHT HERE! LET EVERYONE KNOW OUR PRESIDENT IS A FRAUD AND YOU WANT HIM OUT!
ONE SHIRT PER PERSON!
IMPEACH VOTE FOR PEDRO
PRESIDENT
A school without Pedro = SAD
I SHOULD HAVE LISTENED TO MY LAWYER.
PRESIDENT
Absolute power ROCKS
"HOW CAN YOU GIVE THEM A PLACE TO STAY, CARLINDA? THESE FOLKS ARE ACCUSING ME OF MURDER!"
"FER CRYING OUT LOUD, RICO..."

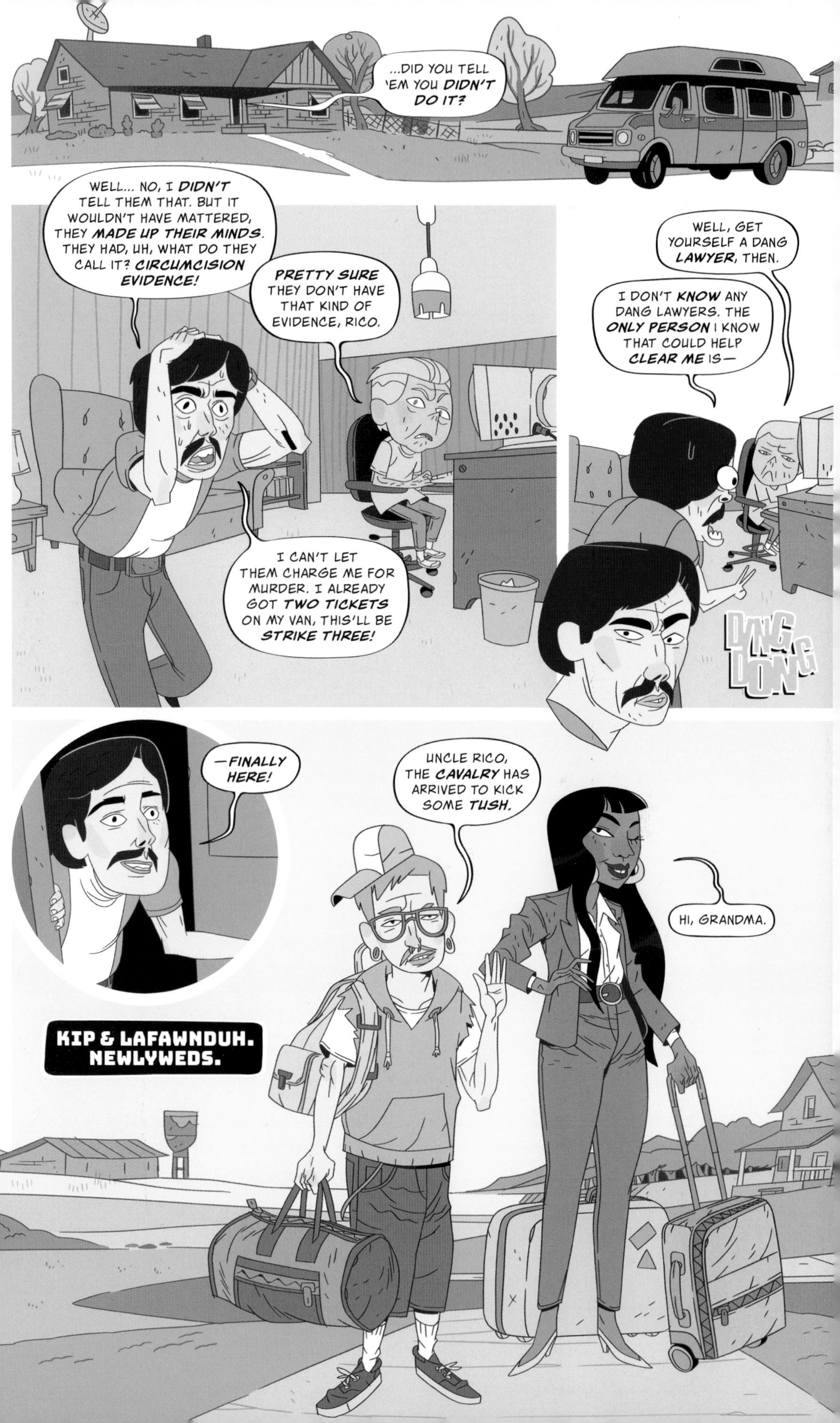

...DID YOU TELL 'EM YOU DIDN'T DO IT?
WELL... NO, I DIDN'T TELL THEM THAT. BUT IT WOULDN'T HAVE MATTERED, THEY MADE UP THEIR MINDS. THEY HAD, UH, WHAT DO THEY CALL IT? CIRCUMCISION EVIDENCE!
PRETTY SURE THEY DON'T HAVE THAT KIND OF EVIDENCE, RICO.
I CAN'T LET THEM CHARGE ME FOR MURDER. I ALREADY GOT TWO TICKETS ON MY VAN, THIS'LL BE STRIKE THREE!
WELL, GET YOURSELF A DANG LAWYER, THEN.
I DON'T KNOW ANY DANG LAWYERS. THE ONLY PERSON I KNOW THAT COULD HELP CLEAR ME IS—
DING DONG
—FINALLY HERE!
UNCLE RICO, THE CAVALRY HAS ARRIVED TO KICK SOME TUSH.
HI, GRANDMA.
KIP & LAFAWNDUH. NEWLYWEDS.

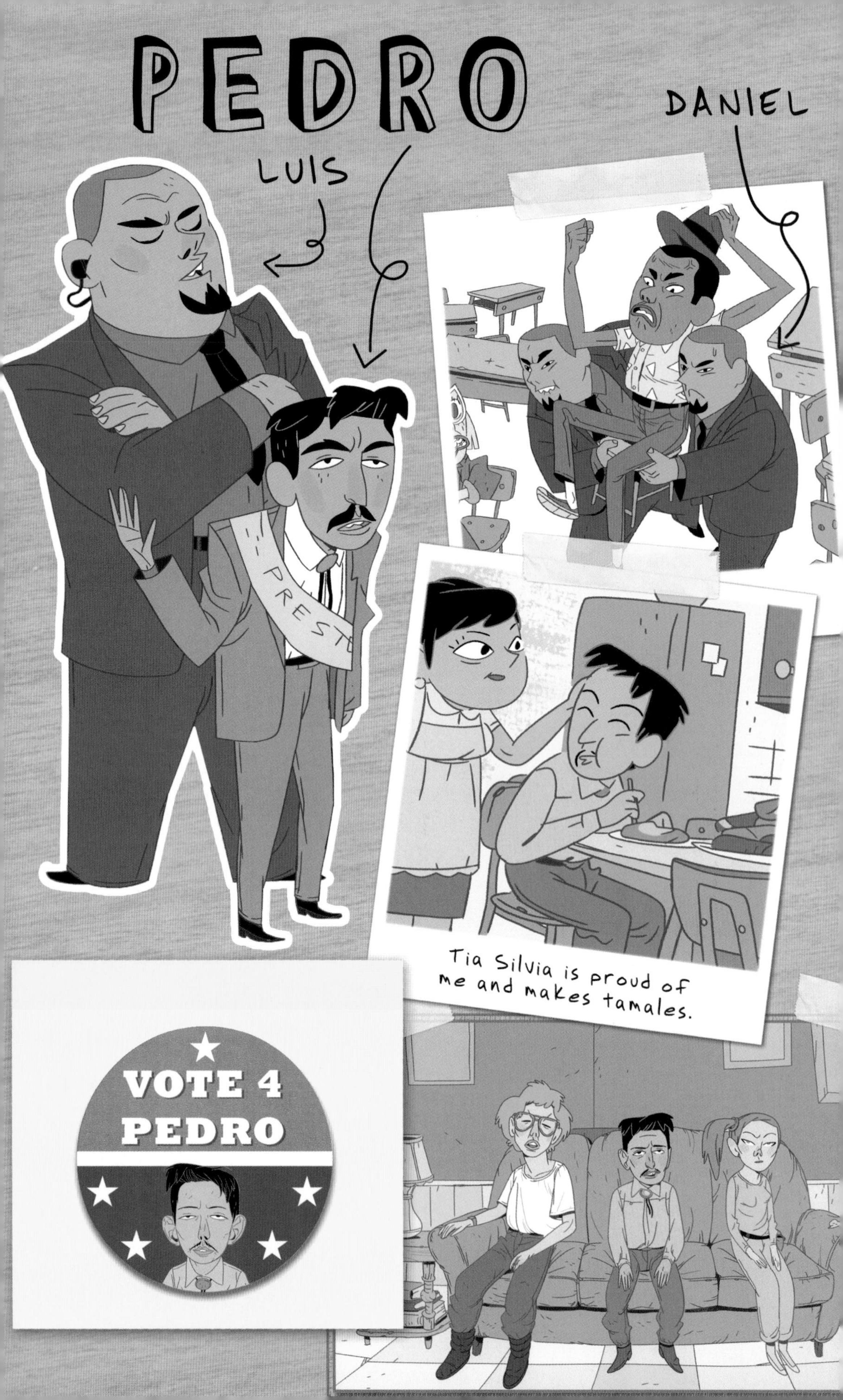
PEDRO
LUIS
DANIEL
Tia Silvia is proud of me and makes tamales.
VOTE 4 PEDRO

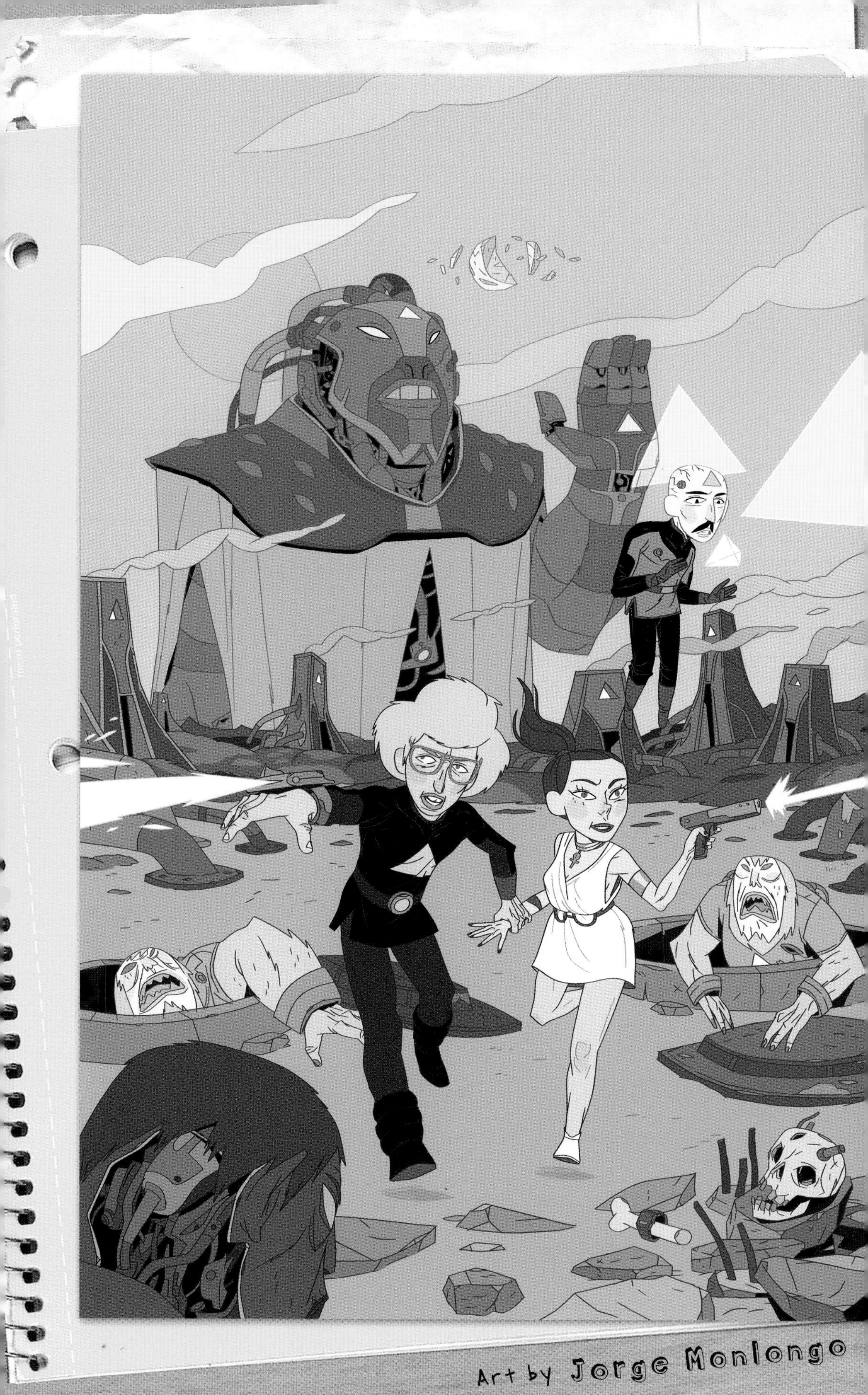

Art by Jorge Monlongo

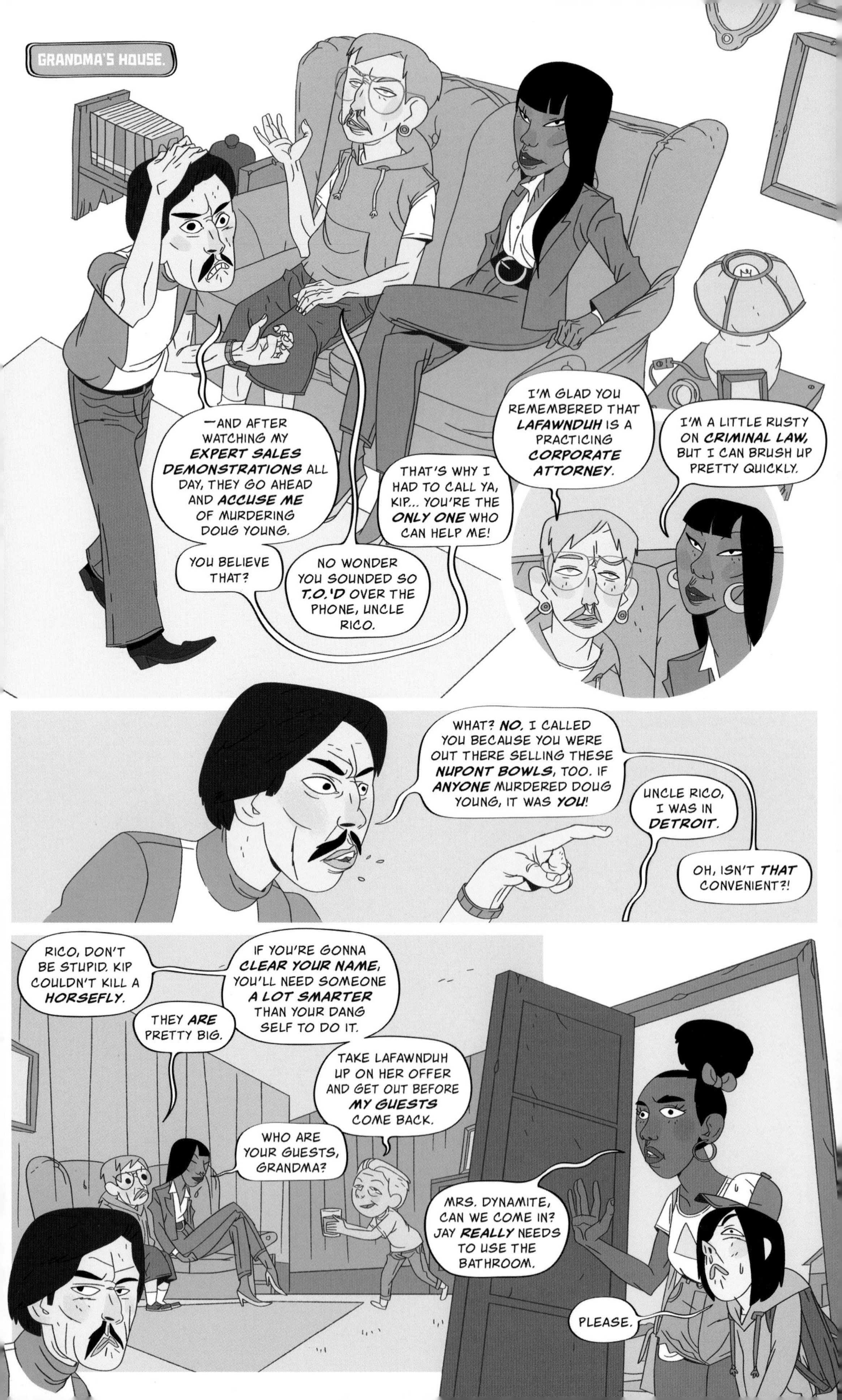
GRANDMA'S HOUSE.
—AND AFTER WATCHING MY EXPERT SALES DEMONSTRATIONS ALL DAY, THEY GO AHEAD AND ACCUSE ME OF MURDERING DOUG YOUNG.
YOU BELIEVE THAT?
NO WONDER YOU SOUNDED SO T.O.'D OVER THE PHONE, UNCLE RICO.
THAT'S WHY I HAD TO CALL YA, KIP... YOU'RE THE ONLY ONE WHO CAN HELP ME!
I'M GLAD YOU REMEMBERED THAT LAFAWNDUH IS A PRACTICING CORPORATE ATTORNEY.
I'M A LITTLE RUSTY ON CRIMINAL LAW, BUT I CAN BRUSH UP PRETTY QUICKLY.
WHAT? NO. I CALLED YOU BECAUSE YOU WERE OUT THERE SELLING THESE NUPONT BOWLS, TOO. IF ANYONE MURDERED DOUG YOUNG, IT WAS YOU!
UNCLE RICO, I WAS IN DETROIT.
OH, ISN'T THAT CONVENIENT?!
RICO, DON'T BE STUPID. KIP COULDN'T KILL A HORSEFLY.
THEY ARE PRETTY BIG.
IF YOU'RE GONNA CLEAR YOUR NAME, YOU'LL NEED SOMEONE A LOT SMARTER THAN YOUR DANG SELF TO DO IT.
TAKE LAFAWNDUH UP ON HER OFFER AND GET OUT BEFORE MY GUESTS COME BACK.
WHO ARE YOUR GUESTS, GRANDMA?
MRS. DYNAMITE, CAN WE COME IN? JAY REALLY NEEDS TO USE THE BATHROOM.
PLEASE.

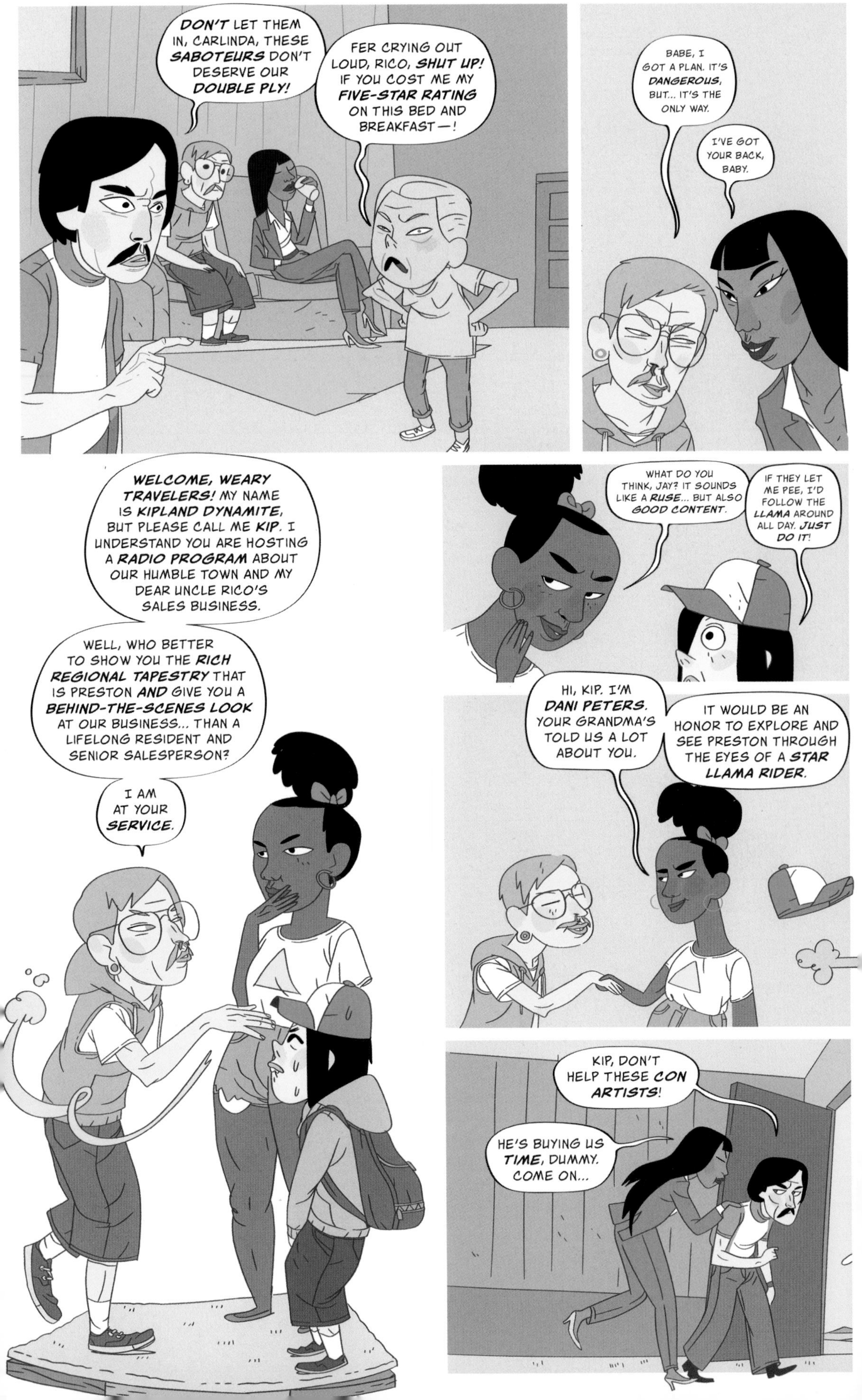
DON'T LET THEM IN, CARLINDA, THESE SABOTEURS DON'T DESERVE OUR DOUBLE PLY!
FER CRYING OUT LOUD, RICO, SHUT UP! IF YOU COST ME MY FIVE-STAR RATING ON THIS BED AND BREAKFAST—!
BABE, I GOT A PLAN. IT'S DANGEROUS, BUT... IT'S THE ONLY WAY.
I'VE GOT YOUR BACK, BABY.
WELCOME, WEARY TRAVELERS! MY NAME IS KIPLAND DYNAMITE, BUT PLEASE CALL ME KIP. I UNDERSTAND YOU ARE HOSTING A RADIO PROGRAM ABOUT OUR HUMBLE TOWN AND MY DEAR UNCLE RICO'S SALES BUSINESS.
WELL, WHO BETTER TO SHOW YOU THE RICH REGIONAL TAPESTRY THAT IS PRESTON AND GIVE YOU A BEHIND-THE-SCENES LOOK AT OUR BUSINESS... THAN A LIFELONG RESIDENT AND SENIOR SALESPERSON?
I AM AT YOUR SERVICE.
WHAT DO YOU THINK, JAY? IT SOUNDS LIKE A RUSE... BUT ALSO GOOD CONTENT.
IF THEY LET ME PEE, I'D FOLLOW THE LLAMA AROUND ALL DAY. JUST DO IT!
HI, KIP. I'M DANI PETERS. YOUR GRANDMA'S TOLD US A LOT ABOUT YOU.
IT WOULD BE AN HONOR TO EXPLORE AND SEE PRESTON THROUGH THE EYES OF A STAR LLAMA RIDER.
KIP, DON'T HELP THESE CON ARTISTS!
HE'S BUYING US TIME, DUMMY. COME ON...

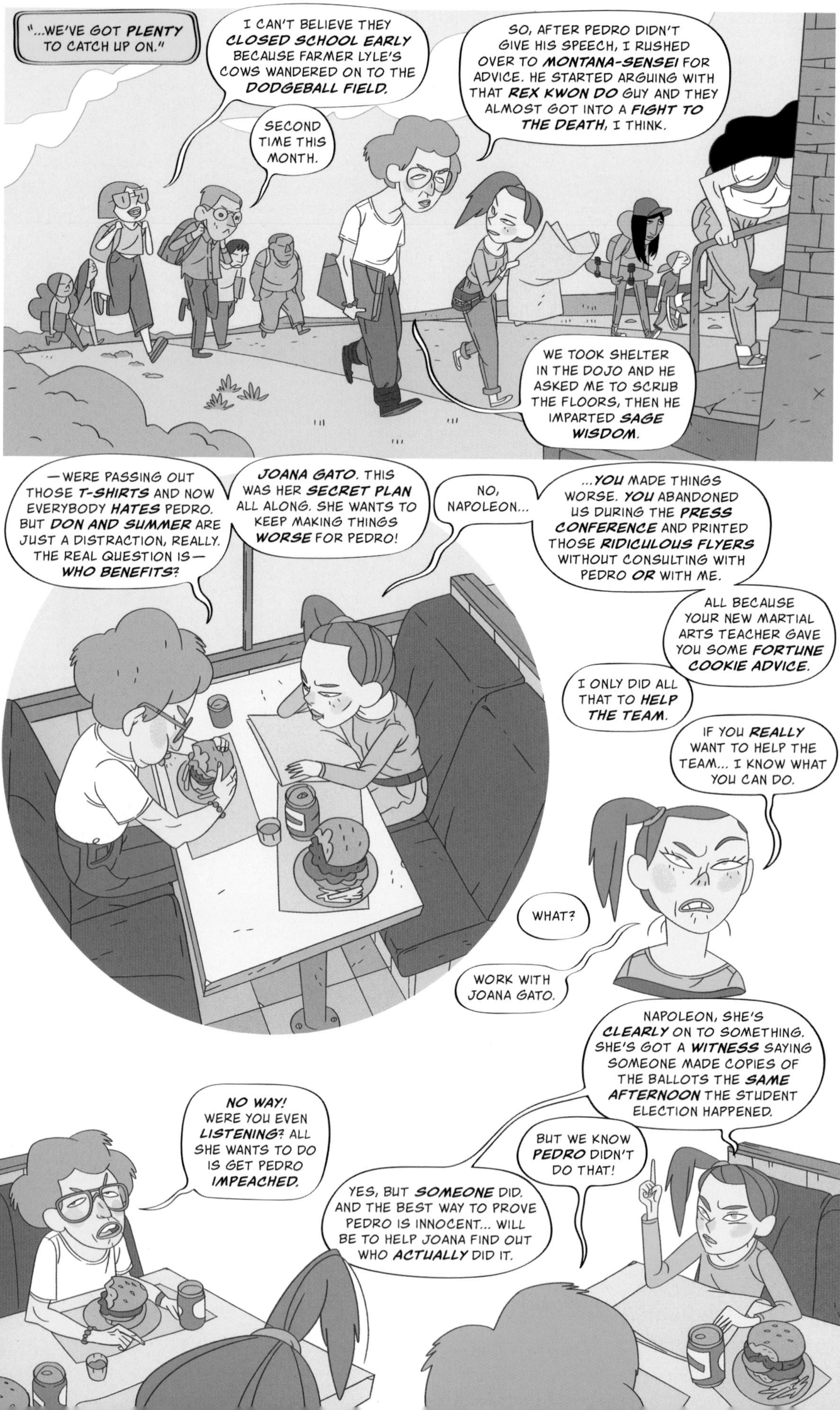
"...WE'VE GOT PLENTY TO CATCH UP ON."
I CAN'T BELIEVE THEY CLOSED SCHOOL EARLY BECAUSE FARMER LYLE'S COWS WANDERED ON TO THE DODGEBALL FIELD.
SECOND TIME THIS MONTH.
SO, AFTER PEDRO DIDN'T GIVE HIS SPEECH, I RUSHED OVER TO MONTANA-SENSEI FOR ADVICE. HE STARTED ARGUING WITH THAT REX KWON DO GUY AND THEY ALMOST GOT INTO A FIGHT TO THE DEATH, I THINK.
WE TOOK SHELTER IN THE DOJO AND HE ASKED ME TO SCRUB THE FLOORS, THEN HE IMPARTED SAGE WISDOM.
—WERE PASSING OUT THOSE T-SHIRTS AND NOW EVERYBODY HATES PEDRO. BUT DON AND SUMMER ARE JUST A DISTRACTION, REALLY. THE REAL QUESTION IS—WHO BENEFITS?
JOANA GATO. THIS WAS HER SECRET PLAN ALL ALONG. SHE WANTS TO KEEP MAKING THINGS WORSE FOR PEDRO!
NO, NAPOLEON...
...YOU MADE THINGS WORSE. YOU ABANDONED US DURING THE PRESS CONFERENCE AND PRINTED THOSE RIDICULOUS FLYERS WITHOUT CONSULTING WITH PEDRO OR WITH ME.
ALL BECAUSE YOUR NEW MARTIAL ARTS TEACHER GAVE YOU SOME FORTUNE COOKIE ADVICE.
I ONLY DID ALL THAT TO HELP THE TEAM.
IF YOU REALLY WANT TO HELP THE TEAM... I KNOW WHAT YOU CAN DO.
WHAT?
WORK WITH JOANA GATO.
NAPOLEON, SHE'S CLEARLY ON TO SOMETHING. SHE'S GOT A WITNESS SAYING SOMEONE MADE COPIES OF THE BALLOTS THE SAME AFTERNOON THE STUDENT ELECTION HAPPENED.
NO WAY! WERE YOU EVEN LISTENING? ALL SHE WANTS TO DO IS GET PEDRO IMPEACHED.
BUT WE KNOW PEDRO DIDN'T DO THAT!
YES, BUT SOMEONE DID. AND THE BEST WAY TO PROVE PEDRO IS INNOCENT... WILL BE TO HELP JOANA FIND OUT WHO ACTUALLY DID IT.

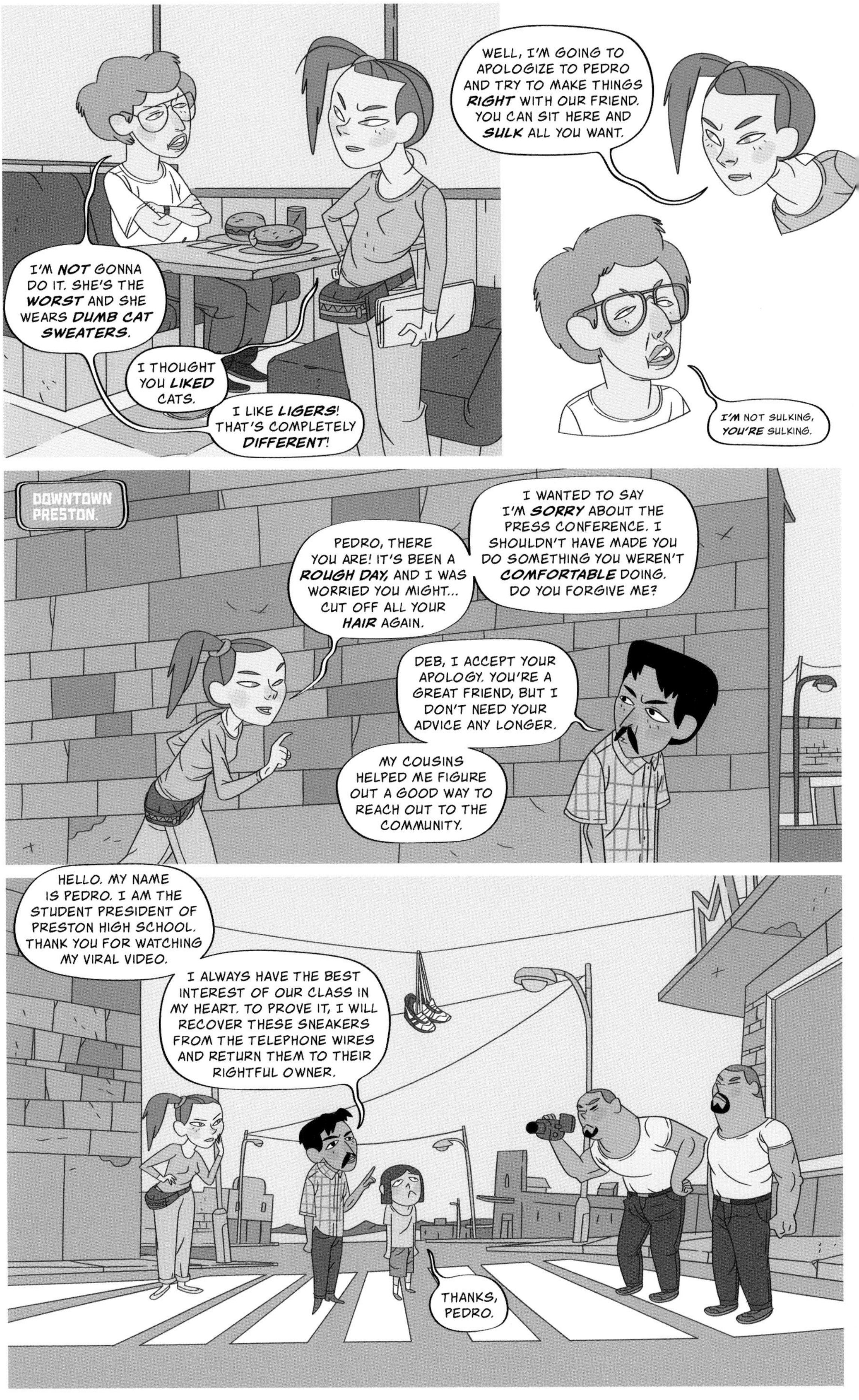
I'M NOT GONNA DO IT. SHE'S THE WORST AND SHE WEARS DUMB CAT SWEATERS.
I THOUGHT YOU LIKED CATS.
I LIKE LIGERS! THAT'S COMPLETELY DIFFERENT!
WELL, I'M GOING TO APOLOGIZE TO PEDRO AND TRY TO MAKE THINGS RIGHT WITH OUR FRIEND. YOU CAN SIT HERE AND SULK ALL YOU WANT.
I'M NOT SULKING, YOU'RE SULKING.
DOWNTOWN PRESTON.
PEDRO, THERE YOU ARE! IT'S BEEN A ROUGH DAY, AND I WAS WORRIED YOU MIGHT... CUT OFF ALL YOUR HAIR AGAIN.
I WANTED TO SAY I'M SORRY ABOUT THE PRESS CONFERENCE. I SHOULDN'T HAVE MADE YOU DO SOMETHING YOU WEREN'T COMFORTABLE DOING. DO YOU FORGIVE ME?
DEB, I ACCEPT YOUR APOLOGY. YOU'RE A GREAT FRIEND, BUT I DON'T NEED YOUR ADVICE ANY LONGER.
MY COUSINS HELPED ME FIGURE OUT A GOOD WAY TO REACH OUT TO THE COMMUNITY.
HELLO. MY NAME IS PEDRO. I AM THE STUDENT PRESIDENT OF PRESTON HIGH SCHOOL. THANK YOU FOR WATCHING MY VIRAL VIDEO.
I ALWAYS HAVE THE BEST INTEREST OF OUR CLASS IN MY HEART. TO PROVE IT, I WILL RECOVER THESE SNEAKERS FROM THE TELEPHONE WIRES AND RETURN THEM TO THEIR RIGHTFUL OWNER.
THANKS, PEDRO.

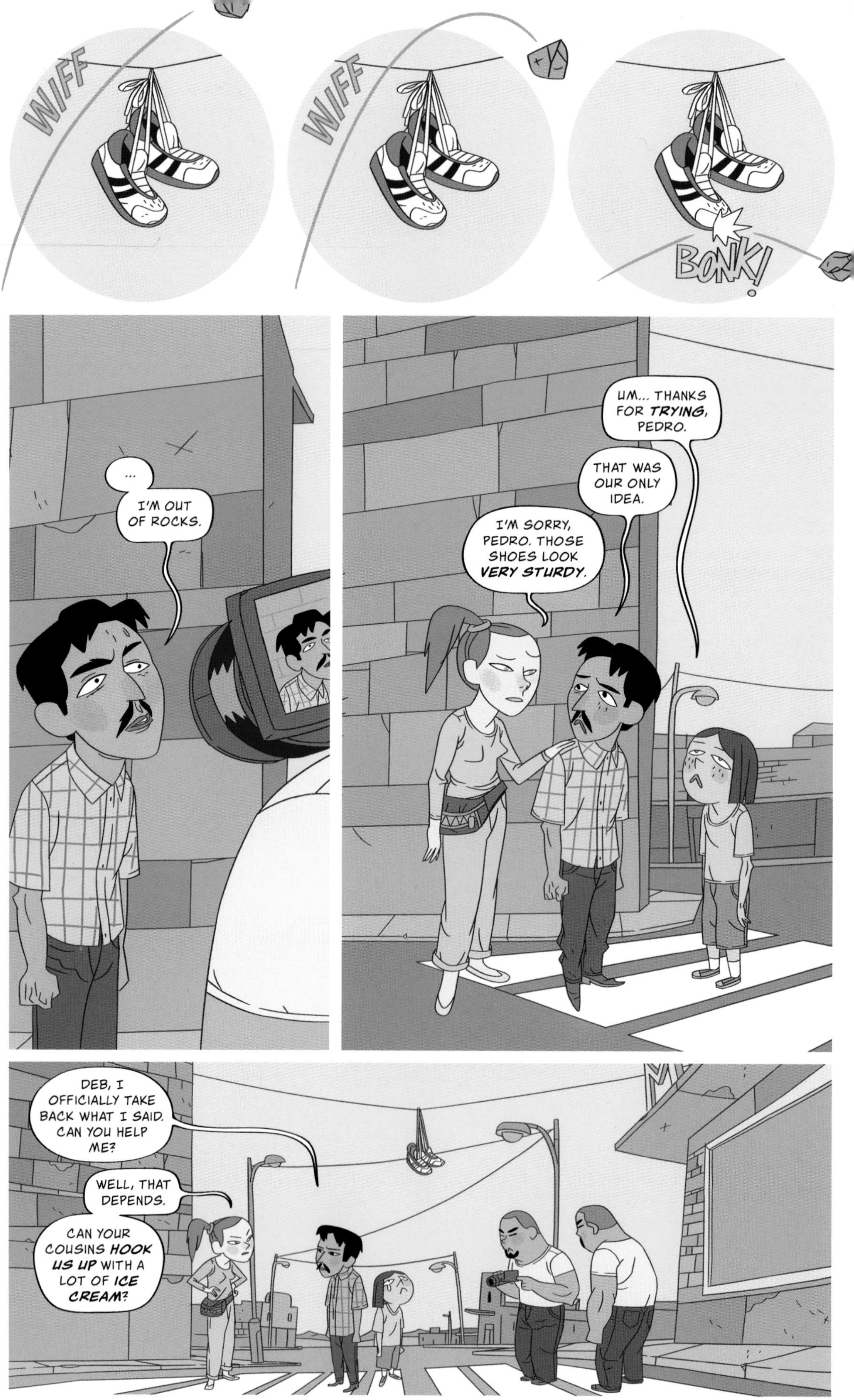

WIFF
WIFF
BONK!
...
I'M OUT OF ROCKS.
I'M SORRY, PEDRO. THOSE SHOES LOOK **VERY STURDY**.
THAT WAS OUR ONLY IDEA.
UM... THANKS FOR **TRYING**, PEDRO.
DEB, I OFFICIALLY TAKE BACK WHAT I SAID. CAN YOU HELP ME?
WELL, THAT DEPENDS.
CAN YOUR COUSINS **HOOK US UP** WITH A LOT OF **ICE CREAM**?

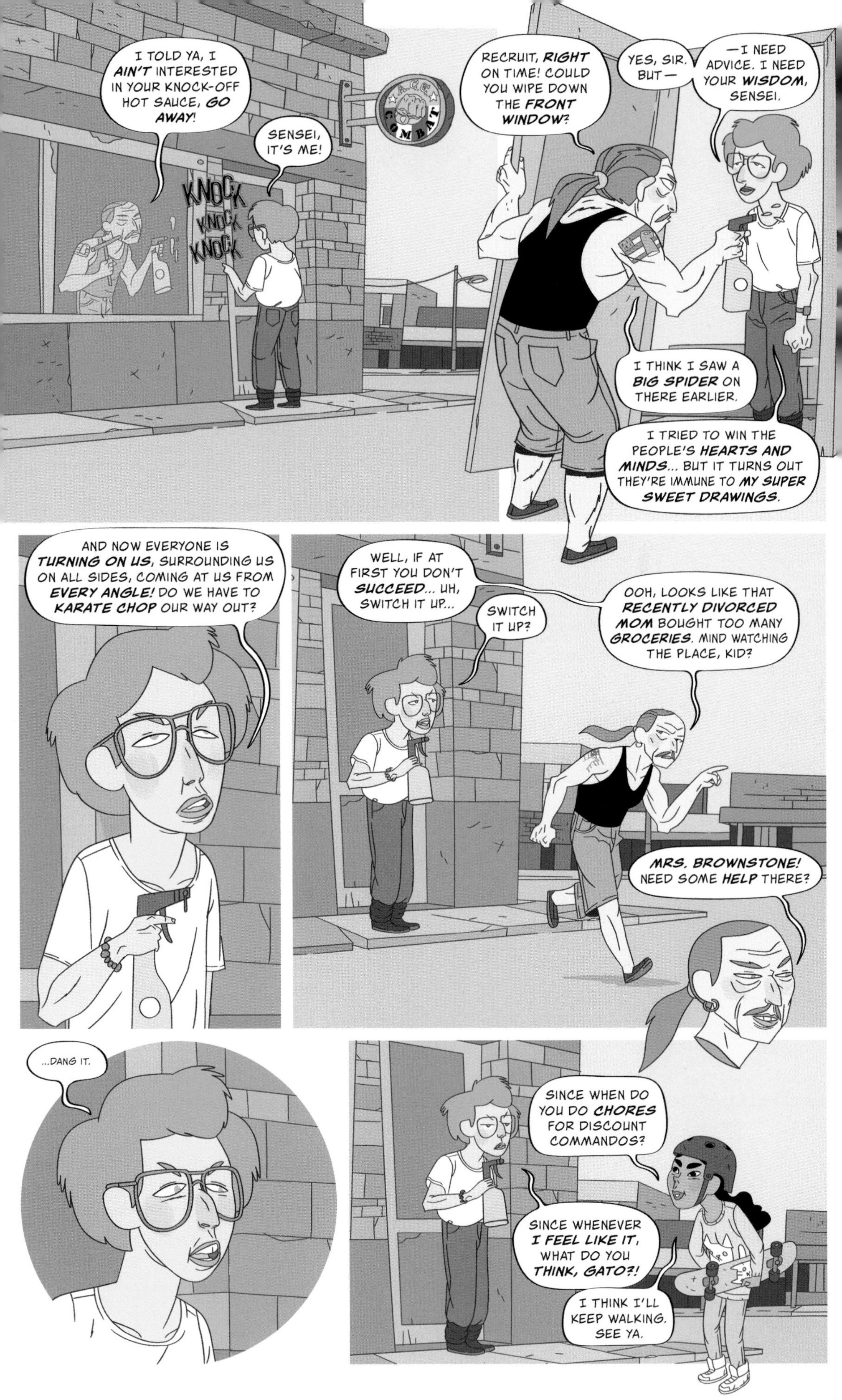
I TOLD YA, I AIN'T INTERESTED IN YOUR KNOCK-OFF HOT SAUCE, GO AWAY!
KNOCK KNOCK KNOCK
SENSEI, IT'S ME!
A.C.E. COMBAT
RECRUIT, RIGHT ON TIME! COULD YOU WIPE DOWN THE FRONT WINDOW?
YES, SIR. BUT—
—I NEED ADVICE. I NEED YOUR WISDOM, SENSEI.
I THINK I SAW A BIG SPIDER ON THERE EARLIER.
I TRIED TO WIN THE PEOPLE'S HEARTS AND MINDS... BUT IT TURNS OUT THEY'RE IMMUNE TO MY SUPER SWEET DRAWINGS.
AND NOW EVERYONE IS TURNING ON US, SURROUNDING US ON ALL SIDES, COMING AT US FROM EVERY ANGLE! DO WE HAVE TO KARATE CHOP OUR WAY OUT?
WELL, IF AT FIRST YOU DON'T SUCCEED... UH, SWITCH IT UP...
SWITCH IT UP?
OOH, LOOKS LIKE THAT RECENTLY DIVORCED MOM BOUGHT TOO MANY GROCERIES. MIND WATCHING THE PLACE, KID?
MRS. BROWNSTONE! NEED SOME HELP THERE?
...DANG IT.
SINCE WHEN DO YOU DO CHORES FOR DISCOUNT COMMANDOS?
SINCE WHENEVER I FEEL LIKE IT, WHAT DO YOU THINK, GATO?!
I THINK I'LL KEEP WALKING. SEE YA.

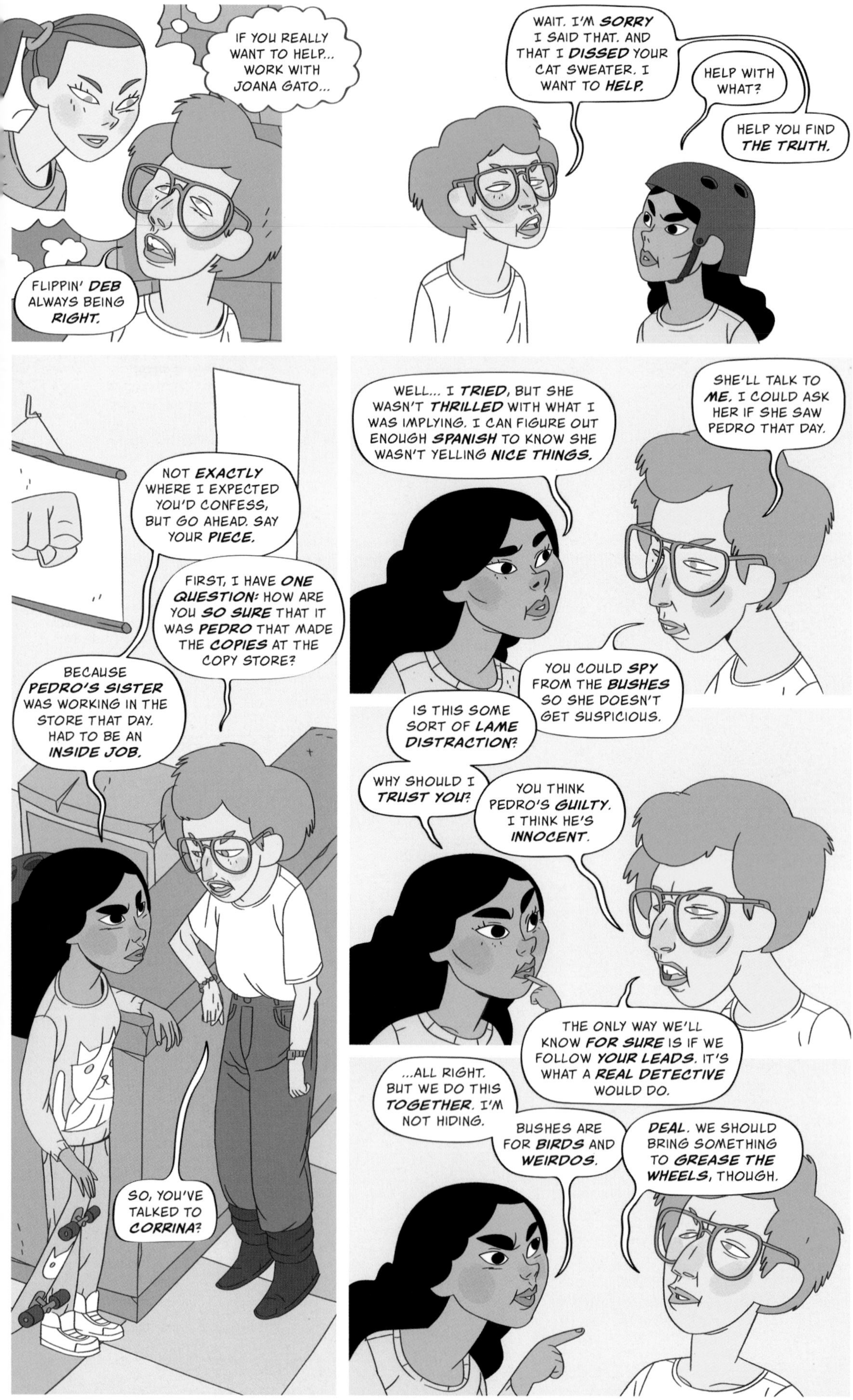
IF YOU REALLY WANT TO HELP... WORK WITH JOANA GATO...
FLIPPIN' DEB ALWAYS BEING RIGHT.
WAIT. I'M SORRY I SAID THAT. AND THAT I DISSED YOUR CAT SWEATER. I WANT TO HELP.
HELP WITH WHAT?
HELP YOU FIND THE TRUTH.
NOT EXACTLY WHERE I EXPECTED YOU'D CONFESS, BUT GO AHEAD. SAY YOUR PIECE.
FIRST, I HAVE ONE QUESTION: HOW ARE YOU SO SURE THAT IT WAS PEDRO THAT MADE THE COPIES AT THE COPY STORE?
BECAUSE PEDRO'S SISTER WAS WORKING IN THE STORE THAT DAY. HAD TO BE AN INSIDE JOB.
SO, YOU'VE TALKED TO CORRINA?
WELL... I TRIED, BUT SHE WASN'T THRILLED WITH WHAT I WAS IMPLYING. I CAN FIGURE OUT ENOUGH SPANISH TO KNOW SHE WASN'T YELLING NICE THINGS.
SHE'LL TALK TO ME. I COULD ASK HER IF SHE SAW PEDRO THAT DAY.
YOU COULD SPY FROM THE BUSHES SO SHE DOESN'T GET SUSPICIOUS.
IS THIS SOME SORT OF LAME DISTRACTION?
WHY SHOULD I TRUST YOU?
YOU THINK PEDRO'S GUILTY. I THINK HE'S INNOCENT.
THE ONLY WAY WE'LL KNOW FOR SURE IS IF WE FOLLOW YOUR LEADS. IT'S WHAT A REAL DETECTIVE WOULD DO.
...ALL RIGHT. BUT WE DO THIS TOGETHER. I'M NOT HIDING.
BUSHES ARE FOR BIRDS AND WEIRDOS.
DEAL. WE SHOULD BRING SOMETHING TO GREASE THE WHEELS, THOUGH.

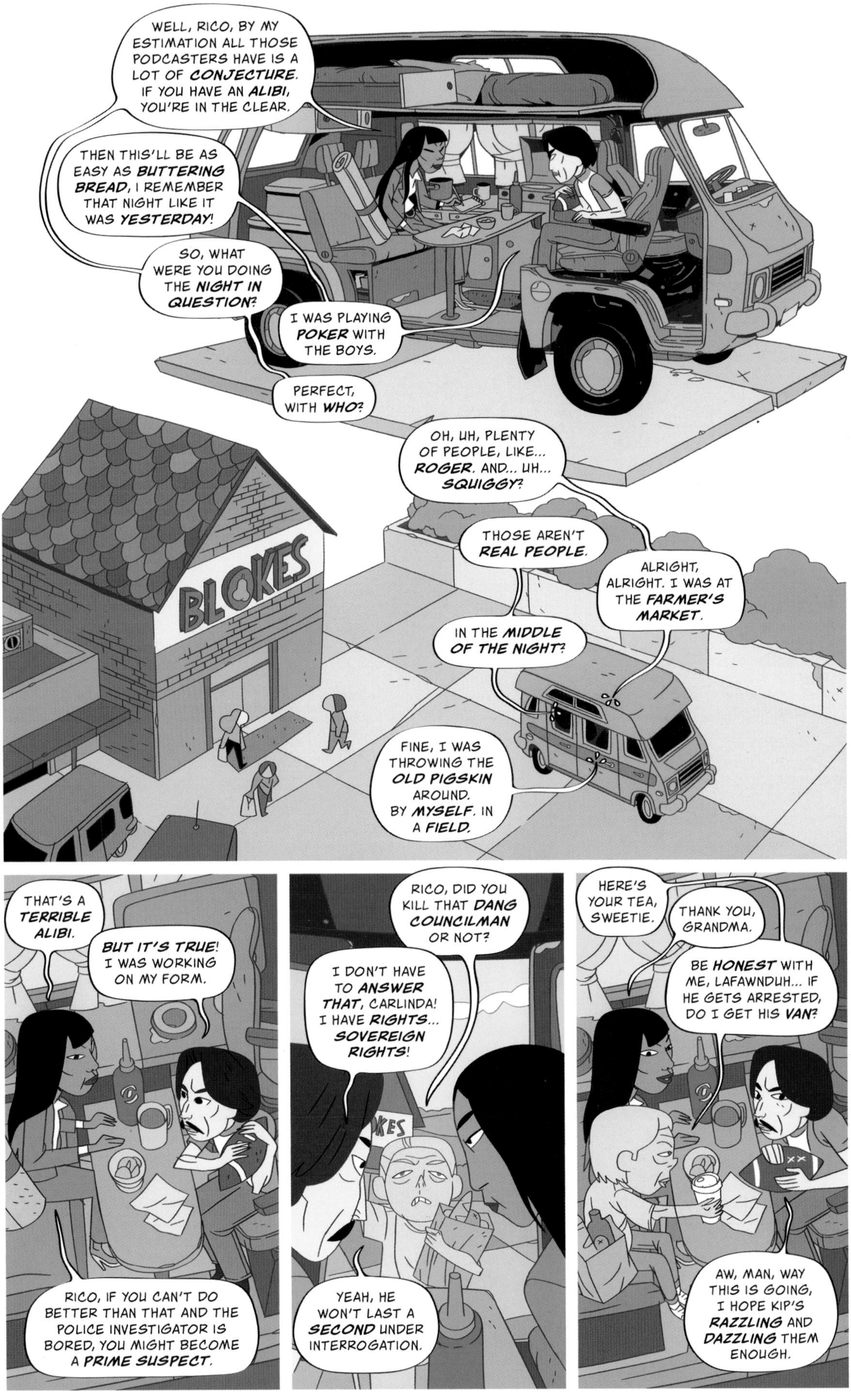
WELL, RICO, BY MY ESTIMATION ALL THOSE PODCASTERS HAVE IS A LOT OF CONJECTURE. IF YOU HAVE AN ALIBI, YOU'RE IN THE CLEAR.
THEN THIS'LL BE AS EASY AS BUTTERING BREAD, I REMEMBER THAT NIGHT LIKE IT WAS YESTERDAY!
SO, WHAT WERE YOU DOING THE NIGHT IN QUESTION?
I WAS PLAYING POKER WITH THE BOYS.
PERFECT, WITH WHO?
OH, UH, PLENTY OF PEOPLE, LIKE... ROGER. AND... UH... SQUIGGY?
BLOKES
THOSE AREN'T REAL PEOPLE.
ALRIGHT, ALRIGHT. I WAS AT THE FARMER'S MARKET.
IN THE MIDDLE OF THE NIGHT?
FINE, I WAS THROWING THE OLD PIGSKIN AROUND. BY MYSELF. IN A FIELD.
THAT'S A TERRIBLE ALIBI.
BUT IT'S TRUE! I WAS WORKING ON MY FORM.
RICO, IF YOU CAN'T DO BETTER THAN THAT AND THE POLICE INVESTIGATOR IS BORED, YOU MIGHT BECOME A PRIME SUSPECT.
RICO, DID YOU KILL THAT DANG COUNCILMAN OR NOT?
I DON'T HAVE TO ANSWER THAT, CARLINDA! I HAVE RIGHTS... SOVEREIGN RIGHTS!
YEAH, HE WON'T LAST A SECOND UNDER INTERROGATION.
HERE'S YOUR TEA, SWEETIE.
THANK YOU, GRANDMA.
BE HONEST WITH ME, LAFAWNDUH... IF HE GETS ARRESTED, DO I GET HIS VAN?
AW, MAN, WAY THIS IS GOING, I HOPE KIP'S RAZZLING AND DAZZLING THEM ENOUGH.

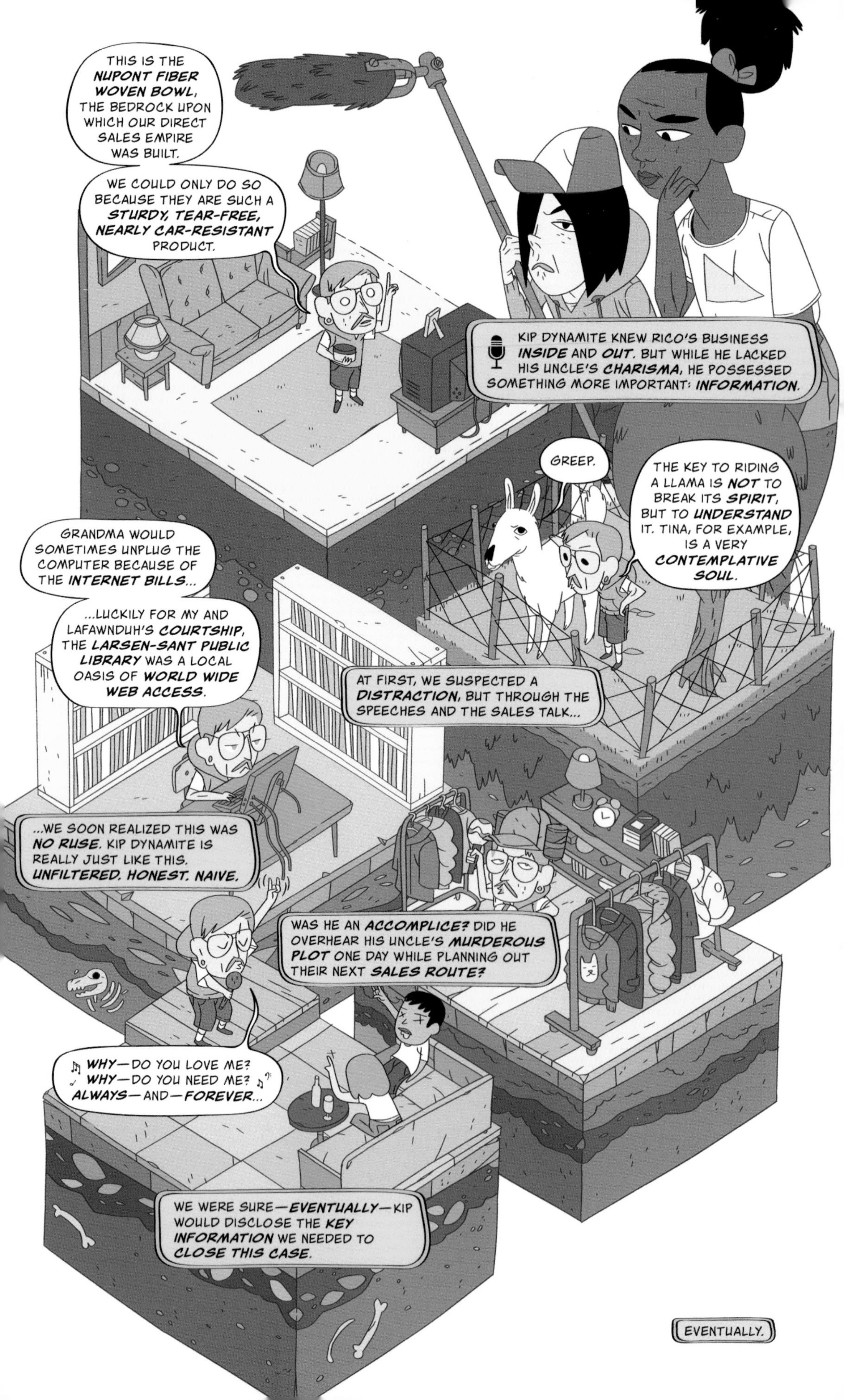
THIS IS THE NUPONT FIBER WOVEN BOWL, THE BEDROCK UPON WHICH OUR DIRECT SALES EMPIRE WAS BUILT.
WE COULD ONLY DO SO BECAUSE THEY ARE SUCH A STURDY, TEAR-FREE, NEARLY CAR-RESISTANT PRODUCT.
KIP DYNAMITE KNEW RICO'S BUSINESS INSIDE AND OUT. BUT WHILE HE LACKED HIS UNCLE'S CHARISMA, HE POSSESSED SOMETHING MORE IMPORTANT: INFORMATION.
GREEP.
THE KEY TO RIDING A LLAMA IS NOT TO BREAK ITS SPIRIT, BUT TO UNDERSTAND IT. TINA, FOR EXAMPLE, IS A VERY CONTEMPLATIVE SOUL.
GRANDMA WOULD SOMETIMES UNPLUG THE COMPUTER BECAUSE OF THE INTERNET BILLS...
...LUCKILY FOR MY AND LAFAWNDUH'S COURTSHIP, THE LARSEN-SANT PUBLIC LIBRARY WAS A LOCAL OASIS OF WORLD WIDE WEB ACCESS.
AT FIRST, WE SUSPECTED A DISTRACTION, BUT THROUGH THE SPEECHES AND THE SALES TALK...
...WE SOON REALIZED THIS WAS NO RUSE. KIP DYNAMITE IS REALLY JUST LIKE THIS. UNFILTERED. HONEST. NAIVE.
WAS HE AN ACCOMPLICE? DID HE OVERHEAR HIS UNCLE'S MURDEROUS PLOT ONE DAY WHILE PLANNING OUT THEIR NEXT SALES ROUTE?
WHY—DO YOU LOVE ME? WHY—DO YOU NEED ME? ALWAYS—AND—FOREVER...
WE WERE SURE—EVENTUALLY—KIP WOULD DISCLOSE THE KEY INFORMATION WE NEEDED TO CLOSE THIS CASE.
EVENTUALLY.

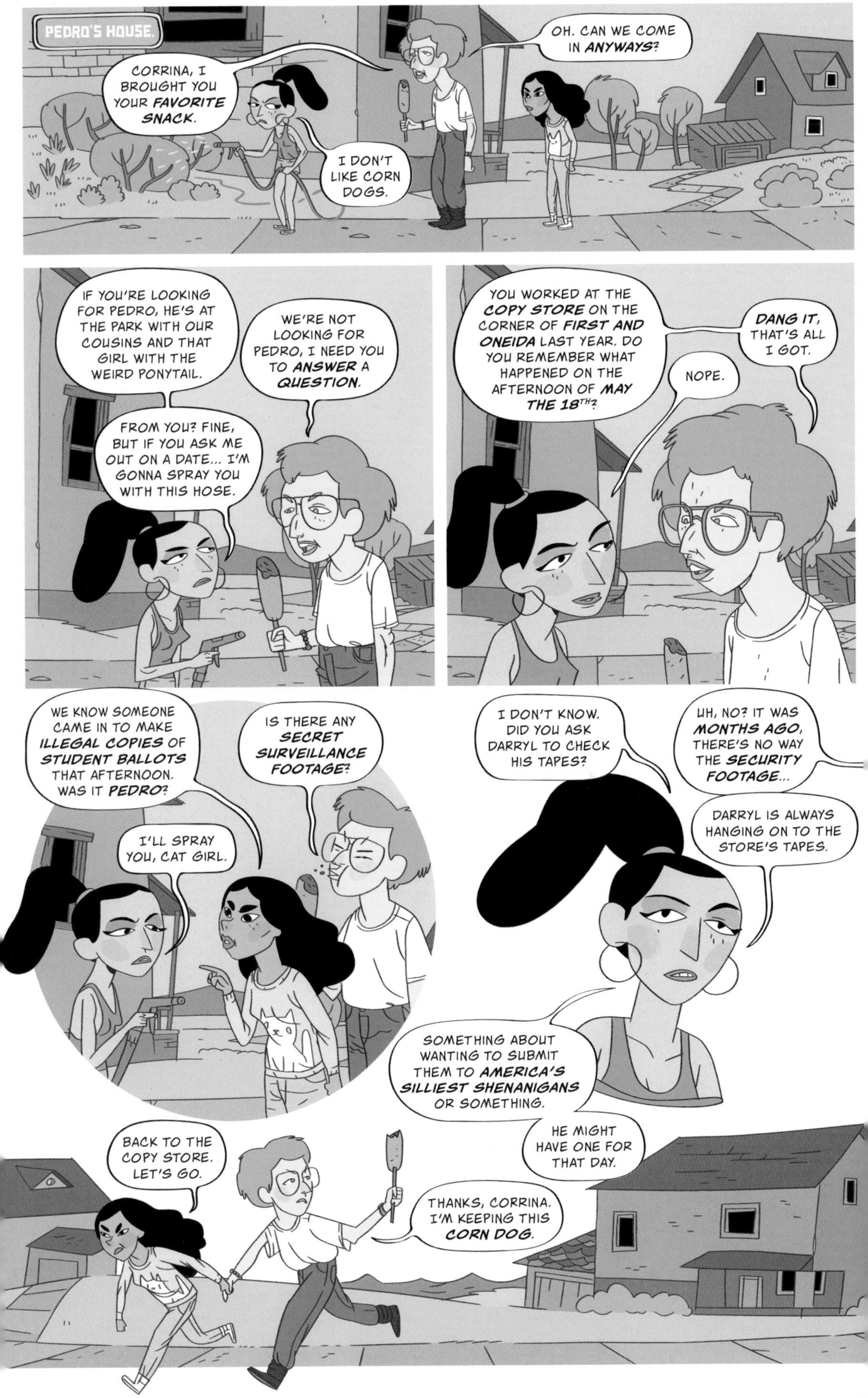
PEDRO'S HOUSE.
CORRINA, I BROUGHT YOU YOUR *FAVORITE SNACK.*
I DON'T LIKE CORN DOGS.
OH. CAN WE COME IN *ANYWAYS?*
IF YOU'RE LOOKING FOR PEDRO, HE'S AT THE PARK WITH OUR COUSINS AND THAT GIRL WITH THE WEIRD PONYTAIL.
WE'RE NOT LOOKING FOR PEDRO, I NEED YOU TO *ANSWER* A *QUESTION.*
FROM YOU? FINE, BUT IF YOU ASK ME OUT ON A DATE... I'M GONNA SPRAY YOU WITH THIS HOSE.
YOU WORKED AT THE *COPY STORE* ON THE CORNER OF *FIRST AND ONEIDA* LAST YEAR. DO YOU REMEMBER WHAT HAPPENED ON THE AFTERNOON OF *MAY THE 18TH?*
NOPE.
DANG IT, THAT'S ALL I GOT.
WE KNOW SOMEONE CAME IN TO MAKE *ILLEGAL COPIES* OF *STUDENT BALLOTS* THAT AFTERNOON. WAS IT *PEDRO?*
IS THERE ANY *SECRET SURVEILLANCE FOOTAGE?*
I'LL SPRAY YOU, CAT GIRL.
I DON'T KNOW. DID YOU ASK DARRYL TO CHECK HIS TAPES?
UH, NO? IT WAS *MONTHS AGO,* THERE'S NO WAY THE *SECURITY FOOTAGE...*
DARRYL IS ALWAYS HANGING ON TO THE STORE'S TAPES.
SOMETHING ABOUT WANTING TO SUBMIT THEM TO *AMERICA'S SILLIEST SHENANIGANS* OR SOMETHING.
HE MIGHT HAVE ONE FOR THAT DAY.
BACK TO THE COPY STORE. LET'S GO.
THANKS, CORRINA. I'M KEEPING THIS *CORN DOG.*

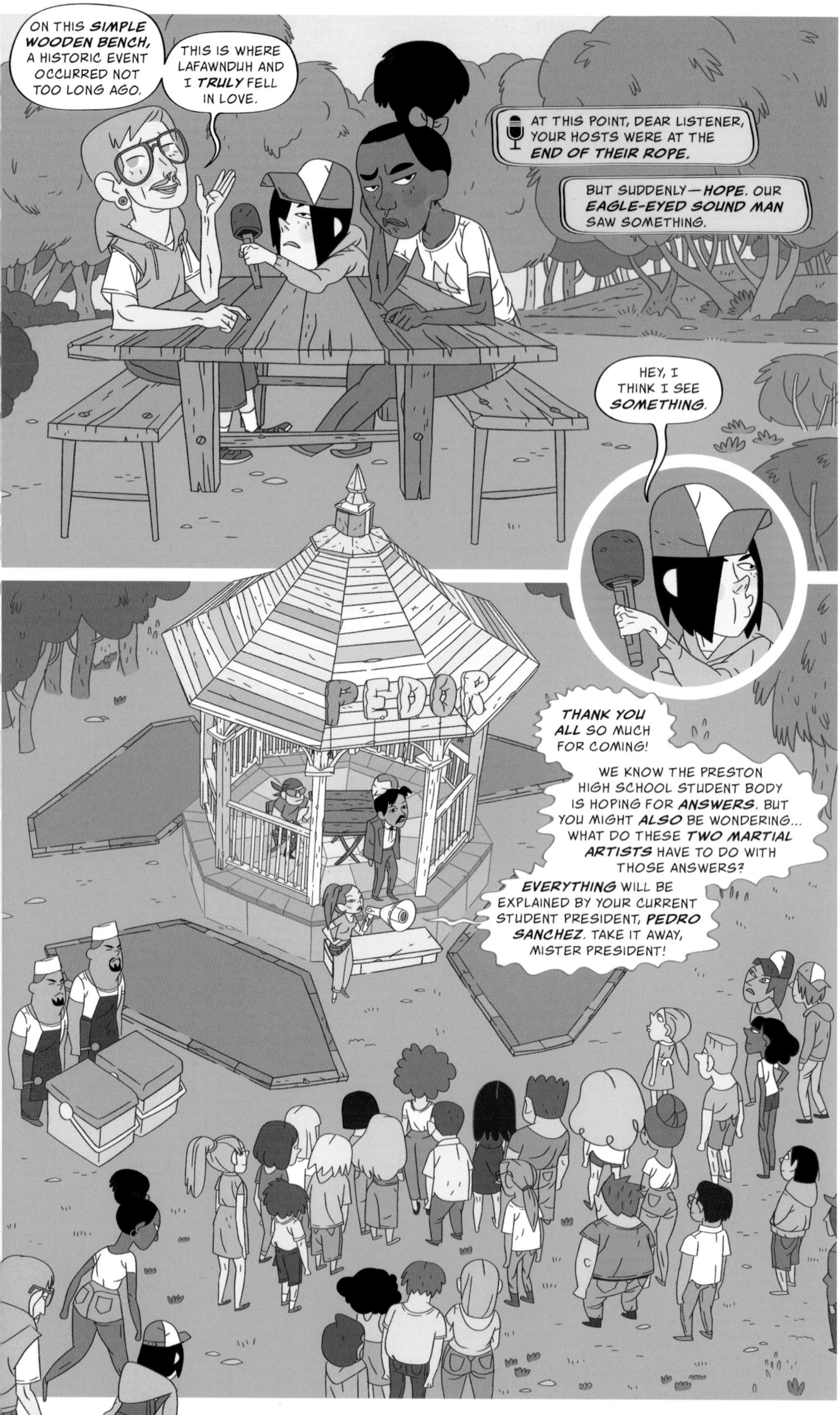

ON THIS SIMPLE WOODEN BENCH, A HISTORIC EVENT OCCURRED NOT TOO LONG AGO.
THIS IS WHERE LAFAWNDUH AND I TRULY FELL IN LOVE.
AT THIS POINT, DEAR LISTENER, YOUR HOSTS WERE AT THE END OF THEIR ROPE.
BUT SUDDENLY—HOPE. OUR EAGLE-EYED SOUND MAN SAW SOMETHING.
HEY, I THINK I SEE SOMETHING.
PEDOR
THANK YOU ALL SO MUCH FOR COMING!
WE KNOW THE PRESTON HIGH SCHOOL STUDENT BODY IS HOPING FOR ANSWERS. BUT YOU MIGHT ALSO BE WONDERING... WHAT DO THESE TWO MARTIAL ARTISTS HAVE TO DO WITH THOSE ANSWERS?
EVERYTHING WILL BE EXPLAINED BY YOUR CURRENT STUDENT PRESIDENT, PEDRO SANCHEZ. TAKE IT AWAY, MISTER PRESIDENT!

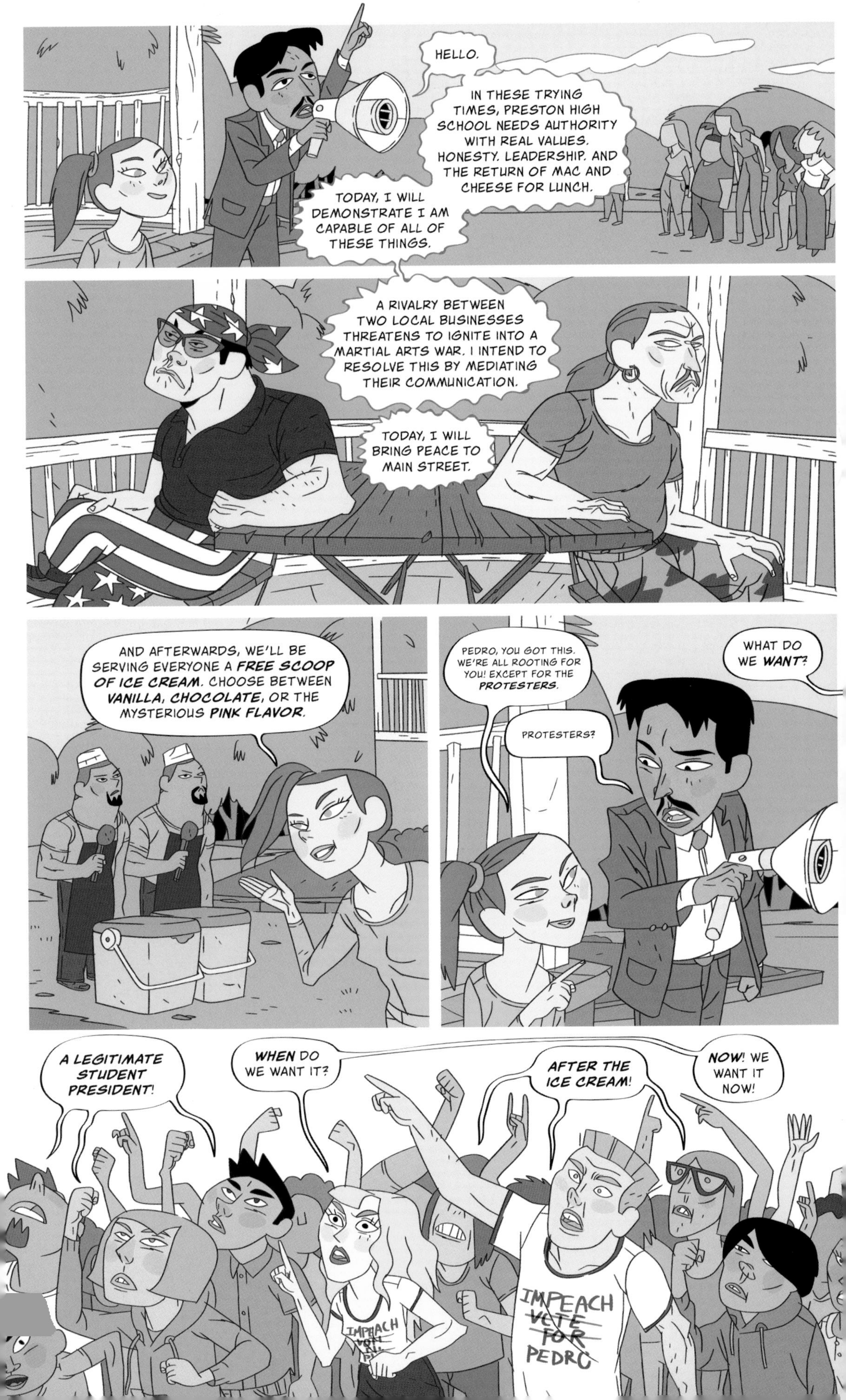

HELLO.
IN THESE TRYING TIMES, PRESTON HIGH SCHOOL NEEDS AUTHORITY WITH REAL VALUES. HONESTY. LEADERSHIP. AND THE RETURN OF MAC AND CHEESE FOR LUNCH.
TODAY, I WILL DEMONSTRATE I AM CAPABLE OF ALL OF THESE THINGS.
A RIVALRY BETWEEN TWO LOCAL BUSINESSES THREATENS TO IGNITE INTO A MARTIAL ARTS WAR. I INTEND TO RESOLVE THIS BY MEDIATING THEIR COMMUNICATION.
TODAY, I WILL BRING PEACE TO MAIN STREET.
AND AFTERWARDS, WE'LL BE SERVING EVERYONE A ***FREE SCOOP OF ICE CREAM***. CHOOSE BETWEEN ***VANILLA, CHOCOLATE***, OR THE MYSTERIOUS ***PINK FLAVOR***.
PEDRO, YOU GOT THIS. WE'RE ALL ROOTING FOR YOU! EXCEPT FOR THE ***PROTESTERS***.
PROTESTERS?
WHAT DO WE ***WANT***?
A LEGITIMATE STUDENT PRESIDENT!
WHEN DO WE WANT IT?
AFTER THE ICE CREAM!
NOW! WE WANT IT NOW!
IMPEACH ~~VOTE FOR~~ PEDRO

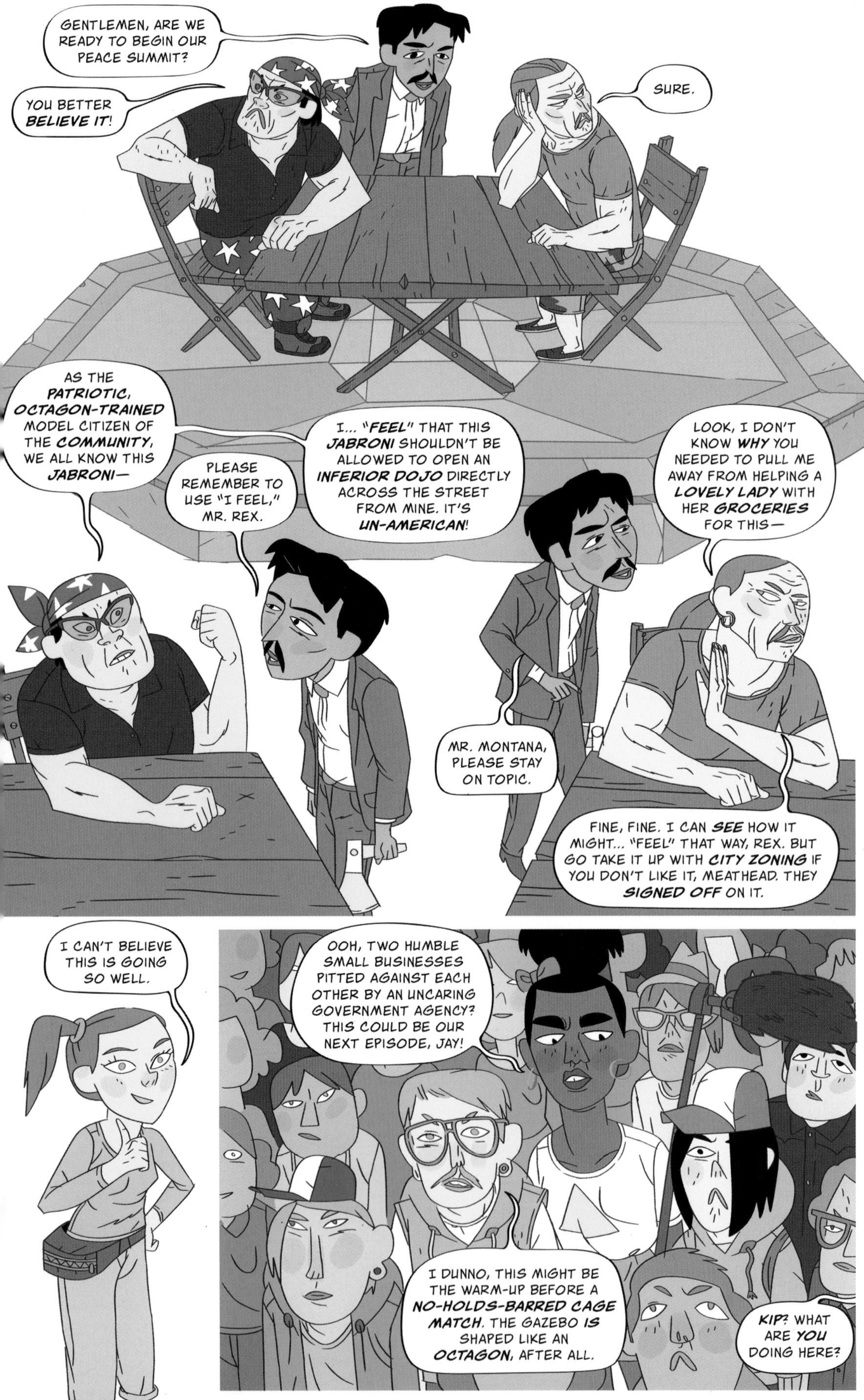

GENTLEMEN, ARE WE READY TO BEGIN OUR PEACE SUMMIT?
YOU BETTER **BELIEVE IT**!
SURE.
AS THE **PATRIOTIC, OCTAGON-TRAINED** MODEL CITIZEN OF THE **COMMUNITY**, WE ALL KNOW THIS **JABRONI**—
PLEASE REMEMBER TO USE "I FEEL," MR. REX.
I... "**FEEL**" THAT THIS **JABRONI** SHOULDN'T BE ALLOWED TO OPEN AN **INFERIOR DOJO** DIRECTLY ACROSS THE STREET FROM MINE. IT'S **UN-AMERICAN**!
LOOK, I DON'T KNOW **WHY** YOU NEEDED TO PULL ME AWAY FROM HELPING A **LOVELY LADY** WITH HER **GROCERIES** FOR THIS—
MR. MONTANA, PLEASE STAY ON TOPIC.
FINE, FINE. I CAN **SEE** HOW IT MIGHT... "FEEL" THAT WAY, REX. BUT GO TAKE IT UP WITH **CITY ZONING** IF YOU DON'T LIKE IT, MEATHEAD. THEY **SIGNED OFF** ON IT.
I CAN'T BELIEVE THIS IS GOING SO WELL.
OOH, TWO HUMBLE SMALL BUSINESSES PITTED AGAINST EACH OTHER BY AN UNCARING GOVERNMENT AGENCY? THIS COULD BE OUR NEXT EPISODE, JAY!
I DUNNO, THIS MIGHT BE THE WARM-UP BEFORE A **NO-HOLDS-BARRED CAGE MATCH**. THE GAZEBO **IS** SHAPED LIKE AN **OCTAGON**, AFTER ALL.
KIP? WHAT ARE **YOU** DOING HERE?

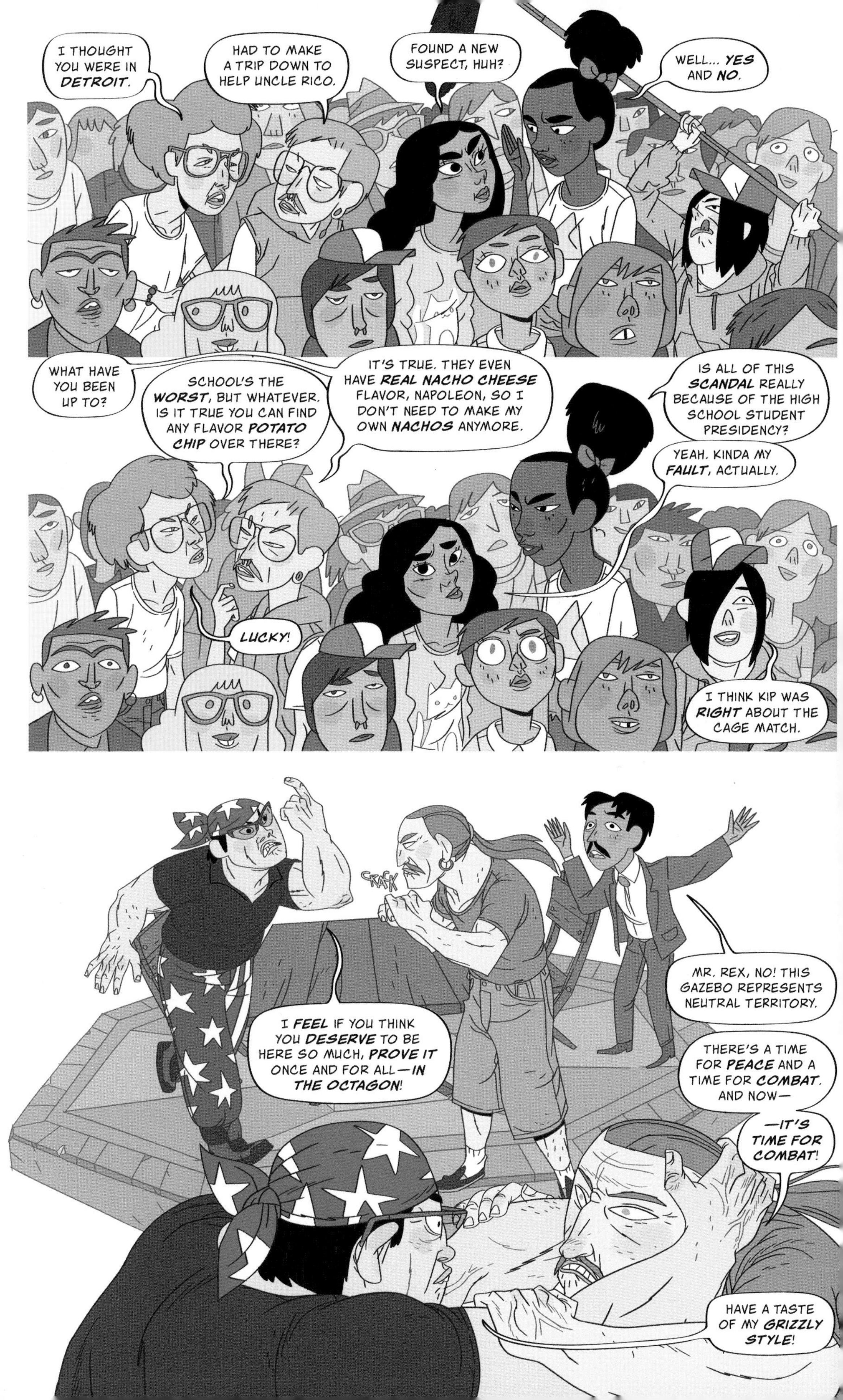

I THOUGHT YOU WERE IN DETROIT.
HAD TO MAKE A TRIP DOWN TO HELP UNCLE RICO.
FOUND A NEW SUSPECT, HUH?
WELL... YES AND NO.
WHAT HAVE YOU BEEN UP TO?
SCHOOL'S THE WORST, BUT WHATEVER. IS IT TRUE YOU CAN FIND ANY FLAVOR POTATO CHIP OVER THERE?
IT'S TRUE. THEY EVEN HAVE REAL NACHO CHEESE FLAVOR, NAPOLEON, SO I DON'T NEED TO MAKE MY OWN NACHOS ANYMORE.
IS ALL OF THIS SCANDAL REALLY BECAUSE OF THE HIGH SCHOOL STUDENT PRESIDENCY?
YEAH. KINDA MY FAULT, ACTUALLY.
LUCKY!
I THINK KIP WAS RIGHT ABOUT THE CAGE MATCH.
CRACK
I FEEL IF YOU THINK YOU DESERVE TO BE HERE SO MUCH, PROVE IT ONCE AND FOR ALL—IN THE OCTAGON!
MR. REX, NO! THIS GAZEBO REPRESENTS NEUTRAL TERRITORY.
THERE'S A TIME FOR PEACE AND A TIME FOR COMBAT. AND NOW—
—IT'S TIME FOR COMBAT!
HAVE A TASTE OF MY GRIZZLY STYLE!

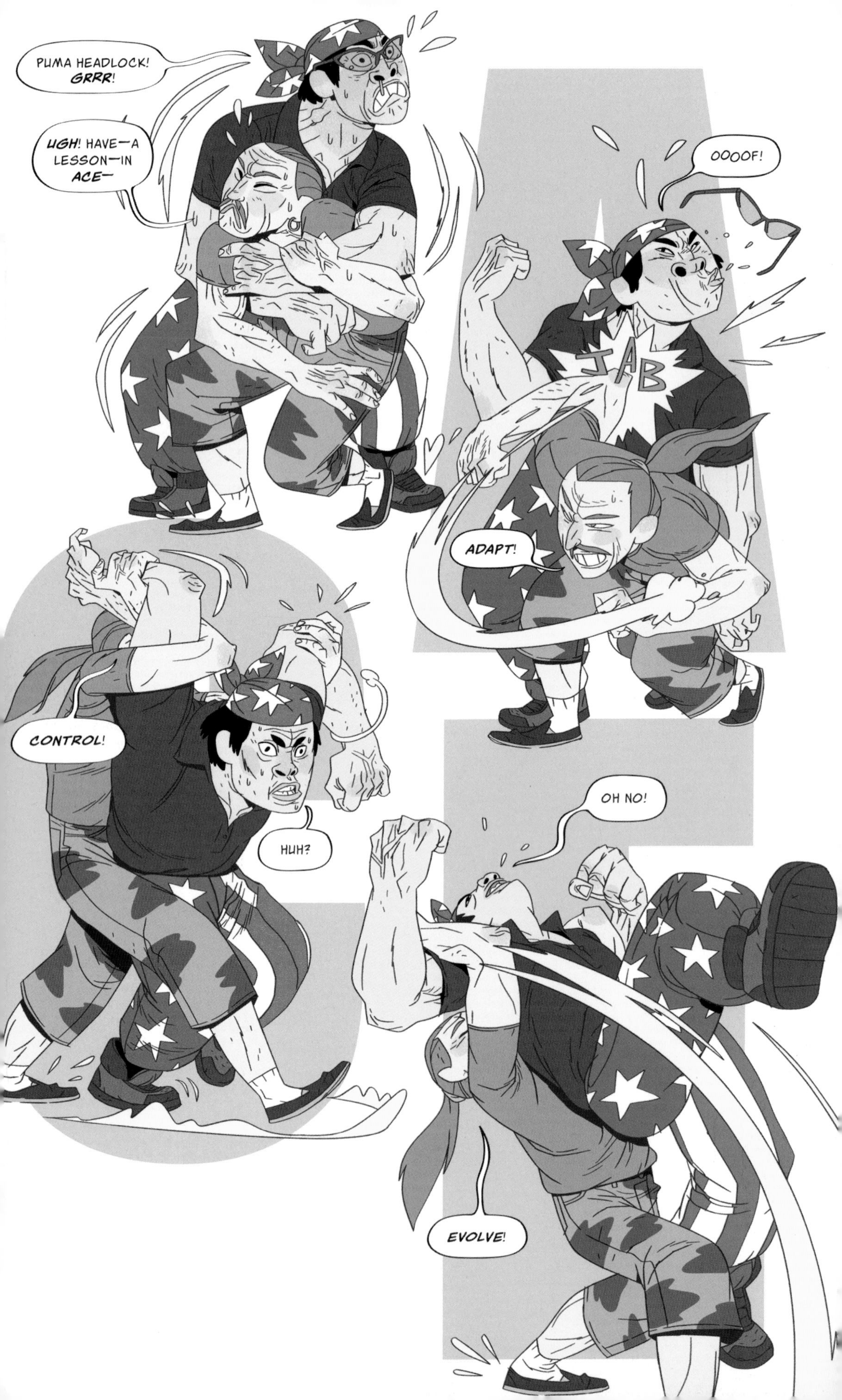
PUMA HEADLOCK! GRRR!
UGH! HAVE—A LESSON—IN ACE—
OOOOF!
JAB
ADAPT!
CONTROL!
HUH?
OH NO!
EVOLVE!

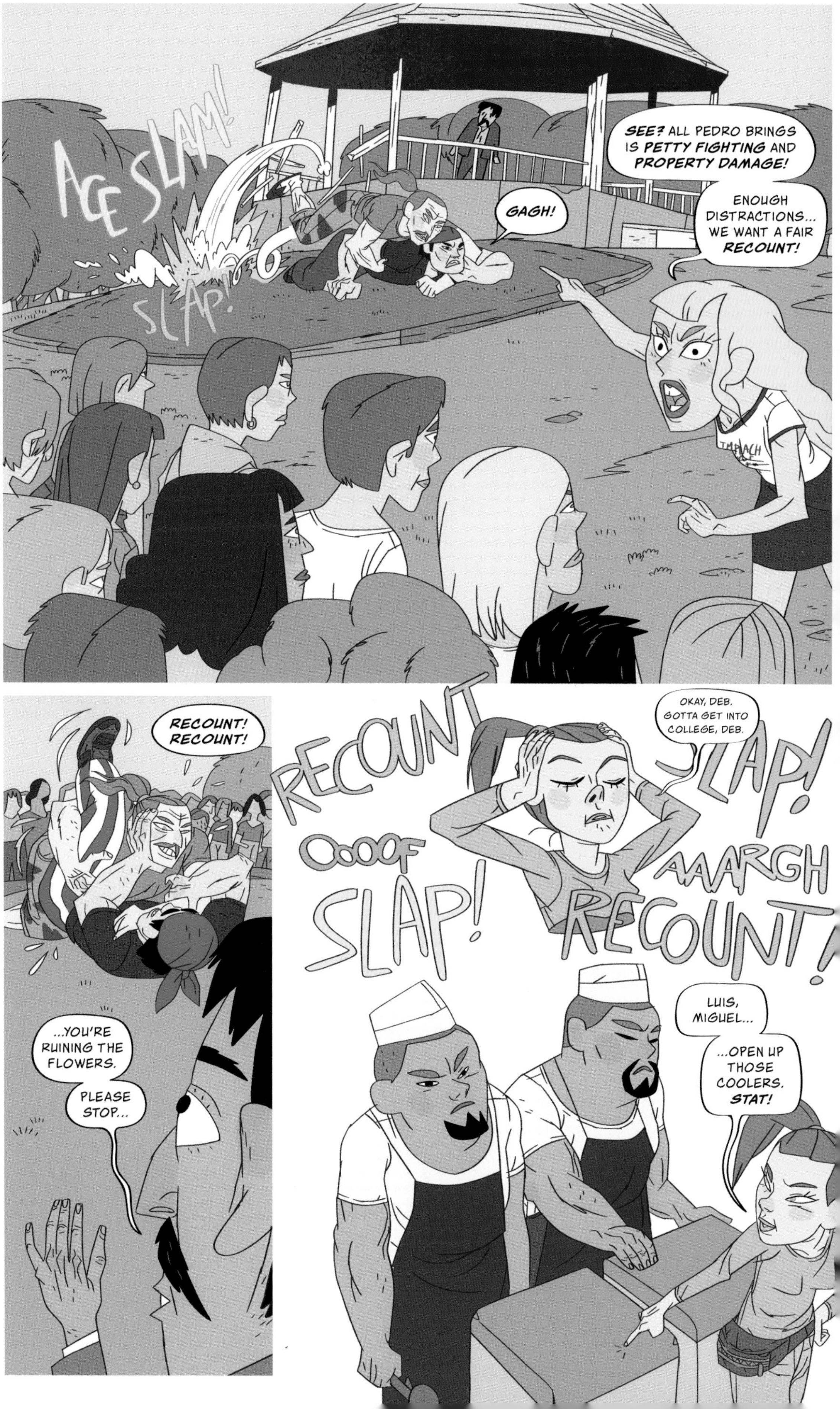
ACE SLAM!
SLAP!
GAGH!
SEE? ALL PEDRO BRINGS IS PETTY FIGHTING AND PROPERTY DAMAGE!
ENOUGH DISTRACTIONS... WE WANT A FAIR RECOUNT!
RECOUNT! RECOUNT!
...YOU'RE RUINING THE FLOWERS.
PLEASE STOP...
RECOUNT
OKAY, DEB. GOTTA GET INTO COLLEGE, DEB.
SLAP!
OOOOF
SLAP!
AAARGH
RECOUNT!
LUIS, MIGUEL...
...OPEN UP THOSE COOLERS. STAT!

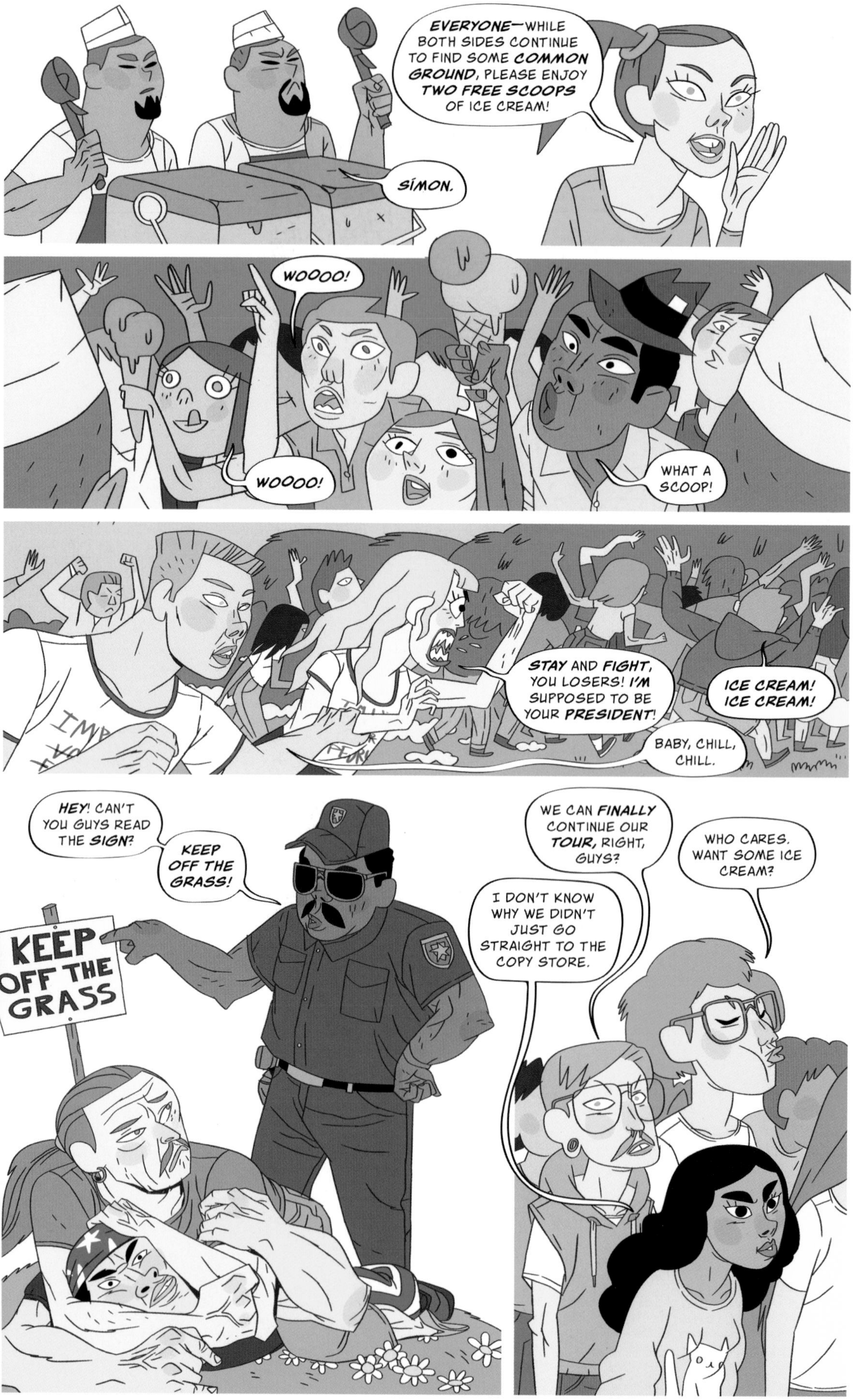
EVERYONE—WHILE BOTH SIDES CONTINUE TO FIND SOME COMMON GROUND, PLEASE ENJOY TWO FREE SCOOPS OF ICE CREAM!
SÍMON.
WOOOO!
WOOOO!
WHAT A SCOOP!
STAY AND FIGHT, YOU LOSERS! I'M SUPPOSED TO BE YOUR PRESIDENT!
ICE CREAM! ICE CREAM!
BABY, CHILL, CHILL.
HEY! CAN'T YOU GUYS READ THE SIGN?
KEEP OFF THE GRASS!
KEEP OFF THE GRASS
WE CAN FINALLY CONTINUE OUR TOUR, RIGHT, GUYS?
WHO CARES. WANT SOME ICE CREAM?
I DON'T KNOW WHY WE DIDN'T JUST GO STRAIGHT TO THE COPY STORE.

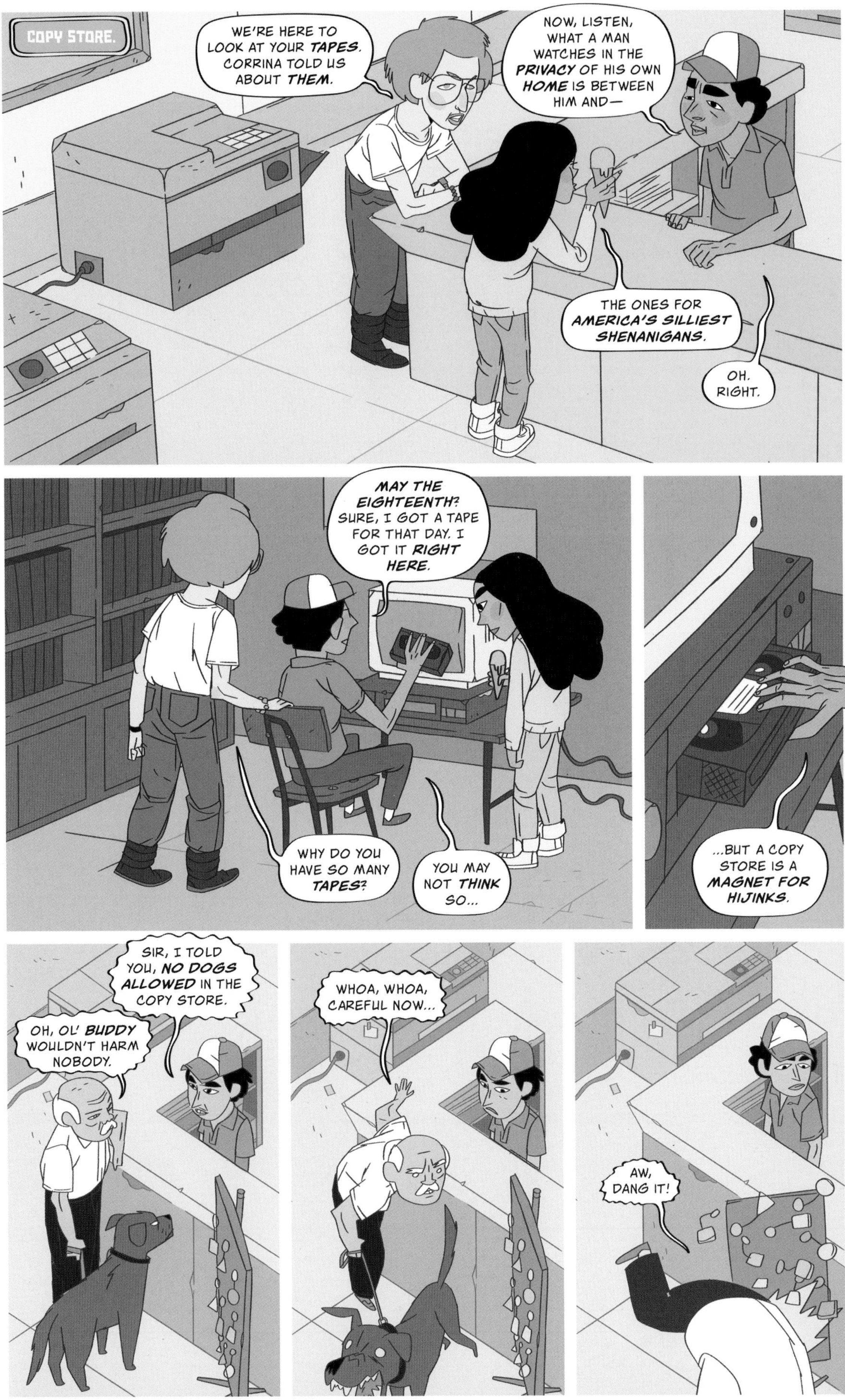
COPY STORE.
WE'RE HERE TO LOOK AT YOUR TAPES. CORRINA TOLD US ABOUT THEM.
NOW, LISTEN, WHAT A MAN WATCHES IN THE PRIVACY OF HIS OWN HOME IS BETWEEN HIM AND—
THE ONES FOR AMERICA'S SILLIEST SHENANIGANS.
OH. RIGHT.
MAY THE EIGHTEENTH? SURE, I GOT A TAPE FOR THAT DAY. I GOT IT RIGHT HERE.
WHY DO YOU HAVE SO MANY TAPES?
YOU MAY NOT THINK SO...
...BUT A COPY STORE IS A MAGNET FOR HIJINKS.
SIR, I TOLD YOU, NO DOGS ALLOWED IN THE COPY STORE.
OH, OL' BUDDY WOULDN'T HARM NOBODY.
WHOA, WHOA, CAREFUL NOW...
AW, DANG IT!

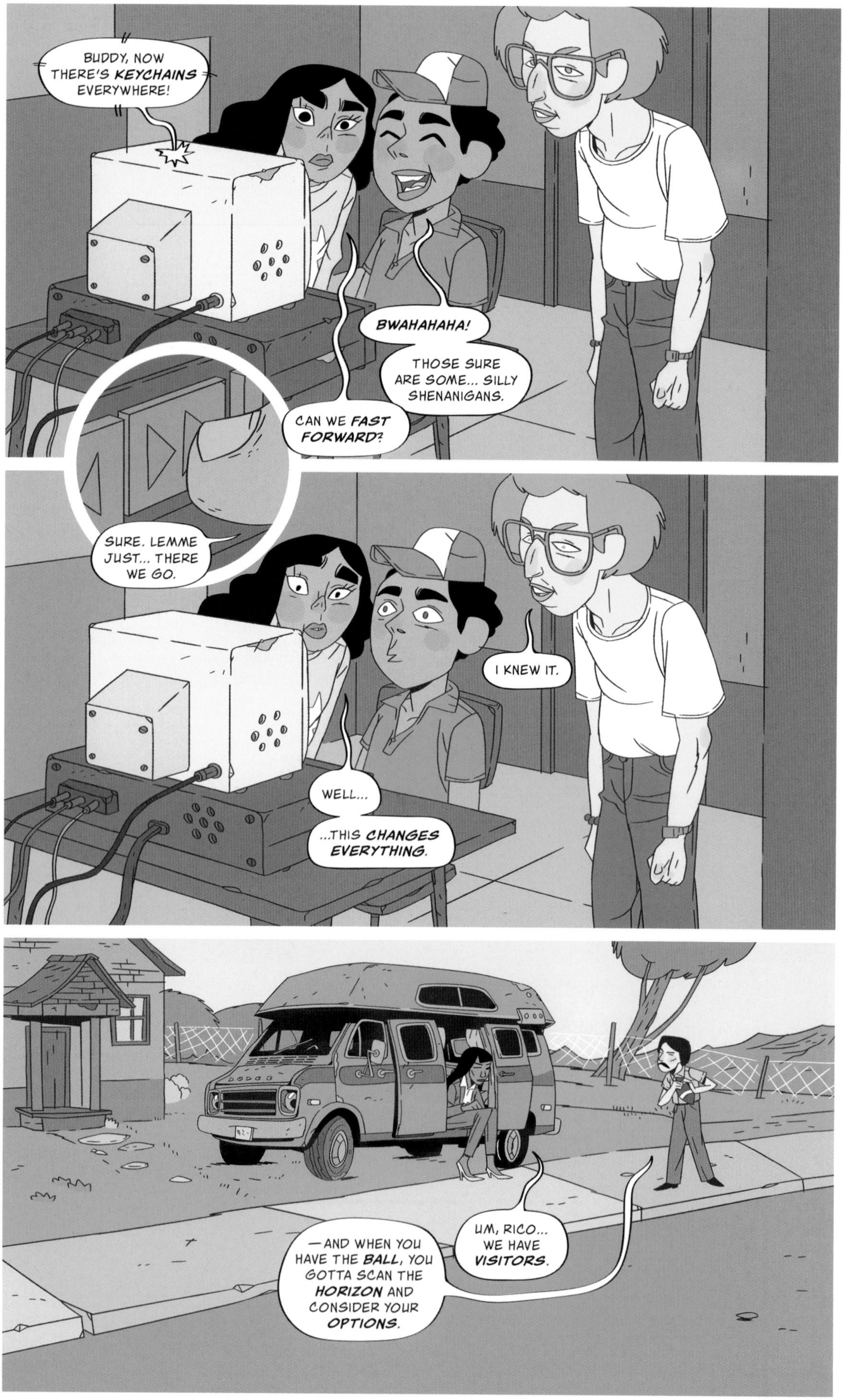
BUDDY, NOW THERE'S KEYCHAINS EVERYWHERE!
BWAHAHAHA!
THOSE SURE ARE SOME... SILLY SHENANIGANS.
CAN WE FAST FORWARD?
SURE. LEMME JUST... THERE WE GO.
I KNEW IT.
WELL...
...THIS CHANGES EVERYTHING.
UM, RICO... WE HAVE VISITORS.
—AND WHEN YOU HAVE THE BALL, YOU GOTTA SCAN THE HORIZON AND CONSIDER YOUR OPTIONS.

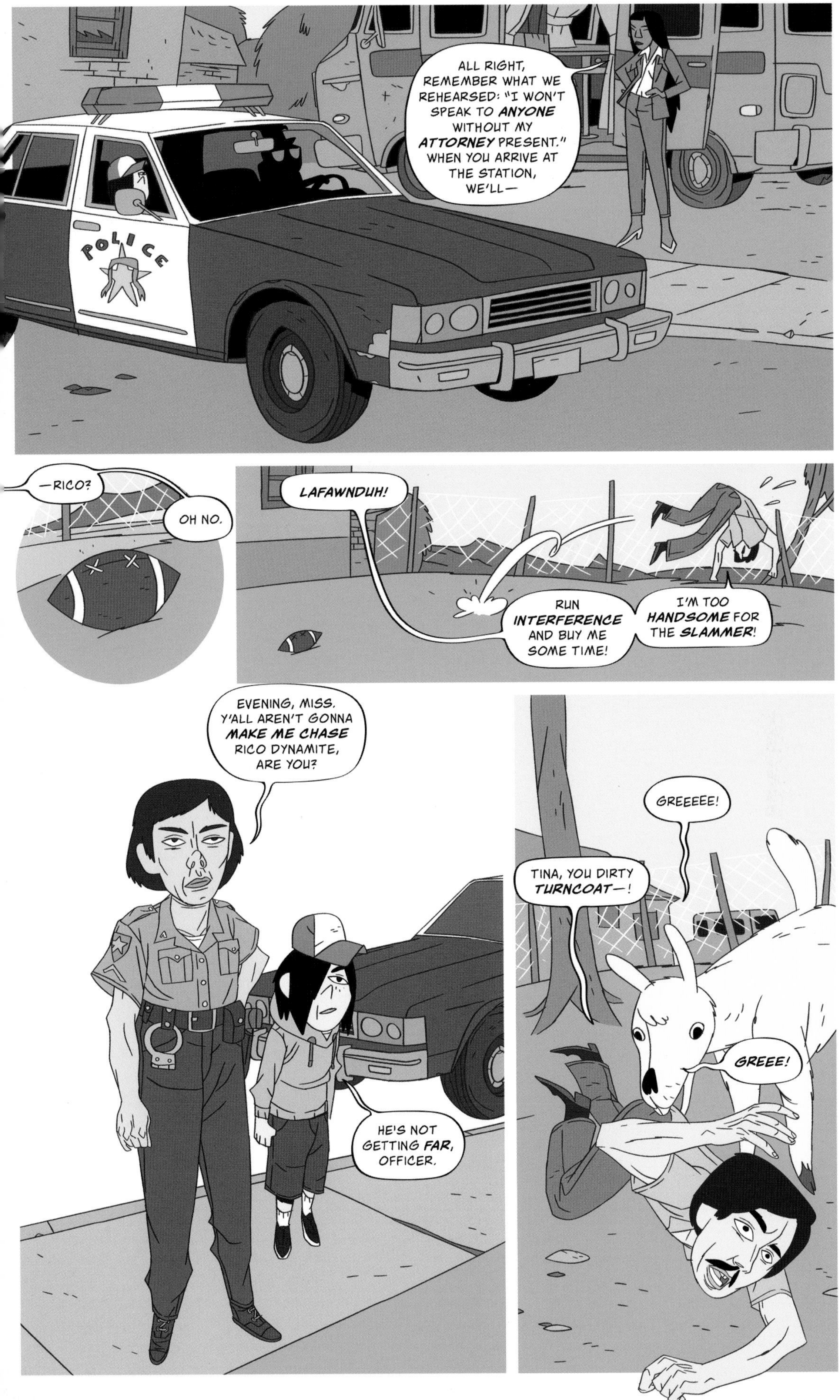
ALL RIGHT, REMEMBER WHAT WE REHEARSED: "I WON'T SPEAK TO ANYONE WITHOUT MY ATTORNEY PRESENT." WHEN YOU ARRIVE AT THE STATION, WE'LL—
POLICE
—RICO?
OH NO.
LAFAWNDUH!
RUN INTERFERENCE AND BUY ME SOME TIME!
I'M TOO HANDSOME FOR THE SLAMMER!
EVENING, MISS. Y'ALL AREN'T GONNA MAKE ME CHASE RICO DYNAMITE, ARE YOU?
HE'S NOT GETTING FAR, OFFICER.
GREEEEE!
TINA, YOU DIRTY TURNCOAT—!
GREEE!

DEB

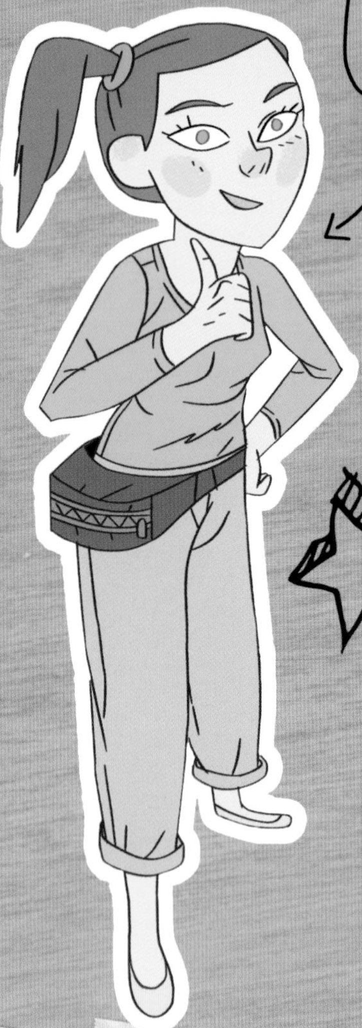

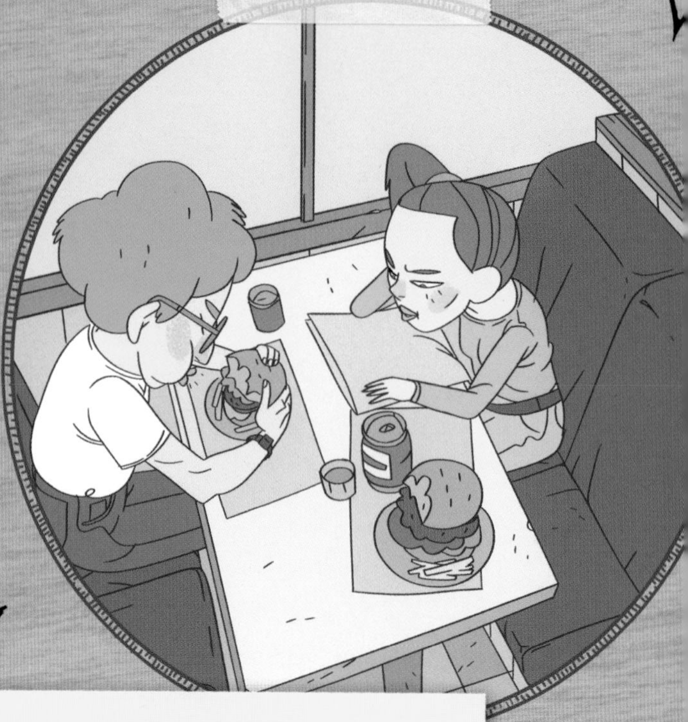

- Help Pedro keep presidency.
- Make bracelets to raise money for college.
- Get into college.
- Ask Gato where she got her cool cat sweater.

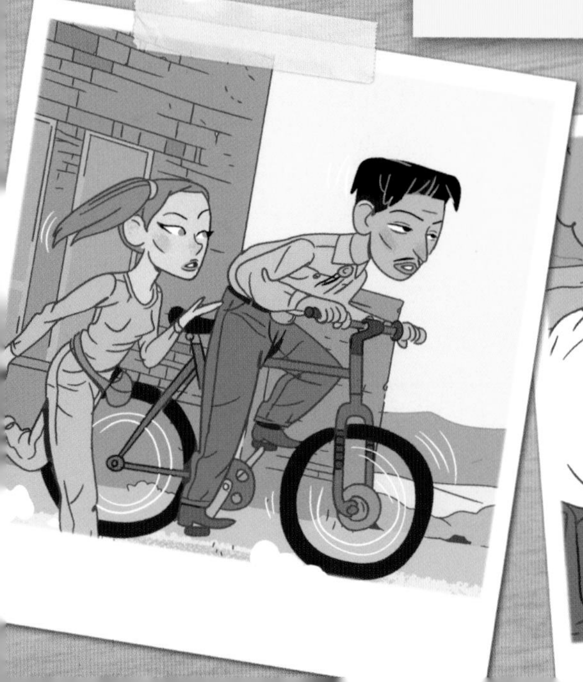

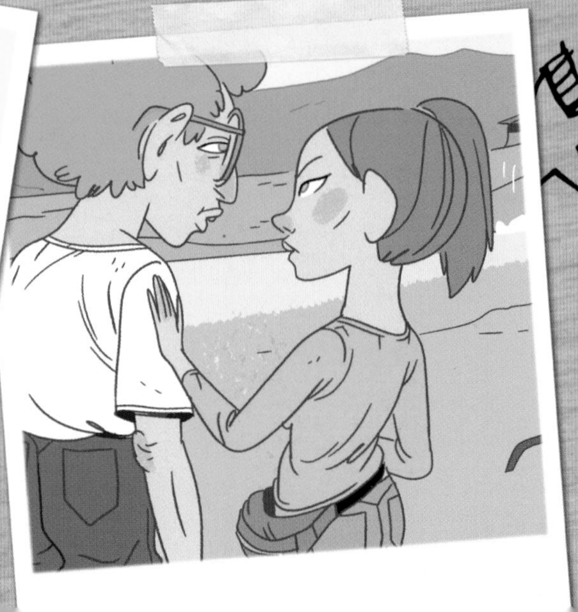

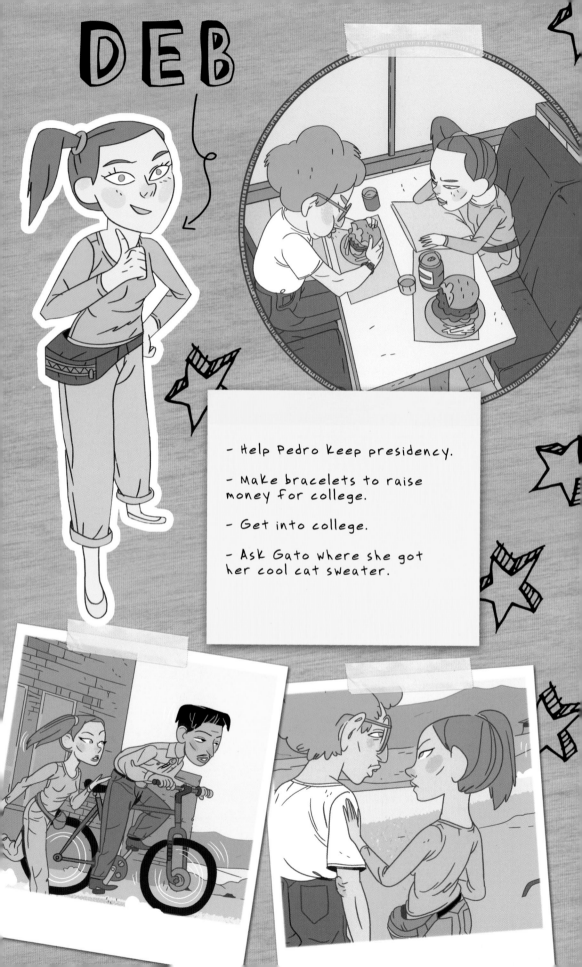

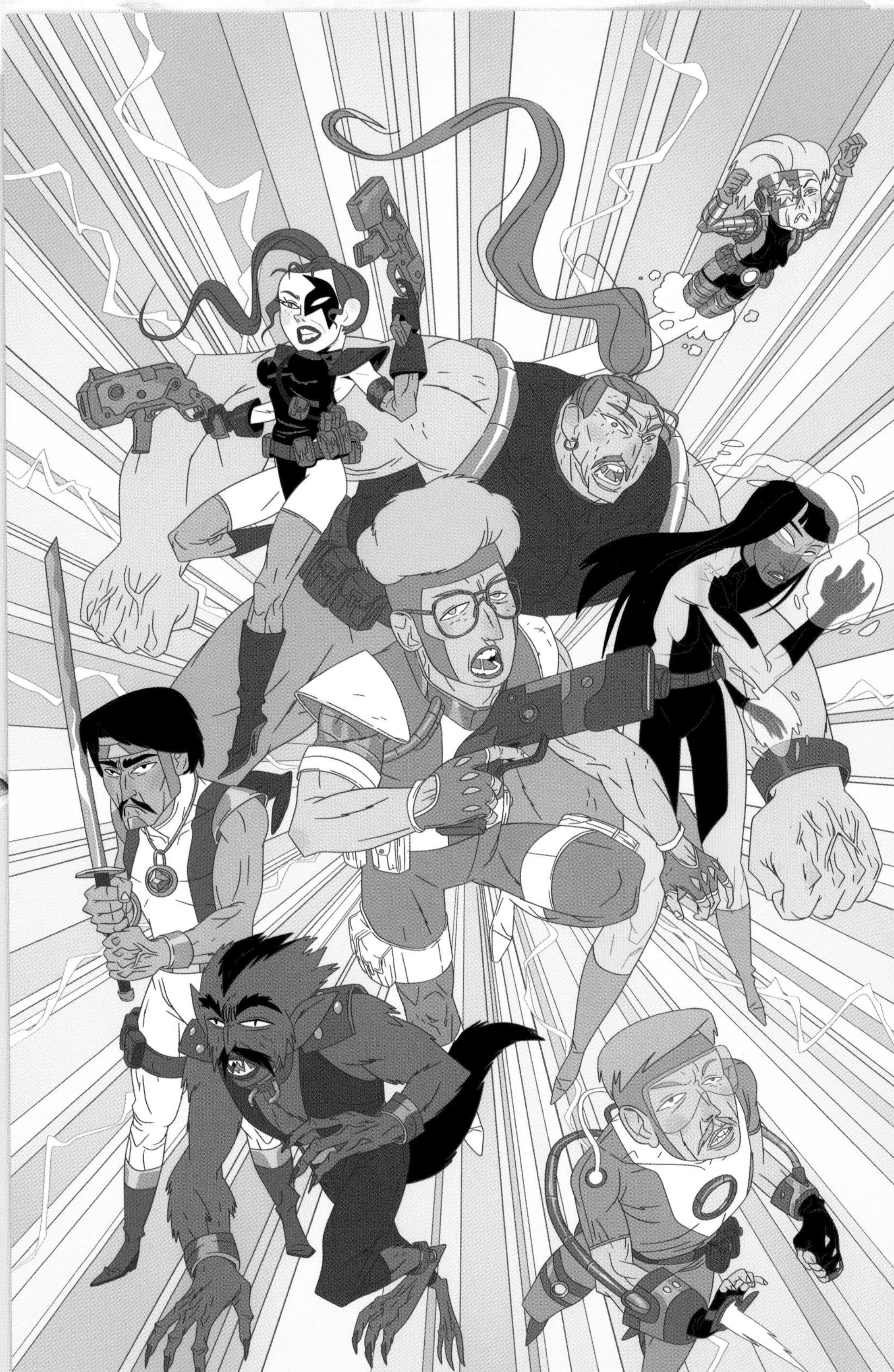

Art by Jorge Monlongo

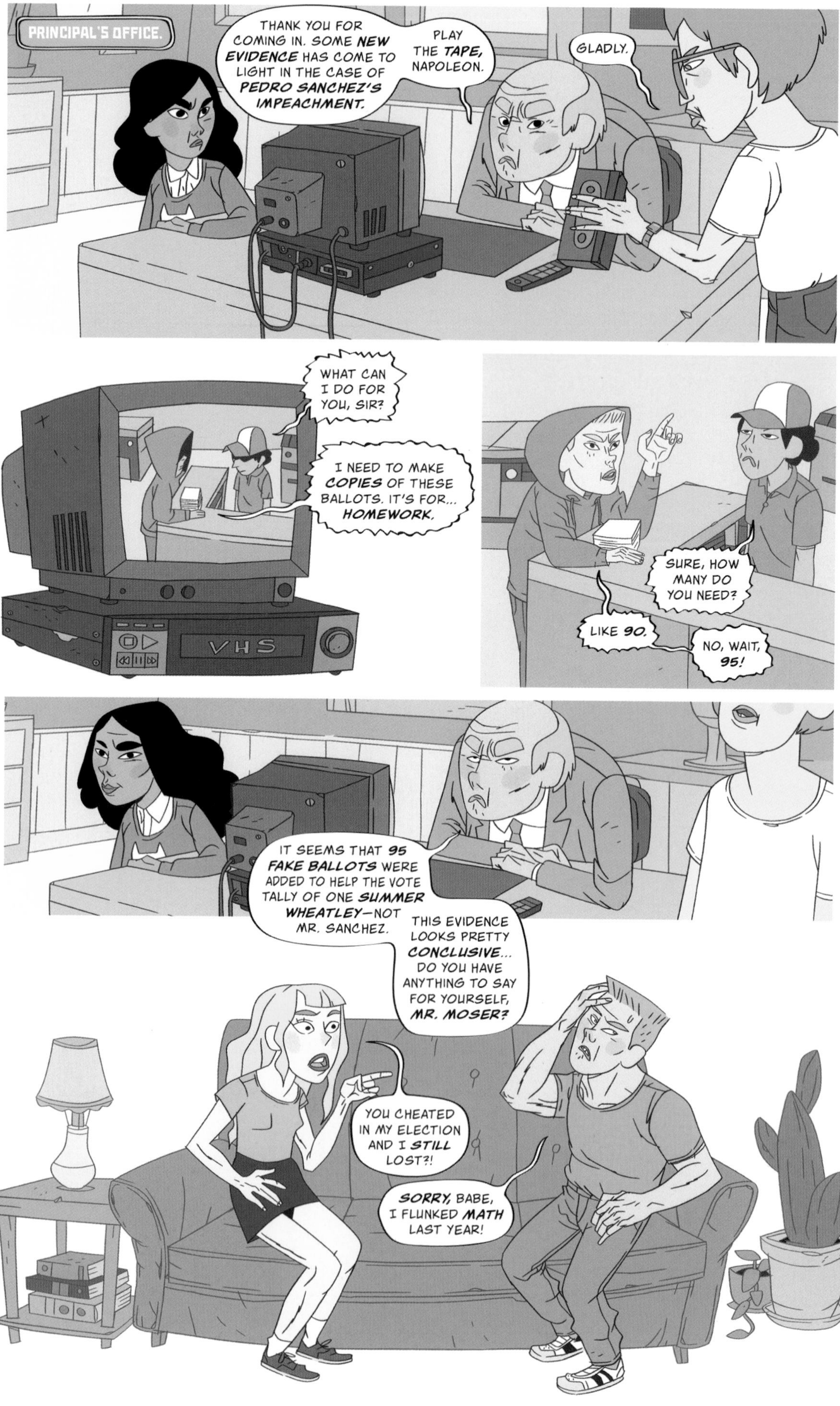
PRINCIPAL'S OFFICE.
THANK YOU FOR COMING IN. SOME NEW EVIDENCE HAS COME TO LIGHT IN THE CASE OF PEDRO SANCHEZ'S IMPEACHMENT.
PLAY THE TAPE, NAPOLEON.
GLADLY.
WHAT CAN I DO FOR YOU, SIR?
I NEED TO MAKE COPIES OF THESE BALLOTS. IT'S FOR... HOMEWORK.
VHS
SURE, HOW MANY DO YOU NEED?
LIKE 90.
NO, WAIT, 95!
IT SEEMS THAT 95 FAKE BALLOTS WERE ADDED TO HELP THE VOTE TALLY OF ONE SUMMER WHEATLEY—NOT MR. SANCHEZ.
THIS EVIDENCE LOOKS PRETTY CONCLUSIVE... DO YOU HAVE ANYTHING TO SAY FOR YOURSELF, MR. MOSER?
YOU CHEATED IN MY ELECTION AND I STILL LOST?!
SORRY, BABE, I FLUNKED MATH LAST YEAR!

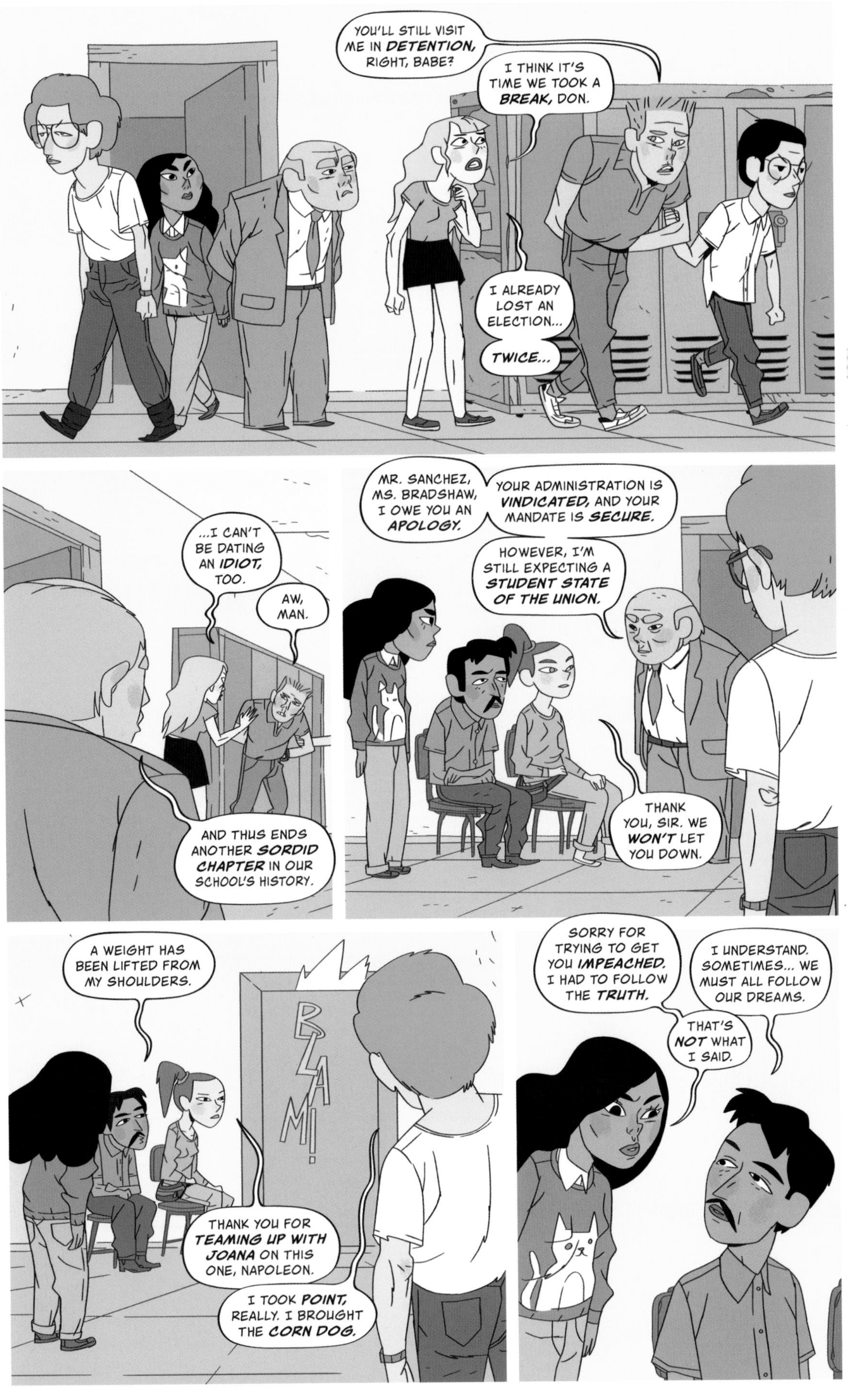
YOU'LL STILL VISIT ME IN DETENTION, RIGHT, BABE?
I THINK IT'S TIME WE TOOK A BREAK, DON.
I ALREADY LOST AN ELECTION...
TWICE...
...I CAN'T BE DATING AN IDIOT, TOO.
AW, MAN.
AND THUS ENDS ANOTHER SORDID CHAPTER IN OUR SCHOOL'S HISTORY.
MR. SANCHEZ, MS. BRADSHAW, I OWE YOU AN APOLOGY.
YOUR ADMINISTRATION IS VINDICATED, AND YOUR MANDATE IS SECURE.
HOWEVER, I'M STILL EXPECTING A STUDENT STATE OF THE UNION.
THANK YOU, SIR. WE WON'T LET YOU DOWN.
A WEIGHT HAS BEEN LIFTED FROM MY SHOULDERS.
BLAM!
THANK YOU FOR TEAMING UP WITH JOANA ON THIS ONE, NAPOLEON.
I TOOK POINT, REALLY. I BROUGHT THE CORN DOG.
SORRY FOR TRYING TO GET YOU IMPEACHED. I HAD TO FOLLOW THE TRUTH.
I UNDERSTAND. SOMETIMES... WE MUST ALL FOLLOW OUR DREAMS.
THAT'S NOT WHAT I SAID.

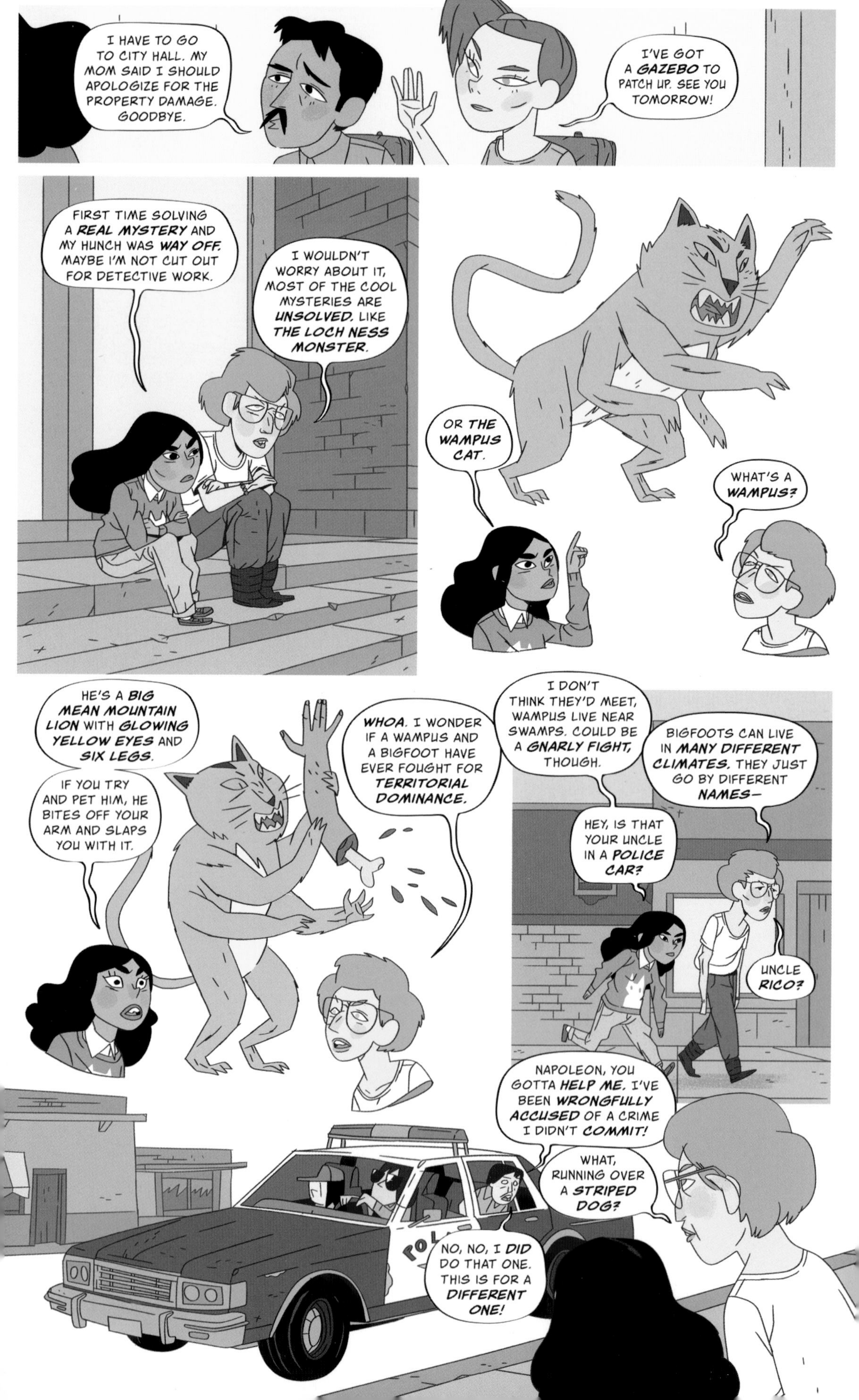
I HAVE TO GO TO CITY HALL. MY MOM SAID I SHOULD APOLOGIZE FOR THE PROPERTY DAMAGE. GOODBYE.
I'VE GOT A GAZEBO TO PATCH UP. SEE YOU TOMORROW!
FIRST TIME SOLVING A REAL MYSTERY AND MY HUNCH WAS WAY OFF. MAYBE I'M NOT CUT OUT FOR DETECTIVE WORK.
I WOULDN'T WORRY ABOUT IT, MOST OF THE COOL MYSTERIES ARE UNSOLVED. LIKE THE LOCH NESS MONSTER.
OR THE WAMPUS CAT.
WHAT'S A WAMPUS?
HE'S A BIG MEAN MOUNTAIN LION WITH GLOWING YELLOW EYES AND SIX LEGS.
IF YOU TRY AND PET HIM, HE BITES OFF YOUR ARM AND SLAPS YOU WITH IT.
WHOA. I WONDER IF A WAMPUS AND A BIGFOOT HAVE EVER FOUGHT FOR TERRITORIAL DOMINANCE.
I DON'T THINK THEY'D MEET, WAMPUS LIVE NEAR SWAMPS. COULD BE A GNARLY FIGHT, THOUGH.
BIGFOOTS CAN LIVE IN MANY DIFFERENT CLIMATES. THEY JUST GO BY DIFFERENT NAMES—
HEY, IS THAT YOUR UNCLE IN A POLICE CAR?
UNCLE RICO?
NAPOLEON, YOU GOTTA HELP ME. I'VE BEEN WRONGFULLY ACCUSED OF A CRIME I DIDN'T COMMIT!
WHAT, RUNNING OVER A STRIPED DOG?
NO, NO, I DID DO THAT ONE. THIS IS FOR A DIFFERENT ONE!

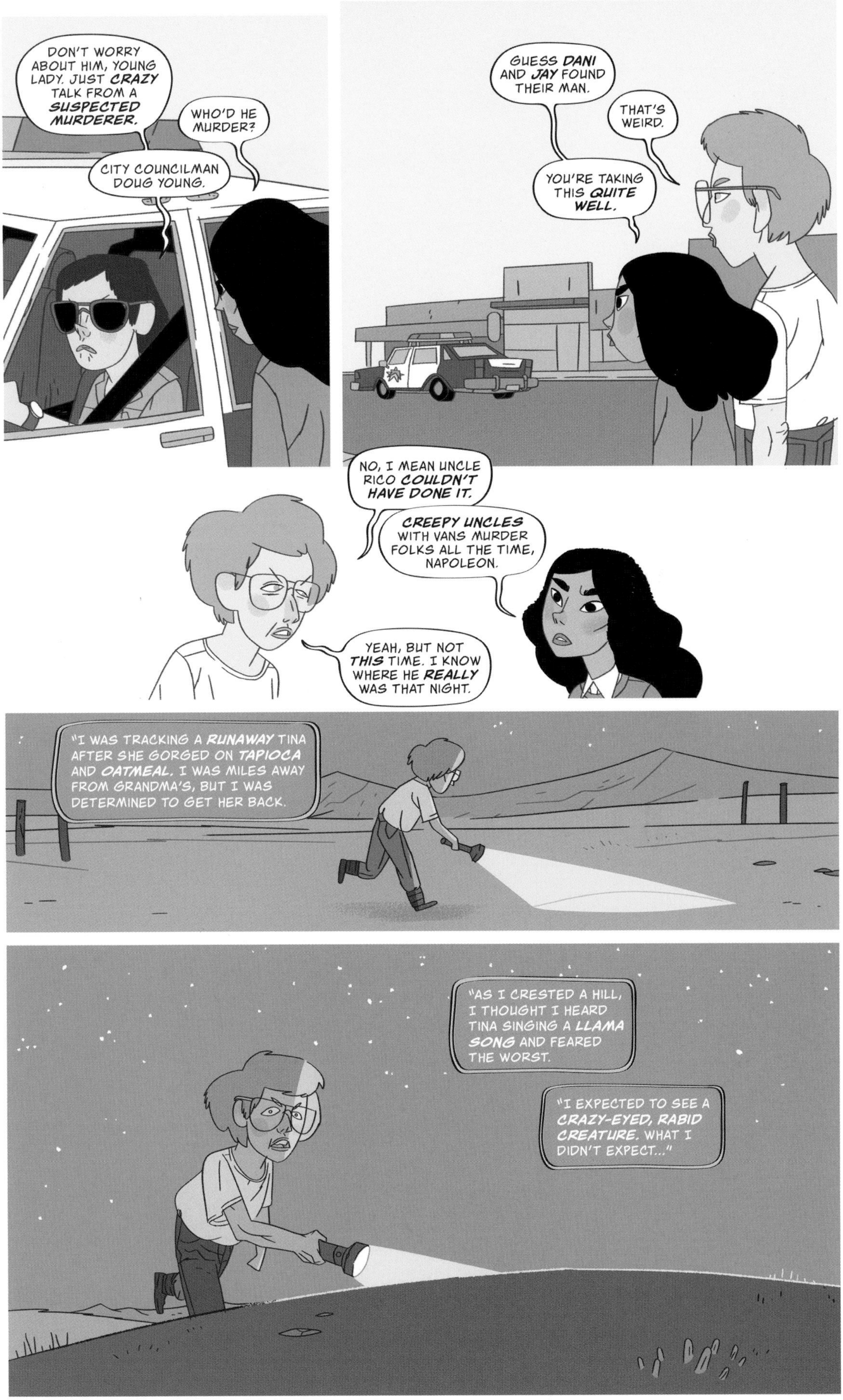
DON'T WORRY ABOUT HIM, YOUNG LADY. JUST CRAZY TALK FROM A SUSPECTED MURDERER.
WHO'D HE MURDER?
CITY COUNCILMAN DOUG YOUNG.
GUESS DANI AND JAY FOUND THEIR MAN.
THAT'S WEIRD.
YOU'RE TAKING THIS QUITE WELL.
NO, I MEAN UNCLE RICO COULDN'T HAVE DONE IT.
CREEPY UNCLES WITH VANS MURDER FOLKS ALL THE TIME, NAPOLEON.
YEAH, BUT NOT THIS TIME. I KNOW WHERE HE REALLY WAS THAT NIGHT.
"I WAS TRACKING A RUNAWAY TINA AFTER SHE GORGED ON TAPIOCA AND OATMEAL. I WAS MILES AWAY FROM GRANDMA'S, BUT I WAS DETERMINED TO GET HER BACK.
"AS I CRESTED A HILL, I THOUGHT I HEARD TINA SINGING A LLAMA SONG AND FEARED THE WORST.
"I EXPECTED TO SEE A CRAZY-EYED, RABID CREATURE. WHAT I DIDN'T EXPECT..."

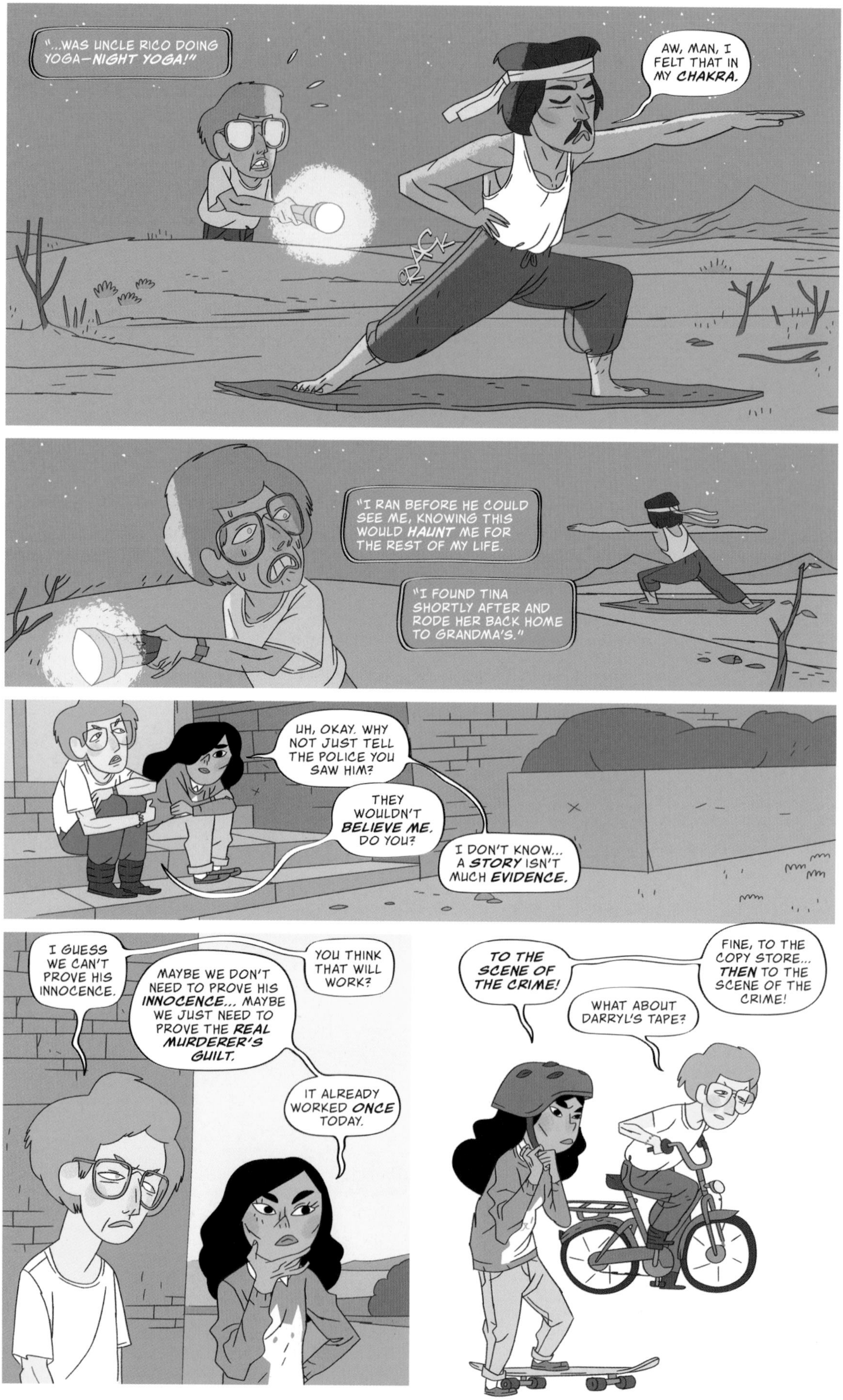
"...WAS UNCLE RICO DOING YOGA—NIGHT YOGA!"
AW, MAN, I FELT THAT IN MY CHAKRA.
CRACK
"I RAN BEFORE HE COULD SEE ME, KNOWING THIS WOULD HAUNT ME FOR THE REST OF MY LIFE.
"I FOUND TINA SHORTLY AFTER AND RODE HER BACK HOME TO GRANDMA'S."
UH, OKAY. WHY NOT JUST TELL THE POLICE YOU SAW HIM?
THEY WOULDN'T BELIEVE ME. DO YOU?
I DON'T KNOW... A STORY ISN'T MUCH EVIDENCE.
I GUESS WE CAN'T PROVE HIS INNOCENCE.
MAYBE WE DON'T NEED TO PROVE HIS INNOCENCE... MAYBE WE JUST NEED TO PROVE THE REAL MURDERER'S GUILT.
YOU THINK THAT WILL WORK?
IT ALREADY WORKED ONCE TODAY.
TO THE SCENE OF THE CRIME!
WHAT ABOUT DARRYL'S TAPE?
FINE, TO THE COPY STORE... THEN TO THE SCENE OF THE CRIME!

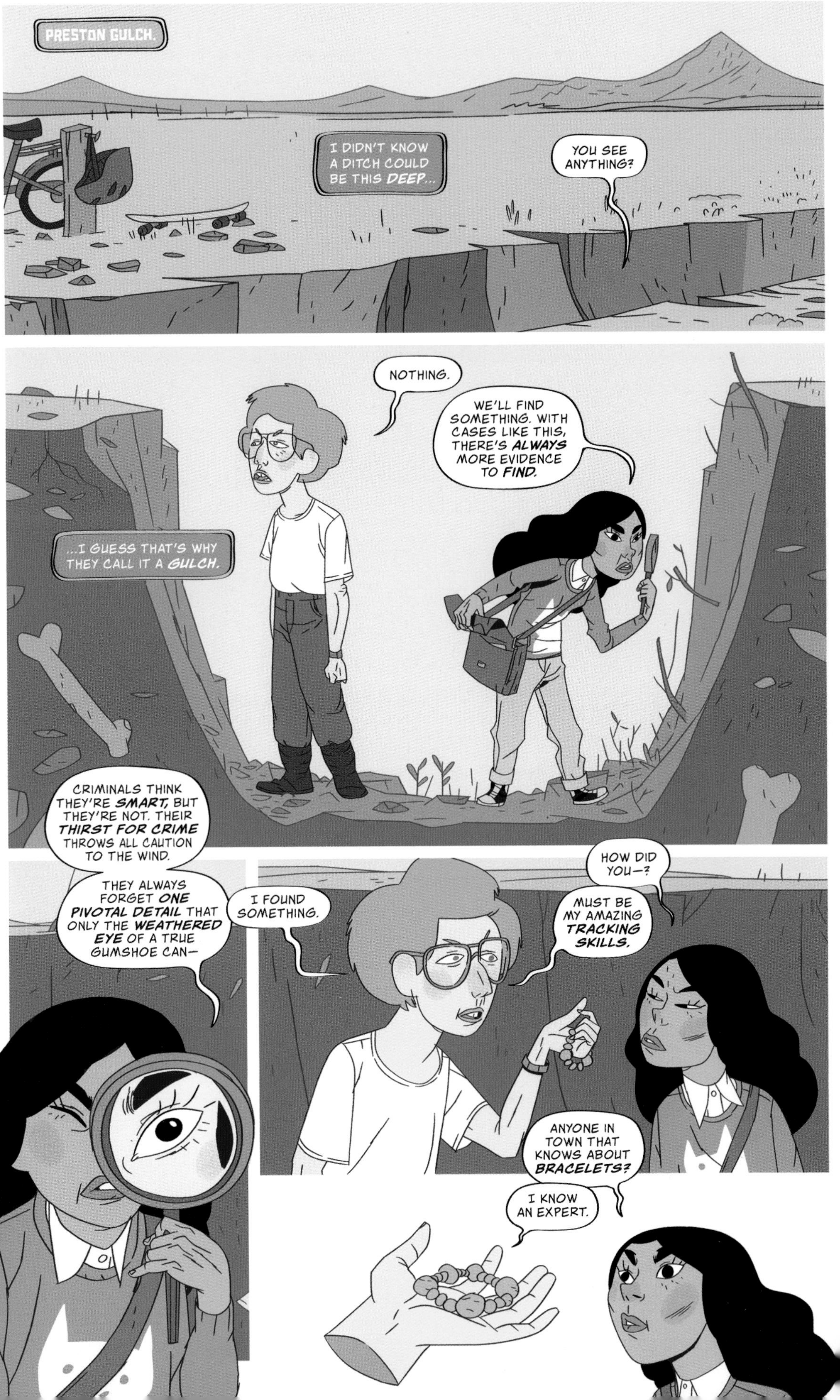
PRESTON GULCH.
I DIDN'T KNOW A DITCH COULD BE THIS DEEP...
YOU SEE ANYTHING?
NOTHING.
WE'LL FIND SOMETHING. WITH CASES LIKE THIS, THERE'S ALWAYS MORE EVIDENCE TO FIND.
...I GUESS THAT'S WHY THEY CALL IT A GULCH.
CRIMINALS THINK THEY'RE SMART, BUT THEY'RE NOT. THEIR THIRST FOR CRIME THROWS ALL CAUTION TO THE WIND.
THEY ALWAYS FORGET ONE PIVOTAL DETAIL THAT ONLY THE WEATHERED EYE OF A TRUE GUMSHOE CAN—
I FOUND SOMETHING.
HOW DID YOU—?
MUST BE MY AMAZING TRACKING SKILLS.
ANYONE IN TOWN THAT KNOWS ABOUT BRACELETS?
I KNOW AN EXPERT.

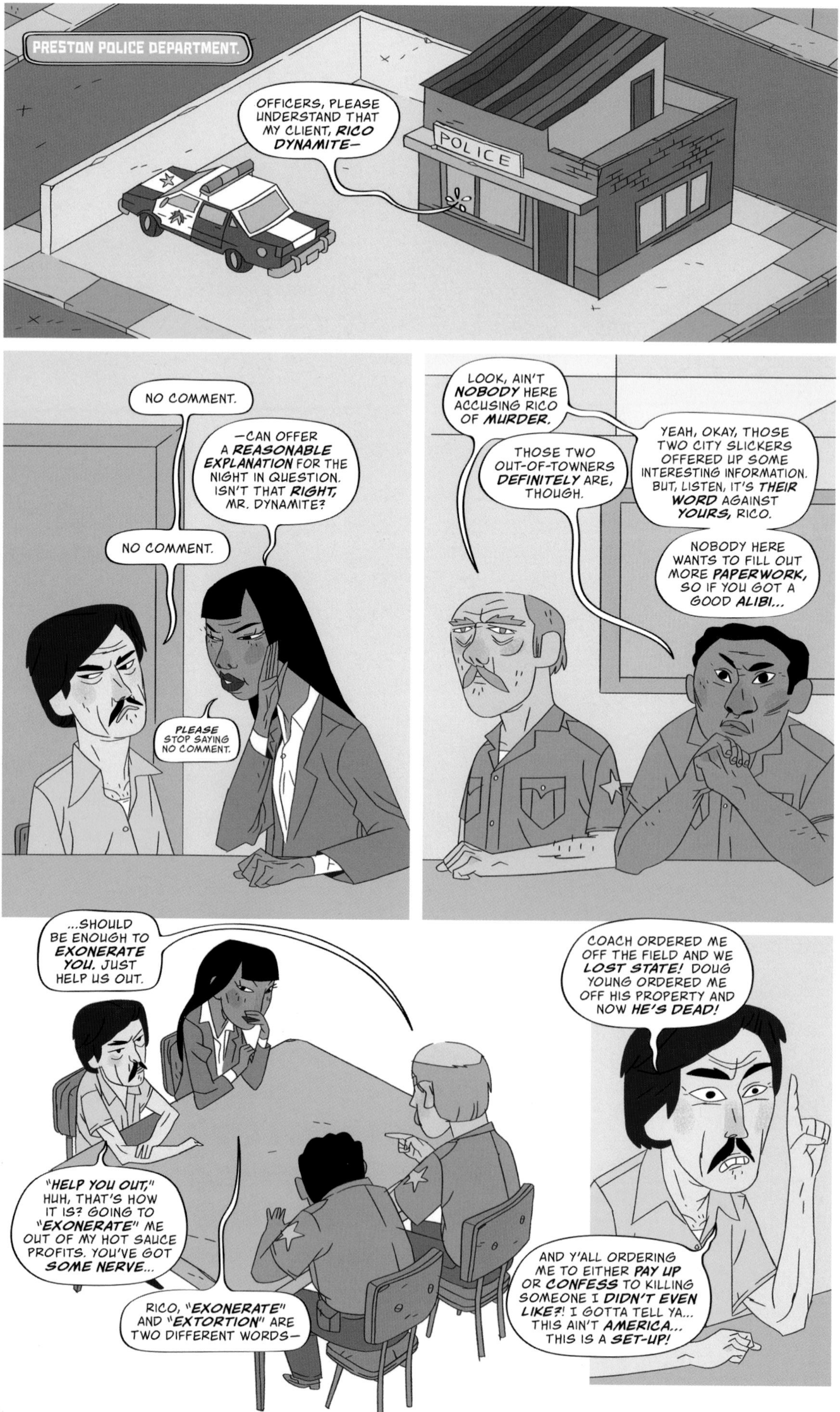
PRESTON POLICE DEPARTMENT.
OFFICERS, PLEASE UNDERSTAND THAT MY CLIENT, RICO DYNAMITE—
POLICE
NO COMMENT.
—CAN OFFER A REASONABLE EXPLANATION FOR THE NIGHT IN QUESTION. ISN'T THAT RIGHT, MR. DYNAMITE?
NO COMMENT.
PLEASE STOP SAYING NO COMMENT.
LOOK, AIN'T NOBODY HERE ACCUSING RICO OF MURDER.
THOSE TWO OUT-OF-TOWNERS DEFINITELY ARE, THOUGH.
YEAH, OKAY, THOSE TWO CITY SLICKERS OFFERED UP SOME INTERESTING INFORMATION. BUT, LISTEN, IT'S THEIR WORD AGAINST YOURS, RICO.
NOBODY HERE WANTS TO FILL OUT MORE PAPERWORK, SO IF YOU GOT A GOOD ALIBI...
...SHOULD BE ENOUGH TO EXONERATE YOU. JUST HELP US OUT.
"HELP YOU OUT," HUH, THAT'S HOW IT IS? GOING TO "EXONERATE" ME OUT OF MY HOT SAUCE PROFITS. YOU'VE GOT SOME NERVE...
RICO, "EXONERATE" AND "EXTORTION" ARE TWO DIFFERENT WORDS—
COACH ORDERED ME OFF THE FIELD AND WE LOST STATE! DOUG YOUNG ORDERED ME OFF HIS PROPERTY AND NOW HE'S DEAD!
AND Y'ALL ORDERING ME TO EITHER PAY UP OR CONFESS TO KILLING SOMEONE I DIDN'T EVEN LIKE?! I GOTTA TELL YA... THIS AIN'T AMERICA... THIS IS A SET-UP!

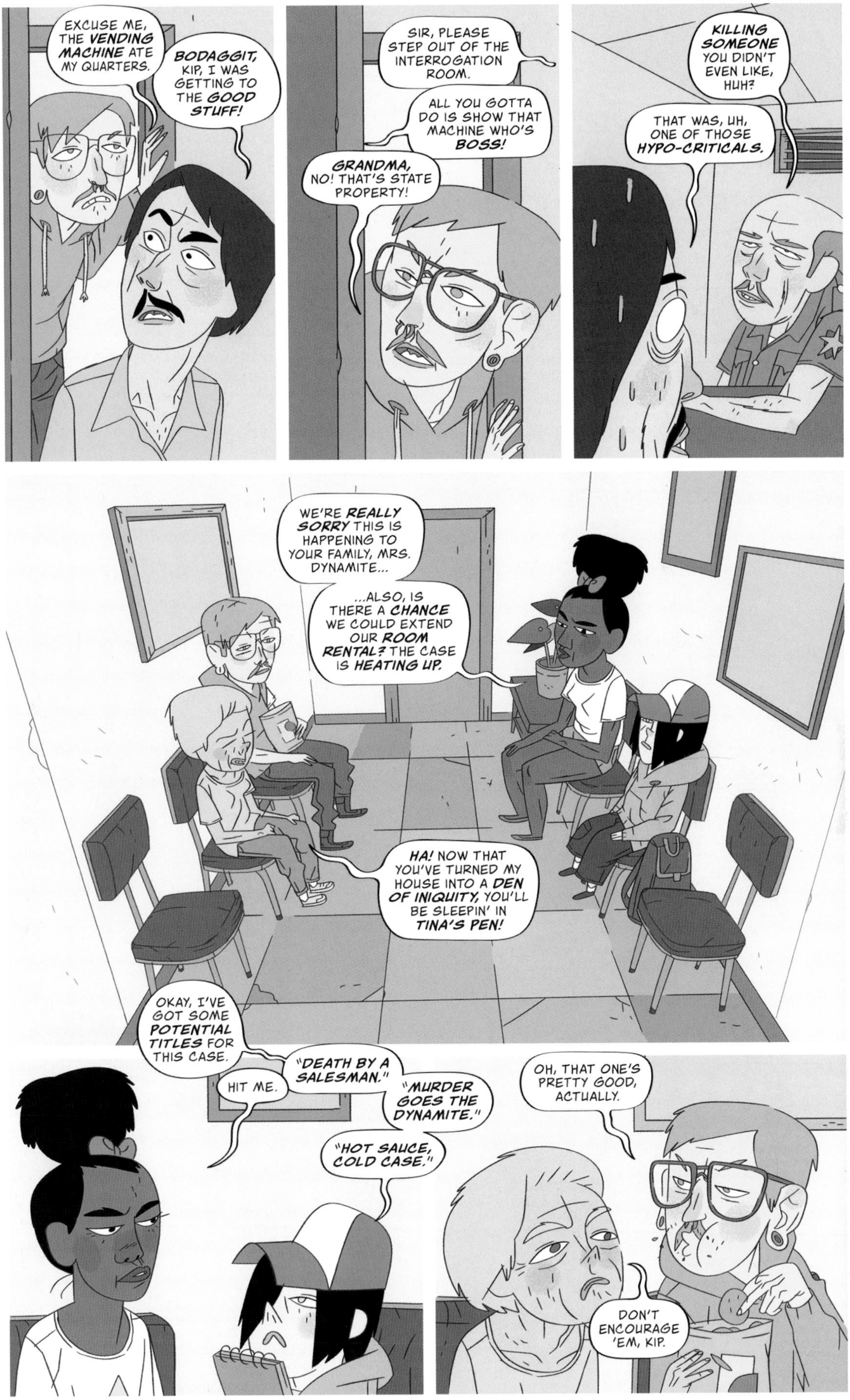
EXCUSE ME, THE VENDING MACHINE ATE MY QUARTERS.
BODAGGIT, KIP, I WAS GETTING TO THE GOOD STUFF!
SIR, PLEASE STEP OUT OF THE INTERROGATION ROOM.
ALL YOU GOTTA DO IS SHOW THAT MACHINE WHO'S BOSS!
GRANDMA, NO! THAT'S STATE PROPERTY!
KILLING SOMEONE YOU DIDN'T EVEN LIKE, HUH?
THAT WAS, UH, ONE OF THOSE HYPO-CRITICALS.
WE'RE REALLY SORRY THIS IS HAPPENING TO YOUR FAMILY, MRS. DYNAMITE...
...ALSO, IS THERE A CHANCE WE COULD EXTEND OUR ROOM RENTAL? THE CASE IS HEATING UP.
HA! NOW THAT YOU'VE TURNED MY HOUSE INTO A DEN OF INIQUITY, YOU'LL BE SLEEPIN' IN TINA'S PEN!
OKAY, I'VE GOT SOME POTENTIAL TITLES FOR THIS CASE.
HIT ME.
"DEATH BY A SALESMAN."
"MURDER GOES THE DYNAMITE."
"HOT SAUCE, COLD CASE."
OH, THAT ONE'S PRETTY GOOD, ACTUALLY.
DON'T ENCOURAGE 'EM, KIP.

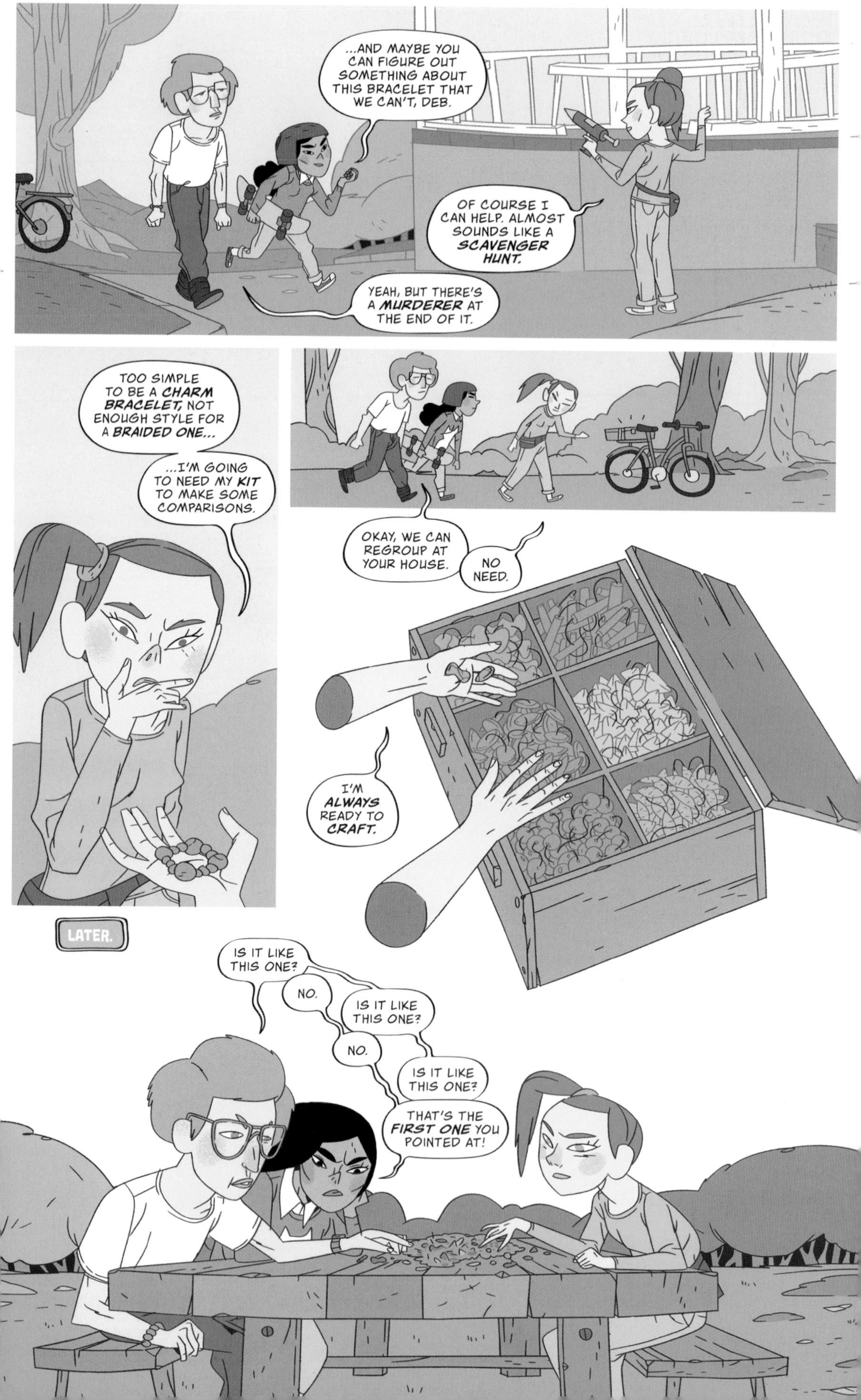
...AND MAYBE YOU CAN FIGURE OUT SOMETHING ABOUT THIS BRACELET THAT WE CAN'T, DEB.
OF COURSE I CAN HELP. ALMOST SOUNDS LIKE A SCAVENGER HUNT.
YEAH, BUT THERE'S A MURDERER AT THE END OF IT.
TOO SIMPLE TO BE A CHARM BRACELET, NOT ENOUGH STYLE FOR A BRAIDED ONE...
...I'M GOING TO NEED MY KIT TO MAKE SOME COMPARISONS.
OKAY, WE CAN REGROUP AT YOUR HOUSE.
NO NEED.
I'M ALWAYS READY TO CRAFT.
LATER.
IS IT LIKE THIS ONE?
NO.
IS IT LIKE THIS ONE?
NO.
IS IT LIKE THIS ONE?
THAT'S THE FIRST ONE YOU POINTED AT!

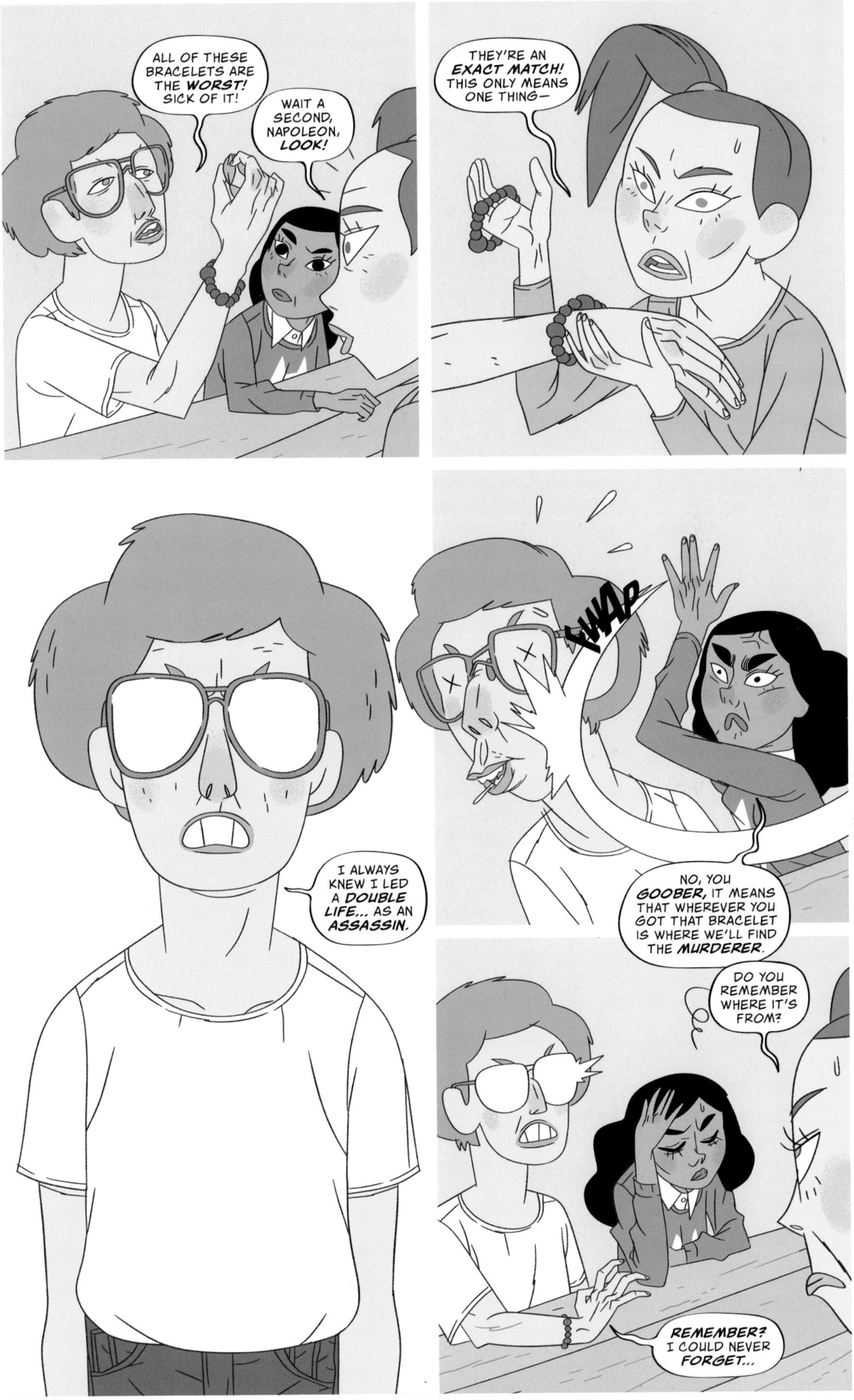
ALL OF THESE BRACELETS ARE THE WORST! SICK OF IT!
WAIT A SECOND, NAPOLEON, LOOK!
THEY'RE AN EXACT MATCH! THIS ONLY MEANS ONE THING—
I ALWAYS KNEW I LED A DOUBLE LIFE... AS AN ASSASSIN.
FWAP
NO, YOU GOOBER, IT MEANS THAT WHEREVER YOU GOT THAT BRACELET IS WHERE WE'LL FIND THE MURDERER.
DO YOU REMEMBER WHERE IT'S FROM?
REMEMBER? I COULD NEVER FORGET...

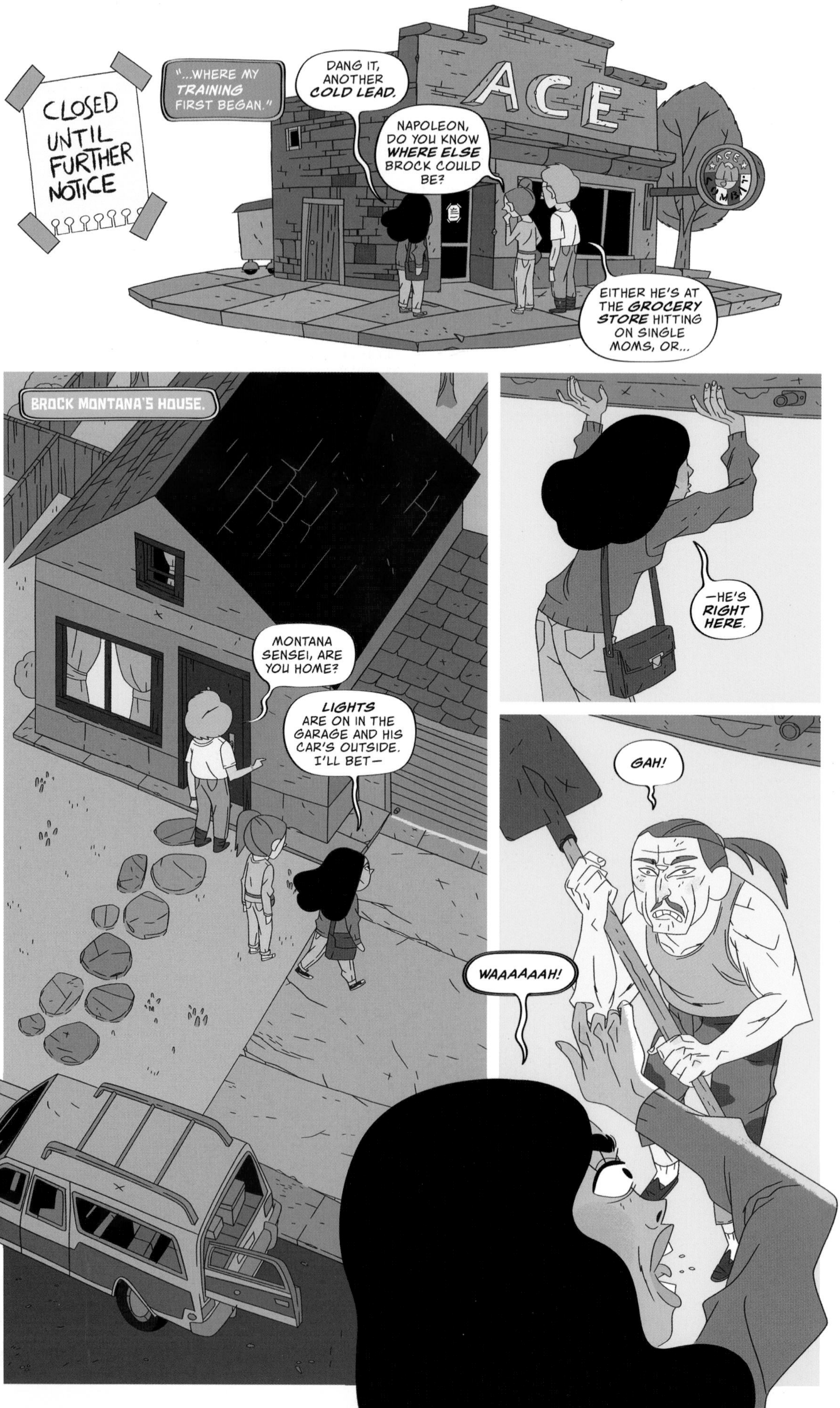
CLOSED UNTIL FURTHER NOTICE
"...WHERE MY TRAINING FIRST BEGAN."
DANG IT, ANOTHER COLD LEAD.
NAPOLEON, DO YOU KNOW WHERE ELSE BROCK COULD BE?
ACE
ACE COMBAT
EITHER HE'S AT THE GROCERY STORE HITTING ON SINGLE MOMS, OR...
BROCK MONTANA'S HOUSE.
MONTANA SENSEI, ARE YOU HOME?
LIGHTS ARE ON IN THE GARAGE AND HIS CAR'S OUTSIDE. I'LL BET—
—HE'S RIGHT HERE.
GAH!
WAAAAAAH!

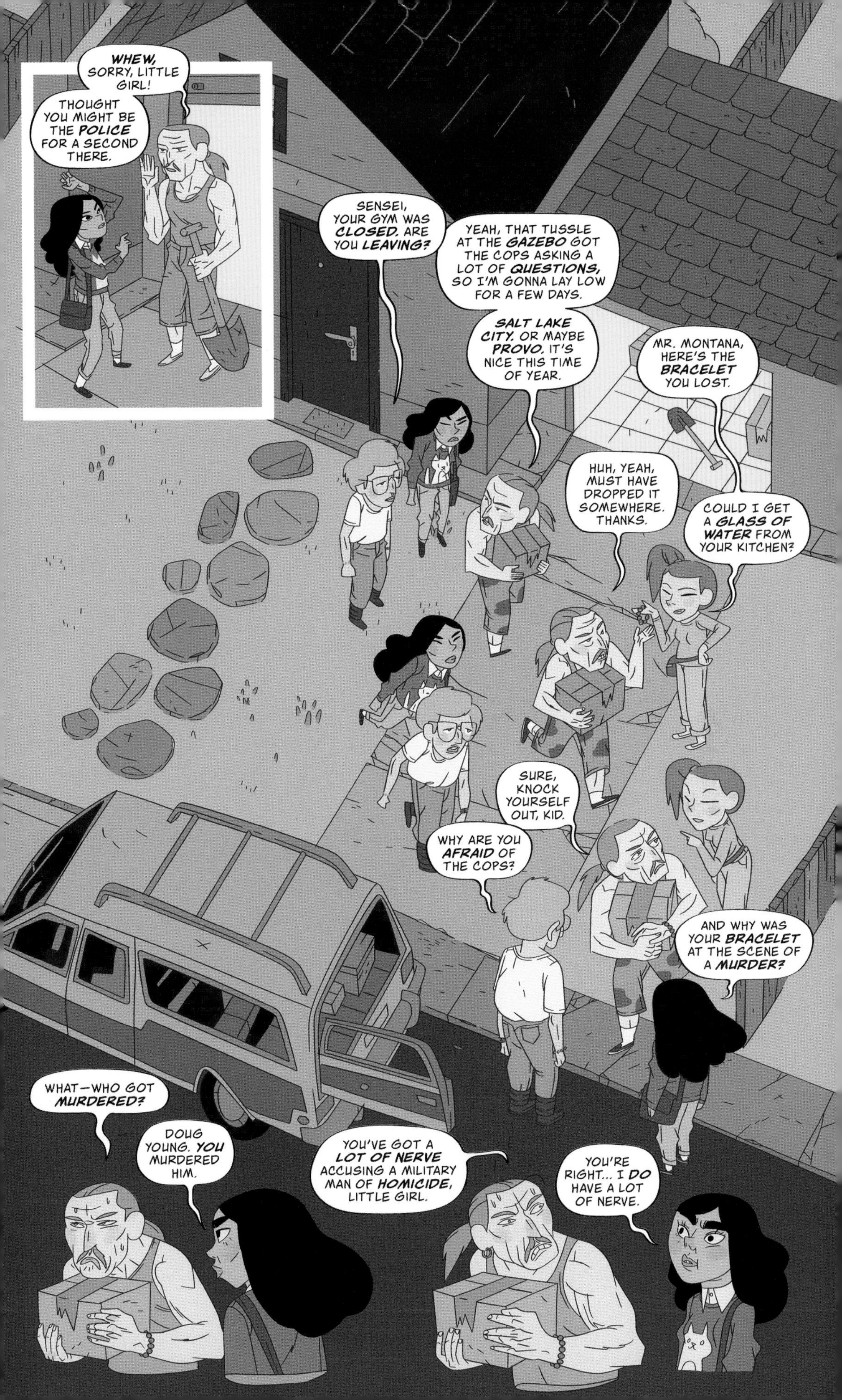

WHEW, SORRY, LITTLE GIRL!
THOUGHT YOU MIGHT BE THE POLICE FOR A SECOND THERE.
SENSEI, YOUR GYM WAS CLOSED. ARE YOU LEAVING?
YEAH, THAT TUSSLE AT THE GAZEBO GOT THE COPS ASKING A LOT OF QUESTIONS, SO I'M GONNA LAY LOW FOR A FEW DAYS.
SALT LAKE CITY. OR MAYBE PROVO. IT'S NICE THIS TIME OF YEAR.
MR. MONTANA, HERE'S THE BRACELET YOU LOST.
HUH, YEAH, MUST HAVE DROPPED IT SOMEWHERE. THANKS.
COULD I GET A GLASS OF WATER FROM YOUR KITCHEN?
SURE, KNOCK YOURSELF OUT, KID.
WHY ARE YOU AFRAID OF THE COPS?
AND WHY WAS YOUR BRACELET AT THE SCENE OF A MURDER?
WHAT—WHO GOT MURDERED?
DOUG YOUNG. YOU MURDERED HIM.
YOU'VE GOT A LOT OF NERVE ACCUSING A MILITARY MAN OF HOMICIDE, LITTLE GIRL.
YOU'RE RIGHT... I DO HAVE A LOT OF NERVE.

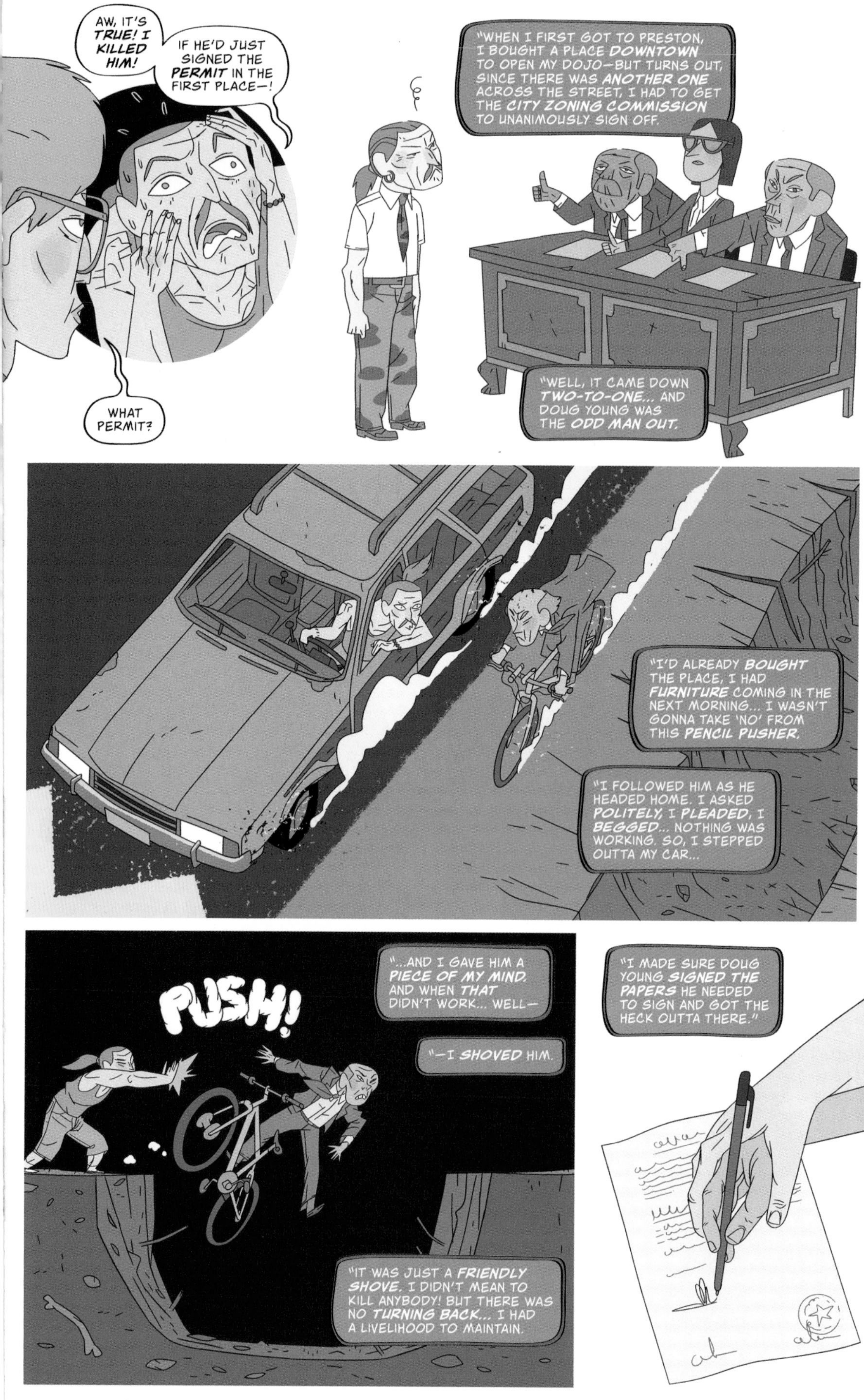
AW, IT'S TRUE! I KILLED HIM!
IF HE'D JUST SIGNED THE PERMIT IN THE FIRST PLACE—!
WHAT PERMIT?
"WHEN I FIRST GOT TO PRESTON, I BOUGHT A PLACE DOWNTOWN TO OPEN MY DOJO—BUT TURNS OUT, SINCE THERE WAS ANOTHER ONE ACROSS THE STREET, I HAD TO GET THE CITY ZONING COMMISSION TO UNANIMOUSLY SIGN OFF.
"WELL, IT CAME DOWN TWO-TO-ONE... AND DOUG YOUNG WAS THE ODD MAN OUT.
"I'D ALREADY BOUGHT THE PLACE, I HAD FURNITURE COMING IN THE NEXT MORNING... I WASN'T GONNA TAKE 'NO' FROM THIS PENCIL PUSHER.
"I FOLLOWED HIM AS HE HEADED HOME. I ASKED POLITELY, I PLEADED, I BEGGED... NOTHING WAS WORKING. SO, I STEPPED OUTTA MY CAR...
"...AND I GAVE HIM A PIECE OF MY MIND, AND WHEN THAT DIDN'T WORK... WELL—
PUSH!
"—I SHOVED HIM.
"IT WAS JUST A FRIENDLY SHOVE. I DIDN'T MEAN TO KILL ANYBODY! BUT THERE WAS NO TURNING BACK... I HAD A LIVELIHOOD TO MAINTAIN.
"I MADE SURE DOUG YOUNG SIGNED THE PAPERS HE NEEDED TO SIGN AND GOT THE HECK OUTTA THERE."

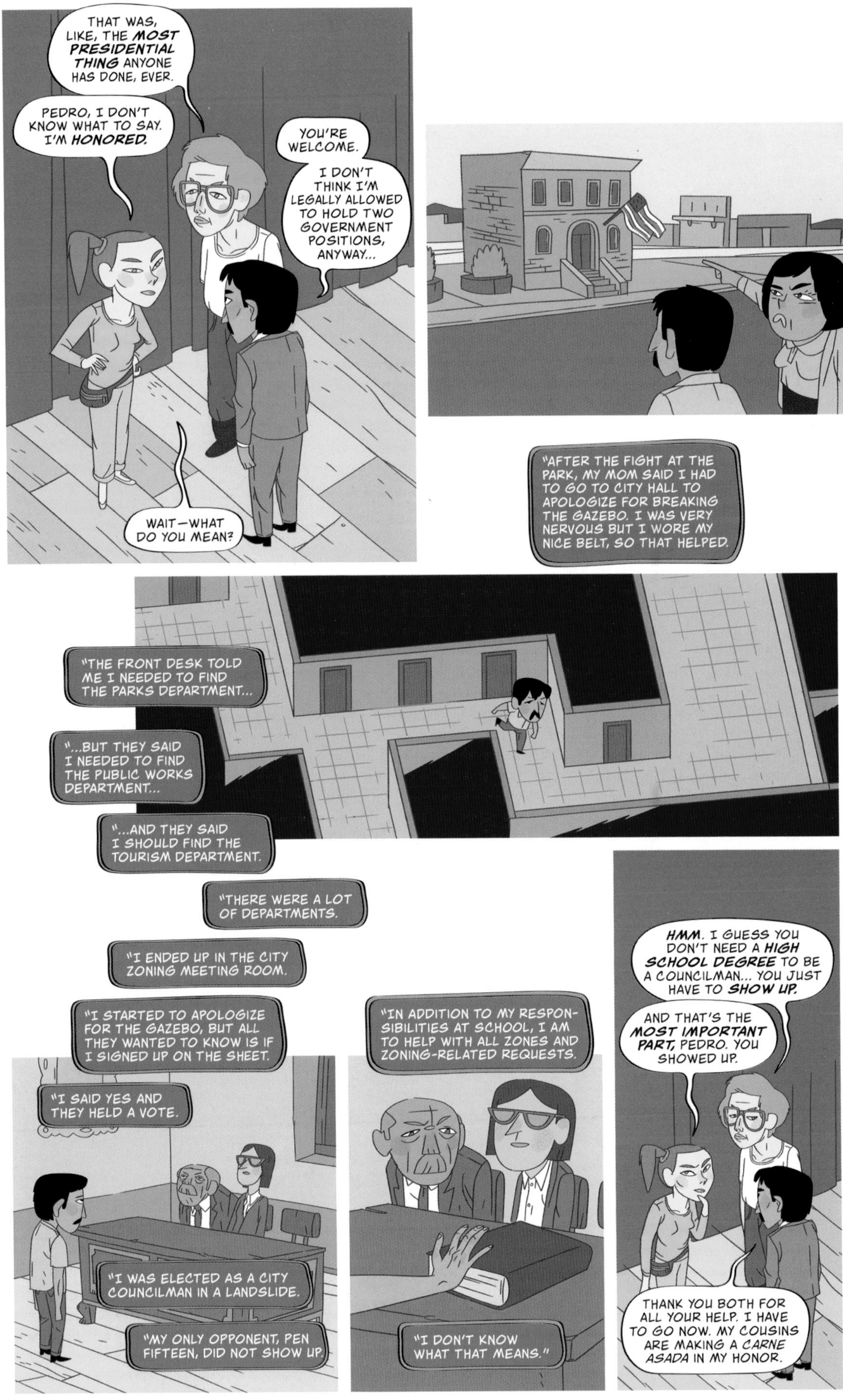

THAT WAS, LIKE, THE MOST PRESIDENTIAL THING ANYONE HAS DONE, EVER.
PEDRO, I DON'T KNOW WHAT TO SAY. I'M HONORED.
YOU'RE WELCOME.
I DON'T THINK I'M LEGALLY ALLOWED TO HOLD TWO GOVERNMENT POSITIONS, ANYWAY...
WAIT—WHAT DO YOU MEAN?
"AFTER THE FIGHT AT THE PARK, MY MOM SAID I HAD TO GO TO CITY HALL TO APOLOGIZE FOR BREAKING THE GAZEBO. I WAS VERY NERVOUS BUT I WORE MY NICE BELT, SO THAT HELPED.
"THE FRONT DESK TOLD ME I NEEDED TO FIND THE PARKS DEPARTMENT...
"...BUT THEY SAID I NEEDED TO FIND THE PUBLIC WORKS DEPARTMENT...
"...AND THEY SAID I SHOULD FIND THE TOURISM DEPARTMENT.
"THERE WERE A LOT OF DEPARTMENTS.
"I ENDED UP IN THE CITY ZONING MEETING ROOM.
"I STARTED TO APOLOGIZE FOR THE GAZEBO, BUT ALL THEY WANTED TO KNOW IS IF I SIGNED UP ON THE SHEET.
"I SAID YES AND THEY HELD A VOTE.
"I WAS ELECTED AS A CITY COUNCILMAN IN A LANDSLIDE.
"MY ONLY OPPONENT, PEN FIFTEEN, DID NOT SHOW UP.
"IN ADDITION TO MY RESPONSIBILITIES AT SCHOOL, I AM TO HELP WITH ALL ZONES AND ZONING-RELATED REQUESTS.
"I DON'T KNOW WHAT THAT MEANS."
HMM. I GUESS YOU DON'T NEED A HIGH SCHOOL DEGREE TO BE A COUNCILMAN... YOU JUST HAVE TO SHOW UP.
AND THAT'S THE MOST IMPORTANT PART, PEDRO. YOU SHOWED UP.
THANK YOU BOTH FOR ALL YOUR HELP. I HAVE TO GO NOW. MY COUSINS ARE MAKING A CARNE ASADA IN MY HONOR.

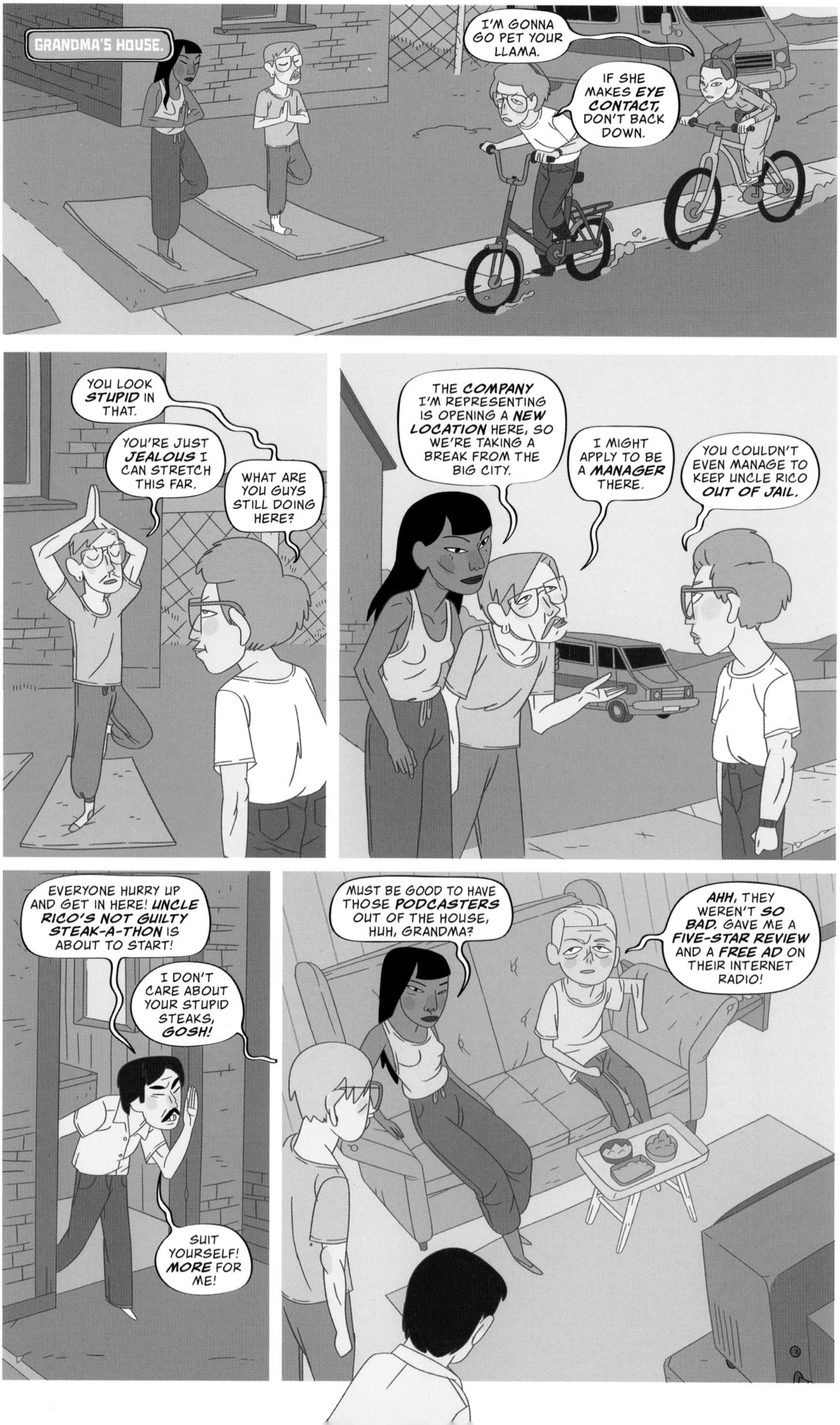
GRANDMA'S HOUSE.
I'M GONNA GO PET YOUR LLAMA.
IF SHE MAKES EYE CONTACT, DON'T BACK DOWN.
YOU LOOK STUPID IN THAT.
YOU'RE JUST JEALOUS I CAN STRETCH THIS FAR.
WHAT ARE YOU GUYS STILL DOING HERE?
THE COMPANY I'M REPRESENTING IS OPENING A NEW LOCATION HERE, SO WE'RE TAKING A BREAK FROM THE BIG CITY.
I MIGHT APPLY TO BE A MANAGER THERE.
YOU COULDN'T EVEN MANAGE TO KEEP UNCLE RICO OUT OF JAIL.
EVERYONE HURRY UP AND GET IN HERE! UNCLE RICO'S NOT GUILTY STEAK-A-THON IS ABOUT TO START!
I DON'T CARE ABOUT YOUR STUPID STEAKS, GOSH!
SUIT YOURSELF! MORE FOR ME!
MUST BE GOOD TO HAVE THOSE PODCASTERS OUT OF THE HOUSE, HUH, GRANDMA?
AHH, THEY WEREN'T SO BAD. GAVE ME A FIVE-STAR REVIEW AND A FREE AD ON THEIR INTERNET RADIO!

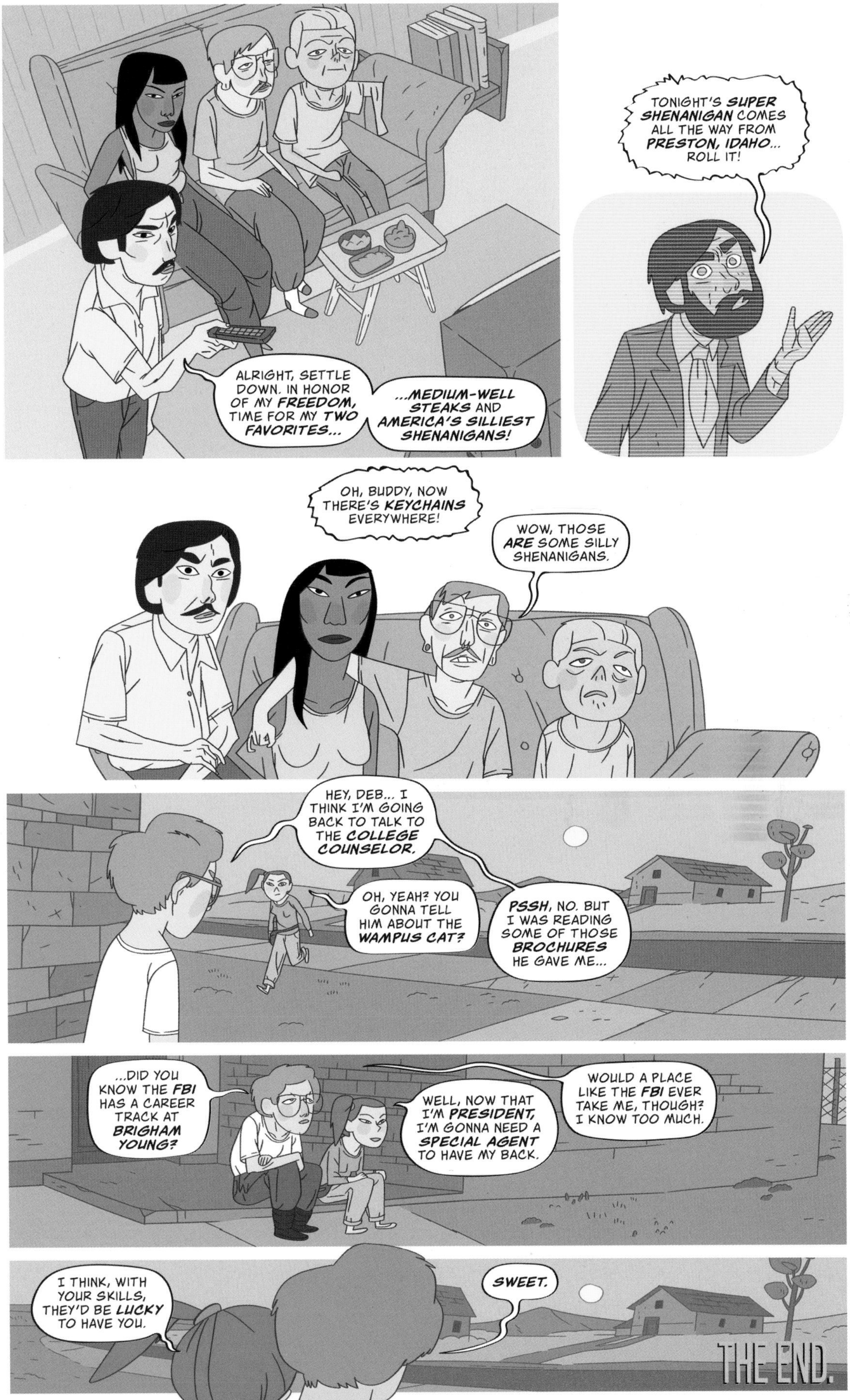
ALRIGHT, SETTLE DOWN. IN HONOR OF MY FREEDOM, TIME FOR MY TWO FAVORITES...
...MEDIUM-WELL STEAKS AND AMERICA'S SILLIEST SHENANIGANS!
TONIGHT'S SUPER SHENANIGAN COMES ALL THE WAY FROM PRESTON, IDAHO... ROLL IT!
OH, BUDDY, NOW THERE'S KEYCHAINS EVERYWHERE!
WOW, THOSE ARE SOME SILLY SHENANIGANS.
HEY, DEB... I THINK I'M GOING BACK TO TALK TO THE COLLEGE COUNSELOR.
OH, YEAH? YOU GONNA TELL HIM ABOUT THE WAMPUS CAT?
PSSH, NO. BUT I WAS READING SOME OF THOSE BROCHURES HE GAVE ME...
...DID YOU KNOW THE FBI HAS A CAREER TRACK AT BRIGHAM YOUNG?
WOULD A PLACE LIKE THE FBI EVER TAKE ME, THOUGH? I KNOW TOO MUCH.
WELL, NOW THAT I'M PRESIDENT, I'M GONNA NEED A SPECIAL AGENT TO HAVE MY BACK.
I THINK, WITH YOUR SKILLS, THEY'D BE LUCKY TO HAVE YOU.
SWEET.
THE END.

JOANA GATO

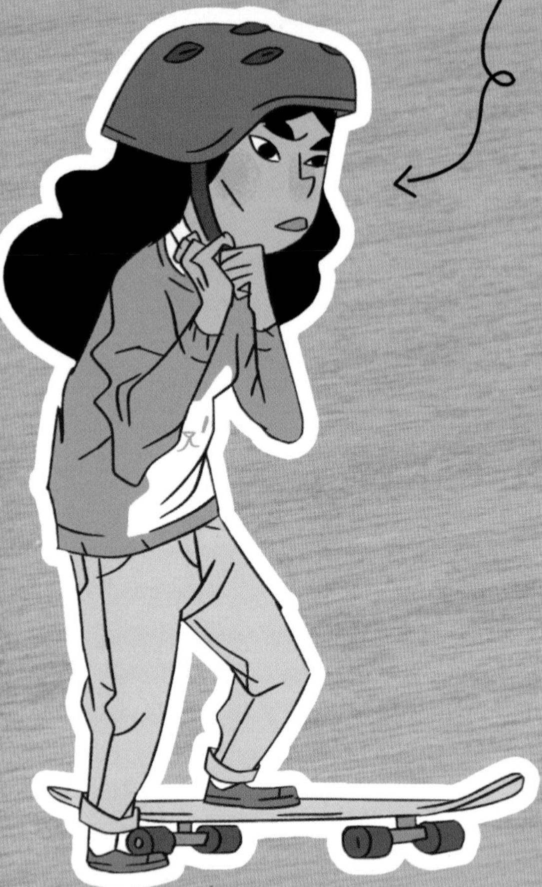

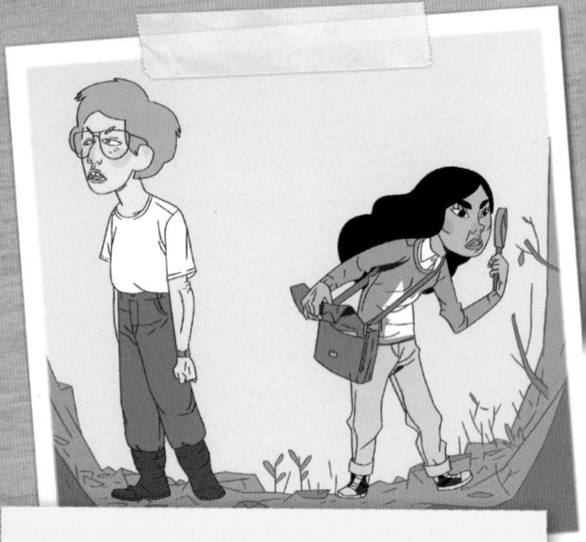

- Solve the ballot mystery.
- Look up if the Wampus cat and Big Foot have ever fought.
- Buy cat sweater in purple.
- Read more books.

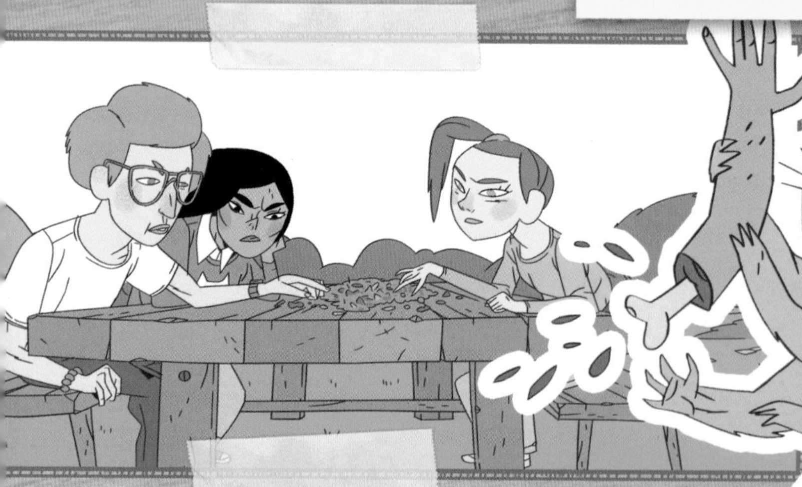

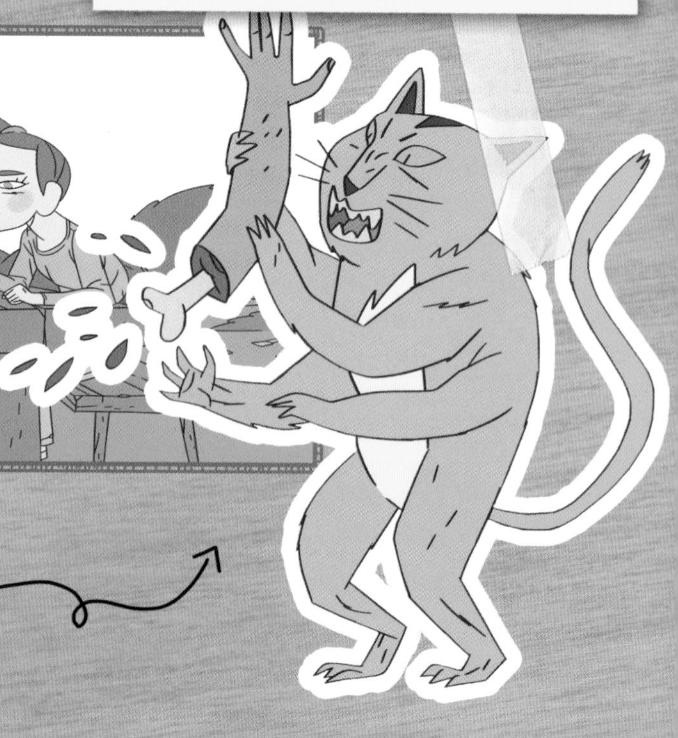

WAMPUS CAT

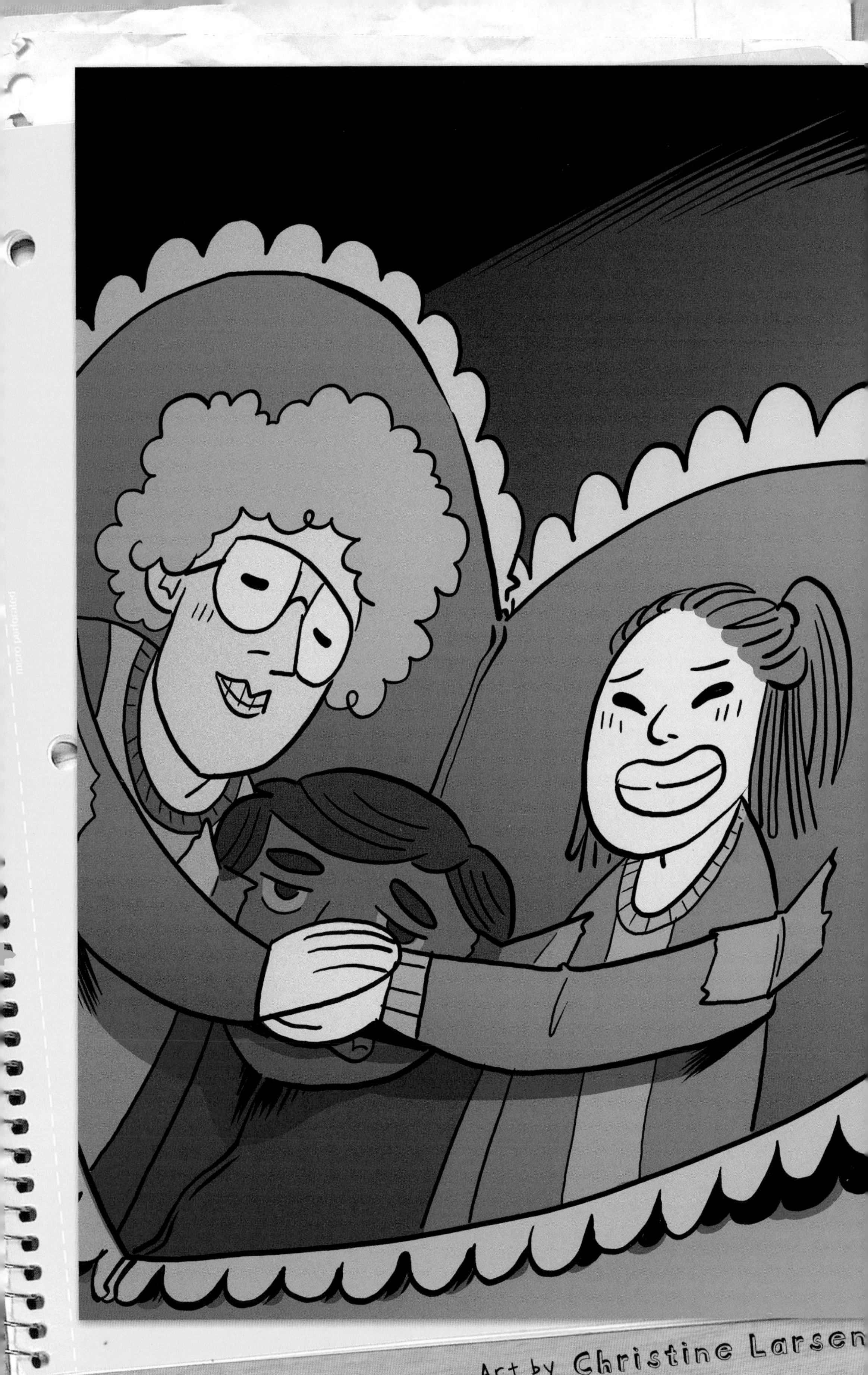
micro perforated

Art by Christine Larsen

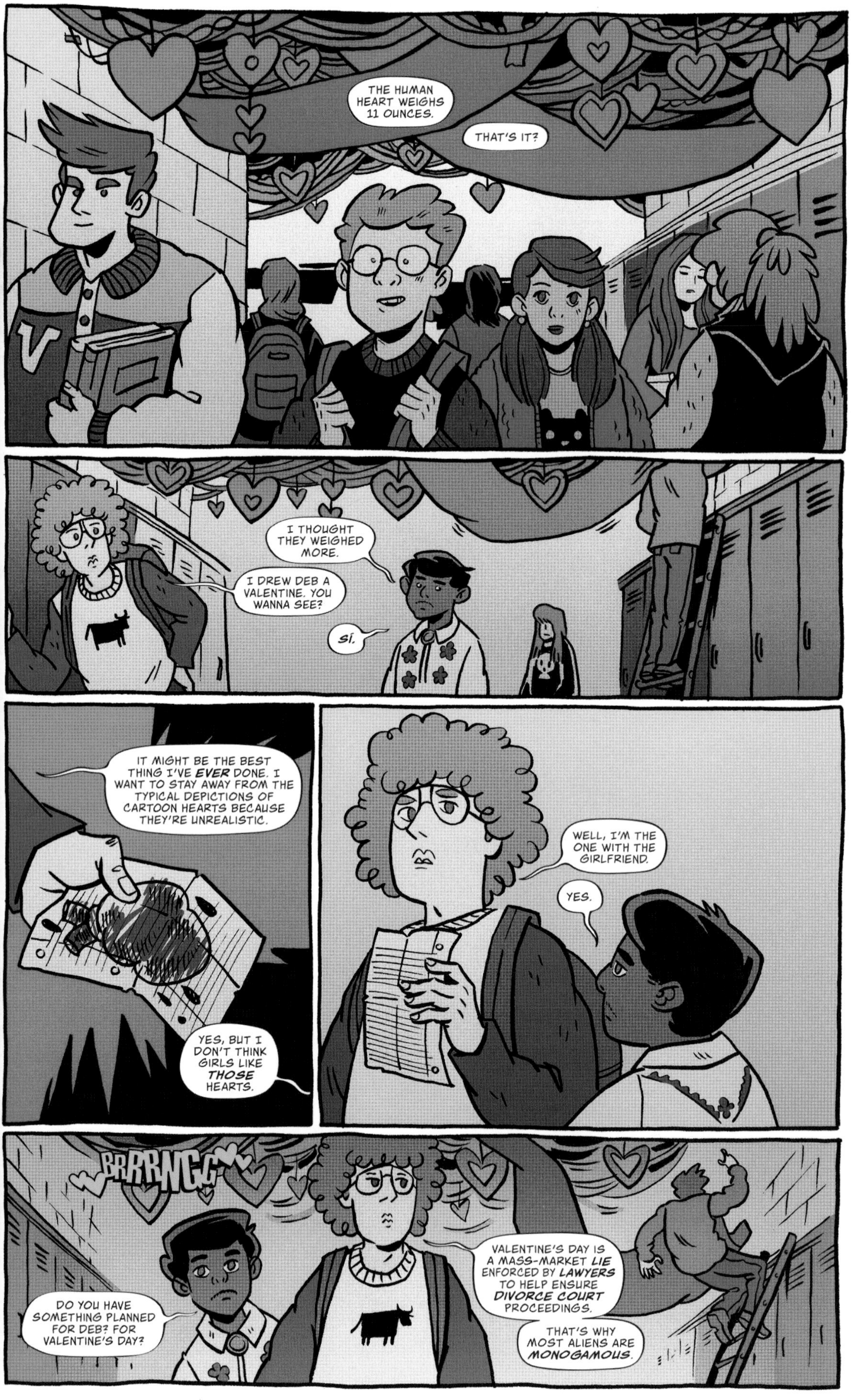
THE HUMAN HEART WEIGHS 11 OUNCES.
THAT'S IT?
I THOUGHT THEY WEIGHED MORE.
I DREW DEB A VALENTINE. YOU WANNA SEE?
SÍ.
IT MIGHT BE THE BEST THING I'VE EVER DONE. I WANT TO STAY AWAY FROM THE TYPICAL DEPICTIONS OF CARTOON HEARTS BECAUSE THEY'RE UNREALISTIC.
YES, BUT I DON'T THINK GIRLS LIKE THOSE HEARTS.
WELL, I'M THE ONE WITH THE GIRLFRIEND.
YES.
BRRRNGG
DO YOU HAVE SOMETHING PLANNED FOR DEB? FOR VALENTINE'S DAY?
VALENTINE'S DAY IS A MASS-MARKET LIE ENFORCED BY LAWYERS TO HELP ENSURE DIVORCE COURT PROCEEDINGS.
THAT'S WHY MOST ALIENS ARE MONOGAMOUS.

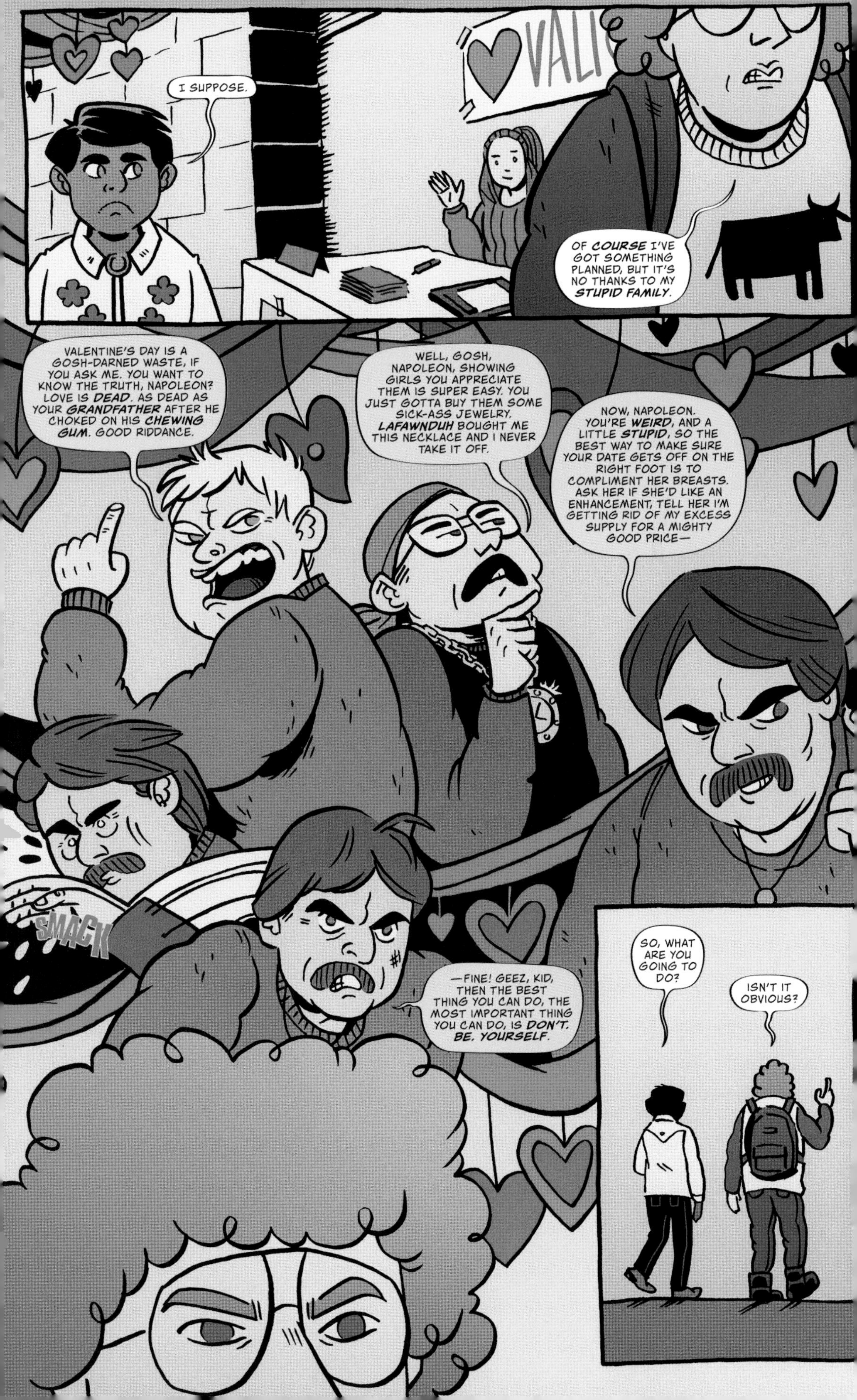

I SUPPOSE.
OF COURSE I'VE GOT SOMETHING PLANNED, BUT IT'S NO THANKS TO MY STUPID FAMILY.
VALENTINE'S DAY IS A GOSH-DARNED WASTE, IF YOU ASK ME. YOU WANT TO KNOW THE TRUTH, NAPOLEON? LOVE IS DEAD. AS DEAD AS YOUR GRANDFATHER AFTER HE CHOKED ON HIS CHEWING GUM. GOOD RIDDANCE.
WELL, GOSH, NAPOLEON, SHOWING GIRLS YOU APPRECIATE THEM IS SUPER EASY. YOU JUST GOTTA BUY THEM SOME SICK-ASS JEWELRY. LAFAWNDUH BOUGHT ME THIS NECKLACE AND I NEVER TAKE IT OFF.
NOW, NAPOLEON. YOU'RE WEIRD, AND A LITTLE STUPID, SO THE BEST WAY TO MAKE SURE YOUR DATE GETS OFF ON THE RIGHT FOOT IS TO COMPLIMENT HER BREASTS. ASK HER IF SHE'D LIKE AN ENHANCEMENT, TELL HER I'M GETTING RID OF MY EXCESS SUPPLY FOR A MIGHTY GOOD PRICE—
SMACK
—FINE! GEEZ, KID, THEN THE BEST THING YOU CAN DO, THE MOST IMPORTANT THING YOU CAN DO, IS DON'T. BE. YOURSELF.
SO, WHAT ARE YOU GOING TO DO?
ISN'T IT OBVIOUS?

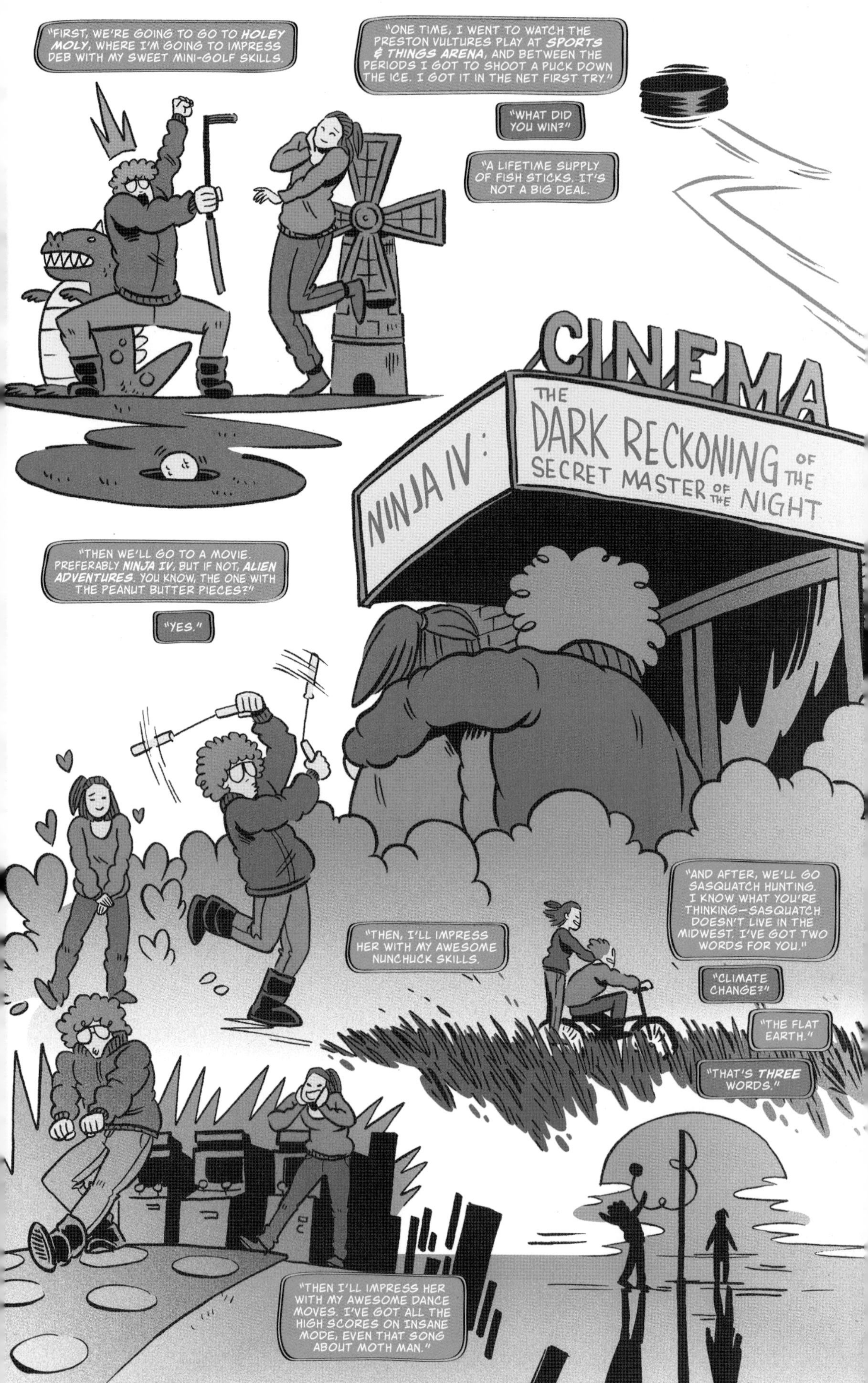

"FIRST, WE'RE GOING TO GO TO **HOLEY MOLY**, WHERE I'M GOING TO IMPRESS DEB WITH MY SWEET MINI-GOLF SKILLS.
"ONE TIME, I WENT TO WATCH THE PRESTON VULTURES PLAY AT **SPORTS & THINGS ARENA**, AND BETWEEN THE PERIODS I GOT TO SHOOT A PUCK DOWN THE ICE. I GOT IT IN THE NET FIRST TRY."
"WHAT DID YOU WIN?"
"A LIFETIME SUPPLY OF FISH STICKS. IT'S NOT A BIG DEAL.
CINEMA
NINJA IV: THE DARK RECKONING OF THE SECRET MASTER OF THE NIGHT
"THEN WE'LL GO TO A MOVIE. PREFERABLY **NINJA IV**, BUT IF NOT, **ALIEN ADVENTURES**. YOU KNOW, THE ONE WITH THE PEANUT BUTTER PIECES?"
"YES."
"THEN, I'LL IMPRESS HER WITH MY AWESOME NUNCHUCK SKILLS.
"AND AFTER, WE'LL GO SASQUATCH HUNTING. I KNOW WHAT YOU'RE THINKING—SASQUATCH DOESN'T LIVE IN THE MIDWEST. I'VE GOT TWO WORDS FOR YOU."
"CLIMATE CHANGE?"
"THE FLAT EARTH."
"THAT'S **THREE** WORDS."
"THEN I'LL IMPRESS HER WITH MY AWESOME DANCE MOVES. I'VE GOT ALL THE HIGH SCORES ON INSANE MODE, EVEN THAT SONG ABOUT MOTH MAN."

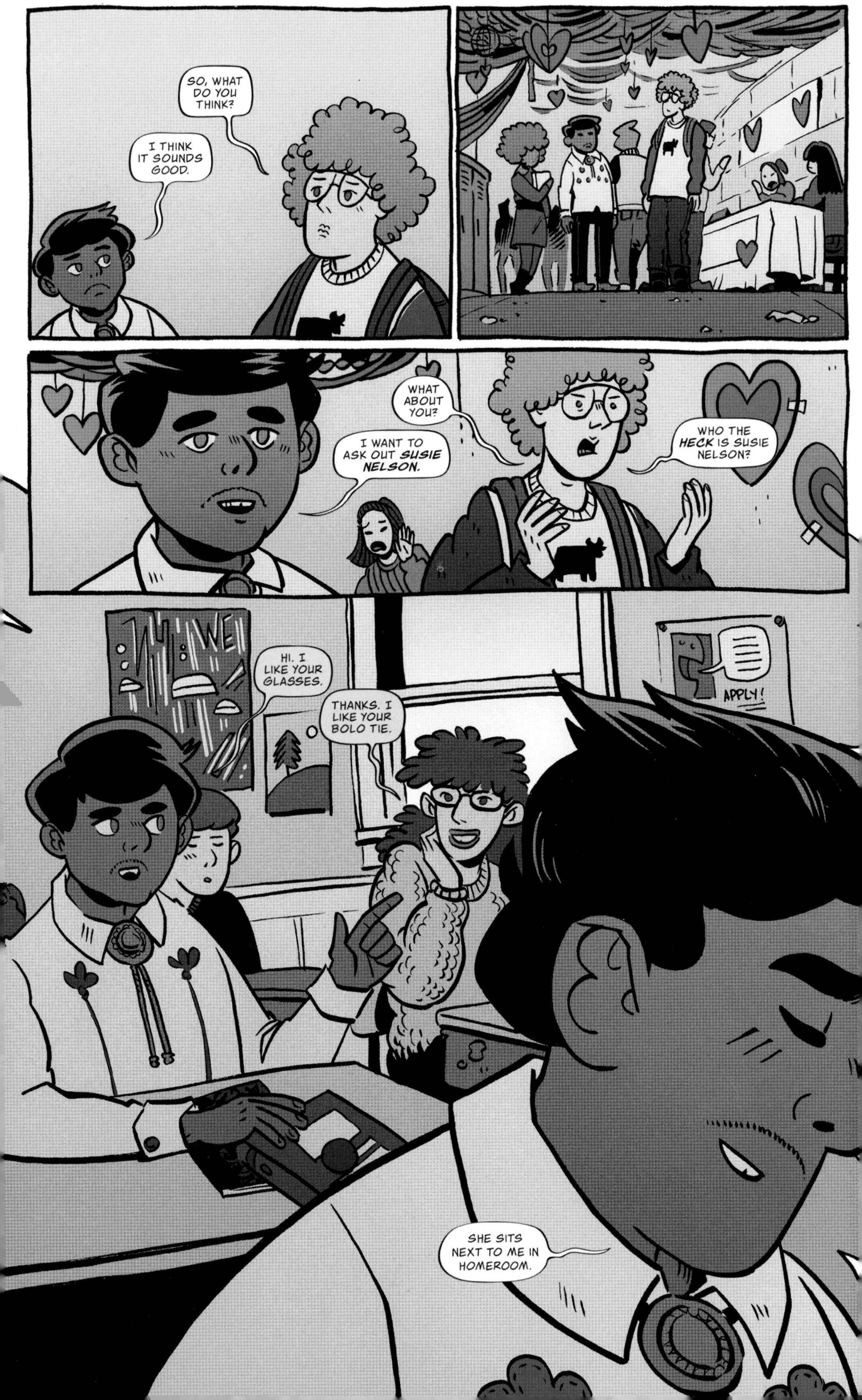
SO, WHAT DO YOU THINK?
I THINK IT SOUNDS GOOD.
WHAT ABOUT YOU?
I WANT TO ASK OUT SUSIE NELSON.
WHO THE HECK IS SUSIE NELSON?
HI. I LIKE YOUR GLASSES.
THANKS. I LIKE YOUR BOLO TIE.
APPLY!
SHE SITS NEXT TO ME IN HOMEROOM.

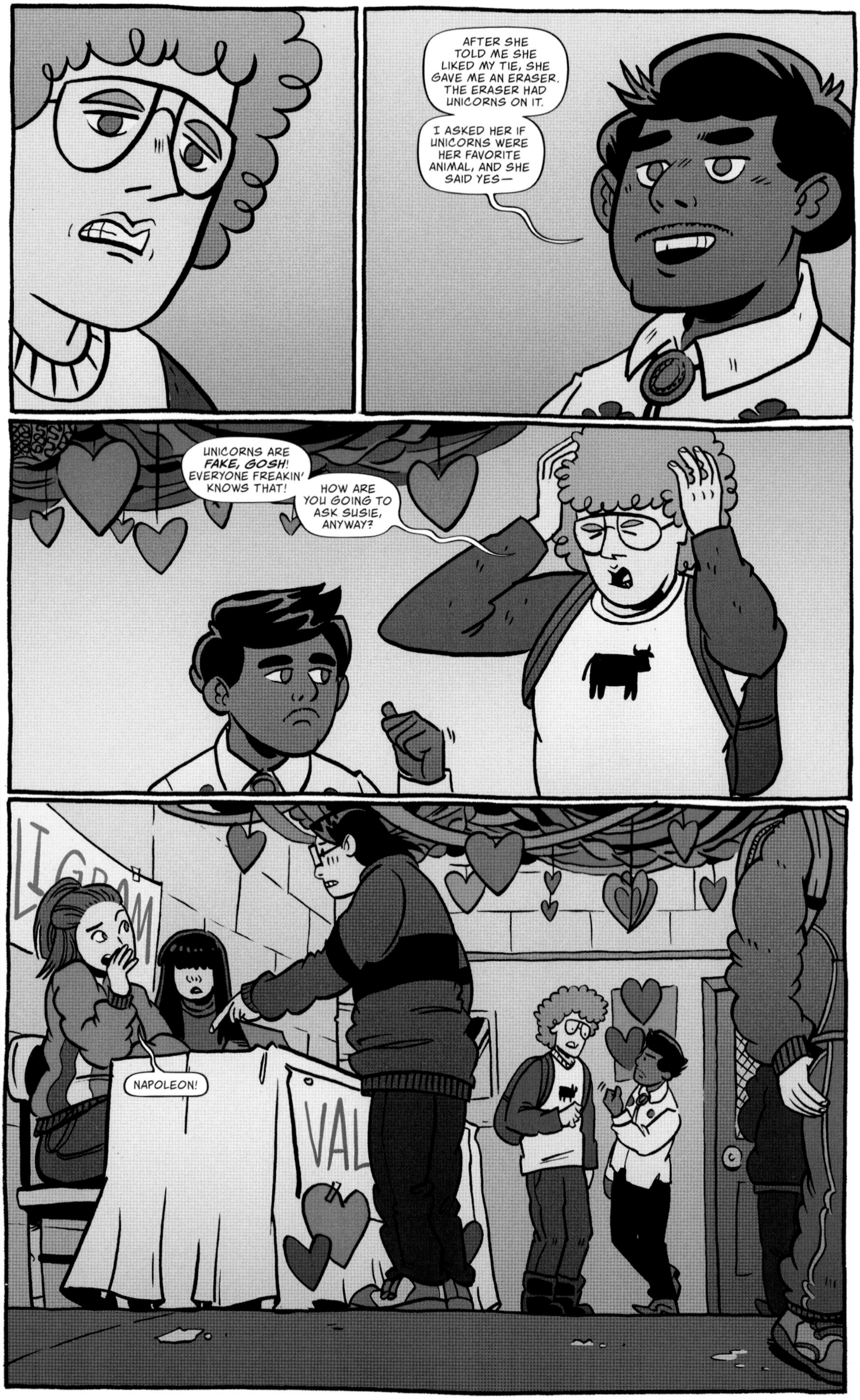
AFTER SHE TOLD ME SHE LIKED MY TIE, SHE GAVE ME AN ERASER. THE ERASER HAD UNICORNS ON IT.
I ASKED HER IF UNICORNS WERE HER FAVORITE ANIMAL, AND SHE SAID YES—
UNICORNS ARE ***FAKE, GOSH***! EVERYONE FREAKIN' KNOWS THAT!
HOW ARE YOU GOING TO ASK SUSIE, ANYWAY?
NAPOLEON!

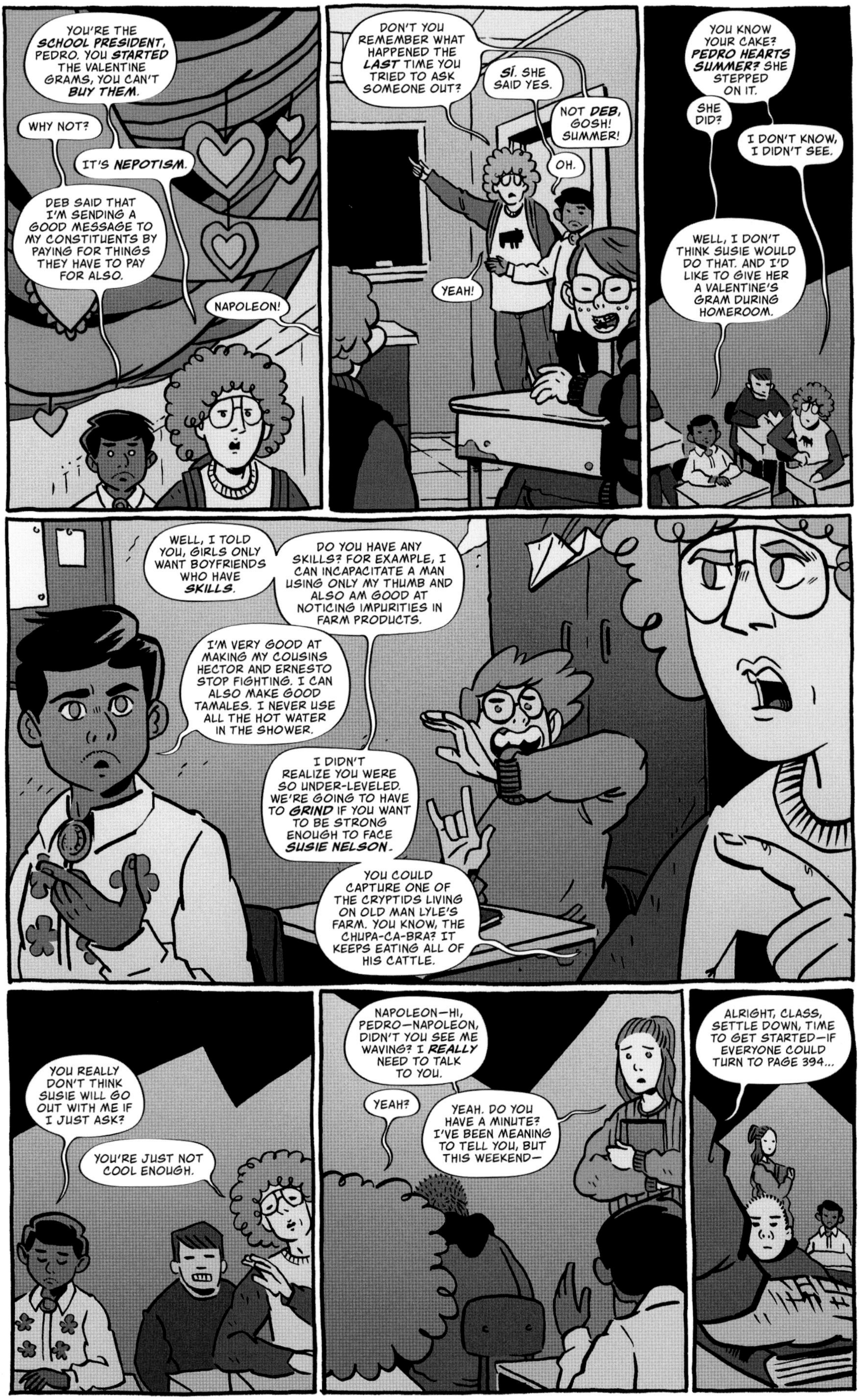
YOU'RE THE SCHOOL PRESIDENT, PEDRO. YOU STARTED THE VALENTINE GRAMS, YOU CAN'T BUY THEM.
WHY NOT?
IT'S NEPOTISM.
DEB SAID THAT I'M SENDING A GOOD MESSAGE TO MY CONSTITUENTS BY PAYING FOR THINGS THEY HAVE TO PAY FOR ALSO.
NAPOLEON!
DON'T YOU REMEMBER WHAT HAPPENED THE LAST TIME YOU TRIED TO ASK SOMEONE OUT?
SÍ. SHE SAID YES.
NOT DEB, GOSH! SUMMER!
OH.
YEAH!
YOU KNOW YOUR CAKE? PEDRO HEARTS SUMMER? SHE STEPPED ON IT.
SHE DID?
I DON'T KNOW, I DIDN'T SEE.
WELL, I DON'T THINK SUSIE WOULD DO THAT. AND I'D LIKE TO GIVE HER A VALENTINE'S GRAM DURING HOMEROOM.
WELL, I TOLD YOU, GIRLS ONLY WANT BOYFRIENDS WHO HAVE SKILLS.
DO YOU HAVE ANY SKILLS? FOR EXAMPLE, I CAN INCAPACITATE A MAN USING ONLY MY THUMB AND ALSO AM GOOD AT NOTICING IMPURITIES IN FARM PRODUCTS.
I'M VERY GOOD AT MAKING MY COUSINS HECTOR AND ERNESTO STOP FIGHTING. I CAN ALSO MAKE GOOD TAMALES. I NEVER USE ALL THE HOT WATER IN THE SHOWER.
I DIDN'T REALIZE YOU WERE SO UNDER-LEVELED. WE'RE GOING TO HAVE TO GRIND IF YOU WANT TO BE STRONG ENOUGH TO FACE SUSIE NELSON.
YOU COULD CAPTURE ONE OF THE CRYPTIDS LIVING ON OLD MAN LYLE'S FARM. YOU KNOW, THE CHUPA-CA-BRA? IT KEEPS EATING ALL OF HIS CATTLE.
YOU REALLY DON'T THINK SUSIE WILL GO OUT WITH ME IF I JUST ASK?
YOU'RE JUST NOT COOL ENOUGH.
NAPOLEON—HI, PEDRO—NAPOLEON, DIDN'T YOU SEE ME WAVING? I REALLY NEED TO TALK TO YOU.
YEAH?
YEAH. DO YOU HAVE A MINUTE? I'VE BEEN MEANING TO TELL YOU, BUT THIS WEEKEND—
ALRIGHT, CLASS, SETTLE DOWN, TIME TO GET STARTED—IF EVERYONE COULD TURN TO PAGE 394...

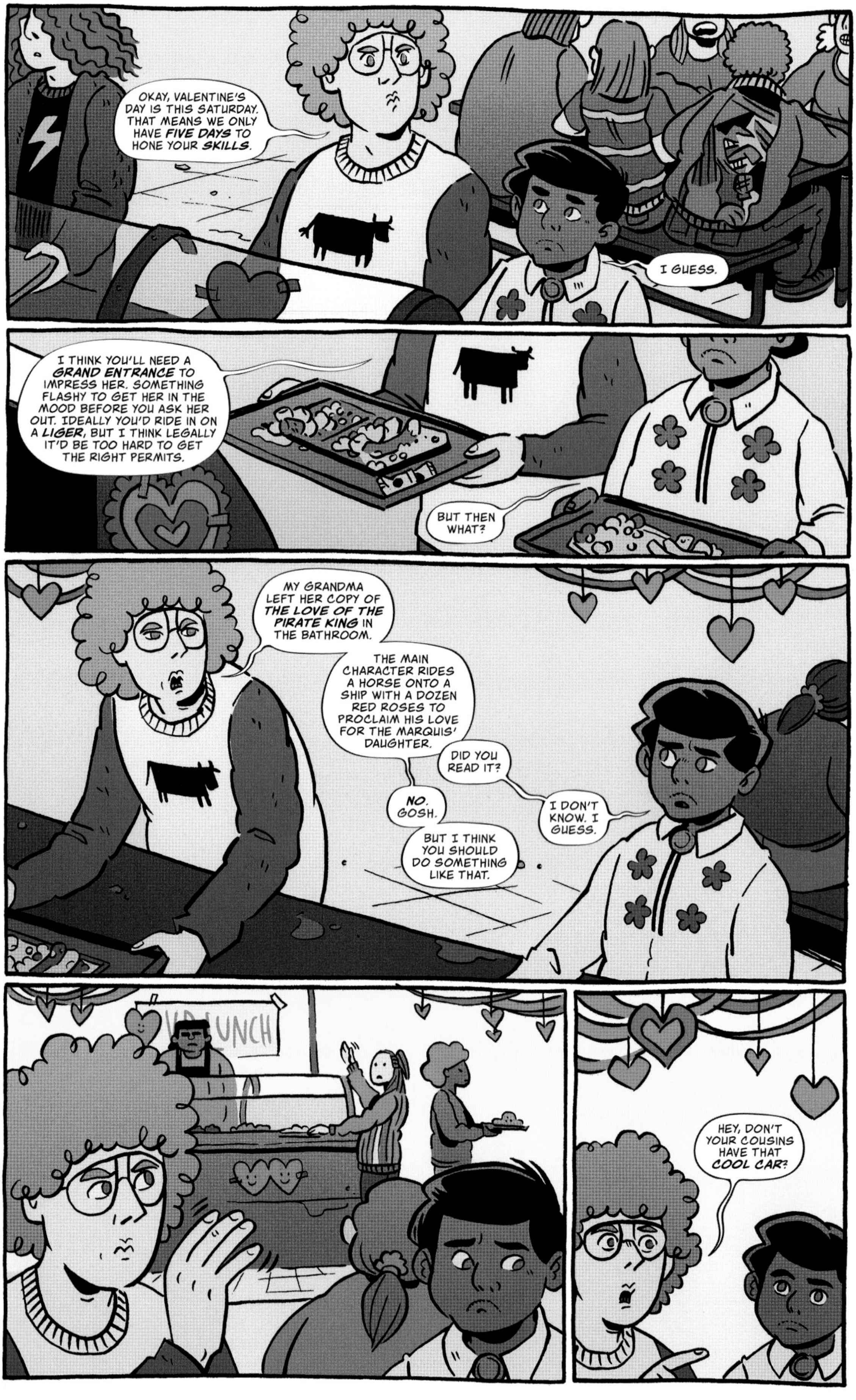

OKAY, VALENTINE'S DAY IS THIS SATURDAY. THAT MEANS WE ONLY HAVE FIVE DAYS TO HONE YOUR SKILLS.
I GUESS.
I THINK YOU'LL NEED A GRAND ENTRANCE TO IMPRESS HER. SOMETHING FLASHY TO GET HER IN THE MOOD BEFORE YOU ASK HER OUT. IDEALLY YOU'D RIDE IN ON A LIGER, BUT I THINK LEGALLY IT'D BE TOO HARD TO GET THE RIGHT PERMITS.
BUT THEN WHAT?
MY GRANDMA LEFT HER COPY OF THE LOVE OF THE PIRATE KING IN THE BATHROOM.
THE MAIN CHARACTER RIDES A HORSE ONTO A SHIP WITH A DOZEN RED ROSES TO PROCLAIM HIS LOVE FOR THE MARQUIS' DAUGHTER.
DID YOU READ IT?
NO. GOSH.
I DON'T KNOW. I GUESS.
BUT I THINK YOU SHOULD DO SOMETHING LIKE THAT.
HEY, DON'T YOUR COUSINS HAVE THAT COOL CAR?

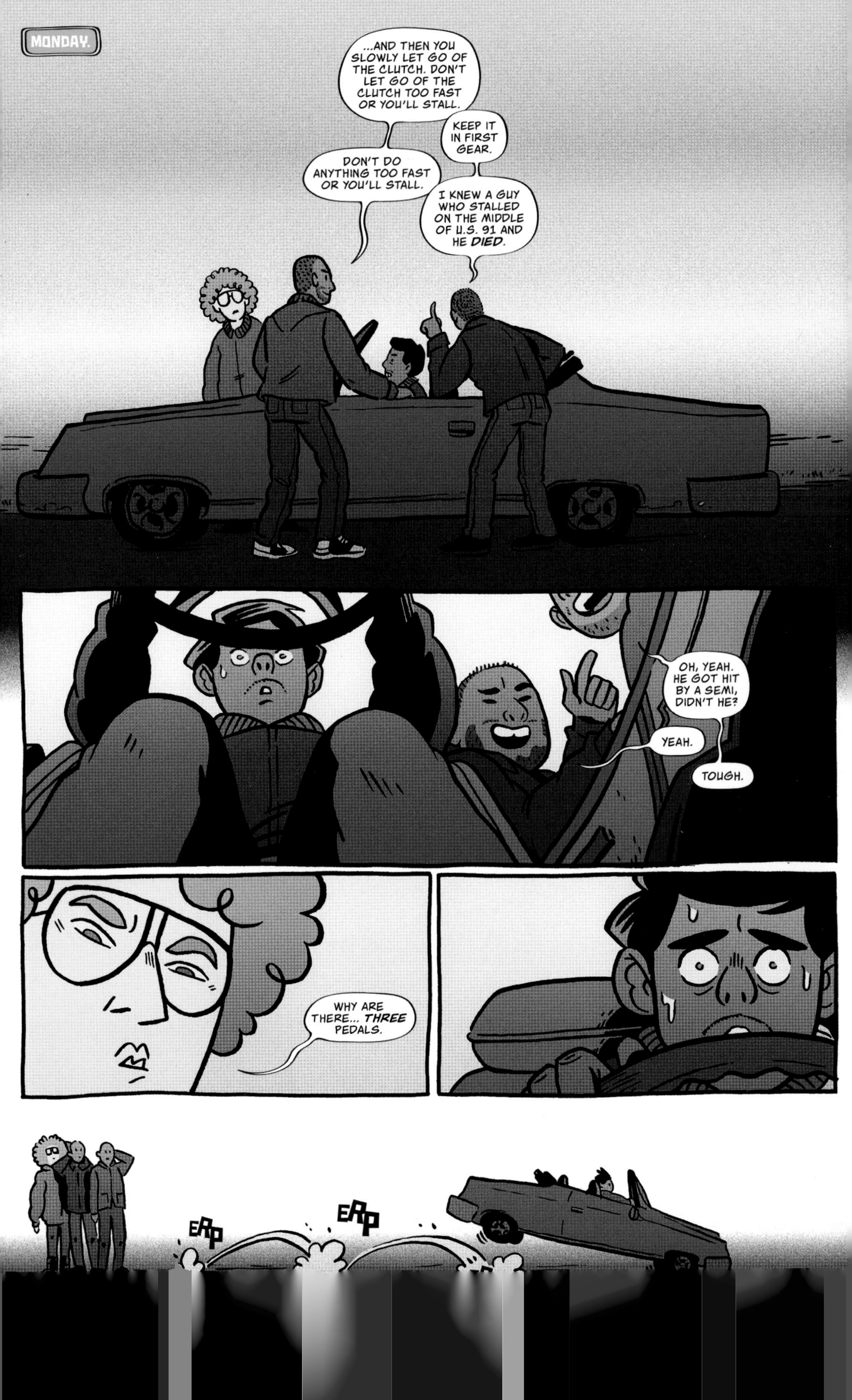
MONDAY.
...AND THEN YOU SLOWLY LET GO OF THE CLUTCH. DON'T LET GO OF THE CLUTCH TOO FAST OR YOU'LL STALL.
DON'T DO ANYTHING TOO FAST OR YOU'LL STALL.
KEEP IT IN FIRST GEAR.
I KNEW A GUY WHO STALLED ON THE MIDDLE OF U.S. 91 AND HE *DIED*.
OH, YEAH. HE GOT HIT BY A SEMI, DIDN'T HE?
YEAH.
TOUGH.
WHY ARE THERE... *THREE* PEDALS.
ERP
ERP

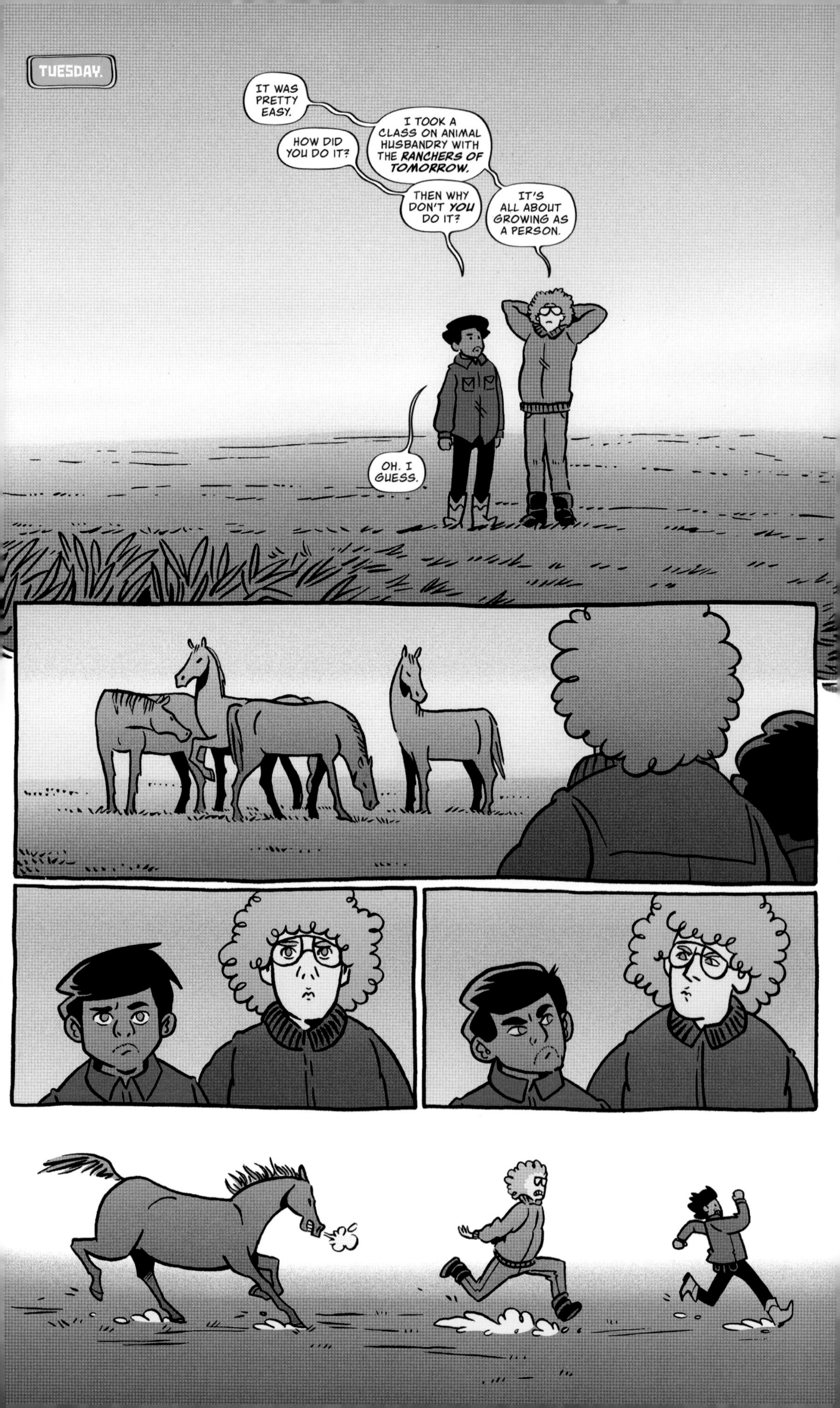
TUESDAY.
IT WAS PRETTY EASY.
I TOOK A CLASS ON ANIMAL HUSBANDRY WITH THE RANCHERS OF TOMORROW.
HOW DID YOU DO IT?
THEN WHY DON'T YOU DO IT?
IT'S ALL ABOUT GROWING AS A PERSON.
OH. I GUESS.

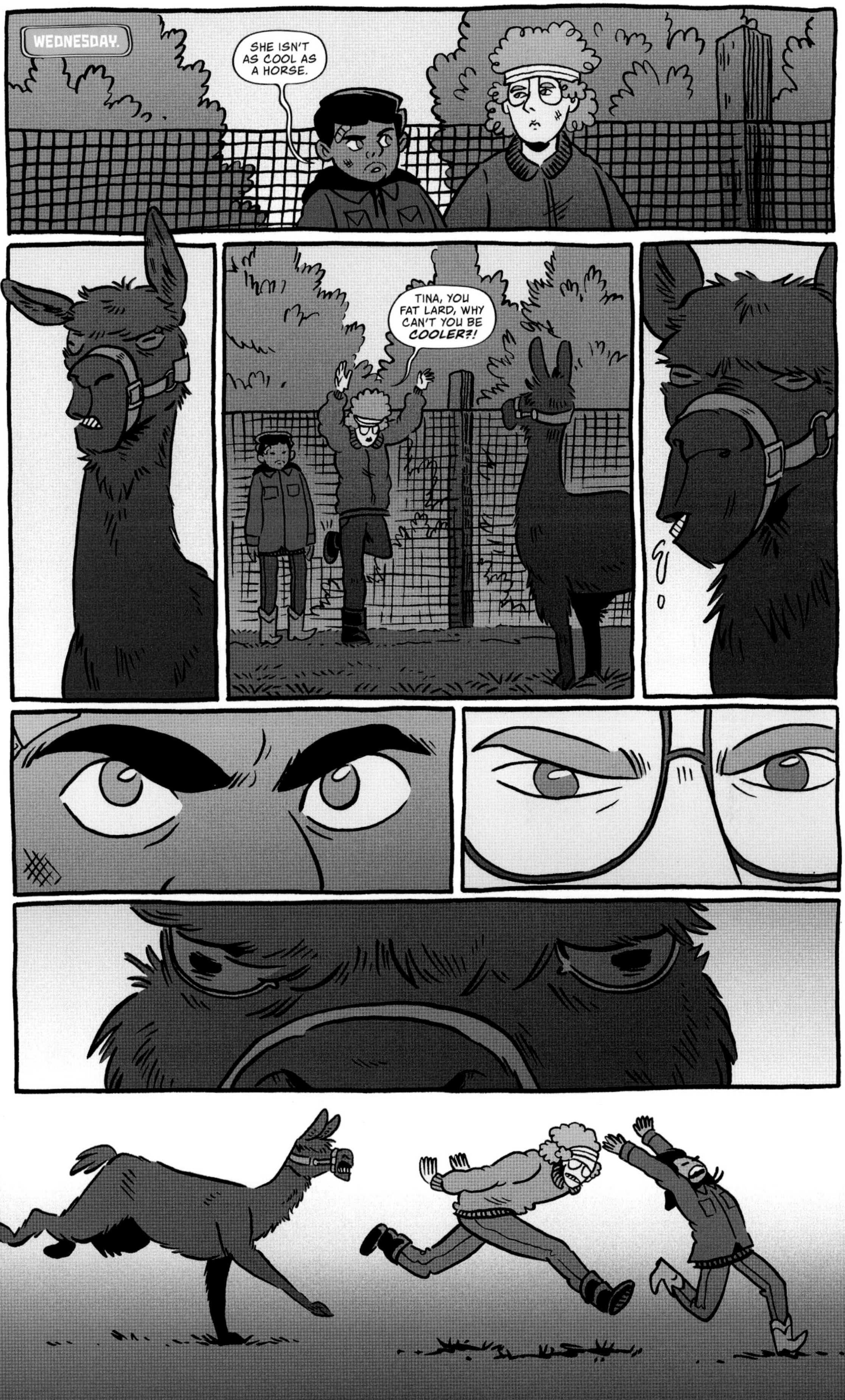
WEDNESDAY.
SHE ISN'T AS COOL AS A HORSE.
TINA, YOU FAT LARD, WHY CAN'T YOU BE COOLER?!

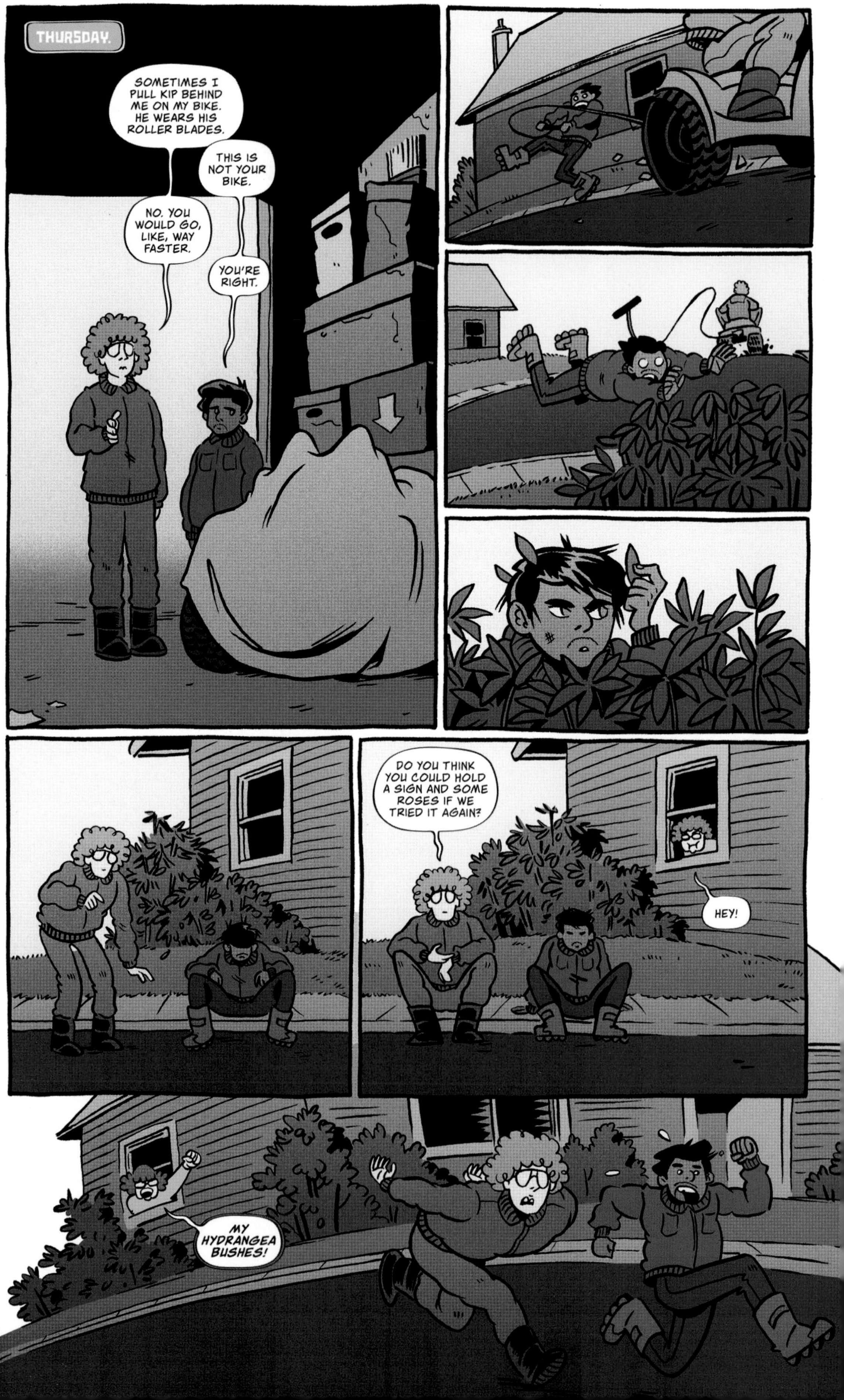
THURSDAY.
SOMETIMES I PULL KIP BEHIND ME ON MY BIKE. HE WEARS HIS ROLLER BLADES.
THIS IS NOT YOUR BIKE.
NO. YOU WOULD GO, LIKE, WAY FASTER.
YOU'RE RIGHT.
DO YOU THINK YOU COULD HOLD A SIGN AND SOME ROSES IF WE TRIED IT AGAIN?
HEY!
MY HYDRANGEA BUSHES!

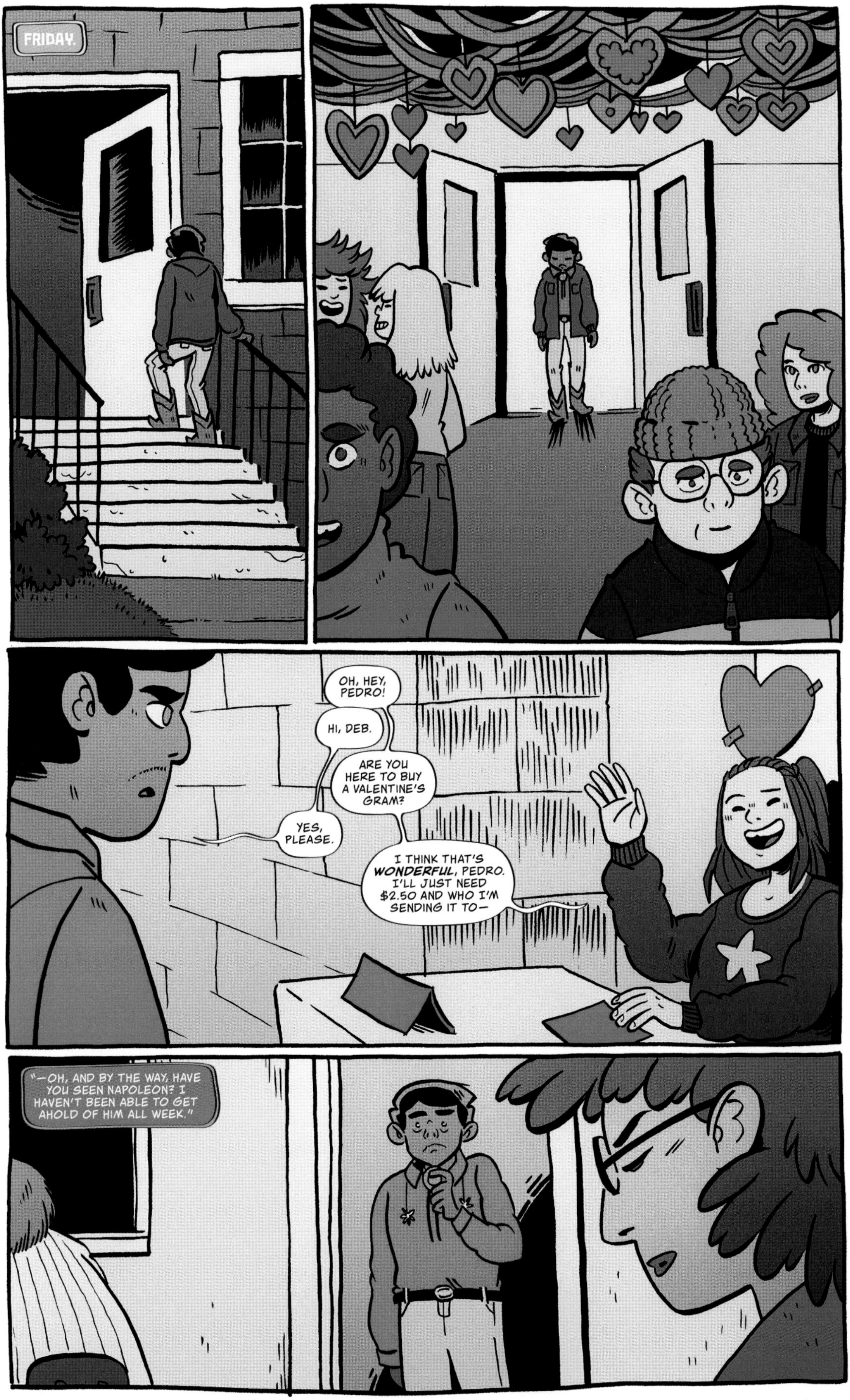
FRIDAY.
OH, HEY, PEDRO!
HI, DEB.
ARE YOU HERE TO BUY A VALENTINE'S GRAM?
YES, PLEASE.
I THINK THAT'S *WONDERFUL*, PEDRO. I'LL JUST NEED $2.50 AND WHO I'M SENDING IT TO—
"—OH, AND BY THE WAY, HAVE YOU SEEN NAPOLEON? I HAVEN'T BEEN ABLE TO GET AHOLD OF HIM ALL WEEK."

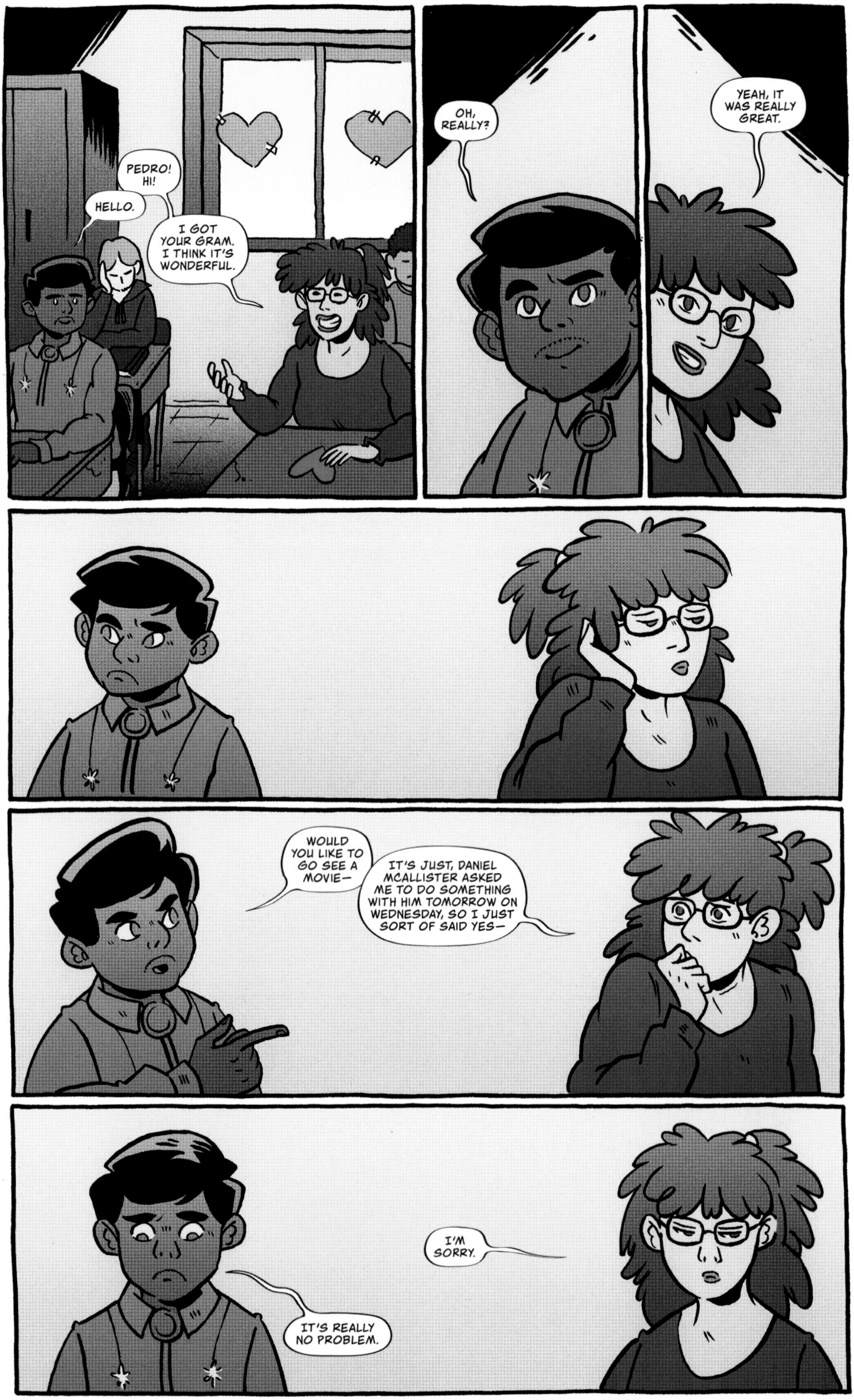
PEDRO! HI!
HELLO.
I GOT YOUR GRAM. I THINK IT'S WONDERFUL.
OH, REALLY?
YEAH, IT WAS REALLY GREAT.
WOULD YOU LIKE TO GO SEE A MOVIE—
IT'S JUST, DANIEL MCALLISTER ASKED ME TO DO SOMETHING WITH HIM TOMORROW ON WEDNESDAY, SO I JUST SORT OF SAID YES—
I'M SORRY.
IT'S REALLY NO PROBLEM.

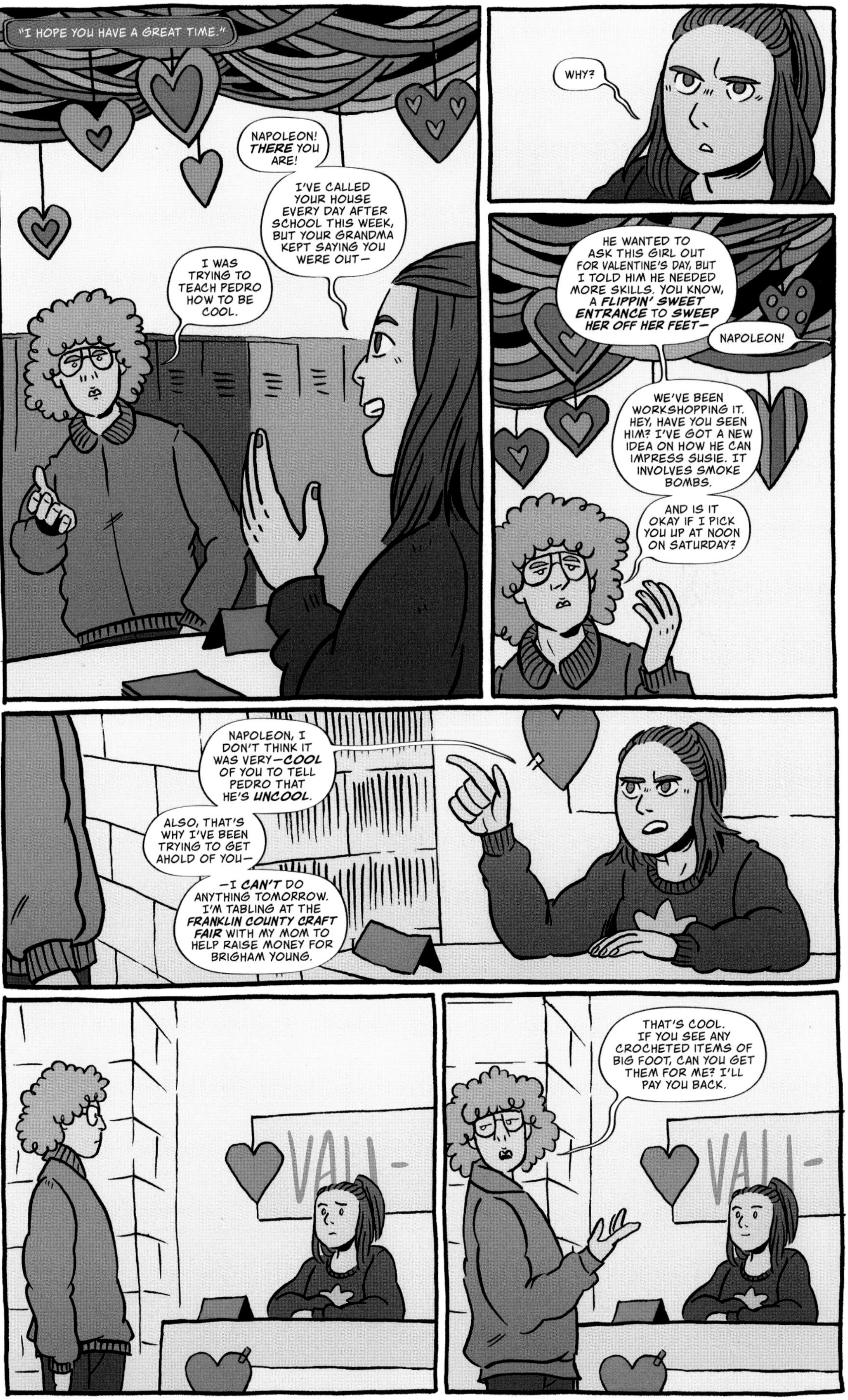

"I HOPE YOU HAVE A GREAT TIME."
NAPOLEON! *THERE* YOU ARE!
I'VE CALLED YOUR HOUSE EVERY DAY AFTER SCHOOL THIS WEEK, BUT YOUR GRANDMA KEPT SAYING YOU WERE OUT—
I WAS TRYING TO TEACH PEDRO HOW TO BE COOL.
WHY?
HE WANTED TO ASK THIS GIRL OUT FOR VALENTINE'S DAY, BUT I TOLD HIM HE NEEDED MORE SKILLS. YOU KNOW, A *FLIPPIN' SWEET ENTRANCE* TO *SWEEP HER OFF HER FEET*—
NAPOLEON!
WE'VE BEEN WORKSHOPPING IT. HEY, HAVE YOU SEEN HIM? I'VE GOT A NEW IDEA ON HOW HE CAN IMPRESS SUSIE. IT INVOLVES SMOKE BOMBS.
AND IS IT OKAY IF I PICK YOU UP AT NOON ON SATURDAY?
NAPOLEON, I DON'T THINK IT WAS VERY—*COOL* OF YOU TO TELL PEDRO THAT HE'S *UNCOOL*.
ALSO, THAT'S WHY I'VE BEEN TRYING TO GET AHOLD OF YOU—
—I *CAN'T* DO ANYTHING TOMORROW. I'M TABLING AT THE *FRANKLIN COUNTY CRAFT FAIR* WITH MY MOM TO HELP RAISE MONEY FOR BRIGHAM YOUNG.
VALI-
THAT'S COOL. IF YOU SEE ANY CROCHETED ITEMS OF BIG FOOT, CAN YOU GET THEM FOR ME? I'LL PAY YOU BACK.
VALI-

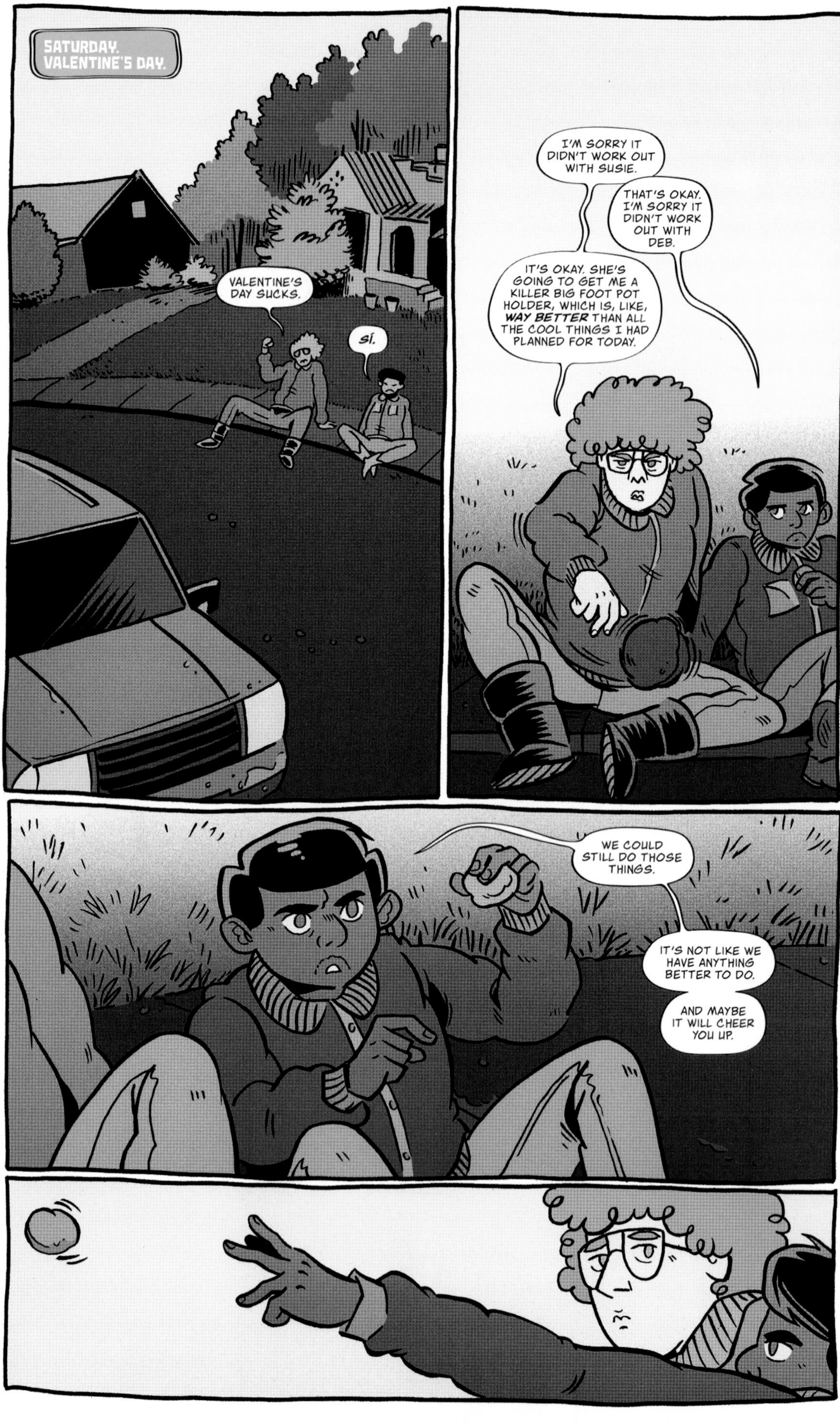
SATURDAY.
VALENTINE'S DAY.
VALENTINE'S DAY SUCKS.
SÍ.
I'M SORRY IT DIDN'T WORK OUT WITH SUSIE.
THAT'S OKAY. I'M SORRY IT DIDN'T WORK OUT WITH DEB.
IT'S OKAY. SHE'S GOING TO GET ME A KILLER BIG FOOT POT HOLDER, WHICH IS, LIKE, WAY BETTER THAN ALL THE COOL THINGS I HAD PLANNED FOR TODAY.
WE COULD STILL DO THOSE THINGS.
IT'S NOT LIKE WE HAVE ANYTHING BETTER TO DO.
AND MAYBE IT WILL CHEER YOU UP.

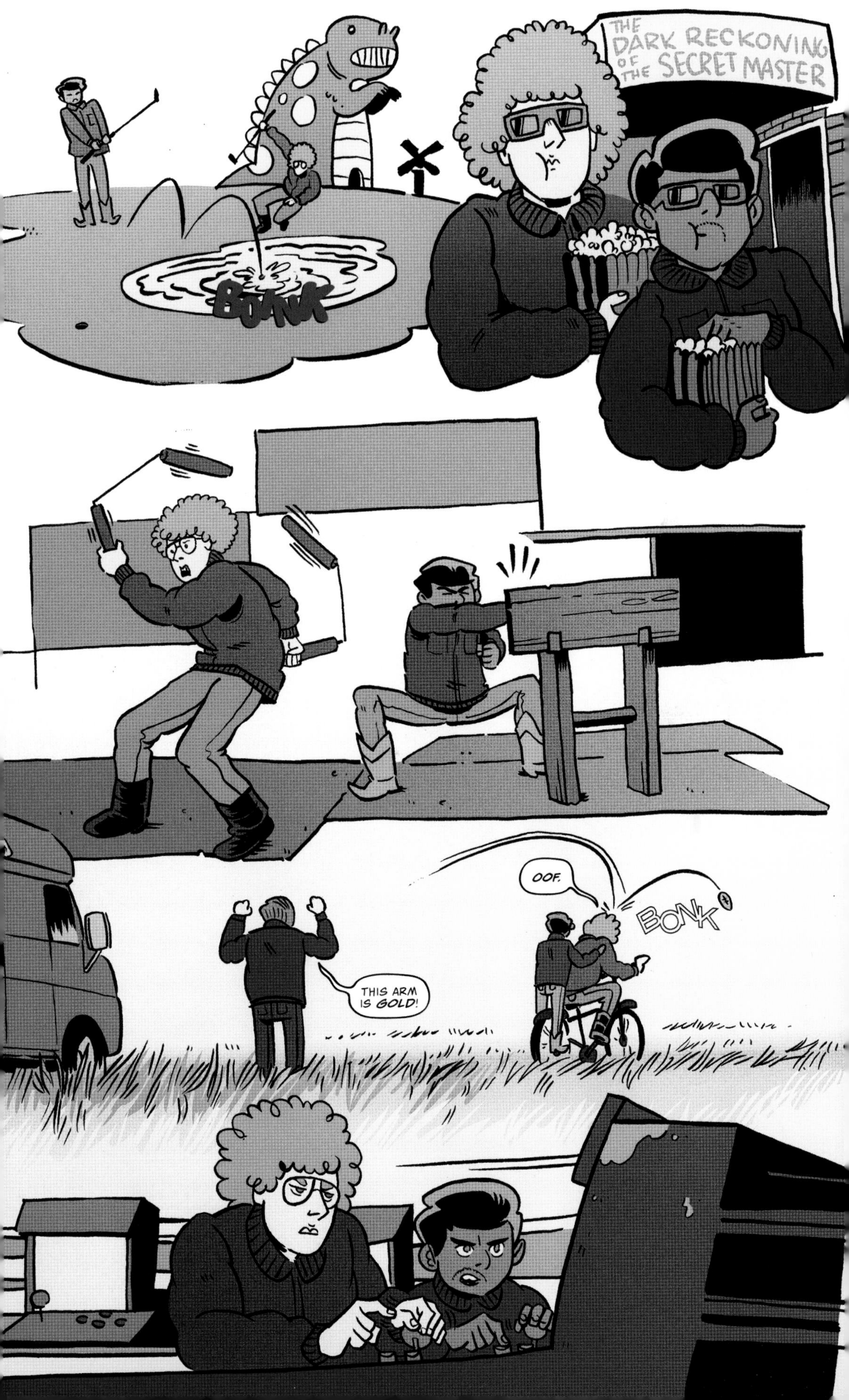

BONK
THE DARK RECKONING OF THE SECRET MASTER
THIS ARM IS GOLD!
OOF.
BONK

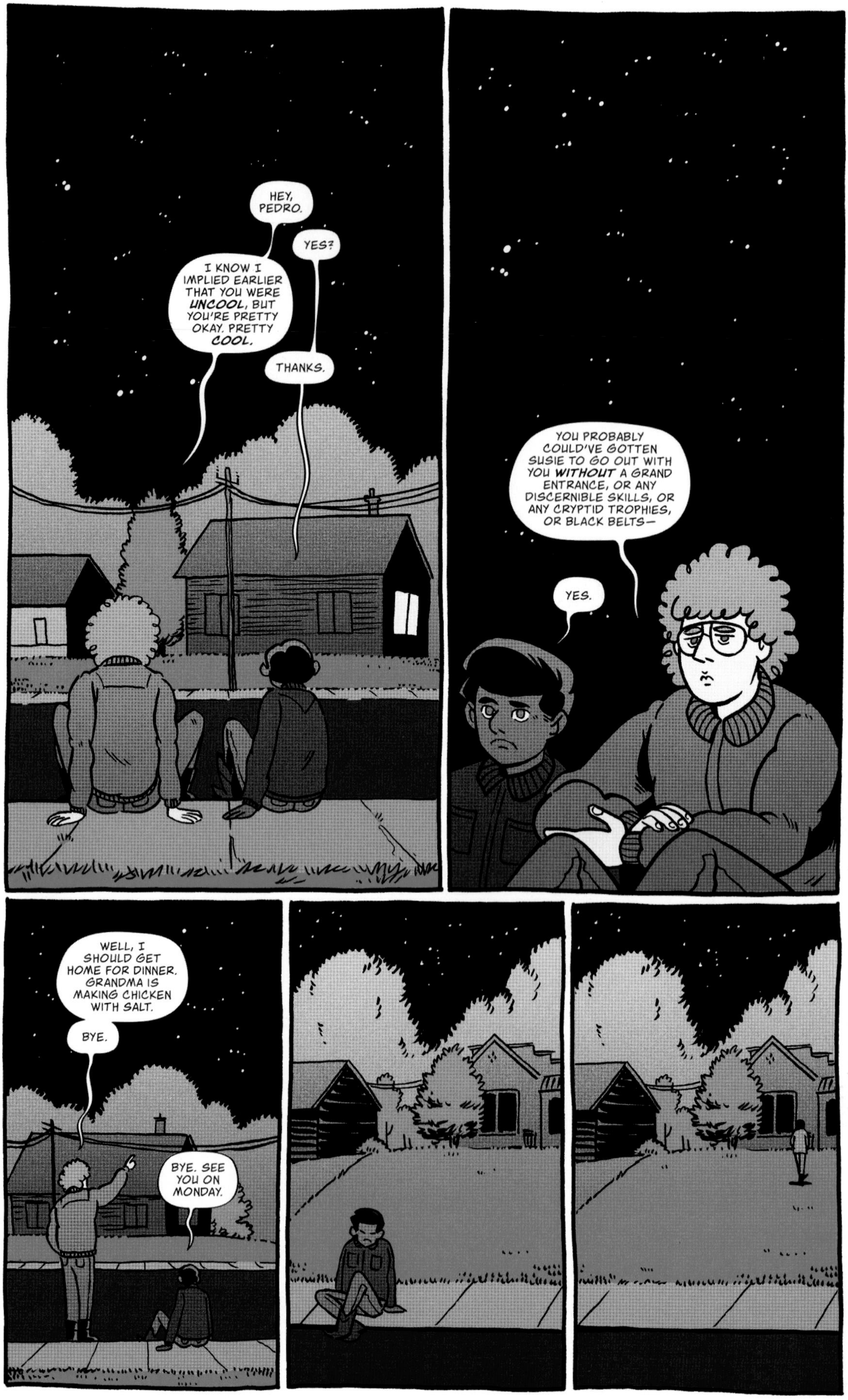
HEY, PEDRO.
YES?
I KNOW I IMPLIED EARLIER THAT YOU WERE UNCOOL, BUT YOU'RE PRETTY OKAY. PRETTY COOL.
THANKS.
YOU PROBABLY COULD'VE GOTTEN SUSIE TO GO OUT WITH YOU WITHOUT A GRAND ENTRANCE, OR ANY DISCERNIBLE SKILLS, OR ANY CRYPTID TROPHIES, OR BLACK BELTS—
YES.
WELL, I SHOULD GET HOME FOR DINNER. GRANDMA IS MAKING CHICKEN WITH SALT.
BYE.
BYE. SEE YOU ON MONDAY.

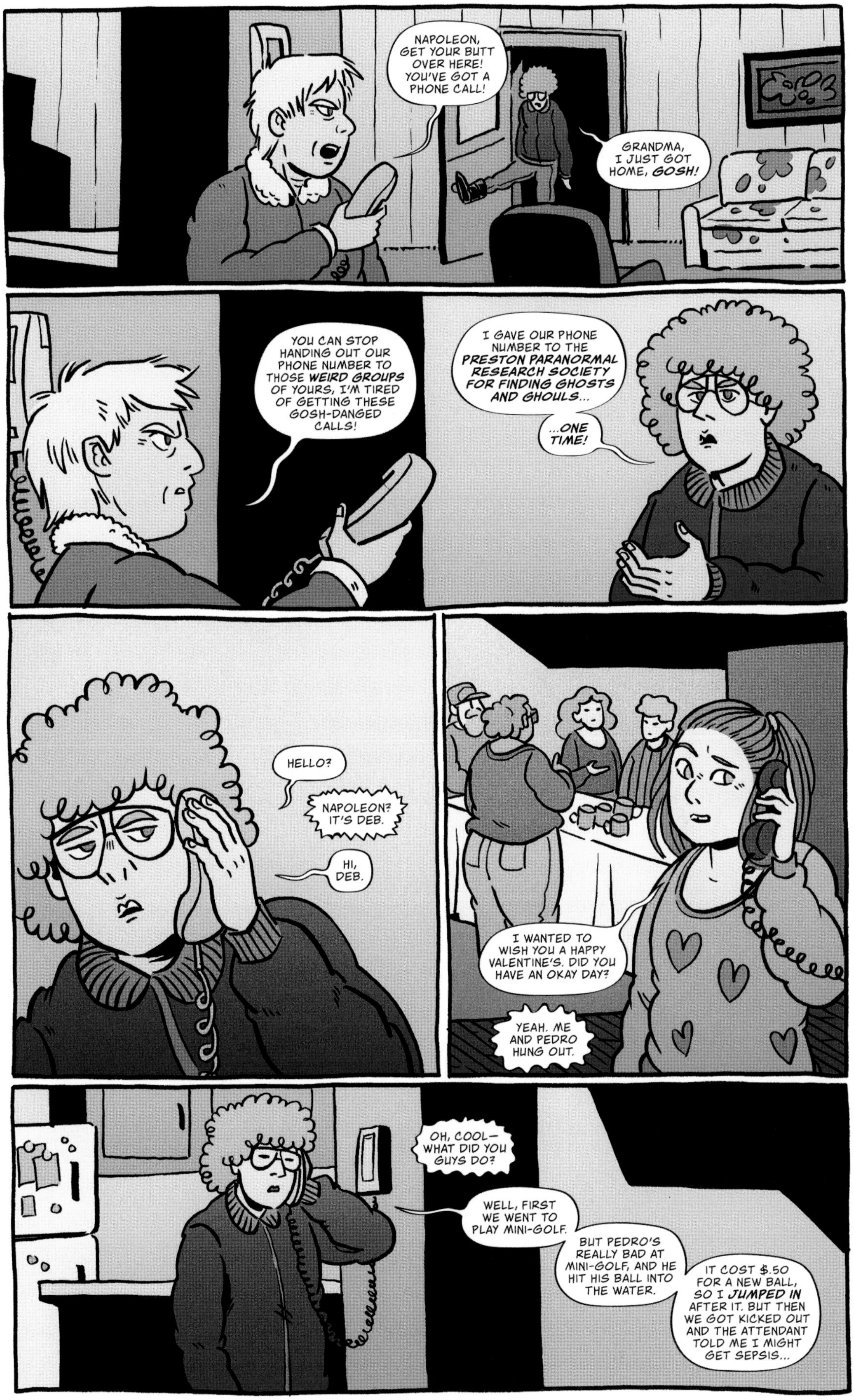

NAPOLEON, GET YOUR BUTT OVER HERE! YOU'VE GOT A PHONE CALL!
GRANDMA, I JUST GOT HOME, GOSH!
YOU CAN STOP HANDING OUT OUR PHONE NUMBER TO THOSE WEIRD GROUPS OF YOURS, I'M TIRED OF GETTING THESE GOSH-DANGED CALLS!
I GAVE OUR PHONE NUMBER TO THE PRESTON PARANORMAL RESEARCH SOCIETY FOR FINDING GHOSTS AND GHOULS...
...ONE TIME!
HELLO?
NAPOLEON? IT'S DEB.
HI, DEB.
I WANTED TO WISH YOU A HAPPY VALENTINE'S. DID YOU HAVE AN OKAY DAY?
YEAH. ME AND PEDRO HUNG OUT.
OH, COOL— WHAT DID YOU GUYS DO?
WELL, FIRST WE WENT TO PLAY MINI-GOLF.
BUT PEDRO'S REALLY BAD AT MINI-GOLF, AND HE HIT HIS BALL INTO THE WATER.
IT COST $.50 FOR A NEW BALL, SO I JUMPED IN AFTER IT. BUT THEN WE GOT KICKED OUT AND THE ATTENDANT TOLD ME I MIGHT GET SEPSIS...

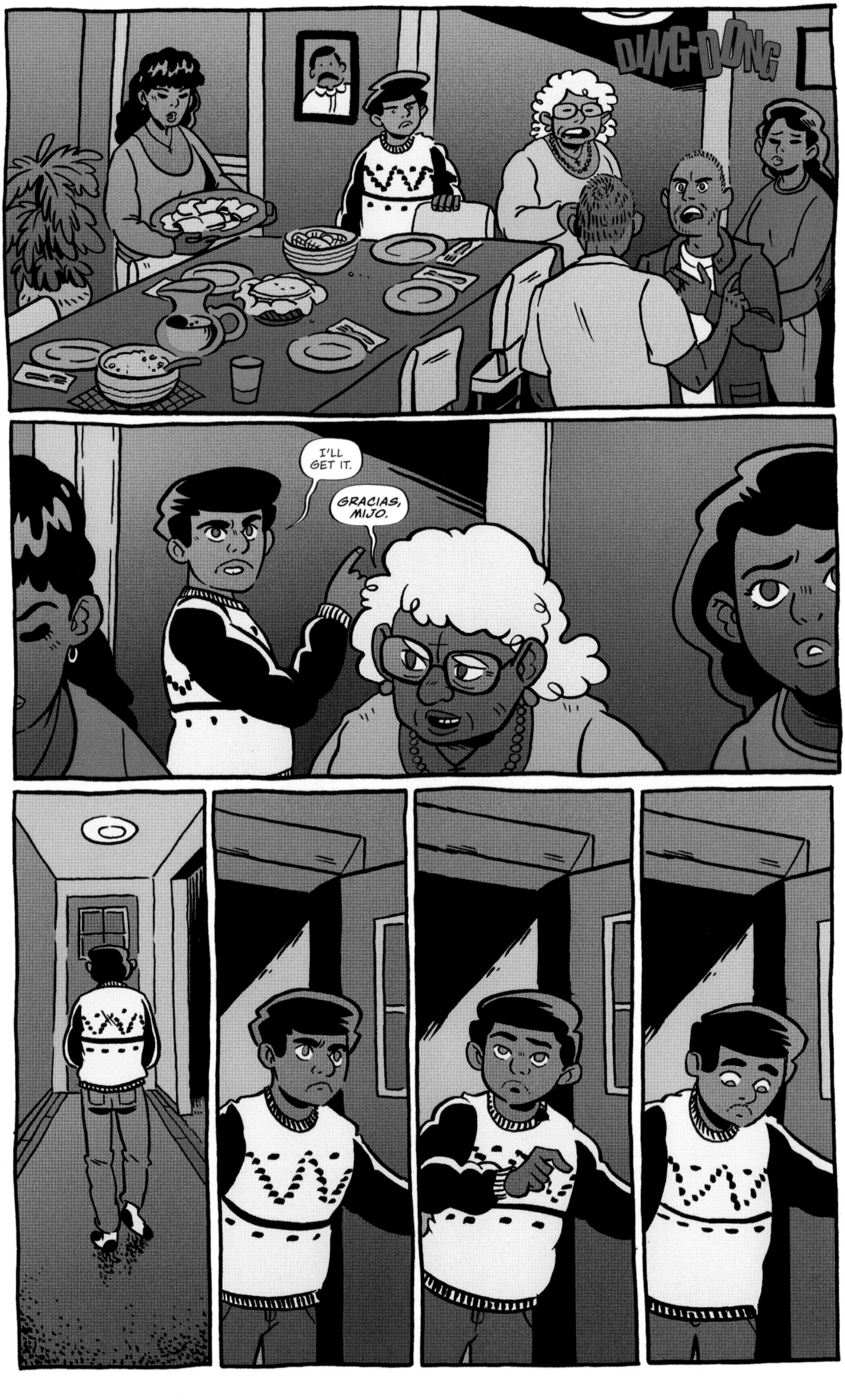
DING-DONG
I'LL GET IT.
GRACIAS, MIJO.

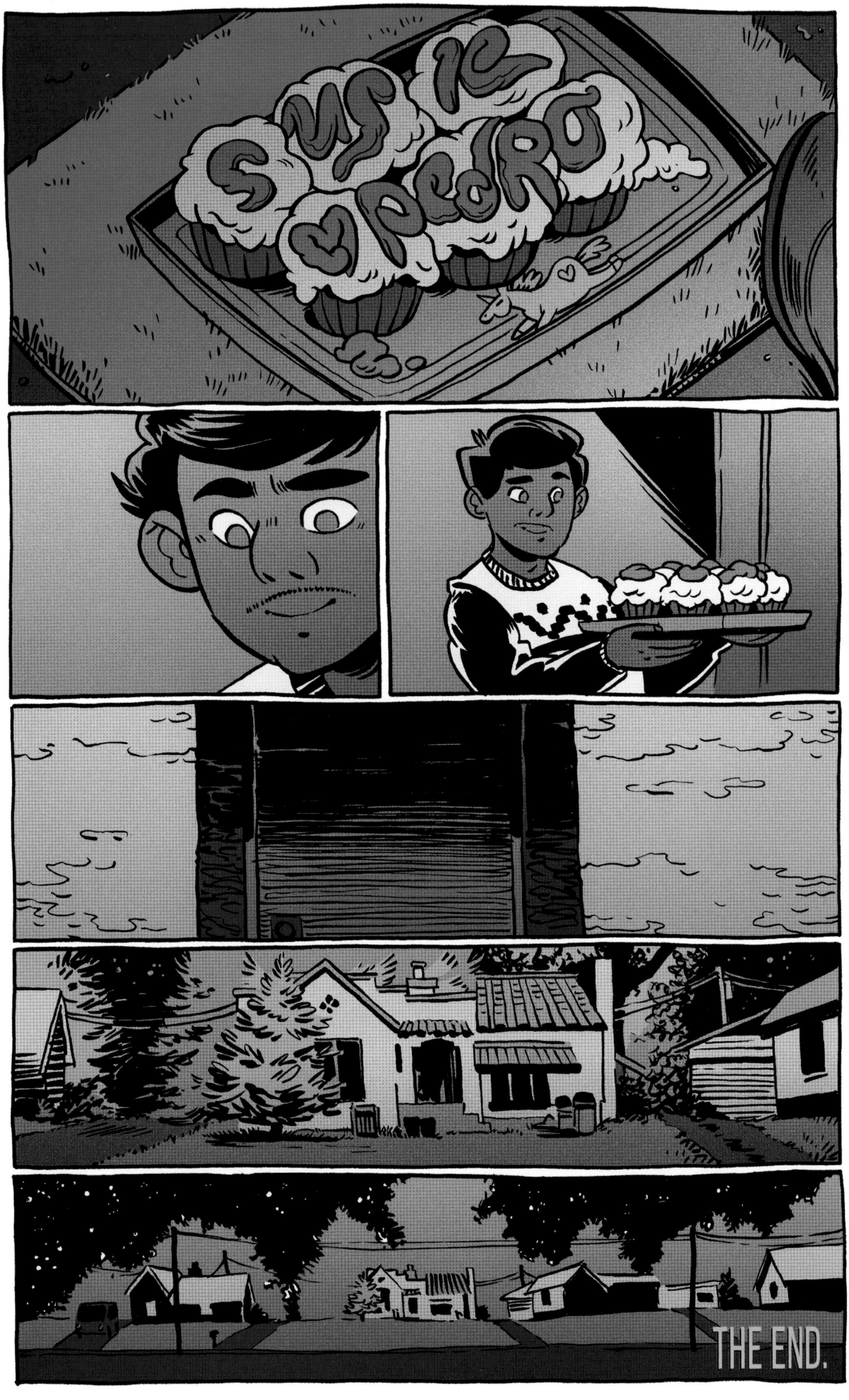
THE END.

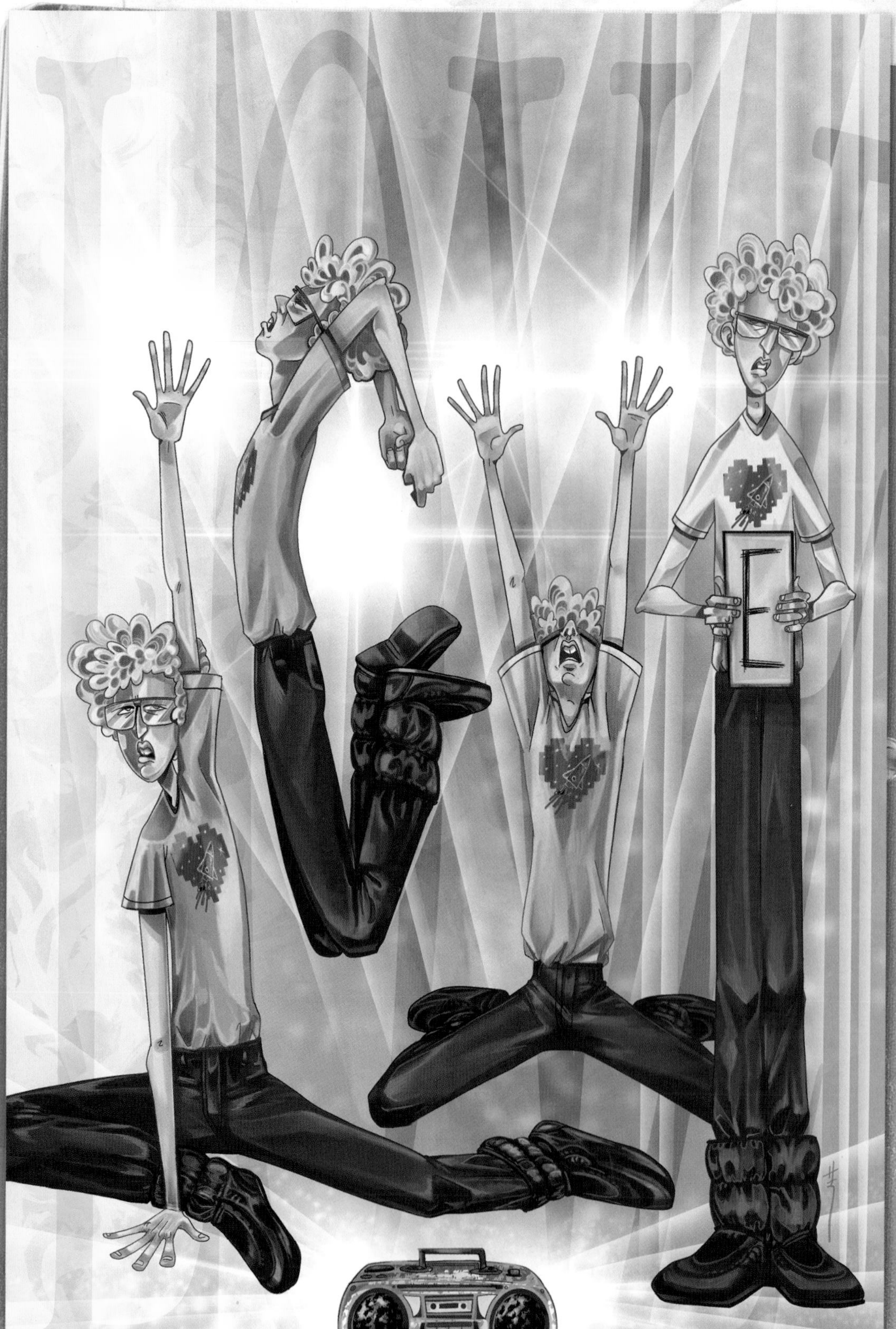
E

Art by Sara Richard

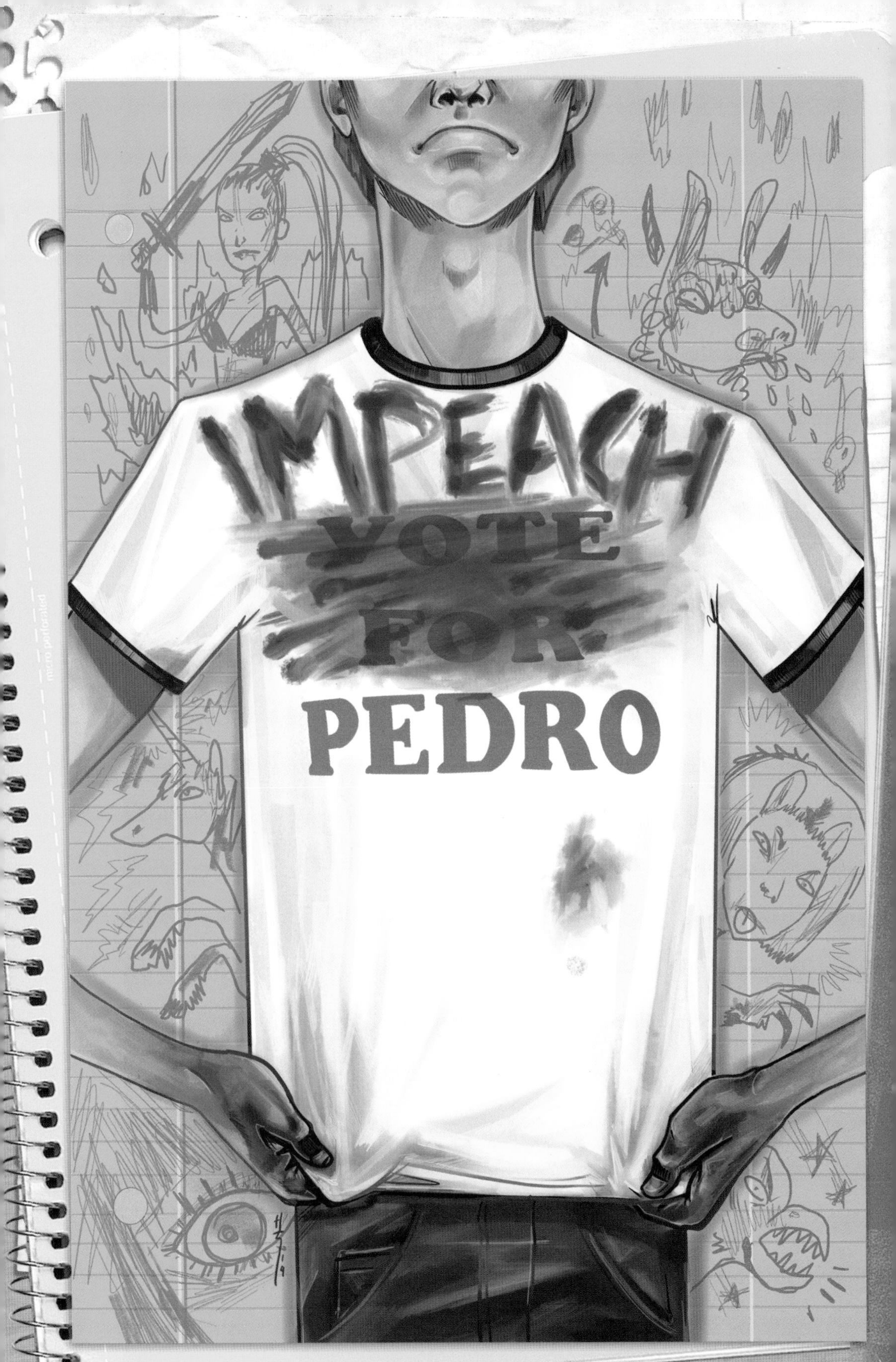
IMPEACH
VOTE FOR
PEDRO

Art by Sara Richard

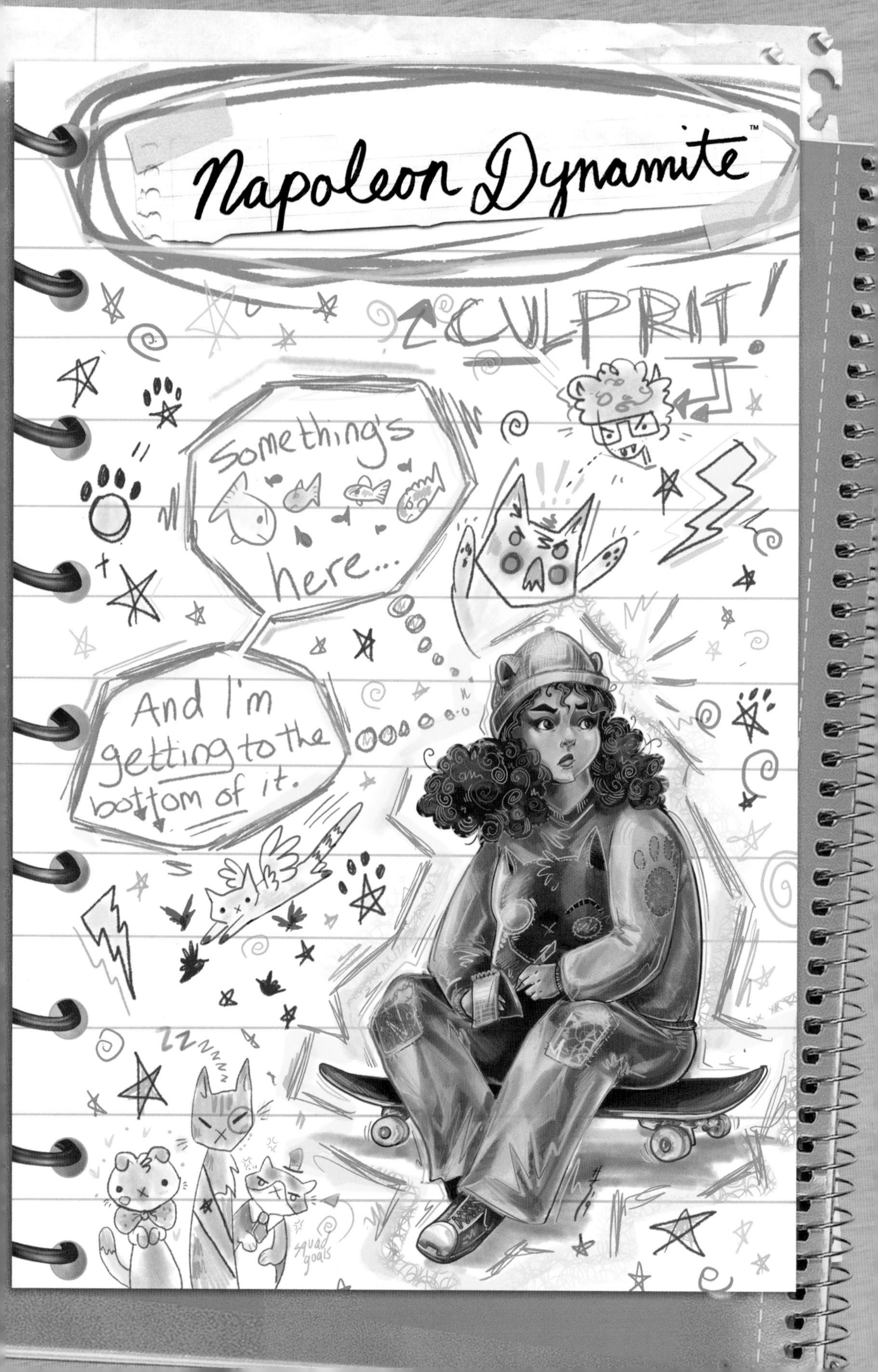

Napoleon Dynamite™
CULPRIT!
Something's here...
And I'm getting to the bottom of it.
squad goals

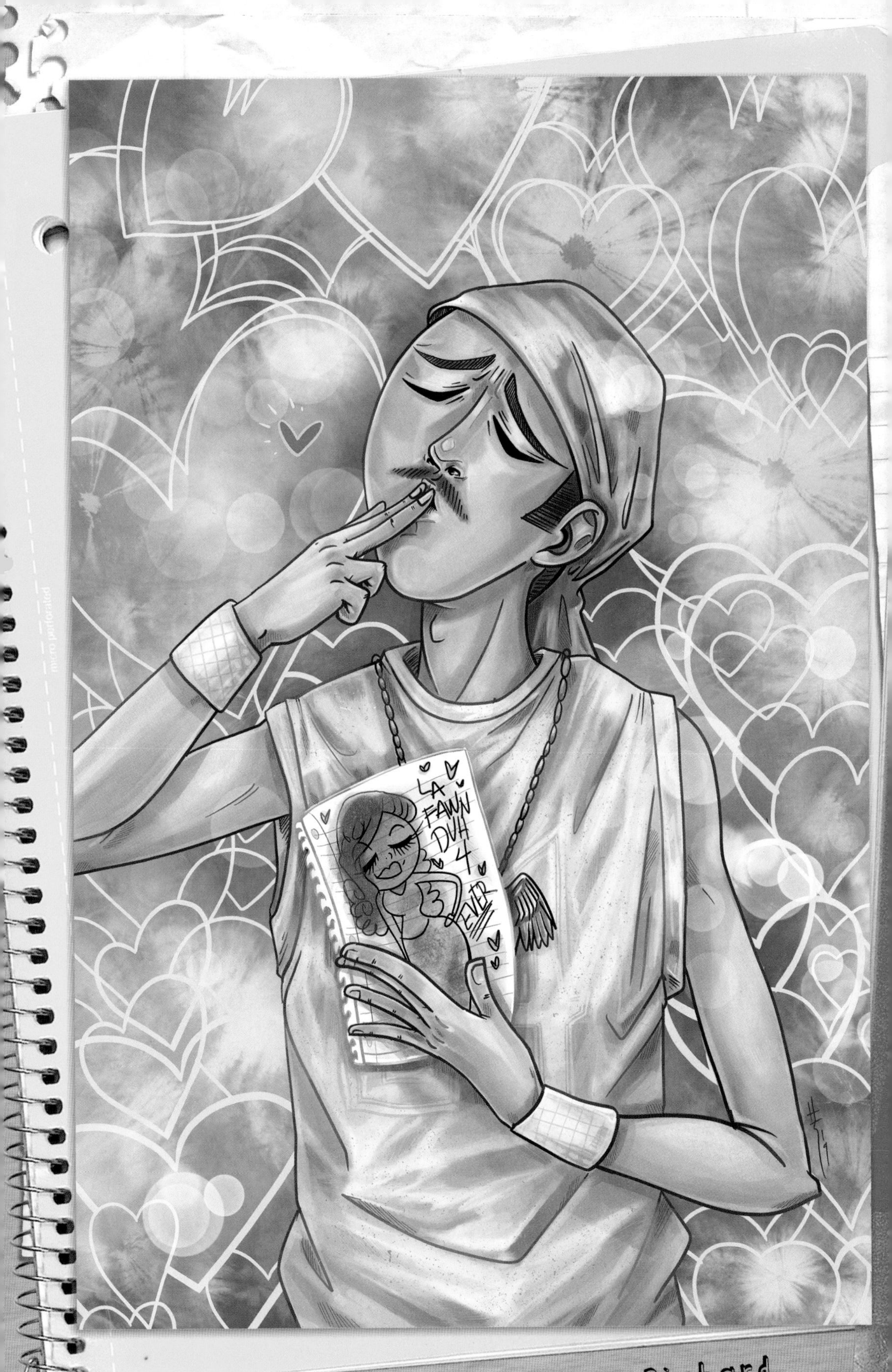
LA FAWN DUH 4 EVER

Art by Sara Richard

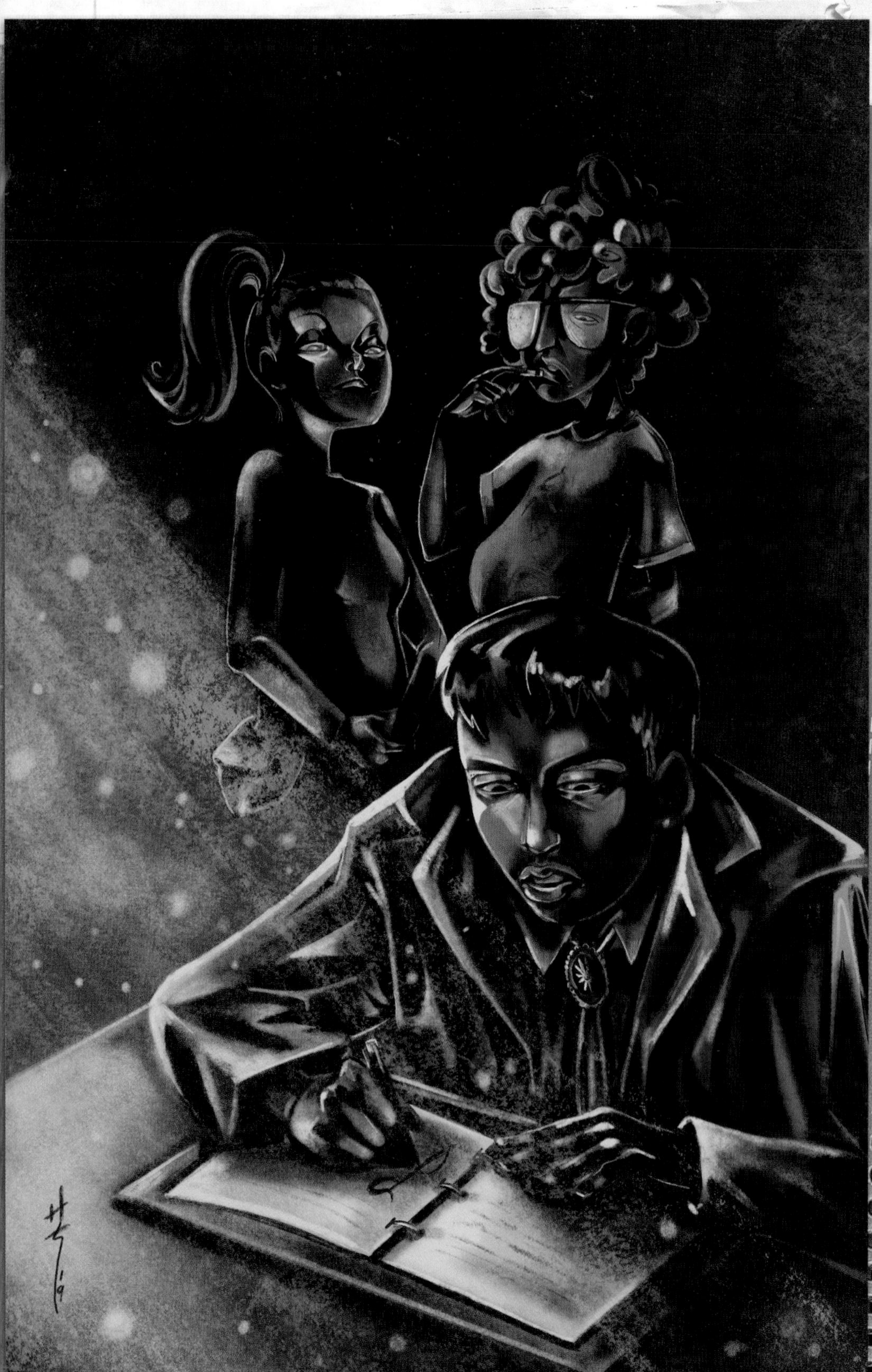

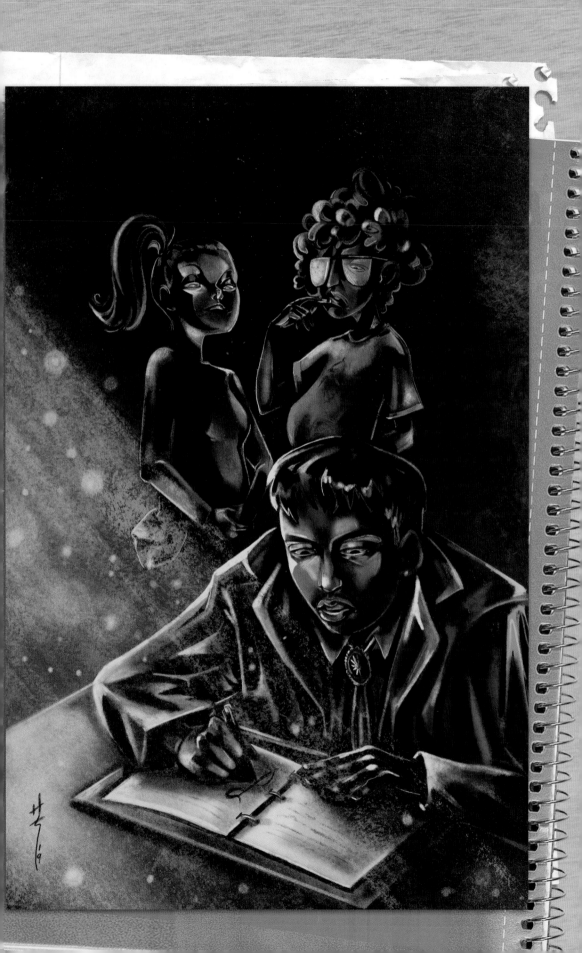

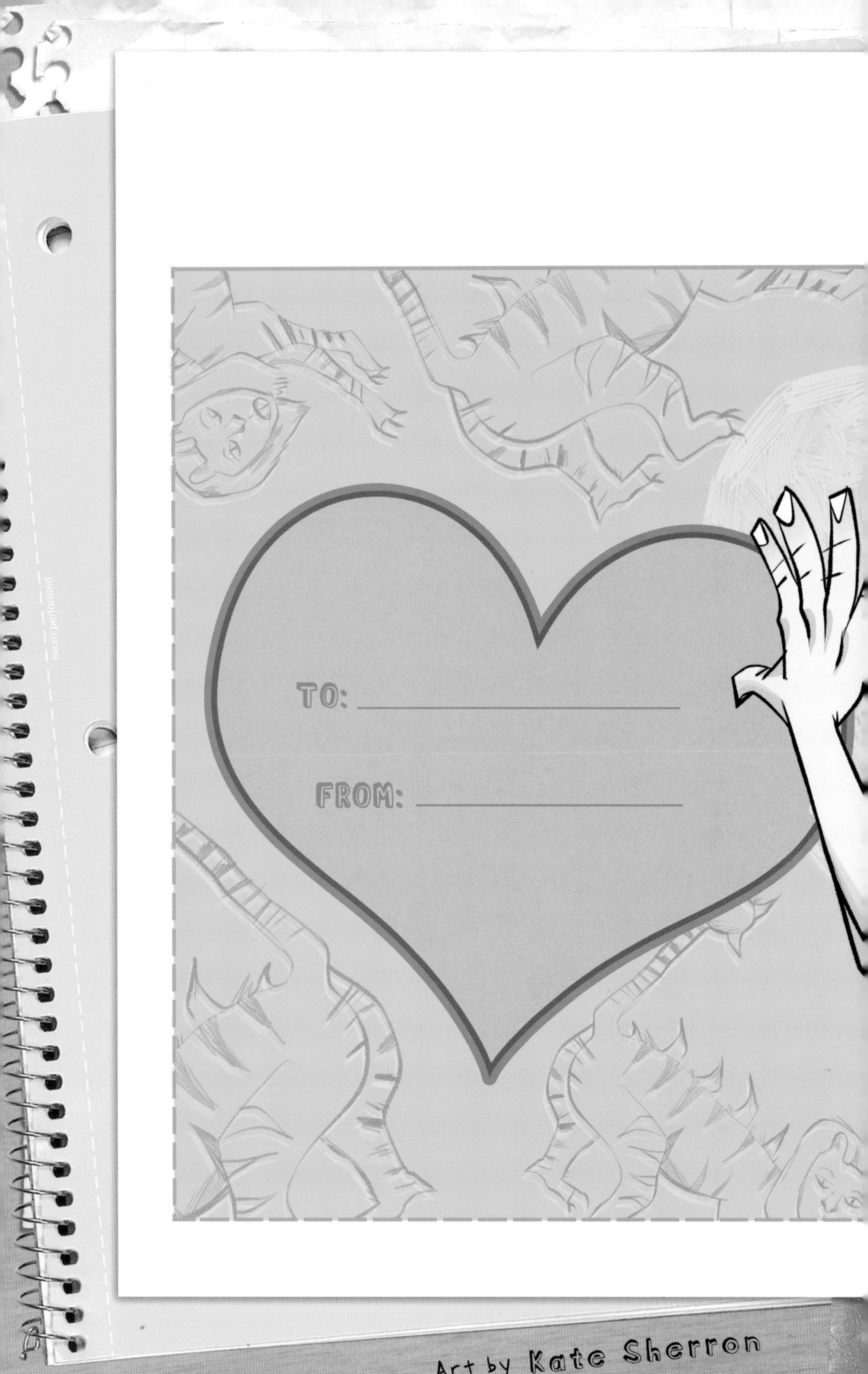
TO:
FROM:

Art by Kate Sherron

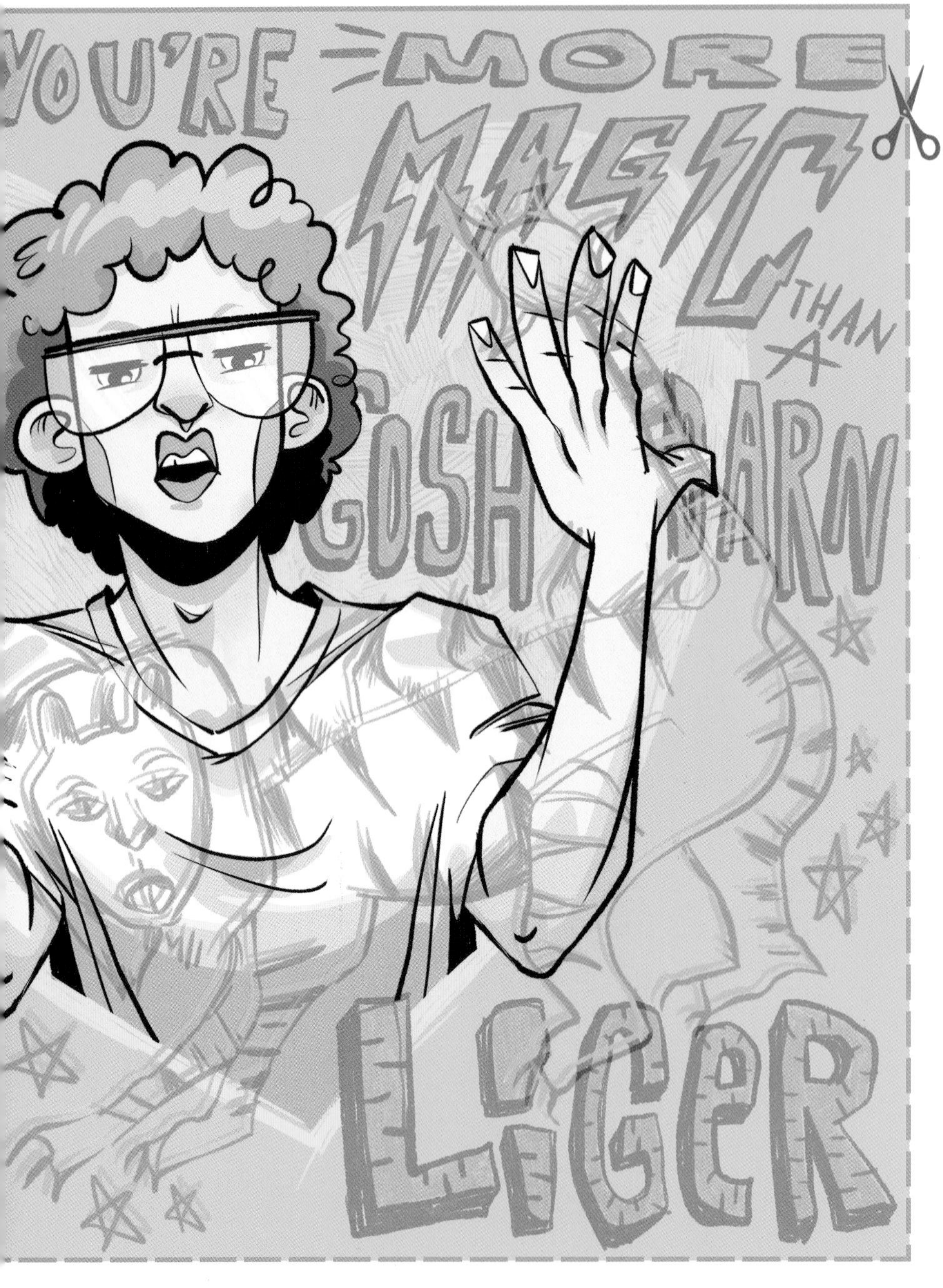
YOU'RE MORE MAGIC THAN A GOSH DARN LIGER

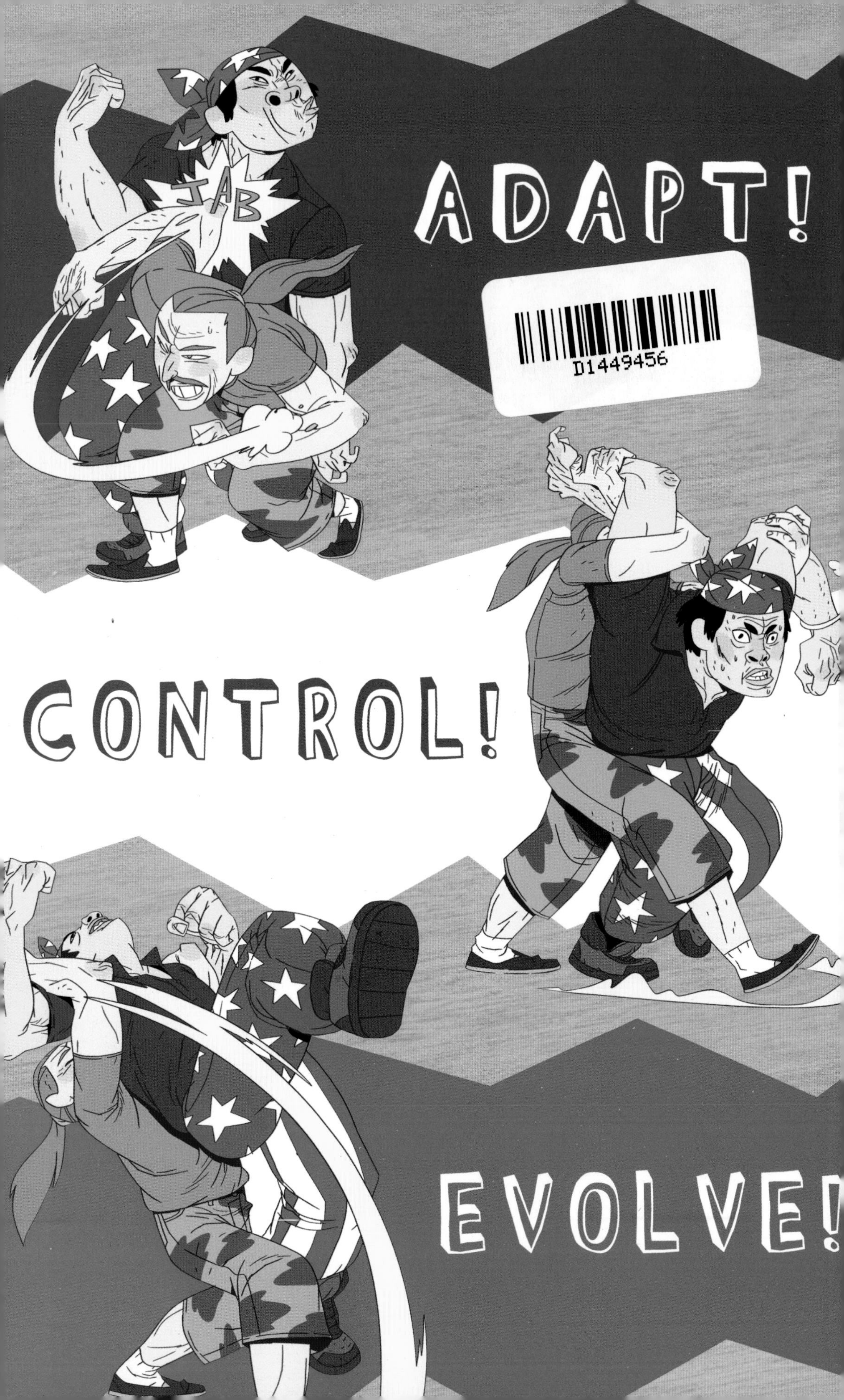
ADAPT!
JAB
CONTROL!
EVOLVE!